Murder at Sunny View

T0349925

GREG MOSSE is a 'writer and encourager of writers' and husband of internationally bestselling author, Kate Mosse. He has lived and worked in Paris, New York, Los Angeles and Madrid, mostly as an interpreter and translator, but grew up in rural south-west Sussex. In 2014, he founded the Criterion New Writing playwriting programme in the heart of the West End and, since then, has produced more than 25 of his own plays and musicals. His creative writing workshops are highly sought after at festivals at home and abroad. His first novel, *The Coming Darkness*, was published by Moonflower in 2022, followed in 2024 by *The Coming Storm*. *Murder at Sunny View* is the fifth book in his successful cosy crime series featuring the charming and perceptive amateur sleuth, Maisie Cooper.

Also by Greg Mosse

The Maisie Cooper Mystery Series:
Murder at Church Lodge
Murder at Bunting Manor
Murder at the Theatre
Murder at the Fair

The Alex Lamarque Trilogy (Moonflower):
The Coming Darkness
The Coming Storm
The Coming Fire

Secrets of the Labyrinth

Murder at Sunny View

Greg Mosse

HODDER &
STOUGHTON

First published in Great Britain in 2025 by Hodder & Stoughton Limited
An Hachette UK company

The authorised representative in the EEA is Hachette Ireland, 8 Castlecourt
Centre, Dublin 15, D15 XTP3, Ireland (email: info@hbgi.ie)

1

A CIP catalogue record for this title is available from the British Library

Paperback ISBN 978 1 399 74067 8
ebook ISBN 978 1 399 74068 5

Typeset in Monotype Plantin by Manipal Technologies Limited

Printed and bound in Great Britain by Clays Ltd, Elcograf S.p.A.

Hodder & Stoughton policy is to use papers that are natural, renewable
and recyclable products and made from wood grown in sustainable forests.
The logging and manufacturing processes are expected to conform
to the environmental regulations of the country of origin.

Hodder & Stoughton Limited
Carmelite House
50 Victoria Embankment
London EC4Y 0DZ

www.hodder.co.uk

For Beth

MAISIE'S MAP OF TROUT LEAP

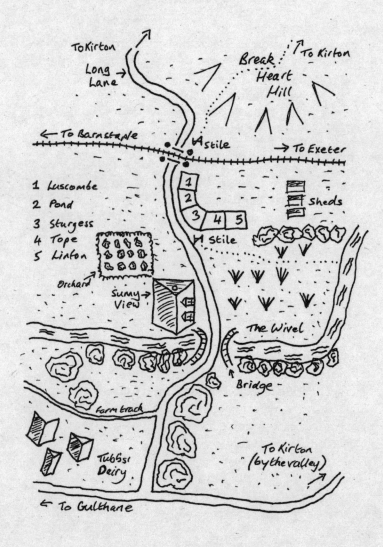

To Kirton

Long Lane

Break Heart Hill

To Kirton

← To Barnstaple

A stile

→ To Exeter

1 Luscombe
2 Pond
3 Sturgess
4 Tope
5 Linton

1
2
3 4 5

Sheds

Stile

Orchard

Sunny View

The Wivel

Bridge

Farm track

Tubbsi Dairy

To Kirton (by the valley)

← To Gulthane

CAST OF CHARACTERS

Maisie Cooper

Russell and Audrey Savage, Maisie's friends, ten years previously her employers, owners of Sunny View Guest House

Fred Luscombe, railway gatekeeper, of number one, Trout Leap

Holly Luscombe, his daughter

Miss Vera Pond, school secretary, of number two, Trout Leap

Timothy Sturgess, 11, of number three, Trout Leap

Mrs Geraldine Sturgess, seamstress, his mother

Petunia Sturgess, her daughter

Shane Tope, agricultural inspector, of number four, Trout Leap

Jane Tope, his wife

Deborah Tope, 10, their daughter

Patrick and Marthese Linton, recent arrivals from Malta, of number five, Trout Leap

Pawlu (known as Paul), 18, and Marija (known as Maria), 16, their children

Floyd Tubb of Tubb's Dairy Farm, driver of the milk lorry

Norman and Stella Tubb, his parents

Herbert Peckham, editor of the *Kirton Courier*

Vincent Brent, a paying guest at Sunny View

Ida Anderson, a paying guest at Sunny View

Clive and Cherry Atwill, shopkeepers

Constable Jasper of the Kirton police

Canon Greig, of the 'Collegiate Church of the Holy Cross and the Mother of Him Who Hung Thereon', in Kirton

Special Constable Salmon, a volunteer with the Kirton police

PROLOGUE

The small Devonshire town of Kirton had few claims to fame. Its medieval bishop so outgrew the place that he upped sticks and went to exercise his missionary zeal in Belgium and Germany, rather than among the soft hills and red dirt of his native lands. The cathedral duly moved away from Kirton to Exeter. The prosperous textile industries also left, heading north, following coal and the Industrial Revolution. Decline became ingrained, with only farming and retail as significant employers, plus a little tourism for visitors who loved the green hills, the twinkling rivers and the rust-coloured soil.

Among the vestiges of former grandeur, there remained the grandly named Queen Elizabeth's Grammar School, a co-educational establishment where the daughters and the sons of West Country families were instructed in the standard secondary curriculum – all three sciences, English, maths, history, geography and French. Plus, they had to make a choice between music or art, as if too much self-expression might not be a good thing.

One warm day, in late June of 1972, in a gymnasium converted into an exam hall, the fifth-formers 'put down their pens' at the end of a gruelling two-hour marathon on 'How World War I caused World War II'. At that very moment, three-forty-five by the gymnasium clock, a small, thin-limbed boy of eleven – floppy blond hair, pale skin, long lashes and wary eyes – began his journey through the building, swinging a loud handbell, announcing that the wearisome school day was at an end.

The children spilled out from their labours in his wake, some to board the buses that stood ready at the gates, others to walk or cycle away. What awaited them? Orange squash and bread-and-butter for a snack, *Blue Peter* or *Magpie* on the telly, beans on toast, fish fingers with chips and peas, sausage with mashed potatoes and onion gravy.

The small, thin-limbed boy was almost the last to leave – apart from those in detention for various misdemeanours – once he had returned the handbell to the school secretary, a nervy lady of advanced age called Miss Pond. Thanks to her weekly visit to the grandly named Kirton Coiffeur, Miss Pond's unnaturally black hair was curled and sculpted in such a way as to cling round her windburned face like an improbable wig.

'Thank you, young Sturgess,' said Miss Pond.

'Good afternoon, miss,' said the boy, accustomed – as were all the Grammar School children – to being referred to by his family name.

He went outside. The sun was still high in the western sky. His arms ached from the weight of the bell. A few groups of Kirton children had yet to disperse, some of them in his class. He knew them but they didn't seem to feel his lonely gaze upon them, enjoying their own private communion from which he was inexplicably excluded.

'Young Sturgess' had a five-pence piece in his pocket, what his mother still referred to as 'a shilling' or 'a bob' in pre-decimalisation language. He crossed the road to the newsagent and, for just three pence, bought a Curly Wurly, a chocolate bar made of strands of caramel, covered with milk chocolate, like intertwined sticks.

Back outside on the narrow pavement, he didn't open the white wrapper straight away. He was hesitating between two routes home. One went over the top and then down the precipitous far side of Break Heart Hill: it would be tiring on the ascent, his legs aching in his grey cotton shorts; it would be jarring on the descent, his toes pushed forward and pinched in his tight school shoes. The other choice was known as Long Lane.

The harder way was – inevitably – the safer way, but that was a lesson that life hadn't yet found time to teach him.

He chose Long Lane, passing the sign that said the road was closed to vehicle traffic after eight o'clock each evening and six on Sundays, winding between tall and bedraggled hedges, buzzing with summer insects. As he went, he teased his Curly Wurly out of its wrapper, nibbling the soft chocolate and caramel.

One day, he thought, *I'll make it last all the way to the railway gates at Trout Leap.*

Not today, though. Five or six minutes later, he licked his fingers and, guiltily, pushed the empty waxed paper deep into the brambles and walked on.

There were bees on the hedgerow flowers, close at hand, and a dusty smell of ripening barley. Somewhere, not too far away, a farmer must have been muck-spreading, because there was a whiff of pig manure in the air, too. Just then, he heard the toot of the milk-lorry driver, probably thanking the railway gatekeeper for opening up to let him pass. Then came the intimidating crescendo of the approaching diesel engine, accompanied by the rattle of the churns, lined up like soldiers on parade on the flatbed behind.

Like any child born to country roads, 'Young Sturgess' knew to press himself back into the hedge, despite the brambles scratching at the tender skin on the backs of his bare knees, despite the worry that there might be a bee right there, by his ear or on the nape of his neck, and he would be stung.

The milk lorry came lurching round the corner, going too fast. The boy caught a glimpse of the driver's face – it was Floyd Tubb – whose set expression of weary inattention suddenly transformed into focused action. Floyd tugged on the wheel, running the nearside tyres up onto the opposite verge.

It was a close-run thing, but he passed safely by, albeit upsetting one of the churns. It fell from the flatbed and landed on its side. The metal lid dislodged and the rich milk sloshed out across the tarmac.

'Young Sturgess' watched Floyd Tubb swing open the cab door and jump down, wondering if this – like most calamities that took place within his orbit – would turn out to be his fault.

'What're you doing, Tim? Do you want to get killed, then?'

'No, Mr Tubb.'

Floyd rubbed a dirty hand over his floppy blond hair, not dissimilar to Timothy's.

'And I've gone and lost one,' he said, looking ruefully at the fallen churn. 'Where's the lid?'

'It rolled down there,' said Timothy, pointing.

'That's a mercy,' said Floyd, stomping off to fetch it. When he came back, the boy hadn't moved. 'Ain't you got no home to go to?'

'But look, Mr Tubb. There's a rat.'

It was true. In the neck of the fallen churn, there was the unmistakable shape of a drowned rodent, its fur slick, its eyes glassy. Timothy Sturgess looked from the dead animal to the willowy dairyman. Something important had happened. He knew that from the aggressive – and also wary – look in Floyd's eye. But he didn't know exactly what.

'Goodbye, Mr Tubb,' he said.

'No, you don't,' said Floyd, putting a heavy hand on Timothy's frail shoulder. The boy's blue eyes opened wide. Floyd demanded: 'Who are you going to tell about this?'

Timothy gave it only a moment's thought. The answer was obvious.

'No one, Mr Tubb.'

The dairyman's blue eyes returned to the awful incriminating evidence of the rat in the milk.

'That's right,' he said. 'Not no one. Go on. Be on your way.'

With relief, Timothy walked on, round two bends to the railway barrier, held closed to traffic because the regular train services that passed through the hamlet of Trout Leap were more common than lorries and tractors and cars. He pushed open the pedestrian kissing gate, designed to be beyond the wit of errant cattle or sheep, looked left along the track towards Exeter and right towards Barnstaple. Finding his way clear, he crossed the rails and pushed through the corresponding gate on the far side.

Trout Leap was made up of five cob cottages in the shape of an L, with thick walls made of sand, straw and red Devonshire clay, plus a brick-built guest house known as Sunny View – by the bridge over the river Wivel – and a dairy farm on the hill beyond.

He went inside number three, the corner cottage, and found his mother kneeling on their oppressively dark Axminster carpet, laying out a dressmaker's pattern of tissue paper, unfurling a bolt of slippery blue satin.

'Good day?' she asked, the words muffled by her mouthful of pins.

'Yes, thank you, Mother,' said Timothy.

'Any news?'

'No, Mother, nothing at all.'

I

THORNS & BRAMBLES

ONE

A few weeks later, on a hot and stuffy Friday in late July, Maisie Cooper set off from Chichester railway station, a little regretful to be leaving, noisily transported by a slam-door British Rail train. She was thirty-five years old, in the prime of life. The weather was fine. She had a corner seat on the left-hand side, all by herself in a six-seat compartment right at the back. She was heading west, so that was the sunny side, like the port cabins on a cross-Atlantic cruise. The buttoned carriage cloth of the upholstery smelt of cigarettes. The floor was grimy and the windows were dusty and smeared. On the small shelf beneath the glass were her thermos flask of tea and the greaseproof paper wrappings of two rounds of sandwiches.

There was also a letter, sent – as it seemed – out of her own past by the owners of the Sunny View guest house in mid-Devon, where she had been working when the awful news of her parents' deaths had tracked her down, changing her life forever. She picked it up and read it through for the fourth or fifth time.

Dear Maisie,

Audrey and I hope this little note finds you well and in a position to travel down to see us, preferably sooner and certainly not too much later.

I don't want to write down exactly what it is we want to say to you. I'm a careful soul, as you'll no doubt remember.

Perhaps, for the affection you bear us, you'll consider making this small detour out of your busy life. Something has to be done before there's a murder and the police just aren't interested.

Yours affectionately,
Russell Savage

The idea there might be a murder at Sunny View was as far-fetched as it was surprising. She assumed Russell was exaggerating for effect. But Maisie was intrigued by what her old employers had to say to her, so decided she could afford a quick visit.

Anyway, just for now, I have nothing to worry about. Travel is time out of time.

Maisie's fiancé, Jack Wingard, was heading in a quite different direction, north-east to Newcastle for the next phase of his career as a police sergeant in search of promotion. His journey would take longer – up from Chichester to London, across the metropolis on the Tube, then north from King's Cross station. Maisie regretted the fact that they would spend the week at opposite ends of England, but she knew it was for the best.

It's a shame to be apart so soon after finally being together.

She had set off at the crack of dawn, wanting to accompany Jack on his own very early departure, and soon her own journey was three-quarters done. She felt the grip of the brakes taking hold as they began their approach into Exeter Central station, heard the squealing sound as the train began decelerating.

From the luggage rack above her head, she got down her small suitcase – which Jack's grandmother Florence referred to as a 'grip' – and put away the tidily folded greaseproof paper and the now-empty thermos. With the grip in her right hand and her handbag in the crook of her left elbow, she prepared to climb down onto the platform, seeing herself in the grimy glass.

Many younger women don't carry handbags any more. But it's so practical and means you don't have to stuff everything into your pockets and spoil the line of your clothes.

Maisie was wearing a short-sleeved navy-and-white polka-dot summer dress, with a comfortable full skirt that draped below her knees. She was feeling fit, almost athletic, from her regime of early-morning exercise at the swimming baths in Chichester. Her arms were strong and tanned from helping with summer labour in the woods and on the arable farmland at Bunting Manor. She had no need of a jacket or cardigan because it was July and the notoriously unreliable British weather seemed set fair.

The train finally came to a complete stop, hissing and wheezing. She climbed out, slamming the door behind her, discovering that the train had been busier than she had imagined, alone in her isolated compartment at the very rear. The platform was abustle with people of all types and classes. Some hurried while others strolled, reorganising their belongings. Plus, there were the uniformed British Rail staff in their dark woollen jackets, with insignia reminiscent of military ranks.

Maisie presented her ticket at the barrier and emerged onto the pavement, looking for the bus to take her across the city from Exeter Central station to Exeter St David's. Very fortunately, it was there, ready and waiting, a smart dark-green double-decker with a very overweight driver and a friendly guard. She paid her fare of eight new pence – which she thought quite steep given the brief journey – and found herself surrounded by schoolchildren making their way home, their shrill voices shocking after the quiet of her solitary compartment. Very soon, she learned from their excited conversation that it was the last day of term, that the long summer holiday was about to begin.

The roads were busy and they were held by several traffic lights. Twice, after a stop, considerate drivers allowed the double-decker to go first. They pulled up in front of Exeter St David's and Maisie went to one of three open counters to purchase a ticket for Kirton, just eight miles outside the city.

Once again, a connection was ready and waiting. She ran up and over the bridge, worried it would pull out and leave her waiting for twenty minutes for the next service on the Barnstaple line. Her low-heeled shoes made a clip-clopping sound on the tarmac of the platform as an attentive porter held open a door for her, then wolf-whistled.

This was not an unusual occurrence. Maisie cut a striking figure. She was quite tall at five-foot-eight, with a slim physique, short curly hair bleached almost blonde by the summer sun and the chlorine in the water of the public baths. And she had clear skin and large brown eyes – a combination many men found attractive, generally without unwelcome consequences.

In she climbed, finding herself among more schoolchildren – possibly the same ones, making a similar journey to her own – but was able to sit alone in a two-person bay at the front of the short, two-carriage train. The eight miles to Kirton were rapidly eaten up, with a brief stop halfway at Newton St Cyres, making Maisie smile, remembering the characteristic West Country names that she found it hard to say out loud without adopting the local accent.

But that's fair enough, isn't it? For a while, ten years ago, I was local.

As the green hills hurried past, with occasional scars in the landscape revealing the deep red dirt of the iron-rich soil, Maisie summoned memories of those happy times. After two 'tours', she had left the Women's Royal Army Corps, aware that significant promotion was unlikely for a woman in the British military. Uncertain of what direction she wanted her life to take, she had responded to an advertisement for a 'manager' at a guest house called Sunny View and made this very same journey through Exeter and Kirton to meet the owners, Audrey and Russell Savage. She had been deemed 'a proper job' – meaning ideal – and employed on the spot.

We got on so well, but then . . .

Maisie sighed. In 1962, life had taken an unexpected and unhappy turn with the accidental death of her parents in a road traffic accident in a London pea-souper fog and her adored and admired older brother, Stephen, had let her down by turning to drink and dissipation. She had gone to live in Paris to escape her grief and her disillusionment.

And now Stephen's dead, too.

Maisie made an effort to escape both those unhappy memories and the shadow of intrigue in Russell's letter. Happily, at just that moment, she began to recognise features of the landscape: the winding river Wivel; a particular stretch of woodland; an oddly shaped hill, like a currant bun, but studded with sheep rather than dried fruit. Beyond that, the town.

Kirton had one main street that tracked quite steeply uphill, past the Home and Colonial Stores, Townsend's Furniture & Bed Shop, Moore's car showroom, the Churchworkers' Institute, the Masonic Hall, the Liberal Club. Maisie's favourite was the general store, C & C Supplies, run by Clive and Cherry Atwill where, as Dylan Thomas had it in *Under Milk Wood*, 'everything was sold'.

The train, though, pulled in at the bottom of the town, close to the course of the pleasant trout river, the Wivel, that wound through the valley to the south, linking several hamlets, including Maisie's final destination, Trout Leap.

Once more she got her things together, ready to get down, alighting with two dozen children and grown-ups. She shuffled forward with them and showed her ticket to the collector, before stepping out into the warmth of the afternoon, the sun quite dazzling. She heard Russell's voice calling out to her before she saw him.

'There she is, my handsome.'

All at once, he was standing in front of her, in his sagging tweed suit, despite the warmth of the day, his grey shirt – that had once been white – open at the neck and revealing a mass of grey chest hairs. He was beaming, his eyes wide and smiling, framed by his salt-and-pepper whiskers and topped by a thick head of hair the same shade. She realised he must have come early, prepared to wait for hours, if necessary, in order to be there to meet her.

Oh no, I think I'm going to cry.

Despite her outward confidence, Maisie Cooper was a private person. She didn't enjoy sharing her deepest thoughts and emotions. That had been one of the reasons that she and Jack had found it so hard to rekindle their relationship after so many years apart – that and Maisie's involvement in several police investigations, including her brother's murder at Church Lodge in Framlington. The crimes had, at first, erected a barrier between them, one made up of grief and constabulary formality. Now, in the little car park outside Kirton railway station, she was astonished by the depth of her emotion, taking out her handkerchief and dabbing her eyes.

'Oh, Russell . . .'

'Now, then, my lovely,' said Russell. 'What's all this?'

'It's all right. Don't worry. I'm just . . .'

Maisie couldn't finish the thought. It was too complicated to express out loud.

I'm crying because I was happy at Sunny View, ten years ago, before I really knew that life was short and the people you love won't be around forever, like it seemed when I was a child.

But Russell seemed to understand.

'Come here, my lovely.' He put his arms round her and the urge to weep faded, seemingly absorbed into the wool of his tweed jacket that smelt of wear and dust. 'I know how 'tis. Last time you were here at Kirton railway station, it was to go up to that London for your poor parents. We wish we'd had a chance to meet them, Audrey and me both, to tell them the fine young woman they'd made.'

Maisie felt her emotion subside, marvelling at the fact that Russell, talking very directly about her loss, made it much less painful than someone else might have done by beating about the bush. She stepped away.

'It's wonderful to see you. How clever you are.'

'I don't know about "clever", but I know you, Maisie Cooper. You may be what they call "self-contained", but you feel things as deeply as anyone else – more deeply, perhaps.'

'How are you both? You look so well.'

Russell gently contradicted her, repeating his phrase: 'I don't know about "well". It's the years weigh heavy, you know? I don't seem to have the same vim I used to.'

'That's normal, isn't it.'

He sighed and agreed: 'I suppose.'

Maisie frowned, wondering how old Russell actually was. She hadn't seen him for ten years and it was true that his face was much more deeply lined than the image she held in memory.

'Will you soon be drawing your pension?'

'Soon?' He laughed. 'I've had it these last three years – and very welcome after a lifetime's scraping by.'

Maisie swiftly calculated that Russell must be sixty-eight, therefore, but she knew very well that he and Audrey hadn't been 'scraping by'. They were thrifty – 'careful' as they called it – by choice. Their charming four-roomed guest house in the hamlet of Trout Leap had always been a thriving business, so much so that they hadn't needed to open twelve months of

15

the year, making a living by welcoming most of their guests in the peak summer season and the other school holidays.

'You look very well on it,' she told him.

'You've not aged a jot, Maisie. You look healthy and strong and as pretty as Norman Tubb's prize-winning heifer.' Maisie laughed at Russell comparing her to a cow and he quickly qualified what he meant. 'There I go, saying something foolish. You know how it was meant, I hope?'

'Of course I do,' Maisie reassured him. The car park was still busy with departing cars and a single-decker bus in the same dark-green livery as the one she had taken in Exeter, making an awkward turn. 'How's Audrey? Blooming, I hope?'

'Aside from the worry, she's bright as a button. She doesn't seem to feel her years like I do.'

'The worry?' asked Maisie.

'The worry that made me look you up. Like we said in our letter, something has to be done before there's no goodwill left among neighbours and friends.'

The bus pulled away, leaving them alone in the little car park in front of Kirton railway station. Maisie was glad there was no one close by to overhear. She hoped Russell wasn't 'getting silly', as Jack's grandmother Florence would have put it. It was a fact, though. Sometimes, the imaginations of older folks were easily fussed and created all kinds of devilment that had little or no basis in reality.

'Yes, your letter. You know it sounded very melodramatic, Russell. "A murder". Can you really mean that?'

'Perhaps there was a smidge of poetic licence,' he told her. 'But who can tell? I've never known passions to run so high.'

'You must tell me all about it.'

'I will, but not in the car park, here.' Russell bent down to pick up her tightly packed grip and led her to his car, a weary Vauxhall Viva with rust on the sills and wheel arches. 'I'll just put this in the back.'

He slid the passenger seat forward and placed her suitcase on the bench seat behind, then gallantly held the door open for her to get in. She did so. He closed it without slamming and went round to the driver's side, climbing in with an audible exhalation that told Maisie he was glad to be off his feet. The car started first time but, to Maisie's ear, it sounded unhealthy, spluttering as if it was suffering from the same summer cold that had played an unexpected role in her solution to the murder at Bitling Fair.

Russell pulled away, chatting and driving with the nonchalant confidence of someone for whom the narrow country lane was second nature.

'It's been a good year for weeds and everything else the farmers don't want to grow. All that wet in February, March and April, and some even more recent. Have you had the same up Sussex?'

'We have.'

'You see those banks of stinging nettles? They're all over and flourishing like nobody's business. Luckily the dock plants are doing just as well and, as you know, their leaves will take away the worst of the tingle.'

Driving along the country lane, Kirton was above them, out of sight beyond the hill. The windows were open and Maisie began to feel intoxicated with the fragrances of the warm afternoon.

'Are those foxgloves?'

'And parsnip flowers. There was a kiddie taken to hospital up Exeter for eating one or other of them, the daft little mite.'

'Grockles?' asked Maisie, using the West Country word for tourists. 'I suppose the parents didn't know any better.'

'That's the truth.'

The lane followed then crossed a curve in the river, before climbing gently uphill through pasture inhabited by somnolent cows. Then Russell swore and stepped on the brakes as a small, underpowered motorbike came swinging round a bend, almost on their side of the road. It was ridden by a lithe young man in a T-shirt and no helmet, leaning into the corner as he swung past them with a noise like an angry bee.

'Who on earth was that?' asked Maisie.

'Young Paul Linton. There's a chance he might turn out a bit of a tearaway. Time will tell.'

'Isn't there a law about wearing a helmet?' Maisie asked, not completely up to date with UK news, having been living in Paris.

'It might come in next year from what I've heard.'

'I think I would use one. We wear hard hats for horse riding and that's probably a lot less dangerous, even on dry summer roads.'

Russell drove on, remarking: 'Talking of summer, the warm weather means there's ticks hiding in the dry grass, only too pleased to hitch a ride on your trouser cuffs, and they can be the very devil once they latch on to your skin. Some people get the allergy. And battalions of bees and jaspers – you know, wasps? We had a big old nest up under the eaves of one of the dormers.'

'Oh dear. What did you do?'

'I knocked it down onto an old towel, folded it over quick and stomped all over them.'

'Were you stung?'

'Just the once from a latecomer on its way home after a forage.'

'I sometimes wonder what's the point of wasps.'

'And drumbeldrones,' said Russell, using the Devon word for bumblebees. 'But they'll not do you any harm. Not like them gurt hornets – big black blimps, wings buzzing as they drift by.'

'Horseflies, too?' asked Maisie, knowing July was the season.

'Not so many,' answered Russell. 'But biting spiders and adders. Didn't I find a nest of writhing young ones in the culvert under the apple orchard? Oh, that's another thing you don't know. We're making our own brew.'

'How lovely,' said Maisie, who was very partial to a refreshing glass of apple cider.

'It's more on the scrumpy side, though,' Russell told her. 'It comes out something fierce, it does.'

They came to a fork in the road. Straight on went west towards Gulthane and Colthorp, but they swung right, running gently downhill past the gate of Tubb's Dairy Farm, the concrete drive protected by a cattle grid. Up ahead was the little humpbacked bridge over the Wivel and, just visible thought the trees on the left, the dormer windows in the tiled roof of Sunny View. They crested the bridge and Russell stepped on the brake, causing the Vauxhall Viva to skid to a halt.

'What's this then?' asked Russell to himself.

In the middle of the road was a man in swimming trunks with a child of six or seven in his arms and, beside him, a woman in a one-piece bathing costume, with her two hands clasped in shock over her mouth.

Two

Maisie was out of the car more quickly than Russell. She went to ask what was the matter and if she could help. The woman told her that the little girl – 'our daughter, Deborah' – had been chased by cows across the field.

'How frightening for her,' said Maisie. 'I'm trained in first aid. Can I have a look?'

The girl had her face pressed into her father's shoulder but Maisie managed to persuade the man to set her down on her feet. It was quickly apparent that there was nothing seriously wrong with the child, but she had some nasty scratches on her calves from running through some thorns.

'It might be a good idea to get her a tetanus shot,' Maisie told the parents whose panic was subsiding. 'You never know.'

'She's had one of them,' said the father, speaking for the first time. 'She's always finding ways to do herself a damage, this one. Who might you be?'

Russell had finally levered himself out of the tiny car and interrupted by offering to go indoors and 'fetch the Germolene antiseptic ointment from the kitchen drawer'.

'No thanks, Mr Savage, there's no need. We've got some in our picnic basket down by the river,' said the father. 'Our name's Tope,' he told Maisie, with a gleam of inquisitiveness in his eye.

'I'm Maisie Cooper,' she replied.

The little girl whined so he crouched down to comfort her. The mother, Mrs Tope, did the same. The girl – who perhaps, on reflection, was eight or nine but on the small side – was wearing a frilly bikini-style bathing costume in an insipid yellow and her skin was very pale.

'Are you feeling all right, now, Deborah?' Mr Tope asked. 'There was no need to go running off like that, was there.'

'I thought they were going to come after me,' whined Deborah.

'Poor little thing,' said Russell.

'I know, I know,' said Mrs Tope.

The girl had a spoilt look to her, Maisie thought, and was playing her doting parents for all they were worth.

Why not, though? Children ought to be doted over.

'All's well that ends well,' said Russell. 'I'd better get my "Victoria and Albert" out of the road.'

'What's that?' Maisie asked.

'The number plate's VAA 898 H, so I call her my Victoria and Albert. I expect it's silly.'

'Not at all,' said Maisie with a smile.

'Anyway, the milk truck will be coming through soon and Floyd Tubb will start hooting and hollering if he can't get past.'

'Of course, Mr Savage,' said Mrs Tope. 'It's just young Deborah gave me quite the turn, dashing off like that. The cows were quite safe on the other side of the river but one came down to drink and she got it into her head that they were all going to stampede across and trample us under their hooves, so she ran like a rabbit. Thank you for your kindness. Nice to meet you, Miss Cooper.'

'We need that meeting, Russell,' said Mr Tope. 'Where's our money gone?'

'I know, Shane, but Sunday night's soon enough and it's a time everyone can manage. What about old Norman Tubb?'

'I've a good mind to report him to the police, if we only had a service we could properly fall back on, but you know what they're like at the station in Kirton.'

'They do their best, I'm sure,' said Russell. 'Should I have a word with Norman on your behalf? He ought to apologise, after all.'

'I don't know if you'll get through to him,' said Shane with a shake of his head. 'I don't want him manhandling you as well.'

Maisie watched the Topes follow the road away from the humpbacked bridge towards the cluster of five cottages by the railway gates, turning right before them to climb over a stile, through the overgrown hedge, into a field on the near bank of the Wivel. She was interested to know more about Norman Tubb and would have liked to ask Russell about the 'meeting'. However, with a squeal of heavy brakes, the milk truck came to a sudden halt on the brow of the bridge. A young man with a spiteful face, despite his blue eyes and floppy blond hair, leaned out of the driver's window.

'What're you playing at, you old nonsense? Get on with you.'

'All right,' said Russell. 'Keep a civil tongue in your head.'

Russell painfully folded himself back into the Vauxhall Viva and edged forward, taking a sharp left into the narrow drive of Sunny View, between two brick pillars. Maisie followed on foot as the milk truck skimmed past, uncomfortably close. She watched it stop a hundred yards further on at the railway gate. The milk truck driver hooted again – which was quite unnecessary because the gatekeeper had already emerged from the cottage by the tracks. His shoulders hunched, the British Rail employee drew the bolts out of the tarmac and swung the gates back, the near one to the left and the far one to the right, blocking the rails and opening the road. The milk truck drove on, impetuously fast in the narrow lane, Maisie thought, and the gatekeeper closed the lane once more. Russell came to stand beside her at the gatepost.

'Is that still Fred Luscombe in charge of the crossing?' Maisie asked.

'Until he dies, I shouldn't wonder.'

'Was he already quite old ten years ago, or is it just that he seemed so to me because I was younger?'

'Job for life,' said Russell, disapprovingly, then he shrugged. 'I couldn't do it though – at the beck and call of every vehicle from the bang of dawn till the road's closed to traffic.'

'Do I remember correctly?' Maisie asked. 'Eight in the week and six on Sundays?'

'That's the feller.'

The noise of the milk truck's diesel engine faded and it became very quiet in the lane, apart from the occasional rustle of an animal in the undergrowth of the hedgerows, the buzzing of insects and the occasional chirping of songbirds.

'How is Fred's daughter?'

'Dotty as your polka-dotted dress. That'll never change.'

They made their way to the front door, sheltered under an open porch.

'Is that the bicycle I used to use?' asked Maisie, delighted.

'It is. I pumped up her tyres, thinking you might like a bit of freedom.'

'Thank you, Russell.'

'Will you come inside and say hello to Audrey? How does it feel to be back?'

'It feels wonderful,' she told him.

But there was something in the back of her mind – an awareness of a kind of shadow behind Russell's eyes – that told her it wouldn't feel like that for long.

THREE

As it turned out, Sunny View guest house was deserted. Audrey was not in. Russell apologised but Maisie told him that it didn't matter.

'I didn't expect to make all my connections so easily. I was a good hour early. Did you wait long at the station?'

'I had the *Kirton Courier* to read. Herbert Peckham does a good job. I never used to be one for the newspapers. I preferred ancient history, as you may remember. But perhaps it comes with age, becoming interested in other folks' affairs – like those busybodies Shane and Jane Tope.' He laughed. 'Of course, it would all be very small beer if the stories weren't here on our doorstep.'

They were standing at the foot of the stairs in a hallway paved with terracotta tiles, panelled in dark wood beneath the dado rail and painted apple green above. He hung his keys on a set of hooks on a panel by the front door, under an inscription burnt into the grain of the oak: *Bless this house.*

'Didn't you have an idea of writing a memoir about country life?'

'Fancy you remembering that,' said Russell, looking pleased. 'Now, you run upstairs and hang up your things and have a wash. It's very grimy on the trains. If everyone stopped home instead of fossicking this way and that, the world might get on easier. You're in "Caesar".'

Russell followed the corridor to the rear of the property where, Maisie knew, a rather dark but spacious kitchen gave on to a glorious lawn whose left-hand edge sloped gently down to the bank of the Wivel. She took the stairs to a large room on the first floor with a view over the lane through east-facing windows.

Before she unpacked, Maisie had a vivid flash of memory from her interview for the job of manager at Sunny View, when Russell had told her that the four double rooms – two on the first floor and two in the roof with large dormer windows – had been named for great generals from the Roman wars.

'The names will be easy as pie to hold,' he had told her, counting the generals off on his strong fingers. 'People won't be so apt to forget and cause a commotion by going into the wrong one in a strange house. First floor is "Caesar" and "Pompey", second floor is "Scipio" and "Hannibal". I don't remember much about what I was taught in school. I've a notion the teachers at the Queen Elizabeth Grammar School thought they were wasting their time with me, albeit I got my eleven-plus. But the Roman empire stuck in my mind like a thorn in your finger.'

Maisie went to the open window and looked out. The view was partly obscured by the spreading branches of a huge copper beech tree in glorious leaf, making a canopy of maroon and burgundy. But, through the twiggy lower branches, she could see over the hedge and across the pasture to the winding river. The distant trio of Topes were sitting on towels on a patch of beach, opposite a steeper bank that was scooped out by the current. The water twinkled in the summer sunlight.

How lovely.

Leaning out, Maisie could also see the humpbacked bridge up the lane to the right, with the sun behind. Beyond the bridge, the road ran slightly uphill to the cattle grid at the entrance to Tubb's Dairy Farm.

I need to know more about the conflict between Shane Tope and Norman Tubb.

Maisie felt something scratch her hand and realised she had inadvertently brushed her wrist against a sharp stiletto spine on an enormous pyracantha, a well-defended woody shrub covered with orange flowers that had colonised the façade. Jack's grandmother Florence had one below her bedroom window in Chichester and always referred to it as 'firethorn'.

The spine had drawn blood. She went to the bathroom on the landing and ran her hand under a tap, squeezing blood from the wound to make sure that it was clean, then dabbed it dry with toilet paper. Satisfised, she returned to 'Caesar' to hang up her clothes.

Maisie had resisted all the pervasive 1970s advertising for 'drip dry' and 'non-iron' synthetic fabrics. She knew that creases in cotton and wool wouldn't all drop out in the imposing mahogany wardrobe. Because her grip had been so tightly packed, she might borrow Audrey's iron to make some of them presentable.

She laid out a few toiletries on a marble-topped chest of drawers, beside a tray on which an empty flower vase stood. She pressed a hand to the eiderdown to discover – with pleasure – that the mattress was very firm. She returned to the bathroom to wash her face and hands, finding that the puncture to her wrist persisted in oozing a dark-red pearl of blood.

She went downstairs and along the corridor to the kitchen. It was very warm – as was her memory of the room – because the hot water at Sunny View was provided by a massive cast-iron Aga stove, fuelled with coal or coke, delivered in dirty sacks by a business based on a backstreet in Kirton. Russell brought in the fuel from an outdoor coal shed, using a tall scuttle with a curved top lip.

Next to the Aga was a narrow kitchen dresser in pale oak. Maisie remembered that Audrey referred to the top drawer as 'chaos' because it was where she crammed all kinds of useful things in utter disorder. Maisie also remembered Russell offering to 'fetch the Germolene antiseptic ointment from the kitchen drawer' for Deborah Tope's scratches.

She pulled the drawer open and rummaged through an extraordinary assortment: string; paper bags; drinking straws; candles; batteries of various sizes and voltages; light bulbs; two torches, one of which was held together with Sellotape; six or seven packets of over-the-counter medicines; a writhing nest of rubber bands; a corkscrew with a novelty handle in the shape of a monkey; a box of Airstrip plasters; a pair of secateurs; one large and two standard boxes of non-safety Swan Vesta matches; some metal meat skewers; a paper packet of envelopes and a pad of Basildon Bond writing paper.

Finally, Maisie located the Germolene in its cream-and-blue tin, prised it open and dabbed a tiny amount of the pink ointment on her wrist, then applied a small Airstrip plaster over the top. Russell came in from the garden carrying a heavy earthenware cider flask, beige below and rust-brown around the neck.

'I don't know where Audrey's got to,' he said, placing the flask on the elderly beechwood kitchen table, scarred by decades of use. 'Would you like to try this?'

'I would,' said Maisie.

'Have you done yourself a mischief, there?' he asked, indicating her plaster.

'Just a scratch,' she reassured him, fetching two tumblers from the cupboard beneath 'chaos'. 'Will these do?'

'They're a mite small,' Russell told her, stroking his salt-and-pepper whiskers, 'but happen we could refill them.'

'All right then,' said Maisie, smiling. 'What's the vintage?'

'Last autumn's apples, of course. We've been at it four years and there's never been any left over from previous.'

Russell needed two hands to lift and pour from the large earthenware flask. The cider was slightly cloudy in the glass, without bubbles.

'Made with the waters of the Wivel,' he told her as they picked up their tumblers. 'Good health.'

'Cheers,' said Maisie.

They both drank, Maisie sipping and Russell emptying his glass.

'What do you think?' he asked.

'It's absolutely delicious,' she told him. 'I've never known, though, how scrumpy is different from cider.'

'Scrumpy is more the old way, unfiltered, with no extra ingredients. Our apples ferment to alcohol because their skins have a natural yeast. When I started out, I read up on it in the library and, did you know, apples originated from Central Asia, that they're not native to Devon or anywhere else you or I might call home?'

'No, I didn't.'

'The Romans brought them, I believe, then your friends, the Norman French, carried their own trees across with William the Conqueror. You know why it's called scrumpy?'

'Because of scrumping? Because it's made with apples stolen from other people's orchards?'

'That's right. And why shouldn't your native-born Englishman steal a few fruits from under the trees of their new French overlords?'

Maisie laughed and took another sip.

'It really is very good. The dryness in the mouth is balanced by the fruit flavour. How strong is it?'

'About the same as wine, I think.'

'Oh, crikey. Are you sure? Have you had it tested?'

'I've conducted my own in-depth research, as has Audrey,' said Russell with a wink.

'A delicious sort of study, then?' said Maisie, joining in the joke.

'The key finding was two pints good, three pints bad.'

'Three pints? Good heavens,' said Maisie, draining her glass. 'If I have another one of these small tumblers, that'll make half a pint and that'll be plenty.' Russell refilled both. 'By the way,' she went on. 'What's that wonderful smell?'

'That's a brisket in the slow oven. Been in since soon after breakfast.'

Just for a moment, Maisie felt a wave of sadness. A slow-cooked joint of brisket was what Jack's grandmother Florence had cooked – as she admitted later – in an attempt to 'hurry things along and bring you and my sluggish grandson together'. But she made her voice light, replying: 'That's very thoughtful.'

Russell drained his second glass and replaced it on the heavy boards of the kitchen table. Maisie sipped her own, beginning to feel the effects of the alcohol, warming and loosening. She realised that Russell looked worried. His eyes were creased and his right hand was clenched in a fist on the spout of the large earthenware flask.

'I don't know where Audrey's got to,' he said again. 'Perhaps you'd like to see how the cider's made?'

'I would.'

They went outside into the garden, following an intermittent path of grey stone slabs, placed deep in the grass so the lawnmower could run across them without blunting its blades. On the far side of the lawn, under a hazel hedge, was a large wooden shed about five paces by ten. The double doors stood open. Inside were wooden racks with large, shallow shelves, very close together.

'Come autumn,' he told her, 'there'll be five thousand and more fruits on those racks, each one in its own nest of old newspaper.'

He showed Maisie the cast-iron apple press, resembling a very large thick-walled bucket on tallish legs, with a yoke above, through which a threaded plunger pressed down as the top handle was turned, squeezing the juice out of a spout at around knee height.

'All hand-powered,' said Maisie.

'That's right. You tip in about sixty or seventy apples at a time and it can be heavy going.'

He showed Maisie a few more elements of his and Audrey's traditional manufacturing process, then they went back outside. The orchard abutted the garden and was accessed over a stile in a bramble hedge festooned with early, unripe blackberries. Russell panted over first, exhaling with relief once he was across. Maisie followed.

The apples were hanging thick on the trees, though not yet mature by any means. All the same, Russell picked one and broke it in half with his strong fingers.

'Smell that,' he told her.

Maisie took it. 'Delicious,' she pronounced and was about to go on when they heard a thin, desperate voice that somehow seemed to be coming from a thicket in the far corner.

'Is someone there? Can you help me? Please help me.'

FOUR

Maisie dropped the split apple on the rich grass and ran through the trees. It wasn't easy. Their bark was ringed to stunt their upward growth and keep them growing close to the ground so as to make picking easier. That meant she had to bend very low to pass between and beneath the branches.

The thicket in the far corner of the orchard – from which she and Russell had heard the desperate, reedy voice – was made up of spiny hedging plants, hawthorn and blackthorn, plus rampant long strands of bramble, some of them tender with this year's growth, but lots of them older, hard and brown with multiple vicious thorns.

'Hello?' she called. 'Where are you?'

She crouched down on the dry grass, peering into the shadows, locating a boy of maybe ten or eleven, very pale in the gloom. As her eyes began to adjust, she could make out blond hair, pale skin, long lashes and a wary expression.

'Who are you? Am I in trouble?'

'No,' said Maisie. 'Are you stuck?'

'I'm all caught up, even my hair.'

'How awful. My name's Maisie. Mr Savage is on his way, too. We're going to help.'

Russell caught up, coming to a halt beside her with his hands on his knees.

'Well, if it isn't young Tim Sturgess in that old thicket. Maisie, he would have been a baby ten years ago. What did you creep in there for, lad?'

Timothy gestured to a rusty object deep in the brambles.

'I wanted this old oil drum for making a raft,' said Timothy, surprising Maisie, but with a tone that suggested it was the most normal thing in the world. 'Then I got caught up,' he repeated, trying to move. 'Ow.'

'Perhaps you should stay still for a moment,' said Russell, pushing his fingers through his thick grey hair, 'while we have a think about what's best to do.'

Maisie remembered seeing the secateurs in 'chaos' and told them to wait while she fetched them. She dodged back through the low, heavily laden trees to the kitchen and found them in among all the other potentially useful things. Beside the Aga, she noticed a pair of leather fireproof gloves so she brought those too. When she got back, she was glad to hear Russell and Timothy calmly discussing modes of construction for improvised rafts and boats.

The leather fire gloves were very big so Russell put them on, using them to pull away the thorny strands as Maisie snipped them off. Little by little, they cleared a path for Timothy to emerge, but he was still trapped. Maisie bent down on all fours and crept in to help him, delicately removing the barbs that clung in his grey school shirt and his thin blond hair.

Finally, he was free. Maisie exited the thicket in reverse and he followed, dragging his prize behind him – a rusted five-gallon oil drum that someone must have dumped there, possibly years before the brambles grew up and over it. Maisie wondered if it was safe to play with.

'Let's get you indoors.' Russell led them, weaving through the short trees, and pointed out a few loose planks lying over a rectangular manhole that had lost its proper cover. 'Some ruffian crept in and stole it for scrap,' he explained.

'What's underneath?' Maisie asked.

'It's a drain that takes water from the ditches on this side through a culvert under the lawn so it can make its way into the Wivel. It's dry now, though.'

They climbed over the stile, crossed the lawn and took Timothy indoors to look him over. Russell solicitously bathed his scratches with a solution of Dettol and warm water applied with an old flannel, then dried him with a threadbare tea towel. Meanwhile, Maisie took the oil drum – mustard yellow and cherry red with the brand name REDeX – to the big white-china sink. She squirted plenty of Fairy Liquid in through the round hole in the top – there was no cap – added some water from the tap and shook it vigorously. When she poured the contents away down the drain, she was pleased to see that the results looked pretty clean. Meanwhile, Russell was offering to give Timothy an old forklift truck pallet he had no use for.

'It's splintery, mind, so be careful where you sit.' Russell laughed. 'You've already got enough holes in you.'

Timothy smiled uneasily. Maisie thought he was probably more at ease with factual conversation than jolly small talk, so she asked him: 'Who's your favourite teacher?'

Timothy frowned and considered the question.

'You must have one,' Russell chivvied.

'I like woodwork,' said Timothy.

That's not an answer to my question, thought Maisie. *Poor boy. It would be sad if he didn't have a single teacher that he felt was a friend.*

'What have you made in woodwork?' she asked.

'I've made a spice rack and a pipe rack.'

'That sounds like fun,' Maisie approved. 'What tools did you use?'

'A tenon saw and two different chisels.'

'And sandpaper?'

'Yes, and a hammer and glue and pins.'

33

'I'd like to see them. Are they at home? Which number do you live in?'

Timothy recited a description of the hamlet of Trout Leap as if it was a text he had learned, making Maisie wonder if he'd written something similar in English class.

'We're in number three, the corner one. The five cottages are in a shape like the letter L. Number one is Mr Luscombe and his daughter up by the gates, then Miss Pond, the school secretary, is number two. Me and my mum and Petunia are in number three on the corner.'

'Petunia?' asked Maisie.

'That's Tim's big sister,' said Russell with what Maisie thought was an odd inflection.

'On our other side,' continued Timothy, 'is Mr and Mrs Tope and Deborah who is only a girl. After that is the Malta people.'

'The Malta people?' Maisie asked.

'It's an island,' said Timothy. 'In the Mediterranean.'

Russell broke in: 'You read the papers, so you know that Malta's got its independence, like a lot of places Britain used to look after?'

Maisie didn't want to argue about whether the British Empire – and, later, the Commonwealth – had ever really had a mission to 'look after' places like Malta. Instead, she said: 'The prime minister, Mr Mintoff, is a very pugnacious character, isn't he?'

'British citizens sent packing with no more than they could carry and just fifty pounds in their pockets. That's what's happened with the Lintons. Turned up here one fine day last winter – mum, dad, son, daughter – with faces all drawn and sad like a wet August Bank Holiday.'

'And that was the son we saw on the motorbike? How did they end up in an out-of-the-way place like Trout Leap?'

'Yes, that was young Paul. Mr Linton was with the British army on Malta, in the Royal Engineers or working for the

34

regiment on the outside, looking after tanks and trucks and things. I'm not sure. Anyway, Paddy – that is Patrick – told me they wanted somewhere agricultural so he could work maintaining farm machinery. He's got a little van from Moore's car showrooms up in Kirton. Paddy Linton's a dab hand.'

'They've fallen on their feet, then?'

'Money's still dreadful tight with there being four of them, his missus and two teenage children, all relying on him and needing clothes and books for school. And their cottage, number five, being unoccupied for a few years before they moved in, isn't anyone's idea of a palace, not even for people who haven't got a choice. It's cob, of course, like they all are,' Russell concluded, referring to the traditional construction style that resulted in very thick walls, built using a 'cob' of mud, sand, straw and water. 'Of course, the worst of the damp will have been drawn out by the good weather.'

'Do you talk to their children?' Maisie asked the boy.

'Paul and Maria are older than me,' said Timothy.

That means he's tried and they aren't interested.

Russell went back to talking to Timothy about his raft: 'I expect you can get nearly a mile downstream to where the Wivel meets the railway station? What will you call it?'

'The SS *Egruts*,' said Timothy.

Maisie smiled, recognising that it was his name, Sturgess, backwards. Then, he went on, minutely describing the twists and turns of the trout river, the dark pools and overhanging branches, the running shallows. As he spoke, she thought about how quickly the world seemed to be changing. In her accidental investigation into the murder at Bitling Fair, she had met Rayan and Sara Ramsi, a brother and a sister of Indian heritage expelled by the Kenyan government. Everywhere one looked, these days, people – like the Lintons – seemed to be on the move, starting again, strangers in strange lands.

And, so often, change makes people less generous, more grasping, unsatisfied with what they have, jealous of people and ways of life that they don't know or understand.

FIVE

Maisie pushed her gloomy thoughts about 'strangers in strange lands' from her mind, letting Timothy and Russell run on, discussing the geography of the valley and the path of the Wivel, plus various means of attaching oil cans to a forklift pallet. She visualised the five Trout Leap cottages, in their 'L' shape, as Timothy had said, the upright part made up of numbers one and two, three on the corner and then four and five making up the leg that stuck out to the right. She was interested to know more about all the residents.

She could remember the Luscombes in number one, the gatekeeper and his daughter. Miss Pond, the school secretary, in number two would be new to her. In number three, Timothy had referred to his mother – Maisie had known Mrs Sturgess as a younger woman with Timothy as a little-boy baby – and his older sister Petunia. She had just now met the Topes of number four – together with the daughter they doted on, Deborah – in the road. Was that the whole family?

She frowned, thinking about how the Maltese-Brits in the dilapidated number five, at the end of the leg, must have found the isolation of a cold and frosty Devon winter very difficult after the year-round warmth of the southern Mediterranean. Then she noticed that Russell and Timothy's conversation had ground to a halt.

'Is your mother expecting you?' Maisie asked.

'I should go home. I think it's teatime,' said Timothy.

'You run along,' said Russell. 'Take this and keep it upright.'

He passed the boy the oil can that Maisie had left inverted in the sink to drain.

'Thank you, Mr Savage. I'm sorry to have been a trouble.'

'You weren't no trouble,' said Russell.

'Goodbye, Miss . . .' Timothy frowned. 'What's your name?'

'Miss Cooper, but you can call me Maisie.'

'I'm not allowed. I'm supposed to use grown-up names,' said Timothy, simply.

He left, out the back door into the garden and round the side of the house.

'Poor little scrap,' said Russell. The kitchen clock began its musical chime, followed by four decisive strokes. 'Audrey wanted to be here to meet you. I wonder where she's got to.'

'Might Audrey have gone into Kirton for some groceries? Would she have gone over Break Heart Hill or up Long Lane?'

'She struggles on that gurt steep climb. She's better off in the lane, though it's the longer way. Trouble is, Floyd's not alone in driving through there too fast and the truck's nearly as wide as the gap between the hedges and they're that tall no one can't see what's coming up or who's where.' Russell gave an unhappy shake of his head. 'And I wanted her to tell you everything afore of me. Then you'll be set for the meeting.'

'The meeting?'

'We're coming together to discuss things and how they are and the mine,' he told her, confusingly.

Maisie frowned, then a new chime was ringing, the harsh telephone bell. She said: 'Perhaps that's her?'

Russell had been leaning against the chest of drawers. 'Would you mind getting it? I feel all somehow. Maybe that scrumpy in the middle of the day. Skip along, now. Don't let them ring off.'

Maisie hurried out of the kitchen, knowing the telephone was on the wall near the front door, with a dark wood hall-stand beside it that incorporated a box for footwear on top of which one could sit for longer conversations. She picked up and heard a strong, decisive voice that brought back all kinds of happy memories from ten years before.

'Russell, you'd better come up. I'm in number one and there's a funny turn. You know why. And every sort of nonsense.'

'Audrey, it's me, Maisie. Russell's feeling under the weather. Can I help?'

'Happen you might, Maisie,' said Audrey, simply, as if they'd seen one another only that morning. 'Come up to number one and we'll see if you can talk a bit of sense into Holly Luscombe. I've no more patience.'

Maisie hung up and went to explain to Russell what Audrey had asked her to do. He looked grey so she offered him a Garibaldi biscuit from a clay barrel on the dresser and gave him a glass of water, too.

'I'll be all right. You go on,' he told her.

'If you're sure.'

'As sure as eggs are eggs.'

Maisie hurried out the back door and round the side of Sunny View, as Timothy Sturgess had done, remembering the story people told about how Holly Luscombe had 'had a fright when she was little and been silly ever since'. When she had shared the story with Audrey, the older woman had told her: 'Mind, she was silly to begin with.'

The day was still very warm, despite the sun having gone over to the west. The lane was louder with the competing songs of four or five blackbirds. Somewhere nearby, in taller trees, was a rookery from which coarse cawing could be heard.

Maisie hurried up the lane, past the Sturgesses' corner cottage and the narrow in-between home of Miss Pond, the school secretary whom she had never met. Number one, the gatekeeper's cottage, was hard up against the railway line, with a low front door that stood open. At five-foot-eight, Maisie could have squeaked under the lintel without ducking her head, but she did so automatically, stepping into a gloomy hallway with terracotta tiles like at Sunny View, but less well looked after.

'Hello? Is anybody there?'

No answer came.

Maisie peeped into two rooms, a sitting room to the right with a television in a dark wooden cabinet, a very small dining room to the left, with a window overlooking the railway line. There was no one in either. At the end of the narrow hallway, by the doorway into the kitchen, a staircase doubled back upstairs. She stood by the bottom step and listened, suddenly hearing a door slam and running feet on the landing above. Then, Maisie had a peculiar sensation of memory and reality colliding as Holly Luscombe appeared, dressed in a childish blue-and-white-striped pinafore with ribbons on the shoulders and cuffs, as if she was a little girl of eight or ten, rather than a very bony woman of twenty-five or thirty. On her feet were black buckle shoes with blocky two-inch heels, but no socks.

'Hello, Holly,' said Maisie with a broad smile. 'How nice to see you.'

'Who are you?' she demanded in a defiant tone. 'Have you come to take me back?'

'I've come for tea,' said Maisie. 'Is that all right? It's four o'clock, you know, just gone.'

'Tea?' asked Holly Luscombe.

Audrey appeared behind her on the tiny landing, her firmly set grey hair just visible over Holly's bony shoulder, contrasting sharply with Holly's very pale blonde.

'That's Miss Cooper,' said Audrey. 'You remember I told you about her? She was here ten years ago. You'll have seen her on visits, before you came home.'

From the hallway at the foot of the stairs, Maisie watched as a sequence of emotions played out on Holly's narrow face. She pushed her glasses up her nose and widened her eyes, then squeezed them close together as if she was trying to read some very small print, finally deciding: 'She's the pretty one.'

'That's right,' said Audrey. 'Maisie's like a picture in a magazine.'

Holly awkwardly descended the stairs, one step at a time, her weight on the insides of her flat feet, her ankles flexing inwards.

'Have you hurt yourself,' Maisie asked. 'Do you need a hand?'

'I don't like people to touch me,' Holly snapped.

'All right. I'll remember that,' Maisie reassured her in an even tone. 'It was just that you looked like you were finding it hard.'

Maisie was pleased to see that speaking calmly and explaining herself clearly was beginning to have a salutary effect. She had another vivid memory of a desperate Fred Luscombe banging on the door at Sunny View, one afternoon when Audrey and Russell had gone into Kirton for groceries, to announce: 'Holly's gone running up the line, Miss Cooper. She thinks she has to go back there to her doctors to be put right. There's no doctor in Exeter can put her right. What am I to do, with me on duty and everything?'

This speech had been accompanied by yapping from the Luscombes' border terrier, a charming ball of wiry fur that hopped and skipped from side to side under the gate-keeper's feet. Maisie had sent Fred back to attend to his responsibilities and had done the obvious thing. Feeling like a character in the television show *Lassie* – although that was a collie dog, not a border terrier like Bertie, a sort of mobile Brillo pad – Maisie had followed the dog into the field between the cottages and the Wivel and found Holly sitting on the beach of mud and sand, tossing small stones into the water, quite unaware of the fuss she had caused.

'Do you remember,' Maisie asked, when Holly finally reached the ground floor, 'how I take my tea?'

'Lots of tea, lots of milk, lots of sugar,' said Holly in a sing-song voice, her eyes vague with reminiscences of ten years before. Her gaze sharpened. 'Will you make it? Dad says I'm clumsy.'

'It's very easy to make mistakes. Getting things right is always harder.'

'Is that right?' asked Holly, innocently, giving Maisie a fleeting glimpse of the girl she must once have been. Holly produced a surge of unexpected enthusiasm. 'You came to find me with Bertie, throwing pebbles in the Wivel.'

'That's right,' said Maisie, thinking that Holly's sing-song intonation made it sound like a quotation from a poem or a song. 'Is Bertie still alive?'

'No,' moaned Holly with another abrupt change of tone. 'He got stuck down a rabbit hole and no one would help to find him and drag him free.'

'That's not true,' said Audrey, descending the steep staircase with caution. 'We all came out to help and we beat up and down the hedges and everything. It was just that it was a dark night and filthy with sideways rain and his poor little mouth was choked full of dirt and he couldn't bark or whine to make us hear. We all came home drenched and were right sad for you, Holly.'

'Is that right?' Holly asked Maisie.

'Yes, I'm certain that it is,' she confirmed.

Maisie encouraged Holly into the kitchen – a miserable room with a grubby Calor gas stove and a chipped Formica table. There were only two hard chairs with painted plywood seats and tube-steel frames. Holly sat down, twirling her pale blonde hair around her finger. Maisie found the teapot still half full in the sink.

'Perhaps we should all have a little something to eat,' she suggested, looking round in vain for biscuits or bread for sandwiches. 'Is there anything?'

Audrey nodded and told her: 'I'll just nip along for something from ours and tell Russell what's happened.'

She bustled out. Left alone with Holly, Maisie emptied the teapot of its cold leaves into a blue-and-white bowl on the windowsill that was brimming with several days' worth, thinking that silence would allow poor Holly time to get her ideas in order and, perhaps, for her mood to become less changeable. She was wrong. All at once, without warning, Holly was on her feet and shouting.

'I wanted to find the mine; that's what I wanted to do. I read about it in the *Kirton Courier*. Everyone wants to know. But Dad wouldn't let me go out. He locked me up in my room. He's put a bolt on the outside. What do you think of that?'

'I'm sure he wants what's best for you,' said Maisie.

'I shouted down from the window to where he was putting grease on the railway gates and told him that I'd jump out if he didn't set me free. I would, too. I'm not a dog, am I?'

'No, you're not,' said Maisie, soothingly, wondering what Holly could have meant by 'the mine' and what sort of father would put a bolt on the outside of the door of his grown-up daughter's bedroom.

Six

People who are troubled in their minds need to be listened to, taken seriously. Sympathy isn't what they want – or, at least, it's not the only thing they want.

Despite Holly Luscombe's outburst, lurching to her feet and making a commotion, Maisie kept her expression neutral.

'The tea will be a couple of minutes brewing,' she said.

'What's that?'

'You can't hurry it, Holly.'

'I know that.'

'Have a seat, why don't you, while we're waiting?'

'All right.'

Holly sat down again, looking vague, as if she knew she had something important to do or say but could no longer remember what it was.

'What did you mean about the mine?' Maisie asked, lightly.

'Wouldn't you like to know,' said Holly.

'Or you could tell me about what it's like living by the railway line? It must be lovely. The sound of trains going by in the night is very romantic.'

'They don't go by so late.'

'After dark in winter, though?'

'Yes, in winter,' admitted Holly, grudgingly.

Maisie poured some hot water into the pot to warm it, tipped it away then added loose leaves from the caddy. She poured on more boiling water.

'This smells like Lyons Red Label. Is it?' she asked.

'It's tea,' said Holly, before abruptly changing the subject. 'Do you like my dress?'

'I do,' said Maisie. 'It looks quite elaborate, though. Do you know what I mean? I imagine you feel overdressed when you go out and about.'

'I don't go out and about. What do you mean, "overdressed"?'

'I mean for practical things like wooding for the fire or collecting flowers for the vase in the front room.'

'We don't have no flowers.'

'Would you like to have flowers indoors? There are lots in the hedgerows that no one would miss. It would make it nice.'

Holly didn't answer for a few moments, then she seemed to be taking the idea of less fussy clothing seriously: 'What should I wear, then?'

Just then, Audrey returned with a packet of ginger nuts, together with Fred Luscombe, having met him in the road outside. Holly's father had apparently run up the line a quarter of a mile towards Exeter. Now he was back, he was puffing and out of breath. His hair was very pale grey but, seeing him up close, Maisie realised he wasn't as old as she had imagined, even ten years on.

'Hello, Mr Luscombe. It's Maisie Cooper. Do you remember me? Holly and I have just been having a lovely chat about clothes and flowers and things.'

His eyes went from his daughter to Maisie to Audrey and back again. He looked surprised at how calm Holly appeared.

'She won't have any of them biscuits. Holly eats no more than a sparrow.'

'All right, then, Dad?' asked Holly.

'You gave me a fright,' he said.

'How come?' said Holly.

'You were supposed to stay in your room.'

'I didn't want to, did I.'

45

Maisie poured them both a cup of tea in two 'decimalisation' mugs that showed the conversion rates from old money into new pence. Fred sat down, pulling off his grey official jacket to reveal patches of sweat on his unironed off-white shirt. Audrey stayed in the doorway, watching with a kind of frustrated sympathy.

'Anyway, yes, Miss Cooper. I remember you for your kindness,' said Fred. 'But perhaps you and Audrey should leave me and Holly alone.'

A loud motor horn sounded. With a muffled curse, Fred got up to go and open the gates. 'He's the devil himself, that one,' he told them, disappearing along the narrow hall and outside into the sunshine.

'Floyd,' said Audrey.

'Milk lorry,' confirmed Holly.

Maisie thought about how the routines of country living could be – simultaneously – charming and reassuring as well as irritating and restrictive. She considered how thin Holly was and whether she received any kind of treatment for what her father had suggested was a very meagre diet. She was letting her tea go cold without drinking it, ignoring Audrey's biscuits. Maisie glimpsed the milk lorry going by through the low, open doorway.

'I remember Bertie,' she said, hoping this would be a 'safe' topic of conversation. 'It's important to hold on to happy memories, isn't it?'

'I suppose.'

'Was he a good dog?'

'He was my dog,' said Holly, somewhere between wistfulness and truculence.

Fred came back inside. 'You can leave us to it, now,' he said. 'The passion's left her.' He sat down on the second hard kitchen chair, pulling it closer to his daughter. 'That's right, isn't it, Holly? We'll go in and put the telly on and wait for

46

Crossroads, shall we, and find out what them old baggages are up to?'

Holly's narrow face broke into a smile.

'Yes, *Crossroads*.'

She got up and tottered quickly down the short, narrow hallway with the same awkward gait, her ankles bending inwards. She disappeared, closing the door behind her. Fred stayed where he was, gazing at the empty chair.

'She's getting worse,' he said, as if to himself. 'I don't know where we'll end up.'

'Do you have no support from the health service?' asked Maisie.

'Not so's you'd notice.'

Maisie felt very moved by the despair – the defeat, even – in his voice.

'You look done in,' said Audrey. 'Perhaps a finger of brandy might help? Medicinal.'

'You know very well we never have spirits in the house,' he told her.

Fred rose and took Holly's undrunk tea through to the front room. When he re-emerged, closing the door behind him, Maisie tried to make him talk about his life, hoping he might feel better for sharing his troubles, even going so far as to wonder aloud if there might be some useful paid employment Holly might find. But he wasn't having it. He told both Maisie and Audrey, politely but firmly, that all would be well. Watching the early-evening soap opera would 'fill Holly's mind with easier things'.

'Of course,' said Audrey. 'You know you daughter best.'

Maisie thought that Audrey's words were intended for her, too, as a kind of warning not to push too hard.

'It's been a pleasure to see you again after all this time,' she told Fred. 'I have such a lot of fond memories of Trout Leap and all the people who live here.'

'It's mostly change, though, apart from the Sturgess family, the Savages and us.'

'Yes, I suppose it is. Mrs Sturgess was married back then, wasn't she?'

'She were,' said Fred, 'but then the one we're supposed to call "the big sister" came back out of the blue.'

'In addition to Timothy?'

'That's the pigeon. You know what I mean?'

Maisie frowned, putting two and two together, replying: 'Yes, I think I do.' She refrained from commenting further because she didn't like being drawn into gossip. 'I'm sure we'll meet again soon.'

Fred surprised her by replying: 'Six o'clock on Sunday, isn't it, after Long Lane's closed to cars?'

'That's right,' said Audrey. 'I hope everyone will come.'

'There's not one who hasn't given over at least some of their hard-earned savings, so I expect they will,' said Fred.

He escorted them to the front door. The sun was a little lower in the sky, making Maisie narrow her eyes. As the evening drew on, she thought, there would be more and more birdsong. Dew might fall, intensifying the delicious fragrances of the lush hills and pasture. She felt she wanted to climb the stile and go down to the river to look at the sparkling water running over its bed of clean stones. Perhaps she would peer under the humpbacked bridge where, no doubt, trout would be lurking in the shade. Then she realised she hadn't been paying attention and Audrey had been making a bit of a speech.

'So, I'm saying, if she's getting worse and likely to do herself a mischief, Fred, perhaps you can't be keeping her home.'

'You remember how it was, though, up hospital. She screamed the place down and they pumped her so full of drugs she didn't know if it was Tuesday or December. There's no malice in her, though she be silly as a March hare.'

48

'It isn't just for her safety,' insisted Audrey. 'What if she runs off and causes an accident? Young Paul Linton's got himself a motorbike. How about he comes leaning round the corner and she's galivanting in the middle of the road, not noticing who's about.'

'It's easy to imagine bad things happening,' said Fred in a surly tone. 'Doesn't mean they will.'

'It wasn't raining when Noah started building his ark.'

'All right,' said Fred. Maisie heard the distinctive theme music of the nightly *Crossroads* soap opera and Holly singing along in a joyful alto. He told them: 'I'd better join her.'

He left them outside in the lane, closing the front door behind him. Maisie and Audrey shared a glance, then both laughed, dispelling the tension.

'Here's an odd way to be meeting again after all this time,' said Audrey, smiling broadly. 'Me and Russell have thought of you many times and spoken of you often. What a boon you were for us.'

'I have very fond memories of you both.'

'Even with how it ended? I wish you hadn't . . .' Audrey seemed not to have words suitable for her emotion. 'It's a terrible thing to lose a parent. To lose both wasn't fair and—'

'It was a long time ago,' Maisie interrupted.

'And, more recent, your brother, too—' Audrey insisted.

'Let's get back to Sunny View,' Maisie cut in. 'I'll tell you all about what I've been doing these last ten years. Then you can share what you've been up to.'

'Ours is very poor news,' said Audrey. 'Nothing much ever happens in Trout Leap.'

Maisie thought about all she had seen since her arrival: the Topes and their daughter Deborah's drama with the cows; the hints of a serious conflict with the dairy farmer, Norman Tubb; Timothy Sturgess caught in the thicket of brambles; Holly Luscombe having 'a funny turn'; all the gnomic references to a 'mine'. The Lintons' struggles since arriving from Malta was quite the story, too. Then, there was the urgent letter she had received from the Savages, entreating her to visit as soon as circumstances allowed.

'Little things can be just as important as big things,' she said.

SEVEN

At Sunny View, Maisie discovered that Russell had, as Audrey put it, 'taken himself off to bed for a bit of a nap', so the two women sat alone in the kitchen over a pot of strong tea and Maisie told the story of her life from 1962 – when her parents' deaths had dragged her away from Trout Leap – to the present day. Maisie's life in Paris was not especially interesting to Audrey because she had never been abroad and had seldom even crossed Devon's borders either east into Dorset or west into Cornwall.

'I'm not even keen on trips into Exeter. How did you manage foreign travel, all on your own?'

'I received a very small inheritance, just enough to get myself a tiny room for a month and money left over to keep body and soul together. I found gainful employment and things went from there.'

'Isn't Paris very dear, like that London, so they tell me?'

'Yes, it is expensive making one's way in a big city, but in France you live better on the same money, if you see what I mean. And there's so much culture and life and history in Paris. New things are always invigorating. They make you feel alive.'

'Like spring after winter, I expect,' said Audrey, comfortably. 'What was the job you found?'

'I have Mother to thank for teaching me to love languages and the good teaching at Westbrook College in Chichester. I was a tour guide for a rather high-class dragon of a boss called Madame de Rosette.'

'Taking wealthy visitors round the cathedrals and monuments and all that?'

'Yes.'

'Did you like it? I ask because you're not one to suffer fools gladly. How did you manage when they turned out to be rum?'

'They were seldom rum but you're right. I did worry about that now and then, if I heard myself being short or impatient with them, but people seemed to like being organised and told what to do.'

'Like a strict schoolteacher telling them where to look, giving them chapter and verse on what it all meant?'

'Exactly.'

'So, it was only Stephen's death that brought you back to Sussex?'

'Yes, back in this year's miserable, damp February – all power cuts and candles. I wouldn't have come otherwise. I had no reason to.'

Maisie told Audrey the whole story of how she had arrived in Framlington, expecting to meet her dissipated brother with a daydream of helping him to get his life back together, only to discover that he was dead and his urgent but opaque summons had come too late. She explained how shocked she had been to be drawn into the mystery of the murder at Church Lodge, followed by her satisfaction at solving the puzzle, several times confronting physical danger.

Audrey was a good listener and Maisie told her stories with economy and vivacity. Meanwhile, they shared the preparation and cooking of the vegetables to accompany the joint of brisket that had spent more or less all day in the slow oven of the Aga: mashed potatoes with butter and pepper, peas with mint, fried discs of leek, red onion gravy. That gave her time to bring her old friend and employer up to date with the three subsequent mysteries she had helped to solve: at Bunting Manor, at Chichester Theatre and at Bitling Fair. At the end, Audrey remarked: 'I like the sound of that Jack Wingard. From what you tell me, though, he takes no nonsense, he appreciates you and watches over your shenanigans.'

'He does,' said Maisie, demurely.

'Would he be an older gentleman?'

'No, Jack is precisely my age. We were at school together.'

'What a coincidence,' said Audrey vaguely, her mind on the Bisto thickening powder that she was slowly stirring in the roasting pan while the joint rested under a heavy cast-iron lid on the carving board. 'So, he's become a friend of a sort?'

'More than a friend,' said Maisie meaningfully.

Audrey turned away from the stove.

'You don't mean—'

Maisie interrupted by holding out her hand with the modest but lovely engagement ring that Jack had given her – a silver band set with blue stones. She told Audrey: 'This was his grandmother's more than fifty years ago. Did you not notice I was wearing it?'

'I didn't think,' said Audrey, looking delighted. 'These days, young people wear all sorts of jewellery on every finger, as far as I can see, without rhyme nor reason.'

Just at that moment, Russell came downstairs, looking much better for his rest, and Maisie had to repeat much of what she had said, concluding in the same way.

'Jack and I are to be married and I wish you could meet him. Coincidentally, last month, he was down in Exeter on a training programme for promotion, while the mystery at Bitling Fair played out.'

'While you solved it, you mean, and everyone else watched on with not a clue in their heads,' said Audrey.

'For a couple of months, now, he's up in Newcastle for the same reason. If all goes well, we ought to be able to marry next spring and find somewhere to live together, in or around Chichester.'

'And his grandmother?' asked Russell.

'She's very independent,' said Maisie, 'but I hope she'll come with us. Her bungalow is too small for three and it only has a tiny plot so there's no way of extending it.'

'Happen there might be more than three of you soon enough?' asked Audrey.

'Does your Jack like children?' asked Russell.

'He does,' said Maisie, feeling they were putting the cart before the horse. 'We'll see.'

'You'll invite us to the christenings, won't you?' persisted Audrey.

'You could honeymoon here at Sunny View,' said Russell, looking delighted with his idea. 'Then come back with the baby.'

They mean well, Maisie thought, *but their ideas are running on very fast.*

'What about your news?' she asked.

It turned out that Audrey had spoken the truth. While Maisie's life had tumbled down the stream of life like a cork in a torrent, the solid raft of the Savages' existence had drifted with the current of a placid river winding peacefully across a flat plain. Audrey actually used that image, summing up by saying: 'When we're gone, it'll be like we've disappeared at last, you know, like a river meeting the sea. We'll be dead and, soon enough, no one will miss us.'

'That isn't true,' said Maisie, a little shocked.

'We've no kiddies,' said Russell, 'and no one close in blood or geography.'

Maisie felt a ghostly cold.

'You're not ill, either of you?' Her eyes went from Audrey to Russell. 'You'd tell me if you were?'

Russell laughed and his wife replied: 'We're as fit as the years allow.'

All was ready for what they called 'tea'. They put the dishes on the table and tucked in. Maisie enjoyed it enormously, admitting that she'd only eaten two rounds of cheese-and-pickle sandwiches all day. The beef was delicious and melted in the mouth. The vegetables were properly cooked without being mushy and the gravy – made with the wholesome meat juices – was rich and savoury. As she helped herself to seconds, Maisie tried to get them to talk about their letter, the one that had caused her to arrange to come down to Devon while Jack was up in the north-east.

'There'll be time for all that,' said Audrey, giving her husband a little shake of the head. 'Let's have a day without upset.'

'Yes, all right,' he agreed with reluctance. 'Tomorrow will be soon enough for unhappy ideas.'

Because the evening was warm and the kitchen a little overheated by the coal-fired Aga, they had left the front and back doors open. All the time they were eating and, then, washing and drying, not a single car or pedestrian went past.

And it's a Friday evening, surely one of the busier days of the week for people going out and about?

Maisie mentioned this to her hosts and asked: 'Do you have paying guests arriving? The school holidays have just begun.'

'We do,' said Russell. 'They'll be along . . . I forget. Where are we?'

'Today is Friday the twenty-first of July,' Audrey told him in a tone that suggested that she found it a little wearing that Russell used her as an additional memory bank for things he couldn't keep in his head. 'And, before you ask, the sun will be up at half past five and won't go down until after nine.'

Russell laughed and told her: 'I'm surprised you put up with me.'

'Who else would I look to for company?' Audrey riposted, joshing.

'Tomorrow they'll be here,' said Russell.

'A couple?' asked Maisie.

'A gentleman and a lady, separate. I'll put Miss Anderson in "Pompey" next to you on the first floor, Maisie, and Mr Brent upstairs in "Hannibal". That will be more seemly.'

Draping her tea towel over the chrome rail on the Aga, Maisie checked her watch and saw that it was only six-thirty.

'Are you sure you don't want to tell me all about the drama? You're going to have a meeting of all the residents on Sunday night. Have I understood that correctly? And it's to do with a mine? Can that be true?'

Audrey gave Russell the same shake of the head and he repeated his previous phrase: 'We'll explain tomorrow. That'll be soon enough for unhappy ideas.'

'In that case, I feel very full and I've done no real exercise today. The sun won't go down for ages. I've a yen to climb Break Heart Hill and look down on Sunny View from the brow.'

'Rather you than me,' said Russell.

'That sounds like a lovely idea,' said Audrey.

'I've things to get on with in the cider shed,' said Russell. 'You two should enjoy it.'

'I might walk on into Kirton, if that's all right,' said Maisie, 'and come back via the river path. That'll be two miles altogether?'

'Near enough,' said Audrey. 'You don't want to take the bike?'

'Too steep.'

'I'll come with you a little way up the hill before I let you go on.'

'Perfect. Let me just run up and fetch a cardigan in case it feels damp later. Can I help you put things away first?'

'You two get on,' said Russell. 'I'll straighten up.'

Maisie went upstairs to 'Caesar' and found a suitable woollen in the wardrobe and a handful of change – just in case – from the purse in her handbag to put in the pocket of her polka-dot dress. Because the evening was close, she carried her favourite cardigan back downstairs, but found Audrey on the front step, wearing a thin padded anorak in blue nylon.

'Age feels the cold,' she explained.

They set off up the lane towards the railway crossing, pushing through the pedestrian gate. Standing in the middle, between the two sets of steel tracks, Maisie hesitated, looking east towards Exeter and then west towards Barnstaple. The rails were arrow straight and bright in the slant light, the perspective making them narrow into the distance. For a second or two, she felt an uncomfortable sense of being trapped, as if there was no way of escaping where she stood, that a train would soon come hammering through with a raucous thunder of metal wheels and a stench of burnt diesel. Then, she felt and heard a faint vibration from the tracks and realised that an evening service was, indeed, approaching.

With a shudder, she followed Audrey through the second pedestrian gate and found her eating some blackberries from the hedgerow.

'Sharp but almost ripe, some of them. You're taller than I am. You can reach the ones up top where they've had the most sun.'

'I couldn't,' Maisie told her. 'I'm full to the brim.'

The train went by, not fast – no more than twenty miles per hour, the driver taking care – but noisy all the same. They climbed a stile into the field on the right-hand side of the lane and began the long ascent of Break Heart Hill, at first reminding one another of joyful experiences they had shared ten years before, then running out of puff as the slope

57

steepened, their steps slowing to a steady, measured trudge. To her own surprise, Audrey made it all the way to the top. They both turned to look down on Trout Leap and Sunny View, Audrey breathing heavily, Maisie pleasantly puffed.

'It's a picture,' she said.

'It is,' Audrey wheezed.

'But you are concerned?' Maisie asked.

'No,' said Audrey after a moment. 'I'm not, really.'

'In your letter you said—'

'That was Russell. He gets ideas in his head and can't shake them.'

Maisie frowned. 'You don't think there's anything to worry about?'

'There's always things to worry about if you look for them,' said Audrey, breathing more normally. 'Then there's the question of whether or not it's our business.'

'This is all very mysterious.'

'I know, but I think Russell should tell you himself. He was so excited to read about the Chichester cathedral robbery and how you discovered what had happened. That was even in our local paper, the *Kirton Courier*, because there's people remember you from back when. You know Clive and Cherry Atwill at the general store? They want to see you if you've time.'

'I'll make sure I pop in.'

'But he might be right, in the end,' said Audrey, going back to Russell's worries. 'Perhaps it's wishful thinking that makes me want there to be nothing to fret over.'

'Let's talk it through at breakfast, when we're all fresh and apt to look on the circumstances with optimism.'

'Yes,' said Audrey. 'That's a good idea.'

'But can you not tell me anything about the mine, so I can think about it? That sounds very unlikely and mysterious. Even Holly Luscombe mentioned it.'

Audrey sighed. 'All right, but you won't get carried away?'

'Of course not. You know me.'

'Well, you'll not credit it but . . .' Audrey waved a hand vaguely at the lovely landscape of hills and pasture and river valley. 'It's somewhere out there, so they say, within four or five miles of Kirton.'

'What is?'

'The mine, of course. Don't be slow, Maisie.'

'Yes, but what sort of mine?'

'That's what you won't credit but, apparently, it's as true as I'm standing here.'

'Yes, and . . . ?'

To Maisie's surprise, Audrey adopted a broad and rustic American drawl, like a Klondike prospector in a film at the cinema.

'There's gold in them there hills.'

EIGHT

Maisie watched Audrey stomp back down Break Heart Hill, an increasingly tiny figure as she went, only moving out of sight after the railway crossing. In all five Trout Leap cottages, lights were on, not just because evening was drawing in, but because the cob dwellings were dark, with small windows and low lintels. By contrast, beyond the L-shape of five rustic homes, brick-built Sunny View looked almost palatial, though it remained in darkness, with the only glimmer coming from the cider shed in the garden.

Beyond Sunny View and the little humpbacked bridge, Maisie could make out the outline of Tubb's Dairy Farm on the next hill, easily the biggest buildings round about, with a large milking shed and a sprawling farmhouse with single-storey extensions on three sides. She remembered Floyd Tubb from ten years before, a wiry boy with long lashes and very blue eyes, perhaps sixteen or seventeen years old. She had never taken to him because he was the kind who liked to pull the wings off flies to see how they would react, or who didn't trouble to return immature fish to the river to grow and thrive, but left them gasping on the bank.

I hope he's changed.

Frowning, Maisie pictured Norman Tubb, Floyd's father. She had a very clear memory of a fat man – who clearly enjoyed his own butter and cream with a thick mop of dark-blond hair and whiskers. And he was someone she had good reason to despise. She also located a mental image of Norman's wife, Stella, a small, energetic woman with an open smile and an attractive personality, but whose conversation seldom moved beyond the weather, animal husbandry and other staples of farming talk.

Having got her breath back from the steep climb, Maisie turned away from the view and found her way to another stile that led to a well-worn footpath across the top. She followed it through a sheep field with sparse trees until she reached the edge of Kirton via a narrow lane between small workers' cottages at the highest point of the town, emerging onto the High Street opposite the imposing Queen Elizabeth Grammar School. Maisie remembered Timothy Sturgess telling her that the resident of number two, Trout Leap, was Miss Pond, the school secretary.

She followed Kirton High Street downhill with the setting sun behind her, past the Liberal Club and the Masonic Hall, both pretty average early Victorian buildings. She hesitated outside Moore's car showroom, seeing the alleyway alongside that led to a 'service centre' behind ill-fitting wooden gates. That, she remembered, was where Patrick Linton worked, the recently expelled Maltese-Brit who had a son who might or might not be a tearaway.

Next to Moore's was another civic building, the Churchworkers' Institute, with an advertisement in the window for a jumble sale that would take place in two weeks, followed by Townsend's Furniture & Beds and the upmarket Home and Colonial Stores. Finally, she paused outside the chronically cluttered window of C & C Supplies, run by the couple Audrey had mentioned, Clive and Cherry Atwill, who wanted to be remembered to her.

The more inaccessible corners of the Atwills' display shelves were very dusty and Maisie wondered if, ten years before, she had contemplated some of the same unlikely items, perpetually and hopelessly on sale: Dinky Toys, fishing reels, salt and pepper cruets, a pair of blue-glass owl figurines, a cutlery set in a plush wooden box lined with burgundy velvet, a very large can of beer called a Watney's Party Seven, a *Mouse Trap* board game. There were also some scraps of paper and Sellotape on the inside of the glass where some large sheets of newsprint had been stuck and, more recently, taken down.

Maisie walked on, past a run of houses on either side of the road, punctuated by two modest restaurants, one Italian and one Chinese – both doing reasonable Friday evening business – and a closed and locked tea room. Before she arrived at the bottom of the town, she paused outside a plate-glass window belonging to the office of the local paper, the *Kirton Courier*. Despite the late hour, she could see someone working inside, sitting at an architect's sloping desk on a tall stool, arranging pieces of paper that she supposed were next week's news reports. It was a man in shirtsleeves and braces, with wiry steel-grey hair, bent over, looking very closely at his texts. Maisie noticed a name painted on the inside of the plate-glass window by a skilled signwriter and remembered how warmly Russell had spoken of him: *Herbert Peckham, editor.*

Feeling himself observed, the man looked up. Maisie turned away, reminding herself that it was rude to stare.

At the bottom of the town, she cut through the railway station car park – where Russell had met her and called her 'my handsome' – making for a footpath worn by innumerable feet, parallel with the bank of the river, no more than a 'desire line' through the fields. Every few yards she heard the unmistakable plop of frogs or toads throwing themselves into the water in fear of her approach.

Next, came a stretch of path between higher hedges, the air full of midges, but not the biting kind. A large dragonfly was patrolling the tunnel beneath the leaves, zooming back and forth, perhaps indulging in some kind of mating display for a female that Maisie was unable to see. She couldn't help but duck as the impressive insect swung soundlessly over her head.

Emerging from the tunnel of trees, she left the path and headed for the edge of the winding river as it swung away into open pasture, but the going was hard, the long grass full of cow pats, and the light was fading from the sky. She rejoined the hedgerow path, strolling into the glare of the sun's last rays, the sky an impressionist masterpiece of lemons, mauves and pinks. The trees on her right-hand side were twelve and fifteen feet tall, stands of hazel like long fingers rising out of a clenched palm, useful timber for fencing and for heating, coppiced every few years down to the ground. Between the hazels was a thickly woven tangle of thorny bushes, including gorse, its yellow blooms gone over but still exuding a faint fragrance of coconut.

Maisie stopped, seeing a dark shape silhouetted against the fiery sun – a person crouched low to the path or, perhaps, fallen; it was hard to tell.

'Hello?'

The shape moved but only a little, perhaps turning their head towards the sound of her voice.

'It's you,' came a sullen alto.

'Yes, it's Maisie. Who's there?'

'It's me, isn't it.'

'Yes, but who are you?' Maisie came closer, squinting. The dark shape resolved into a pale face framed by light-blonde hair and a blue-and-white-striped pinafore with ribbons at the shoulders and cuffs. 'Ah, hello, Holly. Are you out for a walk?'

'It was under here,' said the gatekeeper's daughter.

'What was under here?'

'Where we lost him.'

Maisie put two and two together and understood that this was where the adorable-though-scampish border terrier Bertie had got stuck in a rabbit hole and suffocated in the dust and dirt of a collapsed burrow.

'That must have been very sad. Do you come here a lot to remember?'

'When I can get out. I used to have the run of the fields before Dad got told off.'

'Who told him off?'

'The council woman. After that, I had to keep close.'

'Of course,' said Maisie, thinking of the wiry hippy Steve Weiss, the social worker who had tipped her the wink with some vital clues to unravelling the mystery of the murder at Bunting Manor.

'Then, when Dad changed his ways, he was told off for locking me in, so I reckon he can't do right for doing wrong. Don't you think?'

'Can I help you up? You must be damp with the dew that's falling.'

'I am – and cold.'

Maisie still had her cardigan in her hand. She hadn't needed it because she had kept warm by walking quickly.

'Here, let me put this over you.'

Holly stood up, docile as a small child, and Maisie draped the soft grey wool over her bony shoulders. Close up, she could see the dirt on Holly's thin cheeks and the tracks of her tears through the grime.

'If I was allowed another dog,' Holly told her, 'I'd care for it.'

'I expect you would.'

'Dad won't never let me though.'

'Dogs can be a lot of bother, especially if they're out worrying sheep and running down the road in front of cars.'

'Not if they're well behaved,' said Holly. 'Like I am.'

For a moment or two, Maisie thought she saw a ghost of a wink or a twinkle in the gatekeeper's daughter's eye. She promised herself she would find out more about Holly's background and more recent experiences. She had only sparse memories of her from ten years before, when she had been an intermittent visitor from a residential home.

'Shall we walk back together?'

'I see all sorts when I'm out late,' said Holly, with another faint twinkle.

'Do you want to tell me what?'

'No, I don't think I do.'

'Fair enough. Well, your father is probably wondering if you're . . .' Maisie stopped, not wanting to say 'safe' because that sounded melodramatic. 'He might be wondering if you'd like something to eat or drink before bed.'

'I like ice cream.'

'Do you have any?'

'No. Only when the van comes through. And do you know what? When I came here to live, out of the home, Dad told me that when they rang the bell that plays the tune, that meant they were all run out and they were on their way back to the depot for some more. And every time that happened and they came through, with the song playing out, and perhaps little Deborah Tope had a Ninety-Nine or a Strawberry Mivvi, he said there wasn't one left for me. That was what he told me and that was what I believed. And, though people say I'm daft and silly, that made me wonder what else he might be fibbing about.'

Maisie was disconcerted by the bitterness in the poor woman's tone, much more like a child that finds itself hard done by than a grown adult. And her father's behaviour seemed unnecessarily cruel.

'Will you come along with me, then? It's not far.'

Maisie walked on and was relieved when Holly fell into step beside her, finding the uneven path awkward, sockless in her black buckle shoes with their inappropriate blocky heels. But they were soon in the final field with the Wivel away to the left and the cottages in the far right-hand corner. The path became well-trodden and clean, which was handy because it was now properly dusk. They crossed the stile, Holly getting in a tangle when one of her ribbons caught on a twig but without any other mishap.

'Good night, then,' said Maisie, turning left towards Sunny View. Holly followed. Maisie stopped. 'Shouldn't you be getting home?' she asked as gently as she was able.

'I suppose,' said Holly, vaguely, handing back Maisie's cardigan. 'Thank you for coming to find me.'

Maisie wanted to say that she had simply been passing that way, but she thought there was a confusion in Holly's mind about looking for poor dead Bertie several years before and this evening's encounter.

'You're very welcome. I'm sure we'll meet again, soon.'

'I could give you a nice cup of Ovaltine,' Holly suggested. 'But only if you know how to make it. Dad says I always get lumps.'

'It's hard to make it completely smooth,' Maisie sympathised. 'No, thank you. Mr and Mrs Savage are expecting me.'

'I prefer the night.'

'I beg your pardon?'

'When it's dark and no one's around. Dad grumbles because I don't wake up until the afternoon.'

'He might be worried now. You should run along.'

Maisie was relieved when Holly followed this condescending advice, wandering past number three, the Sturgesses' corner cottage, and number two, Miss Pond's dwelling. From both pairs of windows, electric light spilled out between curtains that had been left open to allow in the cooling night air.

Maisie walked away, confident she had done her duty. Finding Sunny View quite dark, she opened the front door and looked into the hall, with its sombre, dado-height panelling and apple-green paint above, gloomy and unwelcoming. She felt a sudden premonition of disaster, like seeing a road accident about to happen, a collision between two inattentive drivers, inevitable and catastrophic, but with no way of doing anything to prevent it.

But it's not like a road accident. That would be easier. This is much more complicated.

She called out for her hosts: 'Audrey, Russell, are you about?'

No answer came.

I wish I knew who is about to collide with whom.

II

Ticks & Bulls

NINE

In the end, Maisie didn't go in through the front door of Sunny View. She went down the side of the house, her short curly hair catching in one of the lower twiggy branches of the copper beech. Emerging onto the back lawn, there was a little more light in the sky, but the orange glow in the window of the cider shed stood out brightly in the shadows. She crossed the lawn, managing to plant her feet squarely on the slabs of stone sunk into the dewy grass. The door was slightly ajar so she pushed it open and was about to step inside when she heard raised voices and her own name being spoken with frustration or even disappointment.

Silently, Maisie hung back, out of sight beyond the door frame. She didn't like to eavesdrop but felt she had no choice. Audrey and Russell had been so obscure in their hints and evasions that she was feeling very uneasy. Plus, the encounter with the decidedly odd Holly Luscombe on the dusk path had upset her more than she liked to admit – even to herself.

'You shouldn't have laid it all at Maisie's door,' said Audrey. 'Poor thing. She doesn't want to think of our troubles. She's affianced and good luck to her, with a life of her own to live and no need to get involved in others' business.'

'When I wrote to her you weren't so very against it,' Russell replied in a curt tone that Maisie didn't remember ever hearing him use.

'I was and you know it. You just weren't prepared to listen. Or maybe you listened but you didn't hear.'

'I thought you were with me,' said Russell. 'I'm not used to you thinking different.'

'Poor old man,' said Audrey with a chuckle.

Russell responded in kind: 'I am a poor old man.'

'You worry more than you ought. Come here.'

Maisie heard a shuffling of feet and peeped round the frame. In the lovely soft light of a hurricane lamp, Audrey and Russell were embracing one another. Because they were in profile, she could see that Audrey's eyes were closed and there was a smile of sympathy on her homely features. Russell's eyes, by contrast, were open and fixed on nothing, or perhaps on the cobwebs in the rafters of the big cider shed.

'Hello,' Maisie called, taking a step inside as if she had just that moment arrived. Audrey and Russell sprang apart like guilty teenagers. 'It smells wonderful in here,' Maisie told them. 'Have you been bottling up?'

'That's right,' said Russell.

Self-consciously, Audrey patted her firmly set grey hair and Russell moved one or two bits of paraphernalia on his workbench. Alongside was a large wooden barrel on some heavy breeze blocks to raise it off the floor. The top was nearly as high as Maisie's eye level. At the bottom, a golden liquid was slowly dribbling out of a brass tap set in the barrel's end boards. From there, the scrumpy passed through a large galvanised funnel lined with muslin into one of six half-gallon earthenware flasks, like the one Maisie had seen Russell serving from earlier that afternoon.

'It's lovely to see you both at work in this noble old trade,' she told them truthfully.

'How was your walk?' Audrey asked. 'Did you go further than you meant?'

'No, but I did take my time, looking in the windows of the shops and so on. Oh, and I met Holly Luscombe on the path.'

'Was she out looking at where her poor Bertie died?' asked Russell with sympathy.

'Yes. Does she do that often?'

'Every chance she gets,' said Audrey.

'She said something about leaving "the home" and was quite lucid on the difficulties her father had to cope with, you know, being told what to do and what not to do by the authorities.'

'It's the cuts, isn't it,' said Russell.

'Cuts?'

'To the healthcare. She was happy up Exeter and looked after and what are her dad's taxes for if not for the NHS to keep her safe, poor Holly, who's not capable of looking after herself? I know old Fred worries she'll outlive him and that's a terrible burden for a parent, knowing there's a limit to what he can do and what'll become of her. I once ran into him on the way out of church and he asked me: "Do you know what I was praying for, Russ?" I says to him: "No, Fred, I don't. Was it world peace?" That was just to try and make light of it, to raise a smile, he looked so sour. "No, I was selfish," he tells me, as glum as a donkey. "I was praying for the Good Lord to let me live just a day longer than my poor Holly." It's a sad story and no mistake.'

'It does sound so,' said Maisie. 'I never met Mrs Luscombe, did I?'

'Fred's wife died of a heart attack not long before you came,' said Audrey. 'She'd always been weak that way and the doctors thought she might get over it, but she never. Picked her up and carried her off in a weekend or perhaps a fortnight – I don't remember exactly.'

'He's seen a lot of sadness, hasn't he.'

'Poor old Fred,' said Russell.

'No wonder he's so hard to bring out of himself,' said Maisie. 'Is he kind to Holly?'

Russell yawned and Maisie was able to see his big teeth, several of the back ones with substantial silver fillings.

'He does his best, I expect. Now, it must be half past nine.'

Maisie glanced at her watch and confirmed his guess. Audrey said she would make them all 'a nice malty Horlicks' to take upstairs to bed, reminding Maisie of Holly and her Ovaltine. They went indoors and talked of tomorrow's weather and how the river had become so swollen back in the spring that it had come up over the lawn and they'd had to put sandbags at the foot of the door of the cider shed. When the milk was hot and the drinks mixed, Audrey and Russell crept away up the back stairs to their bedroom above the kitchen.

'We're cosy up there in winter with the warmth that rises,' said Russell.

Maisie said goodnight and went up the much grander front stairs to 'Caesar'. The moon had risen in the east and was shining in through the window glass, casting a moon-shadow of the mullions, like a cross on the floorboards.

Feeling an ache in her legs from her walk, uphill and down, she sat on the end of the bed and took a few moments to make certain that she hadn't acquired any ticks from the dry grass, checking her ankles and calves. Then she reviewed the events of her long day: up with the lark, taking her bittersweet leave of Jack, the pleasant interlude of her unhurried journey to Exeter, the sudden fuss and kerfuffle of taking the bus and changing trains, arrival in Kirton and driving along the winding lane in Russell's sickly 'Victoria and Albert' Vauxhall Viva, the near miss with the Linton boy on his motorbike, hearing Russell enumerate the dangers and snares of country life. She had met the Topes, Floyd Tubb, Timothy Sturgess and the Luscombes, before a delicious dinner, then had taken a stroll down memory lane, over Break Heart Hill, into the town and back by the river.

She heard footsteps on the road outside and got up off the end of the bed to lean out of her open window, realising she was not at all surprised to see Holly Luscombe once more, skipping and twirling on the tarmac, easily recognisable in her fussy striped pinafore in the bright moonshine.

She told me she prefers the night, after dark, when no one's around.

The hem of Holly's skirts got caught up in the thorny hedge and she had to bend down to release it, before skipping and twirling away over the humpbacked bridge and – who knew – perhaps on as far uphill as Tubb's Dairy Farm. But the heavy tread of Fred Luscombe came thumping after her, calling out for Holly to wait – which, apparently, she did, because soon Fred came back past with his daughter on her arm.

Maisie stayed where she was, leaning on the sill, thinking about people's secret lives and what they had to cope with, often alone.

Silence returned, so deep that she could hear her own breathing and the pulse of her own blood in her ears. Maisie peeled off the Airstrip plaster to allow the air to get to the small puncture wound. A ghostly white shape rose above the hedge opposite and would have startled her, had she not straight away recognised it for what it was: the pale underside of a barn owl on its nocturnal hunt. It swooped and perched among the thorny branches of the pyracantha, no more than six feet away from her.

She wondered how the barn owl managed to balance so easily among the thorns without doing itself a mischief or getting caught up like Timothy Sturgess or Holly Luscombe. Then, she smiled.

Because it owns this patch of ground, these bushes and these trees. If there were none of us humans here – 'fossicking about' as Russell would say, worrying at one another and striving for things we haven't got, forgetting the value of what we have – that barn owl wouldn't give two hoots.

TEN

Lying in her bed in Sunny View, Maisie couldn't know it, but the moment of disaster had nearly arrived. The bright moon didn't last long. A bank of clouds rolled in from the south-west, shutting out the stars and darkening the skies, but keeping the temperature high and the atmosphere close.

In number five, Trout Leap, Patrick Linton was out of bed, unable to sleep, tormented by the thought of all that he and his family had lost: the mild Mediterranean climate, a lovely whitewashed home with a view of the sparkling sea, a cosmopolitan circle of friends, a good job, savings. Above all, he was frustrated that he hadn't seen it coming – the expulsion.

He was sitting in their dismal front room on a dirty dining chair with a rush seat that they had found in the property when they moved in, next to a nice beechwood dining table that Audrey and Russell Savage had donated to help them out. His right arm was on the deep windowsill and his chin was on his arm, looking out through the glass at the untidy garden, vaguely visible in the darkness.

He blamed himself. He knew one or two people who had managed to obtain Maltese nationality, renouncing all links to Britian, but he had left the future to chance and, when it came, it had shaken like an earthquake.

Life in mid-Devon, though, he had to admit, might be worse. The relocation service had offered him employment on the North Sea coast of Scotland, in Aberdeen, the 'granite city' that was, these days, an unlikely 'oil town'. But he had decided it would be too great a shock, living so far north, with the long winter of pitifully short days and interminable nights.

And Trout Leap was undeniably pretty. His job with Moore's was secure and paid enough to keep the wolf from the door. Things would go better if Marthese, his diffident wife, could find a job somewhere, too. But the truth was that Kirton wasn't thriving. There were only three industries: farming, retail and intermittent tourism. Plus, of course, the local council and all the related state services, but Marthese didn't have good enough English for that.

Marthese was warm and attentive. She could cook and sew. But she wasn't strong. Plus, her father – God rest his soul – had taken it into his head when she was small to take the opposite path to the one Patrick wished he had found. Despite being Maltese to her bones and in her blood – like many islanders, a delicious cocktail of Italian and Spanish and North African – she was the proud possessor of her own British passport.

Idly, Patrick pushed an oil-stained forefinger into a soft area of the window frame. Not only did the wood give way beneath the slight pressure, but the movement disturbed a colony of woodlice. They came trundling out like tiny black tanks, visible against the white-painted sill. He sat up, unnerved by the scurrying, and added it to his list of jobs whose completion was essential before summer's end, before the wet and cold weather returned.

Uncharitably, he wished that Marthese could manage to be more practical, 'handy' as Russell Savage would put it. That would actually make more difference than her finding a job.

If she were even vaguely competent in DIY, he thought, *she could help improve this dilapidated hovel.*

In order to give pleasure to Marthese and to her father, a well-to-do hotelier, Patrick had agreed to baptise their children with 'proper Maltese names'. Both had come home from their first day at Queen Elizabeth Grammar School with a request to go by anglicised versions. Thus, Pawlu had become Paul and Marija had become Maria, even to Patrick. Only Marthese persisted in using their true given names.

Patrick stood up. He felt reasonably well in himself, despite the financial anxiety that clung to him like a tick, spreading poison into his blood. The summer weather agreed with him and his work included enough physical activity to satisfy his rapid metabolism, keeping his physique slim and athletic, despite his thirty-eight years.

Or, it used to . . .

At many of the farms he visited in his little Moore's van with his bags of tools and boxes of common spare parts – spark plugs, union clips, rubber hoses, gaskets, bearings – he was often made welcome with hearty snacks. Sometimes, he ate so well that he wasn't ready for Marthese's brave attempts to preserve her own Mediterranean culinary culture. Only that evening, he had pretended to have an upset stomach when she had served *stuffat tal-fenek*, a kind of rabbit stew served with spaghetti. Happily, Pawlu and Marija – Paul and Maria – had eaten up every scrap, unaware that he still had the taste of a magnificent steak and kidney pudding in his mouth, prepared and served by Stella Tubb.

Stella's a dear little thing – and born to this life.

Patrick tried and failed to push the image of Stella Tubb out of his mind.

She's small but strong with eyes as blue as cornflowers and not a thought in her head that isn't for the grass, the cattle, the sun and rain. And a worker, never off her feet from dawn till dusk. Marthese still thinks afternoons are for siestas . . .

Patrick went into the porch to put on his wellington boots. As silently as he was able, he lifted the rustic door latch.

That's another job – we need a proper lock, not just a bolt seized up with ancient paint and rust.

Outside, he found a very fine rain falling, warm and pleasant on his upturned face. Just beyond number five, at the end of the leg of the 'L' of cottages, was a lean-to shed, inside which was a 50cc motorbike, a moped really, that he had found abandoned at the back of Moore's service centre. In his spare time – breaks and lunches and, now and then, after work and at weekends – he had refurbished it. The motor was sound, the brakes reliable.

Paul already loves it. He'll need it if he's to get a job.

Patrick would have loved it himself, at eighteen, the promise of freedom and independence.

Freedom. That's what I no longer have. I'm tied to this life with no room to grow and will be till I draw my pension like old Russell Savage and live out my days, scrimping and saving . . .

He shut the door of the shed and went back indoors, trying to convince himself that he was doing the right thing, working hard, making a better life for his children. That was his task: to lay the foundations for Paul and Maria to thrive, like a farmer preparing a field over the long winter, secure in the knowledge that spring planting would bring forth new abundant life.

Back upstairs, Patrick peered into his and Marthese's room. Only half awake, she spoke low to him from under the covers – donated, as were the bedclothes on Paul's and Maria's beds, by their compassionate Trout Leap neighbours – appealing for comfort and companionship.

'*Inħobbok, ir-raġel,*' she murmured.

I love you, husband.

To Patrick's shame, her words just made him think about Stella Tubb once more. He went back downstairs.

★

Around the same time, in number four, Trout Leap, Mr and Mrs Tope were also up late. For Shane, rising late on a Saturday was a kind of recompense for early starts in the week. He was an agricultural inspector with responsibilities that took him fifty miles in every direction, covering pretty much all of central Devon. Often, he would get up with the sun, even in midsummer. Recently, following some routine testing, he had been obliged to act on a 'seizure of milk, liable to spread disease, in accordance with section thirteen of the Agriculture (Miscellaneous Provisions) Act of 1963'. The farmer – Norman Tubb – had cut up rough and given Shane 'a proper shake'. It had made his dental plate rattle and he'd asked Russell Savage to have a word, as a kind of go-between, to avoid any further unpleasantness.

On this Friday evening, while Deborah was in bed, asleep. Shane was sitting in a chintz armchair, listening to a late programme on the radiogram – BBC Radio Three, of course – a romantic fantasia by a composer whose name he had missed, played by the BBC Symphony Orchestra. Jane came through from the kitchen with a late-night snack of tinned sardines on thin Mother's Pride toast. She sat down in a second chintz armchair and leaned over to put his plate in his hand. They both nibbled their supper, deliciously salty and oily and 'cheap as chips'.

The orchestral music became a background soundtrack as, between mouthfuls, they discussed each of their neighbours, probing one another's knowledge and suppositions, innocently unaware that anyone who heard them would think they were unforgivably nosy and prying.

'So, wasson next door?' he asked, using the Devon contraction of 'what's going on'.

'Someone's up and about in number five,' she told him. 'I heard them opening the front door. The hinges squeak something chronic.'

'Did the footsteps come from the front or the back?'

'Garden side. Man's tread.'

'The husband, then, Patrick.'

'Oh, yes. Then I heard his step on the gravel. He was going to the shed, I expect. What about the other side and the Sturgess tribe?'

'All abed,' said Shane. 'Not a peep nor a creak this past hour, neither the mother nor the daughter nor the boy.'

Jane tittered and replied: 'That's very well put, dear.'

'Thank you, dear, but we know, don't we?' said Shane with a conniving smile.

'We do,' agreed Jane.

Just for a moment or two, finishing up his 'tasty little fish', as it said on the tin, Shane experienced a pang of doubt.

Is it quite ... healthy to be so focused on our neighbours' doings?

Jane cleared the plates, leaving him alone with the soaring strings and the romantic crescendo from the radiogram. He shook his head.

What harm can it possibly do to take an interest in how folks get along?

The radio concert came to an end and the announcer transitioned smoothly into reading the news, beginning with the price of crude oil and a recording of an English member of parliament complaining that the world was being 'held to ransom by OPEC'. Jane returned and sat down. Each reached for the other's hand, suspended in space between the two chintz upholstered arms.

'People are worried, Shane,' said Jane. 'Everyone got carried away. Where will it end?'

'It's gold, dear. Just a tiny amount could buy a car or even a house.'

'Did no one think it too good to be true?' asked Jane.

Shane didn't answer.

It's a good question, though.

The announcer finished the news with a weather report for the next day, dividing the country into such large swathes – 'northern England', 'central southern England', 'the West Country' – that it became meaningless. The forecast was followed by a programme of music suitable for bedtime, beginning with a lullaby arranged for piano by Schubert entitled *The Young Mother*. Jane gave Shane's hand a squeeze.

'Like the daughter next door,' she said with a wink.

Shane tried to laugh. 'You are a one, Jane.'

'Are you coming up?'

'No,' he sighed. 'Not just yet.'

'Don't be long.'

'No, dear.'

She left him alone. Shane stayed behind, more and more a prey to dark thoughts.

*

In the corner cottage, number three, Trout Leap, Mrs Geraldine Sturgess, the strongly built seamstress, was profoundly asleep, alone in her tiny bedroom overlooking the railway. On the other side of the first-floor landing there were two bedrooms that sort of fanned out.

Timothy's room looked west onto the lane. He was sound asleep as well, dreaming about his one-in-thirty-two scale plastic Airfix soldiers and the little pots of enamel paint he wished he could afford to buy from C & C Supplies in order to finish off his platoon of German stormtroopers. The Germans might be the 'baddies', but they definitely had the best uniforms. Unfortunately, he had run out of 'Wehrmacht green' and 'gun-metal grey'.

The Topes had been wrong about the third member of the household, the one they had referred to as 'the young mother'. Petunia Sturgess was still awake, sitting up in bed, reading a lurid romance novel by the light of a forty-watt bulb, set beneath a fabric shade, meaning the dim light strained her eyes.

Petunia was passionately devoted to romance novels, especially the ones that the librarian in Kirton called 'cheap', bemoaning their 'simple plots, clichéd dialogue and hackneyed descriptions'. She had offered Petunia a book that she had described as 'the same but better', with the encouraging title of *Desperate Strangers*, by a writer she had never heard of but would henceforth avoid.

Petunia had been disheartened by a peculiar plotline about being bitten by a tick and being silly about getting treatment. Until the last pages, it hadn't been at all clear which characters deserved a 'happy ending' and which their 'comeuppance'. In fact, having finished, Petunia had reread the ending to make sure she hadn't missed something, so inconclusive did it seem.

'Shouldn't the "desperate strangers" have become lovers, don't you think?' she had asked, returning it.

'Did you not enjoy it?' the librarian had wanted to know.

'Not as much as the ones with pictures on the front,' Petunia had replied.

This evening's book was from a publisher called Harlequin with a lovely illustrated cover of a tall man with thick brown hair and a young woman turning her face upward to be kissed. There was a slight hint that, perhaps, she didn't want to be kissed – or perhaps, better still, that she did, but it wouldn't be right. That was the sort of story Petunia loved best of all.

Tonight, though, there was a tinge of doubt in Petunia's mind. Ten years before, when she had been just sixteen, she had done something foolish herself – something she had desired but regretted, whose consequences were with her still.

Ought I to suffer all my life long for one mistake, though? Mother ought to have taught me better. I was just a child ...

Petunia returned her attention to the soft pages of cheap paper and engaging prose. She finished the chapter – the handsome hero had just helped the pretty heroine to change a tyre on her bicycle then walked away, 'barely acknowledging her dimpled smile of thanks' – and put out the light. After only a few minutes, she found she was too hot and pushed the eiderdown off, feeling a delicious cooling breeze on the bare skin of her legs, hearing the pitter-patter of very light rain through the open window.

Where's my 'desperate stranger'? she wondered. *Why is no one desperate for me?*

Like Maisie, Petunia could see a moon shadow in her room, lying aslant on the bare floorboards.

Mum can look after Timothy. Once I get my share of the gold, I'm gone.

Soon, she was asleep and it was her mother Geraldine's turn to find herself wakeful, coming downstairs to think, in her turn, about money and freedom and how to achieve those long-desired goals.

*

In number two, Trout Leap, Miss Pond, the school secretary, was finding it hard to digest her unwise, sickly supper – tinned pears topped with a synthetic mousse of butterscotch Angel Delight. She was standing very still in her tiny living room whose walls were decorated with a framed Ordnance Survey map of the hamlet, plus five glazed racing prints and a low drinks cabinet, left behind by her late father.

And every one of my neighbours knows that I also inherited his debts.

On the rug in front of Miss Pond was a huge expanse of paper, multiple A4 sheets stuck together on the back with Sellotape, on which the options for the next year's school timetable were laid out in a grid of tiny but clear lettering. Her job was to make sure that the right teachers were in the right classrooms with the right schoolchildren at every hour of every day from September 1972 through to July 1973.

Vera Pond was proud of the fact that she alone was mistress of the immensely complex organisation of the school day and the school year. No one else, she knew, could hold in their head all the varied and intricate considerations. Once complete, the timetable would be a kind of automaton, a work of mechanical art, assigning and directing the actions of four dozen teachers, two dozen support staff, nine hundred pupils and even, by extension, the lives of their parents and guardians.

The better to study her work, Vera sat down on a low pouffe made of a patchwork of leather panels, stuffed with horsehair. A little the worse for wear, it saved her fifty-year-old knees from the hard floorboards and the thin synthetic rug. She was hesitating over the use of the gymnasium and the hall, required for concerts by the school band and for theatrical productions by the drama department, in competition with mock and actual public examinations whose dates she did not yet possess.

This was an inevitable problem. This late Friday evening on the very day on which one school year had 'broken up' was not really an appropriate time to be planning twelve months ahead. The headmaster wouldn't expect her to report back for a month, at least. Sadly, though, Vera had nothing much else to think about, to amuse or occupy herself. The long school holidays felt oddly like an unhappy penance for the gratifying pleasure of the rest of the year's busyness and purpose.

She got up off her pouffe and went to stand at the window, watching a fine rain begin to fall, thinking about the mine and the prospect of unearned wealth.

It doesn't seem real . . .

She tried to imagine a savings account that reassured with four- or even five-figure numbers, rather than one whose balance stubbornly refused to grow.

What would I do with it all?

Of course, the first thing would be to pay off her late father's gambling debts, secured on the house in which she lived and, therefore, her responsibility if she wished to remain in occupation.

Then, at least, I'd feel secure in the knowledge that I might die at home, between my own four walls.

Vera shivered, uncertain why she was thinking about death.

It comes to us all, though, doesn't it?

She went to her front door and opened it, standing quiet and still beneath the low lintel.

Will Holly Luscombe go a-gallivanting again, tonight? And, if she does, what will I do?

*

In number one, Trout Leap, Fred Luscombe had spent the evening at the kitchen table, only twice required to open the railway gates before the road closed at eight. Later on, he had heard the front door open and close and been unable to summon the energy to respond.

After a minute, though, he had roused himself and run out, down the lane, past Sunny View, catching up with his daughter on the far side of the humpbacked bridge. He had brought her home and shown her all the kindness his weary heart could muster.

Which wasn't so very much, if I'm honest.

He had escorted her up to her room with a cup of Ovaltine and two ginger nuts from the packet left behind by Audrey Savage. In the morning, he expected to find the biscuits untouched on the chipped saucer beside her bed.

What can I do, though, if she won't eat? She's not a child.

Fred felt bad. He was thinking about the social services people and how it was impossible to please them. He wasn't allowed to keep Holly locked indoors, daft as she undoubtedly was, but he wasn't supposed to let her roam free, either. Where did that leave him?

In the wrong, that's where 'tis.

He was back at the kitchen table. The house was quiet. He hoped Holly was asleep, that she wouldn't sneak out once he himself was abed. He stared at his own reflection in the darkened glass of the kitchen window.

What sort of life is this? If I upped sticks myself and left Holly behind, would she be any worse off? The authorities would have to take her in, wouldn't they?

Fred had an image of himself, in the back of his mind, retired on the Costa del Sol, living frugally but happily on his British Rail pension in a place where the sun always shone. There had been a story in the *Kirton Courier* about a local retiree who had done just that.

He simply packed his bags and started a new life.

On Fred's wrist was a watch, presented to him by British Rail soon after his fifty-fourth birthday, for forty years' service. It was brass but shone like gold in the deceiving lamplight.

The mine – that'll be the change I'm looking for. I did the right thing, there. As long as no one messes it up.

ELEVEN

Just before dawn, as Maisie slept on, enjoying 'the sleep of the just', Holly woke with a start. Someone was out and about from one of the adjoining cottages – or had it been noises from the natural world that had woken her, like the cry of a vixen, a raucous call that resembled an unhappy child in pain?

Holly sat up and drank half her cup of cold Ovaltine, nibbling half of one of the hard biscuits. Taking care not to wake her father, she dressed and went back out.

The lane was still dark. She pushed through the pedestrian gate, onto the railway line, twirled and skipped away in the direction of Barnstaple, until she came to a stretch that was lined with tall nettles, looming over her on either side. She pressed on to a place she knew, another swing gate, that allowed her off the railway line, out into a grassy pasture, with no particular destination in mind.

After perhaps an hour – Holly didn't know for sure because she had never taken to wearing a watch – a fine but warm rain began once again to fall. By this time, she was far from home and the sun was beginning to lighten the sky. Her pinafore became clingy and would have revealed her bony joints and slack skin, had there been anyone close by to witness her dishevelment.

For ten minutes, Holly sheltered under a well-leafed chestnut tree. When the rain ceased, she traipsed on, purposeless, off the lanes and onto a little-used bridleway, eventually coming to a place that was supposed to be secret, concealed from prying eyes in an abandoned corner of a valley where few people ever went any more, among fields too poorly grassed for cattle or sheep and a few uninhabited cottages.

To her surprise, she met someone she knew but who clearly didn't welcome her presence. But that wasn't so very uncommon. There were very few people – if any – who ever seemed truly pleased to see her.

That Miss Cooper had a smile for me today, though, not once but twice.

Unaware of the danger she was in, Holly recognised that she wasn't wanted and turned her back.

*

A little later, Holly was left with her hair plastered to her pale forehead, lying on her back in a place where some innocent passer-by would be bound to find her, abandoned to her eternal rest on a steep bank gouged out by the fast-running spring waters of the Wivel in flood. In the crook of her knee was a shiny black tick, feasting on her blood – but that no longer mattered. There would be no reaction, allergic or otherwise.

Holly's hands were slack, her legs splayed out unnaturally. One heeled buckle shoe had come off and was clinging to the bank, half in and half out of the water, as if wary of embarking on an improvised voyage, unable to commit to floating away downstream.

Holly lay in that unnatural position until well past the moment when most residents of Trout Leap had risen, breakfasted and gone about their business or – for those of school age – wandered out to enjoy a first summer morning of the holidays, disappointed to discover that the weather was cloudy and grey.

The exceptions were Fred Luscombe – who remained at home, on duty, trapped by his responsibilities, unaware that Holly was not in her room – and Maisie Cooper who slept very late, a reaction to the long day's travelling and her evening walk, but also to the drama and emotion of her recent investigation into the murder at Bitling Fair.

More time passed and still, of course, Holly hadn't moved.

The ceiling of summer clouds became ragged, parted then cleared, carried away by the same warm breeze from the south-west that had twice brought mild rain. A hot July sun began shining down on Holly's inanimate body – and on a smear of sticky dark blood in the red Devonshire soil.

TWELVE

Maisie was woken by a bright shaft of sunlight, reflected off something on the bedside table. For a few moments she couldn't fathom what it was, warm and dazzling on her face. Then she worked out that it was the metal base of the table lamp and rolled over to avoid it.

Her travel clock was on the other side, a lovely boxy thing that opened out into a triangle with the analogue dial standing up at an angle, very easy to read.

Good heavens, it's after ten.

Maisie didn't move straight away. She just lay, enjoying feeling completely rested, like on a luxurious Sunday after a late Saturday with friends.

But it's Saturday, today.

She pulled back the covers – just a sheet and a thin woollen blanket because she had thrown off the counterpane in the night – and stood up, her bare feet on the cool tiled floor. In her cotton nightgown, she padded to the bathroom to wash and to brush her teeth, listening for sounds of human occupation in the pleasant house.

Perhaps there's no one about.

Back in 'Caesar', she got dressed, putting on her favourite knee-length black-and-white-check dress, a pair of white ankle socks and her brown leather sandals. She tidily made the bed, folding the counterpane at the foot.

Before going downstairs, she remembered being woken, briefly, in the depths of the night. It had almost seemed like a dream – or perhaps it had melded with a dream – of an angry bee buzzing past. But, of course, it must have been Paul Linton on his motorbike.

Why would he be out so late. I wonder if he has a girlfriend, somewhere?

Downstairs in the kitchen she found the room warm from the Aga but not stuffy because the back door was open. She looked out across the lawn towards the cider-making shed, wondering if Russell might be busy inside, but the door was closed.

She felt as shiver of anxiety for her absent friends and tried, unsuccessfully, to quash it.

Needing tea, she part-filled the whistle kettle, lifted one of the big hinged hot-plate lids and set it to boil. While waiting, she opened all the rustic cupboards and drawers in the old-fashioned kitchen to remind herself where everything was, locating a good quality loose-leaf tea in a Hornsea earthenware caddy, rust-coloured and decorated with black scrolls, with a wooden lid sealed with a rubber gasket. On the draining board she found a silver tea strainer with a short handle and a companion dish to catch drips. Beside that were two other items of Hornsea tableware – a medium-sized teapot, plus a bowl in which Audrey and Russell collected their used leaves, presumably to spread as mulch around the roots of acid-loving garden plants.

The kettle whistled. She poured on the boiling water and, while she waited for the tea to brew, Maisie had a look round.

Downstairs at Sunny View was, essentially, just two large rooms, either side of the front door, separated by the hall and the impressive staircase, with the large kitchen behind. The front rooms both had front-facing windows, of course, but their side windows faced north and south.

On the sunny side was a dining room with French doors that opened onto a gravelly path and a low hedge that separated Sunny View from the Wivel. Maisie opened them and was greeted by a handful of flying insects who had been waiting for just such an opportunity to flutter indoors out of the bright sun.

Maisie stepped out onto the path, running a hand across the top of the close-clipped box hedge, listening to the tinkle and plash of the Wivel as it ran between leaning trees just a few feet away, visible between oak and hawthorn branches as dappled dark pools and sparkling shallow rapids.

She came back inside, leaving the French doors ajar, wondering why the space in the middle of the room – where four imprints of absent table feet had dented the carpet – was empty.

She went to remind herself of the contents of the second room, on the shady side. It felt quite different, dark and slightly damp. The window to the front of the house – that would otherwise have been warmed by the sunrise – was heavily curtained. As her eyes adjusted, she picked out a tall cupboard with a padlock dangling open on a hasp and a television in a mahogany cabinet. A three-piece suite in chocolate-brown corduroy pointed towards the telly. On a tiled coffee table was a vase of dried-out sweet peas. She picked it up and took it away to wash up.

Back in the kitchen, Maisie poured her tea, added some local honey and sat down at the kitchen table. She wondered again where Audrey and Russell had disappeared off to.

A copy of the *Kirton Courier* lay open at an article about some of the summer pests that she and Russell had discussed in the car. The article had been prompted by a child being hospitalised in Exeter with a bad reaction to a tick. Next to the newspaper was an ancient-looking pamphlet. She turned it the right way round to read its title: *Golden Gleanings*.

She frowned, wondering if it had been left out for her to read, noticing first the publication date, July 1888, then its author, a fellow of the Royal Society, a certain Hugh Donnelly Myles.

> *As is well-known, gold has been frequently discovered in a new district by geologists who noticed the similarity of the rocks with those of a country which they knew to be auriferous. Arguing in this way, all probability points to Devonshire as a gold-bearing county.*
>
> *History relates that gold in some quantity has been found in several Devonshire districts, most famously near North Tawton (worked by the Romans), North Molton and Combe Martin. Scattered grains have also been picked up by 'tin streamers' on Dartmoor. Copper miners have also found small specks . . .*

The Victorian pamphlet continued in the same verbose style for some time, discussing the mixed merits of the three locations mentioned. North Molton supposedly provided enough gold to finance a foray into Wales by the thirteenth-century King Edward I of England. Combe Martin was so productive that it encouraged the forced relocation of more than three hundred Derbyshire miners to work it. As Hugh Donnelly Myles went on, however, the author seemed to become less sure of himself, qualifying his history with remarks repudiating the presence of gold, including a categoric negative from an unnamed 'Vicar of Ilfracombe'.

> *Although I have lived here for forty years, I have never heard a whisper of gold being found and, in my judgement, it is pure fable.*

Maisie put the Victorian pamphlet aside, uncovering a page torn from the local newspaper, the *Kirton Courier*, dated several weeks earlier, with the enthusiastic headline: *Is it time to dig and delve?* The column was written in a sensationalist style, quoting the extraordinarily high price of gold on international exchanges and suggesting:

> *This discovery will put Kirton back on the map. Exploratory digging has already been carried out in the 'Kirton trough' and in a second – apparently more promising – secret location with results that must be taken seriously. Experts consider that we are looking at native gold occurring in grains in bedrock belonging to every one of us – and must all be very excited. Shares in the mining company will soon be made available for purchase ONLY by residents of Kirton in order that LOCAL people are the sole beneficiaries of this unforeseen manna.*

Maisie finished her tea with a contemplative expression on her face. It all seemed very far-fetched, despite the historical precedent in the ancient pamphlet and the assertion that, two thousand years before, Roman invaders had found extraction a profitable enterprise.

Surely, the gold would all have been worked out by now?

She was particularly disturbed by the idea of a public share issue, likely to encourage ordinary people – who could have no expert knowledge on which to base their actions – to commit their hard-won nest eggs to what might be an entirely fruitless search for imaginary wealth. She hoped Audrey and Russell had had more sense.

Fred Luscombe's gnomic remark came back to her: *There's not one hasn't given over at least some of their hard-earned savings to it.*

He'd said it in relation to the meeting organised for six o'clock the next evening, Sunday.

Maisie got up to make a second cup of tea, finding it slightly stewed in the heavy Hornsea pot. She drank it standing in the open back doorway, watching a robin turning over the previous year's fallen leaves, looking for insects beneath.

That's gold for a robin, right there.

She finished her tea and washed up her cup, leaving it upside down on the wire rack on the draining board, then went out into the garden, round the house and out into the lane, noticing the Vauxhall Viva wasn't on the short gravel drive. Maisie found that reassuring.

Audrey and Russell must have gone out on some chore, together.

She hadn't been given any keys and Russell's weren't on the hooks by the front door so she didn't lock up.

Scaling Break Heart Hill once more seemed a bit much for the warm morning, leaving her a choice between turning right over the humpbacked bridge and away up the winding country lane towards the Tubbs' dairy farm, or over the stile into the field on the Wivel. She chose the latter. Climbing over the rough wooden structure, she saw the frail form of Timothy Sturgess some way ahead of her, carrying his raft down to the water. She decided to follow.

There was a well-worn desire line through the wiry grass, too tussocky and mixed with weeds to be cut for hay. Because he was moving slowly, encumbered by his home-made embarkation, she caught up with Timothy just as he reached the little gravelly beach.

'That looks like a wonderful raft,' she told him. 'Do you remember me? My name is Maisie.'

'Yes, I remember, Miss Cooper.'

'So, this is the SS *Egruts*?' she asked with a smile.

'Yes. Can you help me with the knots?'

'The knots?'

'I'm not very good at knots so I'm worried the oil cans with come off.'

'I'll have a look, if you like.'

He put down his raft, upside down on the shallow bank, and Maisie inspected his work.

'Ah, yes, you've not done a bad job but reefs and grannies aren't good enough. You really need a knot that self-tightens as you pull it. Shall I show you?'

'Yes, please.'

Timothy was wearing only his swimming trunks and hadn't brought a towel or anything to eat or drink. He wasn't exactly shivering but he looked very weedy and white and thin. Yesterday's scratches stood out strongly as red lines, though none looked infected, thanks to Russell's application of Dettol antiseptic.

'Are you warm enough?' Maisie asked.

'Yes, thank you. I don't get cold easily.'

'You're very lucky.'

One of the many advantages of Maisie's background in the Women's Royal Army Corps was acquiring a wide range of practical skills. She crouched down and took a couple of minutes to undo the slack cords that Timothy had tied.

'I'm going to use a taut line hitch. It's a knot that can slide so you can adjust it, and it tightens when pulled. When I was in the army, we often used it.'

'Why were you in the army?' asked Timothy, watching her nimble fingers closely.

'Because my brother joined up and I wanted to be like him,' said Maisie. 'You don't have any brothers and sisters, do you?'

Timothy didn't answer and Maisie got the distinct impression that he hadn't welcomed the question. He bowed his head closer to what she was doing and asked her to undo it and tie it a second time. She did so, then left it undone for him to try. He took hold of the rope – Maisie thought it might be old sash cord from window weights – created a loop at the end as she had done and made a pretty good job of fashioning his own 'taut line hitch'.

'That's splendid,' she said. 'Now pull there.'

The cord tightened round the oil can, slightly squeezing the metal, which indented under tenson.

'That's much better,' said Timothy. 'Thank you.'

'Can you do the others?'

'Yes, I think so.'

Maisie watched his thin fingers and bitten nails teasing and winding and wrapping the cord around itself and the timbers of the raft. When it was done, he carried the whole contraption into the stream, wading in up to his knees. He placed it on the water, holding on so it didn't float away on the current, bouncing it up and down against the buoyancy of the cans.

'It's brilliant. Thank you, Miss Cooper.'

Maisie decided she might be able to ask Timothy a question that would seem like prying were he an adult.

'Before you go, will you tell me something?'

'Yes, miss,' he replied.

'Do you know what happened between Mr Tope and Mr Tubb?'

Obediently, Timothy told her about an incident in Long Lane when a churn had fallen from the milk lorry, revealing a drowned rat.

'But I didn't tell anyone. It was Mr Tope's regular testing showed that there was . . . contamination.' He said the word carefully, as if he had only recently learned it. 'Mum says they had a "set-to" about it. Can I go now?'

'Yes,' said Maisie, smiling her thanks. 'You can.'

She watched him gingerly climb on board, wondering if he ought to have a bit of blanket or carpet on the rough timber so as not to get splinters. Then she internally rebuked herself.

You'd never have worried about splinters when you were a girl. Stop being so middle-aged.

Timothy got his balance and the raft began to move away with the stream, scraping a little over a shallow bit before picking up speed where the water was deeper.

'*Bon voyage*,' she called.

'*Merci*,' he surprised her by replying.

Maisie guessed he must be eleven and had therefore started secondary school, including French lessons. She watched him drift out of sight, round a bend overhung with green-leaved branches of oak and hawthorn, and smiled.

This really is a lovely spot.

Maisie was undecided what to do next. Opposite where she stood, the far bank of the river was a vertical slice three or four feet tall, cut into the red clay. On the grass atop the bank, a solitary member of the dairy herd stood stolidly chewing the cud, watching her with big brown eyes.

Was that the over-friendly cow that so frightened spoilt little Deborah Tope?

Something in the water caught Maisie's eye, something black with a fragment of silver, bobbing in the current, close to the far bank, a few yards away from her, under the vertical slice of red dirt. Then it swerved across the stream on an eddy, coming close to where she stood, catching in the edge of the shallow rapids where Timothy had just managed to scrape past on his raft.

Very quickly, Maisie took a step onto a smooth stone a foot or so out in the stream and, with great agility, leaned out and snatched the object out of the water, just before it bobbed away. It was wet but not sodden so she didn't think it had been in the stream for long. And she thought she recognised it for what it was.

Is this one of Holly Luscombe's buckle shoes?

Then another thought intruded.

And Audrey and Russell are still nowhere to be found.

THIRTEEN

Maisie was in a quandary, precariously balanced on a slippery stone a foot or so out into the flow of the Wivel, with cool water seeping into the toe of her clean white sock through the bands of brown leather of her sandal. In her right hand she held a black buckle shoe that, at first glance, she had thought to be the spitting image of those she had seen on Holly Luscombe's feet.

But is it?

Timothy – whose opinion she might have asked – was gone, out of sight, beyond the dark pool of deeper water beneath the spreading trees, happy on his raft. A solitary dairy cow – whose opinion was moot – was observing her from the opposite bank of the Wivel, placidly chewing the cud.

Maisie adjusted her centre of gravity and pushed off, back onto the gravelly beach, the buckle shoe still dripping. She looked round, across the field towards the cottages, wondering if she ought to go and ask if Holly was up and about.

Could she have lost it when Fred came running out to fetch her back, late last evening? I don't want to cause a fuss.

Maisie examined the shoe more closely. It had a blocky heel with uneven wear, which matched Holly's gait, characterised by very flexible ankles that sort of rolled inwards as she walked. Turning the shoe over in her hands, Maisie saw that it was creased from wear across the toes and the padded inner had swollen from being in the water.

How long for?

Not too long or it might have begun to come apart. Also, given the speed of the water flowing along the Wivel – walking pace, at least – it had to have gone in recently or it wouldn't have ended up so close to home.

Maisie frowned.

When we were at the Luscombes' house, Audrey warned me off prying or outstaying my welcome. How much worse would it be for me to go causing upset about this, not knowing what's what?

It occurred to her, too, that she needed to be on everyone's 'right side' if she was to help Russell with his unhappy worries.

I suppose Holly might be somewhere upstream and, having lost a shoe in the water, she'll find it very uncomfortable making her way home only partly shod. I'd be doing a good deed if I could find and help her.

Wishing she knew where her friends and hosts had got to, Maisie decided she could do worse than follow the Wivel against the current. It would be a pleasant way of rediscovering the countryside on foot and it would almost certainly bring her to Holly.

She set off, walking the fringe of the field where it sloped down to the water. Quite soon this brought her under the humpbacked bridge close to Sunny View and she had to duck her head to pass beneath it, reflecting that a couple of months earlier she would have found herself walking through deep water. In July, though, she could creep beside the diminished stream without getting her feet any wetter.

She emerged from the shadows of the bridge on the far side of the lane, below the French doors that she had opened from the dining room at Sunny View – from which the table had gone missing. The riverbank was very overgrown and she found it easier to continue by climbing up onto the edge of the lawn.

'Anyone about?' she called and was disappointed to receive no reply.

She crossed the lawn, past the cider shed to the end of the garden where a stile allowed her access to the adjacent field. She thought about going back for the bicycle in the front porch, but decided against it. The terrain was too difficult.

Maisie stayed very close to the edge of this particular pasture because she could see two bulls in the far corner, maybe forty or fifty yards away, pulling hay from a manger, close to the fence that separated them from the railway line. She tried to move quietly, but there was quite a lot of dry bracken and twigs underfoot. The noise soon got the animals' attention. They lifted their heavy heads – one brown and one white – and observed her, then began moving slowly in her direction, slobber dripping from their thick lips.

Maisie kept going, hoping she wouldn't interest the huge animals as bringing either food or sport. If they ran at her, she would have to make a break for it across the river but, at this point, the Wivel looked quite deep and sludgy and awkward to cross.

And who's to say that those bulls don't make a habit of wading through it themselves?

To her relief, up ahead, she saw a low bridge made of heavy planks supported by what looked like railway sleepers standing on end, driven down into the riverbed. The surface of the horizontal timbers was only ten or twelve inches out of the water and she could see that the planks were worn smooth by the water running over them in winter, but she was able to cross quite securely because they were wrapped in chicken wire to give a grip underfoot.

On the far side, Maisie turned and was surprised to see both bulls had come silently down close to the water. The dark brown one had impressive ivory horns that protruded aggressively forward. The white one was shorter but more heavily built. Its horns stuck out sideways from its heavy head.

I expect they want me to feed them. They probably only see people when the farmer brings their hay.

Maisie pressed on. The southern bank of the river was easier going, with no hedges or stiles to negotiate, just a long grassy pasture close-cropped by sheep, almost as if it was mown. Maisie walked on, swinging her arms, no longer thinking about the wet shoe she held in her right hand. She felt happy and free in the green countryside with an occasional scar of red dirt, the sun high in the sky and a soft breeze on her cheeks. She walked so far that, when she came to a dry-stone wall and turned to look back, she could barely make out Sunny View in trees more than a mile away.

Where the dry-stone wall met the water, a post was firmly set in the bank with strands of barbed wire stretched across the water to a similar contraption on the far side. Hanging from the vicious rusting barrier, over the middle of the stream, was a piece of plywood painted with a barely legible warning, worn away by several seasons' weather.

Something to do with fishing permits, I think. In any case, Holly won't be any further this way. Unless she climbed the dry-stone wall ...

Maisie knew that climbing a dry-stone wall was bad manners because of the precarious way they were built, without mortar, meaning the rocks were easily dislodged. She looked around for fallen stones, evidence that someone – perhaps Holly – might have disobeyed this unwritten rule. There were none.

She contemplated the shoe and looked back downstream towards Sunny View, along the sheep field. The Wivel flowed almost dead straight, without notches or bends or eddies in which something floating along might be caught up.

If this is, indeed, Holly's shoe, she either lost it very recently and has since skipped away somewhere, without me running into her. Or, she lost it much further upstream, beyond the barbed wire.

Maisie saw that she was faced with a choice. She could either retrace her steps – something she hated – or follow the dry-stone wall uphill. She chose the latter path.

The sun was warmer still and the climb was taxing. Over perhaps half a mile she gained fifty or sixty feet in altitude. Nearing the top, she turned and looked back down on the hamlet of Trout Leap. Just then a train came through, its racket mitigated by distance, but still easily the noisiest thing in the landscape.

Maisie completed the climb, over a slight brow, coming to a farm track leading away to the west, into the hills through a gate in the dry-stone wall, or east towards the dairy farm. The track was well used with two ruts, worn deep by the wheels of agricultural vehicles, either side of a ridge of grass.

Thinking she oughtn't to be out too long without Russell and Audrey knowing where she was, she took the direction homewards, with a tall hedge on her right, at the end of which she came in sight of the Tubbs' farmhouse and some more modern agricultural buildings.

Hoping she wasn't trespassing or likely to disturb the working day, she walked more quickly, preferring to slip past without being seen. As she approached the farmhouse and garden, protected by a low fence overgrown with blackberry brambles, a small woman with a very generous and open face emerged from the low back door with a basket of laundry on her hip, ready to hang out on her washing line. She and Maisie locked eyes.

'Can I help you, love?' asked the small woman.

'I'm sorry to intrude,' said Maisie, simultaneously.

The small woman laughed.

'I'll go first, then, shall I? I'm Stella Tubb.'

'I thought you must be but it doesn't seem possible,' said Maisie. 'You don't look a day older.'

'Older than what?' said Stella Tubb, coming closer with her wicker basket of wet sheets on her hip.

'Older than when I last saw you. I'm Maisie Cooper.'

Stella's eyes widened. 'Well, I never did, so you are.'

'We've not seen one another for a decade but you've not changed a bit.'

'Neither have you, Maisie, except to seem a mite more grown-up-looking, but just as pretty.'

Maisie indicated the washing. 'Can I help you with that?'

'Happen I could do with an extra pair of hands. It's the big sheets and they do flap about when you're trying to get them pegged out. Come round. There's a gate in the fence round the corner.'

Maisie did as she was told, finding the hinges split and the broken-down gate just pushed into the gap. Feeling silly carrying the wet shoe, she put it down on the ground under the ragged hedge, pushed through and carefully closed up behind her, in case she inadvertently let out a dog or some hens. She went to meet Stella who had put her basket down on a very rickety garden table and was standing with her hands on her hips, the better to observe her guest.

'We share a birthday, of course,' said Maisie, for want of anything better.

'I do remember that, my handsome. St George's Day. You'd be thirty, now, or a bit more?'

'Thirty-five, actually. You look like you're blooming.'

'I am. It's because I love what I do,' said Stella with energy. 'I love the ladies – that's what I call our cows – I love the life. Who wouldn't?'

'I imagine it's a lot of early starts, summer and winter, and no days off?'

'Why would I want a day off? All this . . .' She waved her hand expansively, indicating the farmhouse and the other buildings, then the pasture and hills beyond. 'This is all I ever wanted. Perhaps that's not so common these days? Perhaps you don't often run into people who've properly found their niche?'

Stella pronounced it 'nitch', but Maisie knew exactly what she meant.

'Actually, I do know one or two.'

'Farmers, also?'

'Well, there's Phyl Pascal. She does a bit of farming but, more importantly, late in life, she's turning her house – it's quite big – into a respite home for people who've fallen on hard times.'

'That's very generous.'

'And my friend Adélaïde Amour. She's an actress and she loves life and her dream of being successful on stage has recently come true . . .' Maisie stopped and laughed, then she told Stella: 'These people don't mean anything to you. Why should they? Shall we hang your laundry out?'

'Thank you kindly.' The washing line was supported by a tall clothes prop and was attached to the corner of the house at one end and to a tall fir at the other. Stella said: 'We had that tree in a tub indoors for Christmas a few years ago, then put it in the ground after and now it's twenty feet tall. Would you credit it?'

Stella kept up an amusing, inconsequential narrative of country life as they worked, making sure the bright white cotton didn't trail on the ground. Once all the sheets – and two worn towels – were on the line, Stella used the prop to raise it all high up to catch the almost imperceptible breeze. Maisie found she was very thirsty and was glad when Stella invited her into the kitchen for, inevitably, Maisie thought: 'A nice glass of milk.'

Maisie followed Stella inside, thinking about how her host seemed brimful of life and goodness. She was not a conventionally attractive woman, but her personality was magnetic.

The lintel over the kitchen door was low and Maisie had to duck where Stella didn't. Also, it was rather gloomy inside, especially after the bright July sun in the garden. It took Maisie a few moments to realise they were not alone, experiencing a combination of emotions, beginning with a huge wave of relief.

'Good heavens, Russell.'

'Maisie, wasson? It's not trouble, is it?'

Before she could explain how worried she'd been at his and Audrey's absence, a second man who Maisie recognised as Stella's husband and Floyd's father, Norman Tubb, replied.

'We don't need any more of that.' He said it with a kind of snarl, squeezed into a large wooden carver chair, his fleshy bulk almost pinned by its two leather-padded arms. He was even bigger and heavier than Maisie remembered him, his hair and whiskers unbrushed. He added two expletives then asked: 'How many do I have to put up with, sucking my blood like ticks?'

'Now, now,' said Russell.

'Don't you "now-now" me, you old fool. What do you know? I'll talk how I like in my own kitchen. Didn't I have Shane Tope in here laying down the law and threatening my livelihood?'

'He's got his job to do, Norm. You know that.'

'It's the countryside. You can't pretend there'll never be a rat clever enough to get in at your corn or your milk. It's nature. They can squeeze through a gap no wider than a florin.'

'You mean a ten-pence piece,' said Russell with a smile, trying to defuse Norman's anger.

Maisie caught a glimpse of Stella's pained features as she slipped without a word into the pantry. In the same moment, she had a vivid memory of a horrid conflict that she had found herself caught up in, one in which Norman had been central.

'Good morning, Mr Tubb. I'm Maisie Cooper,' she told him. 'Perhaps you don't remember me but, let me tell you plainly, I remember you.'

FOURTEEN

There was an awkward pause, during which Maisie held Norman Tubb's gaze and his expression went from truculence to guilt and back to anger.

'What are you doing back?' he demanded.

'No manners, still, I see,' said Maisie. Norman looked undecided, then dropped his eyes. 'Russell, will you be long?' Maisie asked.

'No, er, perhaps we're all done, then, Norman.' He got up from the cluttered kitchen table. 'Remember, Shane has his responsibilities, like we all do. We'll see you tomorrow night?'

The dairy farmer nodded, gazing at his hands gripping the table edge as if he feared it might float away.

Stella emerged from the pantry with a metal jug of unpasteurised milk. She put it on the table with the same pained expression on her face.

'Isn't it all a long time ago?' she said to Maisie with a kind of childish appeal. 'Whatever it was, there's no need to drag all that out of the past. Norman didn't mean anything by it, did he?'

Maisie felt unable to smooth things over, but she didn't want to make things any worse.

'I must get on. Here I am intruding on your working day and I know that Saturday is no different for you from any other day of the week.'

'But you'll take a glass before you go,' said Stella. She poured the creamy milk into one of four glasses set ready on a tray on the heavy farmhouse table. 'Tell me what you think.'

'Thank you,' said Maisie, politely, and drank.

'It's this morning's, of course,' said Stella, 'so it's not been refrigerated and it might be a bit warm for your taste.'

It was. Maisie found it quite difficult to swallow. The experience reminded her of the little bottles of milk she and all the other children had been given each day at morning recreation at school – a paternalistic government initiative to improve standards of health. Sometimes, in winter, the crates of small bottles froze and the milk had to be defrosted on the classroom radiators.

'It's like a meal in a glass,' said Maisie, putting the empty tumbler back on the table. 'Thank you very much. Goodbye, Stella. It was a pleasure to see you again. Goodbye, Mr Tubb.'

Maisie went out through the low doorway into the fenced and untidy garden, with the bright white bedsheets flapping on the line. A warm breeze was getting up, suggesting a change in the weather. As she reached the broken gate, she heard Russell's voice.

'Hold up, there, I don't move as quick as you do.'

She waited for him to step through the gap, carefully sealed it with the fragile timbers of the broken gate, then they set off down the track towards the cattle grid and the tarmac lane.

'I'm sorry, Russell. I imagine I've brought up unhappy memories.'

'How's that, then?'

'Of Norman Tubb.'

'I don't know what you mean.'

'But surely—' Maisie began. She stopped, thinking hard. 'Oh, you never knew. It was just before I left.'

'What was? I've never seen Norman Tubb so cowed, to coin a phrase.' Russell laughed at his accidental pun at the dairy farmer's expense. 'He had nothing left to say for himself.'

In memory, Maisie saw Norman, furious and threatening, leaning over his frail father.

'I'm not sure I should tell you. He's a friend of yours, isn't he?'

'I don't know about friend. I mean, you've got to be friendly, isn't that right, with the people around you? Otherwise, the world's a sad place and no mistake. But there's a difference between friendly and friends, isn't there?'

'Had you been there long?'

'No, not really. Ten or fifteen minutes perhaps.'

'And I didn't interrupt and pull you away?'

They had reached the cattle grid and had to pay attention so that their feet didn't slip between the metal bars. Russell, despite his stiff limbs, did it very daintily in his heavy boots. He answered her question with one of his own.

'Did you read the bits and pieces that I left out for you?'

'I did.'

'I thought you might like to see the *Kirton Courier*. But the other items, what did they make you think?'

The deep lane ran downhill to the humpbacked bridge. The air felt heavy between the tall hedges.

'They made me worried for anyone who would put their life savings into such a venture,' she said carefully.

'But what if it's true?' asked Russell in a small voice.

'Yes, there's that, I suppose,' said Maisie, her heart sinking. *So, Russell and Audrey have put money into the mine.*

'Sometimes you have to take a chance,' he told her weakly. *Or perhaps Russell alone and Audrey doesn't even know?*

'If you must gamble,' she told him, 'speaking generally, not meaning you specifically, you should only wager what you can afford to lose.'

'That's God's truth,' he said, following it up with a sigh.

Maisie – though she meant well – felt she was in danger of becoming condescending. She decided to ask outright: 'How much have you put into it?'

'A tidy sum,' he murmured.

'Enough to make a difference to your lives, you and Audrey?'

'Oh, yes,' he told her, his eyes on the tarmac. 'For better or worse.' They had reached the bridge. Russell stood with his hands on the brickwork of the parapet. 'Perhaps we should talk it all out. Audrey was all for waiting for after the meeting tomorrow night, but—'

He didn't finish his thought because he was interrupted by a voice calling out to them.

'Oy, Russ, have you seen her?'

Maisie's heart sank. It was Fred Luscombe, stomping up the lane past Sunny View, gesturing widely. She realised with a lurch of guilt that she had left the drowned buckle shoe under the ragged hedge by the broken gate, back at the Tubbs' farm.

'Has she gone a-gallivanting again?' Russell called back.

'Yes, she has, and I don't know when or where,' Fred replied, breathlessly. He came to meet them on the brow of the bridge. 'I thought she were abed. When I looked in because lunch was long past, her room was empty. You've not had sight nor sound of her, I suppose?'

'We'd have said if we had,' Russell told him.

'And you, Miss Cooper?' Fred asked in a hopeful tone. 'She told me last night about running into you and you made a strong impression on her once more. You've got a manner.'

'Maisie's a calming influence on all and sundry,' said Russell, trying to make light of the situation. 'When would Holly have slipped out?'

'I'm not sure. I was busy on the gates, you know, from early. One of them's been playing up and sticking.'

'I saw you come chasing after her latish last night,' said Maisie. 'She seemed very happy.'

'Night-time's when she's at her most foolish,' said Fred, looking glum. 'I expect you wanted what was best, but you put ideas in her head.'

'I did? How?'

'I mean talking to her about her old dog and all the time that's passed. She doesn't know which end is up at the best of times and . . .' He stopped and sighed, then concluded: 'Perhaps it's not your fault. Meeting you and having all those memories stirred her up, though . . .'

Maisie wasn't sure how to reply. She tried to remember if she had said anything that might have encouraged Holly to go 'a-gallivanting' as Russell had said, but could think of nothing. She had been about to tell Fred about finding the shoe in the river. Now, she was concerned she'd just be stirring up more trouble.

I'll go and fetch it from the dairy, bring it back and show it to him. That way, there'll be no confusion about whether it's truly hers.

'Did she go quietly to bed, though,' Maisie asked, 'when you brought her back indoors?'

'Like a lamb,' said Fred.

Maisie remembered the sound of an angry bee in the night. *Perhaps the Linton boy might have seen her?*

'Are you saying,' Maisie asked, 'that she couldn't have gone back out? Was she locked in?'

'No, she wasn't,' said Fred, lowering his eyes.

Maisie turned to Russell. 'Would you excuse me. I left something behind.'

She set off quickly, before either of them could ask her why, up the lane towards the entrance to the dairy farm, picking her way across the cattle grid. As she made her way up the track, she noticed the massive figure of Norman Tubb, diminished by distance, in a parched pasture beyond the farm buildings, opening a gate and chivvying a herd of 'ladies' – as Stella had referred to them – through onto fresher grass.

A little breathless from hurrying, she reached the fence of the kitchen garden and bent down to pick up the wet buckle shoe. It was almost dry from being carried about and then sitting in the warm sun. Standing, she saw Stella Tubb picking some salad leaves from one of the untidy borders. Feeling Maisie's eyes upon her, Stella looked up and came directly to the broken gate.

'If you came back for Norm, he's up in top field.'

'No, it was something else. But I'm sorry to have brought back an unhappy memory,' said Maisie.

'It were ten years ago,' said Stella. 'What's past is past. Norman was ever so regretful.' She saw the shoe in Maisie's hand and – as Maisie had done – recognised it. 'What's Holly been getting up to now?'

'I wish I knew,' said Maisie. 'Will you be at the meeting at Sunny View tomorrow?'

'Not at Sunny View. At the Masonic Hall in Kirton.'

'Oh, I just assumed . . .' Maisie began. 'Never mind. So, you'll be there?'

'We all will. Norman and Floyd and me.'

'Was that what Norman and Russell were discussing?'

'Yes, and Shane Tope's inspection. He wrote us up for the ministry, making our lives more difficult for no good reason. Norman was furious. He thinks Shane's got a grudge against us though I couldn't say why.'

'Have you and Norman put money into the gold mine, too?'

'Why shouldn't we? It's a scheme could make a difference to all the local people. And isn't it right that the wealth under our feet, under our own hills and vales, should come to us?'

Maisie thought Stella's words naive.

But naivety is often a counterpart to openness and generosity of spirit.

'Do you know where Holly might have lost her shoe? I found it in the Wivel, floating along, maybe an hour and a half ago.'

'Upstream,' said Stella. 'I've seen her, late at night or early morn, when I've been up and about, tending to a sick lady.'

Maisie reminded herself once more that Stella was referring to a cow.

'Is that why Fred took to locking her in?' she ventured.

'Until the social worker told him he couldn't, that he would be taken to court over it.' The sun went behind a cloud and Maisie felt a cooler breeze on her neck and on her legs. Stella told her: 'Showers maybe, later. Good for the grass.'

'Yes, of course.' Just for a moment, Maisie had a vision, a kind of montage of images of Stella's life: hanging out the washing, tending to the herd, washing out the milking shed with a hosepipe, preparing meals for her husband and son in her gloomy kitchen. 'People don't realise how hard a farmer's life can be,' she said, not certain why.

'We talked about that before,' said Stella. 'But a person will always find way if it's the life they want.'

'And your husband? Is it the life he wants?'

Stella sighed. 'I don't know why you're asking when you know as well as I do that he'd have given his right arm to get away from it all, but he couldn't and it's to his credit that he stuck, whatever he might have done.'

'Do I know that?' Maisie asked.

Stella frowned and said: 'No, perhaps we didn't know one another so well, after all, from ten years ago.'

Maisie once more relived the horrid memory – more complete this time – of Norman Tubb's spittle landing on his poor old dad's face as he chastised him for soiling his bed. Maisie had come up to the farm to collect milk and . . .

She shook her head to dispel the image, telling Stella: 'I won't mention what I saw again.'

'Thank you. Everyone needs a clean slate at some point in their lives. What's past is past,' she repeated.

Maisie said goodbye and walked back down the track, her eyes on the dusty dirt before her feet, thinking about how it was true that difficult circumstances can make good people do bad things to one another. Then she rebelled against the idea.

No, there's always a choice.

She tried to agree with Stella's desire for a 'clean slate', but couldn't.

That's a very naive idea as well. We drag our pasts along after us – including the things we wish we hadn't done – whether we want to or not.

FIFTEEN

Back at the cattle grid, Maisie stepped aside for a mustard-coloured Ford Escort van, recognising the lettering on the side that spelled out Moore's, the garage in Kirton where the father of the Maltese family worked. The driver – wasn't his name Patrick Linton? – gave her a look that mingled curiosity with impatience, rattling over the bars. She held up a hand and he politely stopped.

'Good afternoon—' she began.

'Is there a problem?' he interrupted. 'Are you lost?'

'No, I just thought I'd say "hello". My name is Maisie Cooper. I used to work for the Savages and they're putting me up for a few days.'

Maisie saw Patrick's eyes travel the length of her body, then he said: 'I'm glad to meet you. Perhaps you'd like to have a drink some time.'

'And meet your wife?' said Maisie. 'I'd be delighted.'

Patrick held her gaze. He looked surprisingly well turned out for a mechanic on a visit to a farm – clean-shaven and dressed in a collar and tie beneath his overalls, smelling of aftershave. Thinking about how he had just looked at her, Maisie wondered if perhaps he had smartened himself up for Stella's benefit.

'Trouble at the dairy?' she asked.

'I suppose I'm about to find out,' said Patrick. 'Goodbye, Miss Cooper.'

He engaged first gear and pulled away on the climb up to the Tubbs' farmhouse.

Maisie walked away down the lane, worrying that she was alienating the friends and neighbours she might need to ask for help. Russell was still standing on the brow of the bridge, leaning on the brick parapet, looking down into the crystal-clear waters of the Wivel.

'Where did Fred get to?' she asked.

'He had to open the railway gates for Patrick Linton on his way through from Kirton.'

'Why don't people come the other way round, like we did, from the railway station at the bottom of the town?'

'Folks often do, but it's a lot more direct to just shimmy down Long Lane,' said Russell with what sounded like forced jollity. 'What's that you've got there?'

Maisie felt like a scratched record as she repeated her story of finding the buckle shoe in the water and then heading upstream to see if she could locate its owner.

'I had to turn uphill away from the water when I came to a barrier of barbed wire stretched right across. Was that about fishing rights?'

'Happen so,' confirmed Russell. 'If you're looking for trout, upriver's the proper job, much better than through Trout Leap to Kirton, whatever the name might suggest. Norman Tubb has private rights upstream of that mark for a couple of miles, not that he uses them. Never see him with a rod in his hand, that one.'

'I suppose he doesn't get time. It's remorseless work, dairy farming.'

'Worse than having paying guests,' said Russell with another weak attempt at humour. 'No, though, you're right enough. And he never wanted the farm.'

'Will you tell me more about that?'

'He inherited, didn't he, precocious like, when his poor old dad went senile.'

'Was it dementia?'

'What's that, then?'

'A condition that affects the brain – memory above all.'

'I don't know. The doctor just called it senile, you know, like a lot of old people get, but he were much younger, poor man.'

'How old was Norman's father, then?' Maisie asked. 'How old is Norman now?'

'You'll need to ask Audrey. She's better with dates and birthdays.'

'But Norman looked after his dad, didn't he?' suggested Maisie, carefully, aware that Russell didn't know all that she knew.

'He did – and not so many men would have had the patience and . . .' Russell stopped, glancing up from the water at last, looking her in the eye. 'Ah, was that it?'

'Was what it?'

'Did you see something unkind between Norman Tubb and his old dad.'

'I did,' said Maisie. She hesitated and he fixed her with a beady inquisitive eye. 'All right, this is what happened – ten years ago, as you know. I went up to the dairy because one of our guests had spilt the milk and we'd need some for the next morning. It was evening or the end of the day, something like that. I got to the farmhouse and heard shouting and I thought someone had fallen and couldn't get up and, I suppose, that was right, in a way. Except it was Norman leaning over his old dad, shaking him and shouting in his face, and I could see in the old man's eyes that he had no idea what he'd done wrong, broken something or wet his bed or I don't know what. Norman saw me. I told him all I needed was some milk and he came over all regretful and said it had never happened before and would never happen again and begged me not to tell and I haven't until this day.'

'Well, I never did,' said Russell.

'What I saw was bad enough but it made me worry that there might have been worse, you know, when no one was about. What happened to Norman's mother?'

'Oh, that was a long time ago, soon after Norman was born. She left his old dad for an American soldier soon after the war.'

'She didn't,' said Maisie, astonished.

'Went off to Kentucky or somewhere like that, a place with horses, leaving Norman's dad alone in charge of the dairy farm with his strapping son who grew up and, back then, he was different man.'

'Norman was a different man?'

'He was optimistic. He seemed to love his work. He was a big strong handsome feller and, after a few years, he got himself a wife a good deal younger than he was and pretty as a picture or . . .' Russell stopped and Maisie thought he was thinking something similar to her own mental correction earlier on. 'No, well, not pretty as such, you know, Maisie? Not like you. But Stella's just got something like a : . . like a lovely tomato. Do you know what I mean?'

'I do,' said Maisie very seriously. She didn't want to spoil the confessional mood by laughing. 'So, you think I should ask Audrey to put things in chronological order for me, with dates.'

'Why do you want that?'

'The habit of a tidy mind,' Maisie told him. 'What about now, though? Are they hard up?'

'I don't think so. And they've got high hopes that things will improve in the EEC. You remember there was a vote at the beginning of the year and we're going in, like it or not?'

Living in Paris, Maisie knew very well from reading the papers the pattern of events. Despite the UK being the first country to sign up for the forerunner of the European Economic Community, the European Coal and Steel Community, President Charles de Gaulle of France had twice vetoed the UK's application to join the EEC. Prime Minister Edward Heath had taken advantage of de Gaulle leaving office to agree a new treaty, with full accession planned for January 1973 in six months' time.

'You're saying Norman Tubb thinks it will be good for farmers. You don't agree?'

'I can't rightly say,' said Russell, 'but you worry about them over there telling us over here what to do, don't you?'

Maisie thought 'them over there' – the continental Europeans – mostly made a better job of things than the alternating Conversative and Labour governments of the UK, but she didn't want to argue pointlessly about things outside of her and Russell's control.

'Is Audrey back? Where did you both go, by the way?'

'She peeped in on you this morning, wondering if you might like to go with her to the market in Kirton, but you were sleeping like a baby.'

'It's the country air,' said Maisie with a smile. 'Did you go with her?'

'I drove her in and I delivered some cider to the Masonic for tomorrow night.'

'For the meeting?'

'That's right.'

'Do you expect a good turnout?'

'I do.'

'But she's back now?'

'Yes. And it'll be lunchtime,' said Russell. 'I dare say she's put things out. I hope she has.'

'Should I go and talk to Fred?'

'Let him cool off for a bit. Fred knows where to look for Holly. It's not as though this goes against her habits. She'll turn up.'

★

Audrey served lunch in the garden behind Sunny View, using a table and chairs stored folded in the cider shed that Maisie wiped down with Domestos to remove cobwebs and insect eggs. They ate under the trees that lined the Wivel because the sun was high and, though it was obscured now and then by intermittent clouds, hot. The meal was a copious ploughman's lunch that Maisie enjoyed enormously after her unusual morning, at first slovenly, in bed very late, then full of vigorous exercise and, finally, the unsettling confrontations with Norman Tubb and, to a lesser extent, Patrick Linton.

'Russell told me you would put me straight on what happened when in the Tubb family,' Maisie remarked to Audrey.

'You mean dates and things?'

'Yes, and anything else?'

'Why's that then?'

'I'm interested in people,' Maisie told her.

'Well, Old Man Tubb would have died before you came.'

'In the Fifties?'

'Where are we now?'

Maisie laughed and told her: 'We're nineteen-seventy-two.'

'No, I mean generations. There was Old Man Tubb, then Norman Tubb whose farm it is today, then he married Stella who was a lot younger than him, and they had Floyd who you knew as still in school ten years ago. I'd need a pen and paper to work it all out.'

'I don't expect the exact dates are important, but Russell told me that Norman had a much more attractive personality before his father developed dementia – became senile – and he had to cope with all that?'

'He was, though Russell always likes to see the best. Always a bully, I'd say.'

'But Stella married him?'

'He was well-to-do and I imagine he showed her his better side,' said Audrey. 'And Stella came from nothing. Her dad was a day labourer, living in one of those tiny cottages at the top of the town.'

'Fair enough. And Norman's father brought him up largely alone because Norman's mother went off with an American soldier and never came back?'

'That's right. As you say it, I see it clearer.'

'What was Norman's cuckolded father like, before and after?'

'That's a long time ago,' said Audrey.

Russell piped up: 'My parents already had Sunny View and they used to send me to the Cub Scouts up Kirton on a Saturday morning, come wind or shine, to get me out of the house, and he ran it, Old Man Tubb, and he was a fierce sergeant-major type for us as weren't his children, but he was even harder on Norman. In the end, I asked my parents if I could stop going because no one was happy there and they said: "All right, but what are you going to do to keep from under our feet?" I don't know why, but it just came to me and I said: "We could have an apple orchard and I'll look after it and we'll eat them and make apple sauces and, who knows, scrumpy, too." Of course, I was twelve or something so I was big enough to be useful in the house and garden, too.'

Maisie found this glimpse into Russell's childhood fascinating. She did a swift mental calculation, counting back from his sixty-eight years – by coincidence, the same age as Jack's grandmother, Florence.

'That would have been in the middle of World War I?'

'It was, but unless you had a father or a brother of an age for conscription, we didn't see much of that down in the West Country. I was a child and newspapers weren't such a thing and there was no radio back then. Radio came after the war with the stories for children or the music programme in the evening . . .' Russell's eyes became vague. 'It's years since I've thought of all that,' he said.

Maisie brought the conversation back on track.

'So, Norman wouldn't necessarily have felt much of a debt of gratitude to his harsh father, and then it fell to Norman to nurse him through his senility. How did Old Man Tubb die, in the end?' Maisie asked.

'I think he just didn't wake up one morning,' said Russell.

Maisie didn't say anything for a minute or so. Audrey and Russell were still eating, lavishly spreading the excellent white bread from the market with butter and pickles, adding generous slices of strong cheddar cheese. Meanwhile, she wondered how she would have coped with a parent who was no better than a giant baby, who didn't know where he was or what was happening to him, adrift in a confusing world that no longer made any sense.

Is it possible that Norman lost patience and smothered his poor old dad?

'I know this sounds foolish, Audrey, but I would be grateful if you could work out the approximate dates in all this. Can you? I feel it might be important, somehow,' said Maisie.

'Because?' Audrey wanted to know.

Maisie sighed and looked from one to the other.

'You know I've been successful in helping the police with one or two local incidents in Sussex? I won't go into much detail. That's not important. But, a couple of weeks ago, there was a death, a murder, in a village called Bitling, not far from where I was brought up as a child. I happened to be there and I was able to help in working out what had happened.'

'You helped your fiancé, Jack?' asked Audrey, more interested in romance than sleuthing.

'No, Jack was away, in Exeter, you remember? But his friend – well, a friend of mine, too – Inspector Fred Nairn was in charge. But that wasn't what I was going to say.'

'Go on then,' said Russell.

Maisie made a face, expressing frustration but also resignation.

'I don't know why I've come across several mysteries in just a few months and why I've been in a position to help solve them. It seems such a peculiar coincidence but, then, bad things happen all the time and . . .' She frowned. 'What I mean to say is this. At first, with my brother Stephen's murder and then with the drama at Bunting Manor, Jack was cross with me for getting involved. It came between us and, for a while, I thought we'd never get past it. Because of that, during the third one, he kept his distance and . . .'

Maisie stopped. There had been moments after the murder at Chichester Festival Theatre, helping Adélaïde Amour with her lines, when she had convinced herself that her relationship with Jack was doomed and she should disappear back to Paris.

'But it was because he cared for you,' said Audrey.

'He was looking out for you,' said Russell, nodding.

'That's right,' said Maisie, smiling. 'But I was going to say, at the end of the Bitling Fair mystery, he turned up at the last minute after everything was over and I thought he was going to tell me that . . . that he couldn't after all marry someone who would always run towards danger.'

'What danger?' asked Audrey, very interested.

'I've confronted several murderers alone and unprepared,' said Maisie.

'But what's that got to do with any of this?' asked Russell, waving a hand at the peaceful garden, the sparkling trout stream and the soft hills beyond.

'When Jack arrived, after Bitling Fair – it was back at midsummer, you know? – I wanted to apologise for getting involved yet again. But he wouldn't let me. He told me: "You must never be sorry for being yourself, Maisie. You are who you are, and that's enough for me, wherever it leads." And it made me think: *That's true. You can't fight your own nature. Don't you agree?'*

'I do,' said Audrey.

'Depends on what nature we're talking about,' quibbled Russell. 'Some would do well to curb themselves.'

'Yes, that's true,' said Maisie. 'But the thing is, I realised, in that moment, that my nature is and always will be to see danger and run towards it, not because I'm especially brave, but because there's a chance that I can prevent bad things happening.'

'What bad things?' asked Russell.

'Like you said so shockingly in your letter,' Maisie told him, lightly. 'You said you were worried there might be a murder.'

She took the letter out of her handbag and showed it to Audrey. Once her eyes had finished scanning the page, Audrey said: 'Perhaps it's nonsense, after all.'

'No,' said Maisie.

'How do you mean, "No"?'

'Well, murder is my speciality and I wouldn't be surprised to find myself investigating another one right here at Sunny View.'

'Why do you say that?'

'I wish I could tell you. All I know is, there's a kind of atmosphere that, I think, I must be sensitive to. I can feel it here, in Trout Leap. I suppose it's money at the root? I wish you'd tell me more about the mine, if that's the cause of your worries.'

'It is, maid,' said Russell. 'Does it really exist though? That's the question.'

III

NETTLES & WASPS

SIXTEEN

Once again, there was no time to get to the bottom of the question of the gold mine. Russell had to hurry to 'get off to the railway station and pick up our two paying guests' while Maisie and Audrey cleared away the lunch things. In the big rustic kitchen, Audrey continued reminiscing about the Tubbs, trying to put dates to events. Maisie didn't say much, not wanting to interrupt Audrey's train of thought.

When everything was washed and dried and the cheese and the butter and the pickles were back on the cold shelf in the pantry, the plates in the pale oak dresser and the knives and forks in the drawer, Audrey went back outside to drape the damp tea towels over the garden chairs. Maisie followed. The rogue buckle shoe was beside the table. Maisie decided she shouldn't delay any longer – that she should go and speak to Fred Luscombe.

Never mind that Russell says Fred knows where to look and that Holly will turn up. I wish I'd listened to my own conscience sooner.

She picked up the shoe and carried it indoors. Unfortunately, before she could set off, up the narrow lane to the gatekeeper's cottage, Russell returned to Sunny View in the asthmatic-sounding Vauxhall Viva with the guests.

'Stay for ten minutes to get introduced, Maisie,' Russell entreated her.

'All right.'

The first guest was a man of about fifty who gave his name as 'your good friend, Vincent Brent'. He carried a small grip and a green canvas bag that reminded her of riverbanks and fish, plus a long thin case that, Maisie surmised, contained his rod. On a strap round his neck was a sophisticated camera with a German name that Maisie couldn't read because it was embossed in a complicated gothic script.

The second guest was a very jolly woman of about the same age called Ida Anderson who wore a navy-blue skirt and a yellow twinset and also carried with her the paraphernalia of her hobby: an easel and canvases, a battered wooden box of paints and brushes, plus a large Gladstone bag for her clothes and toiletries and so on.

Audrey insisted that they should all 'leave the bags in the hall and have a nice cup of tea in the garden' which she served, to Maisie's dismay – given they had only just eaten lunch – with some home-made scones with strawberry jam and cream. Maisie left the shoe on the edge of the Aga to finish drying, agreeing to sit with them all because Russell seemed very badly to want her to do so. To make conversation, she asked Ida Anderson how she knew about Sunny View.

'From the RAC listings.'

Audrey became rather fussy, insisting on 'best china' and putting out embroidered napkins in silver napkin rings. They all exchanged a few remarks about their journey to Kirton railway station and the weather forecast, then Russell launched into a new topic in a jolly bantering tone and, as he spoke, Maisie felt more miserable still.

'So, you see, our Miss Cooper – Mrs Wingard as she will be, being betrothed – is famous.'

'Is that so?' asked Vincent Brent, looking interested. 'In what field?'

'You'll never guess.'

'Could it be acting?' asked Ida Anderson.

'No, not acting,' said Russell, enormously enjoying himself. 'Though she's worked very recently in a theatre.'

During this exchange, Audrey went indoors 'to put on some more hot water for the pot', leaving Maisie and Russell side by side on the north side of the garden table. The two new arrivals were on the south side with the bright sun behind them. Maisie could feel herself squinting and wished she had some dark glasses to attenuate the glare.

'Are you a magazine model, you know, for clothes and things?' Ida asked Maisie with a titter. 'I wish I had your figure.' She left a pause, then added, for comic effect: 'And your face and your complexion.'

Everyone laughed politely and Maisie – perhaps because she couldn't see them very well – thought about how both had quite a pronounced London accent.

'No, Miss Anderson, that's not it,' said Russell, delighted.

'Is it to do with how she earns her sausage-and-mash?' Vincent asked, using Cockney rhyming slang for 'cash'. 'A presenter on the radio?' he suggested. 'You have a restful voice, Miss Cooper.'

'Thank you, Mr Brent.'

'Call me "Vincent".'

'I'm really someone quite unremarkable, Vincent. I'm not sure what Mr Savage is getting at—' Maisie began, but Russell interrupted her.

'Murder,' he said, beaming.

'What's that?' blurted Vincent.

'Maisie has solved crimes like you wouldn't believe, getting the police out of trouble when they couldn't see up from down.'

'Well,' said Vincent, more quietly. 'Would you Adam-and-Eve it?'

Because Maisie wasn't properly able to see the new guests' faces, she couldn't really gauge their reactions. But she was aware of a new stillness, perhaps a wariness, as neither spoke and Russell rattled on, revealing that he knew much more about the murders at Church Lodge, Bunting Manor and Chichester Festival Theatre than she had realised, including names and even dates. She was relieved when, in the end, he ran out of steam, remarking: 'There's more to come because there's another story from a midsummer fair in one of them Sussex villages, but I haven't got to the bottom of that one yet. Perhaps, Maisie, you'd like to tell us all now?'

'I'm not sure I ought to,' said Maisie, deciding to employ a white lie. 'The whole business is *sub judice* until it has gone to court. But how do you know all that, Russell?'

'I've had your local paper sent on to me here at Sunny View and I've cut out all the columns and stuck them in a scrapbook.' He laughed. 'I never told you that, did I, Maisie?'

'How on earth did you manage it?' Maisie insisted, keeping her voice light.

'Herbie got me copies of the *Chichester Observer* through the post.'

Maisie remembered seeing the offices of the local paper on her evening walk, with the editor in shirtsleeves at his layout table.

'You mean Herbert Peckham of the *Kirton Courier*?'

'I do.'

'Well, I'm afraid the journalistic reporting has deceived you, Russell. It must have made those investigations sound much more dramatic than they ever really were,' Maisie told him, aware that neither Vincent nor Ida had much spoken since Russell's revelations. 'But this must all be very tiresome for your guests. Would you like to tell us about your hobbies? Fishing and painting, isn't that right?'

Russell laughed and jumped in before they could answer: 'There, you see. Maisie's seen right through the two of you already.'

Again, Maisie felt the remark caused an uncertain pause. She shielded her eyes to observe them more closely. Vincent was filling a pipe from a waxed-cotton pouch of tobacco, his eyes down. Ida was lavishly spreading half a scone with jam. As she added a teaspoon of cream, she finally broke the silence: 'I wish I had an exciting life like you have, Miss Cooper. Nothing ever happens to me.'

She took a huge mouthful of the heavily laden scone, then daintily wiped the corners of her mouth with one of Audrey's embroidered table napkins.

'Do you mind if I light this, Miss Cooper?' asked Vincent.

'Not at all. Please go ahead, Mr Brent.'

'Vincent's the name, please. Can I offer you a pipe, Mr Savage?'

'Call me "Russell".'

'Much obliged. Would you like some tobacco yourself?'

'No, thank you, Vincent. Never have, never will. I'm short enough of puff as it is.'

Maisie watched Vincent strike a match by bending down to scrape it on the nearest stone slab set into the lawn. He drew the flame against the wad of tobacco in the bowl of the pipe by sucking on the stem. She found the action strangely magnetic, then realised that there was something Vincent ought to have said, but hadn't.

Before she could follow up on this idea, though, Audrey bustled back out with more hot water, worried that the new guests would perhaps be wanting to go and lie down after their travels. Vincent told her he was very happy in the garden with his pipe. Ida asked winsomely if there might be another scone 'hiding somewhere'. Russell said there was and went to fetch it from the pantry.

The atmosphere became much more convivial with Audrey and Ida finding common ground in a discussion of baking recipes and techniques. Meanwhile, Maisie felt

Vincent's eyes upon her, between puffs of his aromatic tobacco. Eventually, he leaned towards her and said, his words masked by the ladies' enthusiastic voices: 'There's no need to be so diffident, Miss Cooper. It sounds like you made a very real contribution.'

Maisie felt his words meant something more than their surface meaning.

Was that a veiled warning?

She heard the hoot of the milk lorry, reminding her that she had promised to stay for only ten minutes and that she had easily exceeded that.

'I'm delighted to have met you both,' she said, politely. 'Would you excuse me?' She stood up. Audrey and Ida Anderson's conversation tailed off. 'I'm just going to step out for a few minutes. I'll be back shortly.'

Audrey and Ida spoke over one another. Maisie gave them both a smile and slipped away, down the side of the house, past the pale blue Vauxhall Viva parked on the gravel drive, and away up the lane towards the railway gates. They were open to traffic and closed to trains, the milk lorry rattling over the rails towards her, a platoon of empty churns rattling behind. Maisie squeezed herself against the hedge to allow it to go past, feeling a thorn or a bramble scratch her leg. The hot exhaust of the diesel engine made her hold her breath. The lorry was followed by a little posse of holidaymakers on bicycles – several old-fashioned ones and a couple of smart-looking racing models, with heavy paniers.

Maisie let them all go by then made for the gates. To her surprise, it wasn't Fred Luscombe operating them, but a tall, strong-looking woman with several safety pins attached to her baggy brown cardigan.

'Hello, Mrs Sturgess,' said Maisie. 'Is everything all right?'

'How do you mean, then?' asked the woman.

'I'm sorry. I should have properly reintroduced myself. My name is Maisie Cooper. I'm staying with the Savages and you may remember that ten years ago—'

'Of course. I'm glad to make your acquaintance once more,' said Mrs Sturgess. 'My Timothy told me he'd met you and you were very kind.'

'Oh, yes. I saw him down at the river bend this morning and showed him how to tie some better knots.'

'I don't know about that. I was talking about yesterday when he was stuck in the brambles in the apple orchard. I've not seen hide nor hair of him since breakfast. He'll be gone till he's hungry. Would you excuse me?'

Timothy Sturgess's mother bent down to pull a heavy bolt up out of the tarmac, releasing one of the gates, and swung it into position, blocking the road to vehicle traffic on the Trout Leap side. She did the same with the other gate on the Long Lane side, then strode a little way up the track to action a long lever set in a mechanism beside the rails that raised a signal on a tall post to tell approaching trains that the crossing was clear. She slipped out through the pedestrian kissing gate.

'I was asking if all was well,' said Maisie, 'because I expected Mr Luscombe to be on duty.'

'He'll be back dreckly, I expect,' said Mrs Sturgess, using the Devonian corruption of 'directly', meaning 'soon'. She added, employing the same expression Russell had used: 'Holly's off a-gallivanting. He's looking for her.'

She probably went back out after I saw Fred fetch her home, looking out of my bedroom window.

'Has Mr Luscombe been gone long?'

'I don't know. An hour or so?'

'And Holly?'

'He can't be sure. She's in the habit of not getting up till midday or after, cause she's never abed till the middle of the night or even after the sun.'

'You seem very professional with the gates and the signal.'

'It's not the first time and I don't mind stepping in. We've been neighbours for that long . . .' Mrs Sturgess let her voice drift off, then mused: 'It might be a bit longer than an hour that he's been gone. You see,' she added, apologetically, 'I wasn't called out till just now, you know, by someone hooting, and I do lose track of time when I'm sewing. I broke off because I knew to come up to the gates, waiting for Floyd Tubb because he comes through regular. Can I get you a nice cup of tea?'

'No, thank you,' said Maisie. 'I've just had some. Do you know which way Mr Luscombe went? I have something I wanted to ask him.'

'He'll be looking in her usual places, along the Wivel towards Kirton railway station, you know, where poor old Bertie died, suffocated. Or along the line. She can get it into her head that she needs to go to Exeter to see her doctor, or she sets off Barnstaple way, in the other direction, because that takes her to a pedestrian gate where she can gad about into the country without being stopped by Norman Tubb's barbed wire. Do you know the places I mean?'

'Actually, I do.'

'Well, no peace for the wicked,' said Mrs Sturgess, abruptly, but with a smile.

She strode away, disappearing inside the corner cottage, number three, leaving Maisie standing in the middle of the lane, wondering what to do next.

She wandered slowly back towards Sunny View, feeling a kind of ache in her calf where the bramble or the thorn had scratched her. Looking down, she realised it was, in fact, a tick, its nasty shiny body like a tiny black bead against her smooth skin.

She hurried back to Sunny View, entering through the front door, running directly upstairs. Her washbag was on the windowsill in the bathroom. She rummaged inside, finding a pair of tweezers, putting her foot up on the edge of the bath, realising it hadn't been a very good idea to wear white socks with her sandals because they were filthy.

Maisie positioned the tweezers very carefully, horizontally against her skin, either side of the tick's body. She knew it was very important to be extremely gentle so as to pull the insect's mouthparts out of her skin without leaving any pieces behind. Otherwise, the wound had a good chance of becoming infected.

She was successful, disposing of the tick by squishing it in a piece of toilet paper and flushing it down the loo. She heard Audrey's voice, leading Ada and Vincent upstairs, and slipped away to her bedroom, 'Caesar', leaving the door slightly ajar, observing them on their way past.

Audrey was first, talking about bread making. Ida seemed very interested. Between them, the two women carried all of Ida's things. Russell came next, puffing wheezily, festooned with all of Vincent's gear except the fishing rod in its long narrow case that Maisie assumed had been left somewhere downstairs.

'One more flight, Vincent,' said Russell, jovially. 'Perhaps you'd like to look at the book I mentioned later on? Oh, and we had a wasp's nest up here, in under the eaves of the dormer, but I dealt with that using lethal force.' He laughed. 'Let me tell you about those jaspers. They were maddened like a badger caught in a barbed-wire fence . . .'

Russell's voice faded as they went along the landing, out of Maisie's field of view, then she heard their heavy tread climbing to the top bedrooms, 'Hannibal' and 'Scipio', each with a dormer window in the tiled roof. She could still make out a hum of jolly chatter from 'Pompey' where Audrey and Ida had moved on to the debate over 'jam first or cream first' on scones. She softly shut her door and sat down on the edge of her pleasantly firm bed with two questions in her mind.

First of all, where is Holly Luscombe?

Maisie tried to quell her mounting anxiety as several dramatic scenarios played out in her imagination.

Second of all, if Ida Anderson and Vincent Brent are strangers to one another, why didn't he ask Ida – as well as me – if she minded him smoking his aromatic pipe?

Seventeen

Sitting on the edge of her bed, Maisie examined her calf. The puncture wound from the disgusting but microscopic jaws of the tick was red. She squeezed her skin firmly between her two thumbs, making a pearl of red blood appear, hoping that it might flush out any poison from the insect's saliva. She went back to her washbag in the bathroom and put a dab of witch hazel on a pad of toilet paper to disinfect it. She wondered what she ought to do next.

I wish I could have shown Fred Luscombe the shoe I found floating down the Wivel. Each time I've tried, circumstances have got in my way.

Maisie sighed, feeling guilty.

I still don't know for sure that it's Holly's.

She thought again about the question of why Vincent hadn't asked Ida if she minded his pipe smoke.

It was a natural question to ask. He gave me the opportunity to object – Russell, too, by offering him tobacco from his pouch.

She imagined a simple, innocent explanation.

If the two 'paying guests' travelled into Kirton on the same train – by their accents, presumably down from London – Vincent might already know that Ida wasn't bothered by it.

Maisie went downstairs to the kitchen. The ancient pamphlet about Devonshire gold mining had been put away.

Is that because Russell doesn't want his paying guests to see it?

A wasp was zooming back and forth round the lampshade and she wondered why it didn't simply go outdoors. It settled in one of the teacups, scavenging for sugar. Maisie took the cup outside to encourage the 'jasper' to fly away – it promptly did – then she went back indoors and rinsed that teacup and its fellows, leaving them upturned on the draining board.

The local paper was still there. She turned the pages, hesitating over an article about a man called Collier who had lost his sight in an accident but who travelled around the West Country with a canine companion, raising thousands of pounds for the charity that trained Guide Dogs. Another article spoke about Father Riley of Kirton Roman Catholic Church, reputed to be a charming and engaging preacher, who had recently announced his decision to abandon his Devonshire flock and join a missionary community in West Africa, in Senegal.

Maisie turned another page and found herself reading a full-page advertisement for the St Lawrence Residential Home, cunningly disguised as a newspaper column. She remembered the place, opposite the police station, very clean and tidy, almost too clean, in a way, rather soulless and sad, but with an on-site shop that even had a small section for alcohol, mostly bottles of stout and sweet sherry. The page in the *Kirton Courier* remorselessly celebrated it with glowing testimonies from residents and their younger relatives who had chosen the St Lawrence Residential Home for their elders' long-term care. The food was reputed to be very good, 'always satisfying home-cooked meals'. One contributor mentioned the annual Christmas celebrations and the summer fête which, last year, was opened by a celebrity from Westward Television whose name Maisie didn't recognise.

Maisie heard footsteps coming down the boxed-in back stairs to the kitchen. Russell emerged, a little puffed.

'Ah, you're reading about the old people's home,' he said with a smile. 'Are you wondering when we're going to sell up and move in there, Audrey and me?'

'I was just at a loose end.'

He sat down heavily at the table.

'Would you like me to run you into Kirton? You could have a look round the shops.'

'Do you have nothing else you need to do?'

'There's always something useful to get on with in the garden or the cider shed. And there'll be the evening meal for the paying guests. What did you think of them? For me, they sort of come together. Do you know what I mean? They could be brother and sister.'

Maisie summoned images of Ida and Vincent into her mind, she with her jolly, pudgy face, he much more serious, his eyes sharp and his 'noticing' expression.

'That hadn't struck me,' she decided. 'Can I ask, what do you think of Mrs Sturgess, Timothy's mother? I came across her opening and closing the railway gates. That seems a little haphazard, asking a neighbour to do such an important job.'

'She's reliable, though,' said Russell, as if it was the most normal thing in the world. 'What would you worry about?'

'I suppose that she might forget to set the signal for the approaching train and there could be an accident.'

'But the train has a driver looking out the front window for what's ahead – not just the signal but anything on the line as well. And they always come slowish out of Kirton station because they know about the Trout Leap crossing.'

'Yes, that makes sense. Another thing, Mrs Sturgess told me that she hadn't seen Timothy all morning – well, at least since I saw him just after ten – and he was out and about in his swimming trunks on his raft and . . .' Maisie stopped. Recent experiences in the murder at Bunting Manor had made her very sensitive to the idea of a child being neglected. 'He's a wiry little boy.'

'Could do with feeding up, that's for sure,' agreed Russell.

'Does he have friends?'

'I don't see him with any, but there's no reason that I should. Perhaps he does Cub Scouts or something, out of school? Why do you ask?'

'I was just imagining him spending all six weeks of the summer holiday on his own, exploring the river, creeping through the trees and the bushes, like when we found him all caught up in the thorns and brambles. Is he friends with Deborah Tope?'

'I don't expect so. She's young for her age, isn't she? And there's a big difference between a girl in the juniors and a boy at big school.'

'Does he have a dog?'

'No, but he does have Petunia.'

There was an odd expression in Russell's eye as he said this.

'Do you want to tell me about her?'

'Who do you suppose she is?' he asked with a sly look.

'I think someone told me she's Timothy's older sister. I remember her coming to see her mother when Timothy was just a baby. She was quite a big girl.'

'She was. She's much fitter now.'

'There's no Mr Sturgess, no father, in view? I seem to recall him being in the picture? Is that right, back when I came down here to help you out?'

'You did more than help out. You put Sunny View on a sound footing at last, getting us into tourist leaflets and on the AA and the RAC lists so people knew we were here and available. You set us up.'

'Thank you, Russell, but you were well on your way.'

He shook his head and told her: 'No, we weren't. We were dabblers. You made us professional. And I wish we could have kept you on. Imagine your parents hadn't died. Would you have stopped down here, do you think?'

No, I always wanted to see the world.

'Perhaps,' she told him. 'But Mr Sturgess?'

'Oh, him,' said Russell with disdain. 'He cut up something terrible, all unnecessary over Petunia, thinking he could rule the roost and lay down the law and tell everyone what was what, so Geraldine sent him packing. Silly, really, because he was a pleasant mild man, otherwise.'

Russell left a pause and Maisie connected all the elements.

'I see. Petunia was much bigger back when I knew her because she'd fallen pregnant and come to her mother and father for help. Her mother was willing and her father not. Mrs Sturgess took in her daughter's illegitimate son, passing him off as her own late pregnancy. Her husband wouldn't have it and that was the end of their marriage.'

'That's the ticket. He was already down on Petunia because she had what you might call a "generous" nature.'

'You mean she took lovers?'

'Fly-by-night affairs. She was sixteen. There was no harm, if she was careful – which, I suppose, she wasn't.'

'And people think that Timothy is the son of Mrs Sturgess and that Petunia is his big sister, just far apart in ages?'

'Who would think that?' Russell scoffed. 'No one with eyes to see.'

Maisie felt uncomfortable gossiping, but she asked: 'Did the business cause ructions more generally?'

'Live and let live,' said Russell. 'People accepted it, whatever they knew, and most go along and talk about Petunia being the big sister, especially newcomers.'

'But there aren't so many of those,' said Maisie. 'I wonder if the Maltese family realise.'

'I think he would see it, Patrick Linton. He's the noticing sort.'

'You don't like him?' asked Maisie, responding to Russell's tone.

'Is that how I come across? Perhaps I'm tired.'

'What about Mrs Linton?'

'She's a poor little thing, hardly ever out of doors, doesn't speak very good English or doesn't dare. It's hard to say.'

Audrey and Ida came bustling into the kitchen, still sharing culinary tips and strategies.

'Miss Anderson would like to do some baking. She says she makes a lovely cobbler and could we spare some apples from the cider orchard?'

'Of course,' said Russell, rising from his kitchen chair. 'But they'll need something to sweeten them.'

'I use sultanas and honey,' said Ida.

'We've got the honey but do we have dried fruit?' Russell asked.

'I used it all up for the Christmas puddings and the fruit cake last winter,' said Audrey.

'How about I go into Kirton and bring some back?' suggested Maisie. 'Will you need anything else?'

There was a brief discussion and a list was drawn up on a sheet of Basildon Bond writing paper from the pad in the drawer called 'chaos'. Maisie folded it over and put it in the pocket of her dress. Audrey gave her a wicker basket and Russell wondered: 'Where did I put my keys?'

'In their proper place on the hook by the front door, I hope,' said Audrey.

'I think I'd like to walk, actually,' said Maisie. 'I'll go over the top of Break Heart Hill again.'

'Is that the steep slope up from the railway crossing?' asked Ida. 'I'd love to set up my easel on the crest of the hill and have a go at Trout Leap from above.'

Ida had changed out of her yellow twinset into a lightweight painter's smock.

'You're definitely dressed for it,' said Maisie. 'I'd be happy to help you carry everything up. When I've finished, I'll come back the same way and, if you're still there, give you a hand back down.'

'That would be very kind,' said Ida.

Audrey tried to give Maisie some money for the bits and pieces of shopping, but she refused.

'You're already putting me up free of charge. It's the least I can do to make a contribution.'

She and Ida set off. Maisie had the handle of a wicker basket in the crook of her left elbow and Ida's easel on her right shoulder. Ida carried a canvas, her box of paints and a thermos Audrey had lent her to carry clean water. Maisie was glad to see that Fred Luscombe was back and on duty at the railway crossing.

'Where did you find Holly?' Maisie asked with a smile of relief.

'I didn't,' said Fred. 'I've had to call the police.'

Fred's tone and his words gave Maisie a shiver of guilt.

'Oh, dear. Do you think she's got herself lost?'

'She's a wonderful walker but she's been gone a spell. She might have had a slip-up of some kind.'

'Unless she's gone hiking into Exeter,' said Maisie. 'That was in her thoughts, wasn't it, the idea of seeing the doctor who used to look after her?'

'That's what I told the constable. Exeter's eight miles, but it's flat. She'd take no more than a couple of hours to get there, but she'd find the place where she used to be looked after is closed down and gone.'

'That might be very distressing for her,' said Maisie. 'Is there anything I can do to help?'

'Are you off into Kirton?'

'I am. This is Miss Anderson. She's a paying guest at Sunny View.'

'Pleased to meet you, ma'am.'

'Likewise,' said Ida.

'Are you going up Long Lane?' said Fred. 'You know it can be dangerous with traffic?'

'We're going up Break Heart Hill where Miss Anderson is going to set her easel while I go into town.' Maisie hesitated, then told him: 'I found a shoe in the river this morning, floating along. It was quite like one of Holly's shoes.'

'You did? Why haven't you told me?'

'I tried—' Maisie began.

'I've been at my wits' end and, all this time, you've been keeping back?'

'Mr Luscombe,' said Maisie firmly, 'I twice came to find you, but you weren't here. Now that you're back, I'm telling you.'

'Where did you come across it?'

'At the river bend, just across the field,' said Maisie, gesturing with her head because her arms were busy with her burdens. 'It must have been about ten-fifteen or perhaps ten-thirty.'

'I was here then.'

'I didn't know that and I wasn't at all sure it was hers. Well, at first, it did cross my mind that Holly might have lost it and was hobbling about on one foot, as it were, so I decided to go searching upriver, because that had to be the direction it came from. I went under the bridge and along the fields, up to the barbed wire and the dry-stone wall, then came back via the Tubbs' farm.'

'So, what did you do with it?'

'The shoe is in the kitchen at Sunny View, on the ledge of the Aga, drying out. Do you want to come with me and find it?'

Fred didn't answer and Maisie thought he was listening for something. She heard it, too – the approach of a train, at first just making the rails vibrate and sing, then the thunderous cacophony of the diesel engines and the carriages rattling past. As the commotion faded, Maisie asked again if he wanted her to come with him to Sunny View.

'No,' he told her. 'You've done enough. You put ideas in her head with the way you talked to her, like she's normal and can make her own decisions. She isn't and you should have known better.'

Fred stomped off down the lane.

'That was rude,' said Ida. 'I'm surprised you stood for it.'

'He's very worried,' said Maisie, lost in thought, her eyes down. Then she looked up at her companion and caught a glimpse of an evaluating intelligence in Ida's eye. She had a brief impression – lasting only a second or two – that she was being judged.

'Did you want to say something?' Maisie asked.

'No, dear, I don't think so,' said Ida in the garrulous, amused tone that had – until that peculiar and fleeting moment – been her hallmark.

Who exactly is Ida Anderson? And what is she trying to hide?

Eighteen

Maisie found the steep climb to the top of Break Heart Hill mentally relaxing and physically invigorating. For her, the slope was manageable, even with the heavy easel balanced on her shoulder. Ida, however, found it impossible simultaneously to speak and ascend, so she plodded alongside in what seemed an unwilling and unaccustomed silence.

Unable to question Ida more closely, Maisie's mind drifted to the past, in particular to a difficult 'interview' with a special branch officer, soon after the service of commemoration for her brother Stephen in the parish church in Framlington. Inspector Barden had kept his cards very close to his chest, probing her closely on her brother's character, bringing back painful memories of their estrangement, asking about Stephen's elite-level qualifications in the modern pentathlon, including competing at the Melbourne Olympic Games of 1956.

At the time, Maisie hadn't known that Stephen was a victim of a murderous attack. Later, she realised that Barden was making a judgement on whether he would have been able to defend himself with agility or physical strength. Had he asked her straight out, Maisie's answer would have been negative. At that point, Stephen was a sadly dissipated specimen of softened middle-aged manhood.

In the same conversation, Maisie had confirmed that she, too, was proficient in the five pentathlon disciplines of fencing, swimming, horse riding, shooting and running, encouraged by her time in the Women's Royal Army Corps, but without the validation of official competition because women's events weren't sanctioned. As things turned out, during her amateur investigation into Stephen's murder, she had been forced to employ her fencing and riding skills and, in the climax to the drama at Bunting Manor, her prowess in middle-distance running had been crucial. While the mysteries at the theatre and at Bitling Fair had been intellectual – based in character and the kaleidoscope of potential motives and opportunities – she had developed a routine of early-morning swims at the baths in the centre of Chichester.

Maisie reached the brow of the hill and turned to look back down into the valley, only then realising that she had left Ida thirty paces behind. The older woman toiled painfully slowly up to meet her, while Maisie continued her train of thought, wondering if the neglected fifth skill – shooting – would ever be called upon.

It seems unlikely.

Maisie swung the easel down off her shoulder and splayed out its tripod of legs, each with a metal spike on the end to secure it in the ground. The soil beneath the wiry summer grass felt very firm and Maisie wasn't sure of the best position from which to sketch or paint, so she waited for Ida to plod up the final steep incline before choosing. Puffing and wheezing, very red in the face and slightly bent over, Ida dropped her paintbox on the ground with relief, but kept hold of the fragile thermos.

'I should . . . have brought . . . a stool,' she gasped.

'Or perhaps a shooting stick, you know, with handles that open out to make a temporary seat?'

'Good idea . . . but . . . give me a minute . . .'

Maisie turned her attention to the view. She could see the L-shape of the five cottages of Trout Leap just beyond the railway gates at the bottom of the hill. Further away, Sunny View was partly obscured by the large copper beech.

Beyond that was the bridge and then, a quarter of a mile further on, the gate of the Tubbs' dairy farm.

Maisie's eye followed the river to the west, along the straight run though the long sheep field to the dark line of the dry-stone wall. Beyond that, the land was 'lumpier' and the river disappeared between hillocks and clumps of trees. Overall, the terrain seemed to climb. Maisie wondered if that might be where the secret location of the gold mine would be found. It was isolated enough. She could see no evidence of human habitation – no buildings and no smoke rising from boilers or chimneys – though she remembered that the hamlet of Gulthane was in that direction.

'That's better,' said Ida, dabbing at her forehead with a man's handkerchief.

'It's just not being used to it,' said Maisie. 'If you came this way every day for a week, you'd think nothing of it by the end.'

'Perhaps I'll make that my goal.'

'Where would you like your easel?'

Ida contemplated the landscape, still breathing faster than normal. Her eye seemed drawn by the same area of more dramatic landscape to the west. An excellent French descriptive word came into Maisie's mind – *accidenté* – meaning 'broken up', in this case by geology and time.

'Where you have it, actually,' said Ida. 'That will be splendid. You must have a good eye. Although, perhaps, just turned a little away from the sun, with Trout Leap in the centre of the vista.'

Maisie helped Ida set the easel, leaning on each leg in turn to make sure it was firmly set in the turf. Because Maisie was concerned about the shops shutting early on a Saturday afternoon, she bid a swift 'goodbye' and set off, promising to return 'in an hour or perhaps a little more'.

As before, Maisie crossed the stile onto the well-worn footpath across the top of the hill, following it through a sparsely wooded pasture to the edge of Kirton, entering the town along the narrow lane of workers' cottages – the place where an impoverished Stella Tubb had been brought up. To her relief, the High Street was busy with shoppers, including several young mothers with prams, making her think about Petunia Sturgess and her son Timothy – illegitimate but hidden in plain sight.

I should have asked Russell for more details about the father. And what must that have been like for Petunia? Was she shunned by her neighbours and friends for falling pregnant out of wedlock, or did people take it in their stride as something not so very unusual, whatever the hangover of strict Victorian morality might suggest?

Warm from hurrying, Maisie was pleased to see an ice-cream van at the side of the road. She queued up with some children of secondary school age, a boy and a girl, both very tall and handsome with quite dark skin. They were speaking a foreign language in which Maisie recognised one or two words of Arabic origin and made the obvious deduction.

'Are you Paul and Maria Linton?' she asked. 'I thought perhaps that was Maltese you were speaking. My name is Maisie Cooper. I'm visiting with Russell and Audrey Savage.'

Paul introduced his sister and the two of them were polite enough. Maisie learned that Paul had just left school having completed his A levels and was looking for a job, while Maria was about to go into the sixth form. But they were clearly not interested in making friends with a stranger from an older generation. They bought their Feast ice-lollies and departed.

At the counter, Maisie chose a Ninety-Nine, a cornet with a swirl of vanilla ice cream.

'Do you want chocolate in that, maid?' asked the proprietor, using the traditional Devonshire term for addressing a young woman, offering to add a crumbly flake.

'Yes, please.'

Licking the soft ice cream, Maisie followed the High Street downhill towards the main run of shops, running her tongue round the outside of her cornet to prevent the ice cream from dripping down her fingers. Stopping outside the window of C & C Supplies, she remembered wanting some sunglasses. Smiling to herself, she finished her ice cream and ate the cone, taking out her handkerchief to wipe her mouth and her fingers, then went inside.

The interior of the shop was just as crowded as the window displays, with an extraordinary range of objects for sale, including clothes, tableware, cooking utensils, books, hand tools, garden tools, confectionery in big glass jars, cigarettes, cigars, loose tobacco, boxes of tissues, patent medicines, cleaning products. It made Maisie think, once more, of the celebrated quotation from *Under Milk Wood* about 'Mrs Organ Morgan's general shop' stocked with 'custard, buckets, henna, rat-traps, shrimp-nets, sugar, stamps, confetti, paraffin, hatchets, whistles'.

She approached a young woman at the counter whose eyes were down, fully focused on turning the pages of a paperback novel, paying no attention to her customer.

'Good afternoon, do you sell sunglasses?'

The young woman looked up and Maisie recognised an expression she knew she sometimes displayed herself: a vague glance, unwilling to be pulled out of the imaginary world of a book.

'What's that, my lovely?' asked the assistant.

'I was wondering if you sell sunglasses in amongst all these marvellous things.'

'There a spinner in the corner, behind the buckets and the mops.'

'Thank you.' Maisie went to examine her choices, finding them all very dusty, as if they had been there at least since the previous summer – perhaps longer. She chose a pair with oversized tortoiseshell frames and took them back to the till. 'I'd like these, but they're not priced.'

For a second time, the assistant dragged her attention back to the real world, putting her book down on the counter between a large set of scales for weighing out sweets and an old-fashioned cash register with ornate metal keys.

'I'll go and find Cherry.'

The assistant squeezed out from behind the counter – surprising Maisie with her height, at least an inch taller than she was – and sidled past a hanging rail of working clothes to a wooden staircase, climbing out of sight. Maisie looked at the paperback she had left behind, pressed flat and open, straining the spine. It was called *Liberated Spirit*, from the romance publisher Mills & Boon, by an author Maisie hadn't heard of called Priscilla Worthy. The cover was a rather lurid artwork, depicting a modern young woman in a red minidress with an enormous mane of auburn hair, being watched – or perhaps followed – by a dapper man with a square jaw, wearing a smart cream jacket and a tie that flapped in the breeze, giving an impression of movement and excitement.

The shop assistant returned, quoting a price that Maisie thought was very reasonable. She paid and put the sunglasses on top of her head, pressing them down into her sun-bleached curls. The shop assistant seemed to focus for the first time and said: 'Are you Miss Cooper?'

'I am.'

'You won't remember me because I was only young, but I knew you when you were here before. My name's Sturgess.'

'Oh,' said Maisie. 'Is it Petunia? You do look well.'

'Why are you back?'

'I'm staying with the Savages at Sunny View.'

'But didn't you go to Paris and that?'

'I did,' said Maisie, wondering what Petunia meant by 'and that'. Hopefully, glamour and broadened horizons.

'But circumstances drew me home to Sussex. Now I'm just visiting in Trout Leap.'

'If I ever got away, I'd never come back,' said Petunia.

Maisie contemplated the young woman. Her face was pretty and heart-shaped, with striking hazel eyes in a wind-burned complexion and thick mouse-brown hair. Beneath her shop coat in powder-blue cotton, Maisie could see the neckline of a tired summer dress with a threadbare pattern of roses on a white ground.

'Where would you go,' Maisie asked, politely, 'if you got the chance?'

'Anywhere,' said Petunia, almost resentfully.

'But what would I do without you?' came another voice.

Maisie turned and recognised Cherry Atwill who had come silently downstairs and was straightening the rail of workwear where Petunia had disturbed them. Maisie announced her name and Cherry indulged in the inevitable bout of reminiscence, culminating with a memory of a summer fête with events at the old people's care facility, the St Lawrence Residential Home.

'You remember, Maisie, one of the elderly gentlemen, cloistered in his room, had a flashback to the war from all the noise and called the police and the constable came over from the police station opposite – he's the sergeant, now – and got caught up in the water pistol battle that all the grandchildren were having. You were Carnival Queen. Audrey persuaded you to do it and you were driven round the town on a trailer pulled by a bull, accompanied by the majorettes with their twirling canes.'

Maisie had to acknowledge that, yes, she had been persuaded to parade about in her swimsuit in just that fashion. The memory felt very distant.

Perhaps I suppressed it, being displayed in a bathing costume on a trailer through the streets.

'You paint a very vivid picture, Cherry. How's business?'

'We struggle on, you know.'

'What do you think about the mine?'

'You've heard about that?' asked Cherry, looking uncomfortable.

'There's a meeting tomorrow evening. Isn't that right?' From the street outside, Maisie heard a church clock chiming the three-quarters. 'Good heavens. Please excuse me if I hurry along. I don't want to miss the grocer's shop.'

'You'd better run. They shut at four.'

'Thank you. I will.'

Outside, the day was still very warm. The grocery was quite crowded and she had to wait in line at the till to pay. Then, with her basket full, wearing her new sunglasses, she retraced her steps, wishing instead that she could return by a different route, down Long Lane for example. But she chose the narrow road between the tiny workers' cottages, then the path across the hill with its intermittent trees.

Her first glimpse of Ida Anderson's easel was through a gap in the trunks, entirely unattended, looking lonely and rather sad. Maisie hastened, hoping Ida hadn't left her things for Maisie to carry back down the hill alone. She climbed the top stile, passing her wicker shopping basket over then following. Ida and her paintbox were nowhere to be seen.

Maisie approached the easel. Ida had used a hard black pencil without colour. The work was remarkably detailed, almost of draughtsman quality, with a convincing sense of perspective, something like Maisie imagined the artist Canaletto might have produced for his detailed cityscapes, before committing paint to canvas.

Looking past the easel, she saw why Ida wasn't there. She was down near the railway gates at the bottom of the hill where a small group of local residents had gathered alongside a car of a kind that some people referred to – affectionately or contemptuously – as a 'jam sandwich'.

It was a white Austin Princess police car with a horizontal red band along the side.

Nineteen

The sight of the police car tied Maisie up in a complicated knot of emotions. The vehicle was similar to the Ford Zephyr that her fiancé Jack habitually drove, giving her a warm feeling of reminiscence from their shared adventures – and, if truth be told, her own wilful, solitary adventures. But it also reminded her that, for two long months, Jack was at the other end of the country, three hundred or more miles away.

Ida had taken her painting box and thermos. Maisie trudged down Break Heart Hill, thoroughly laden with the easel and canvas, as well as her wicker basket, her toes pushing forward in her brown leather sandals and grimy white socks. It was hard work. She thought about writing Jack a letter as she had done during the lead-up to Bitling Fair, when she hadn't known for certain that something very bad was about to happen, but had her suspicions, all the same. She had even drawn a map and written out a 'cast of characters', not thinking he would have time to read it or offer sage advice, but as a way of clarifying her own thoughts.

With a frown, she realised she had barely been in Trout Leap for twenty-four hours. Given it was now teatime on Saturday, any letter would have to wait for first collection on Monday morning before setting off on its travels north.

She reached the stile at the bottom of the hill, passed across her burdens and climbed over into the deep lane between overgrown hedges. While she had been descending, the little group of locals had mostly dispersed and she saw the police car disappearing over the humpbacked bridge, closely followed by the Savages' sky-blue Vauxhall Viva.

Because the easel was long and awkward – even when folded on her shoulder, Ida's canvas pinned between wooden blocks – she had trouble navigating the two kissing gates either side of the railway lines, taking care to look up the track each way to make sure there were no oncoming trains. No one noticed her until, on the far side, she found Mrs Sturgess in conversation, looming over a shorter woman whose unnaturally black hair was sculpted into tight curls, presumably the school secretary, Miss Pond.

'Ah, Miss Cooper,' said Mrs Sturgess, once introductions and some small reminiscences had been got out of the way, 'your ears must have been burning?'

Maisie felt a pang. It wasn't exactly guilt. Perhaps a 'sin of omission', as she had learned in her catechism – something she had failed to do, rather than something she had done.

'How so? Is Holly found?'

'No,' said Mrs Sturgess. 'But that shoe you plucked from the Wivel is definitely hers. Fred recognised it, didn't he, Vera?'

'He did, Geraldine,' said Miss Pond.

'He's gone off in the car with the constable. I'm listening out for the railway gates.'

'What did the police say?' asked Maisie.

'Nothing to any purpose,' said Geraldine Sturgess. 'Just that we should all have a look for her in the usual places. But Fred's already done that.'

'PC Jasper did promise to radio Exeter,' said Vera Pond, 'with a description.'

Geraldine Sturgess made a sound of frustration.

'Holly's not a lost dog. You'd think Seth Jasper would be more galvanised into action.'

'The trouble is,' said Vera Pond, 'that it isn't the first time, far from it, and Holly's always turned up before, without being any the worse for wear.'

'But the shoe?' said Maisie.

'Yes, that is a worry, Miss Cooper,' said Mrs Sturgess.

'Please, call me Maisie.'

'And you must call me Geraldine. Yes, a worry, especially if she had to come back via the roads, for example. But she does get some silly ideas. I can imagine her sitting out, eating blackberries, thinking about nothing except the nice weather and how she's free as a bird when she's out in the hills.'

Vera nodded and agreed: 'That's very true.'

Maisie could see they were both quite unworried for their neighbour, almost enjoying the drama, enlivening a dull Saturday.

'I hope she hasn't twisted an ankle or something. I must take all this gear back to Sunny View. I suppose Audrey and her paying guest went back that way?'

'I believe so. Russell went off in the car on his own.'

'Where are people looking?' she asked.

'Well, Miss Cooper,' said Vera Pond, 'I made one or two suggestions, you know, about how to divide up the terrain between the two vehicles, between Mr Savage and Constable Jasper, such that they made best use of their resources. But I fear they didn't pay me much attention. Gentlemen have their own ideas, I find. Don't you?'

Maisie smiled and told her: 'That's probably true, but I've been known to stubbornly follow my own path, too, despite well-meant and well-informed advice.'

'But you have the advantage of your lovely smile and your . . .' Vera's voice faded as she contemplated Maisie, rather as a lepidopterist might examine a striking butterfly, pinned to a corkboard. 'Well, you know what gentlemen are like.'

'What do you intend to do, both of you?' Maisie asked, changing the subject.

'I can't go searching,' said Vera, adding obscurely: 'I have a toe.'

'Still?' exclaimed Geraldine. 'You're a martyr to that bunion.'

'I am,' agreed Vera, sadly.

'And you, Mrs Sturgess?' Maisie asked.

'Geraldine, please. I'm trapped, too, because I've my Petunia and my Timothy back soon for their tea – and the gates.'

'Of course,' said Maisie. 'But I would very much like to help. I realise the cars will cover much more ground, but you mentioned a pathway from the railway line, one that avoids the barbed-wire fence on the river. Has anyone gone that way?'

'No, I don't believe so,' said Geraldine. 'Did you hear it mentioned, Vera?'

'I did not, but – as I said – my opinion was not sought and, though I gave it, is unlikely to have been valued. Miss Cooper, I could—'

'Please,' Maisie interrupted, a little exasperated by the school secretary's self-pity and laborious formality. 'May I call you Vera?'

'Oh, er, on such brief acquaintance, it doesn't seem . . .'

Vera Pond put a hand to her firmly set bottle-black hair.

'I would much prefer you to use my first name,' Maisie insisted. 'Also, I wonder if either of you might have an Ordnance Survey map, one with a good large scale. That would be helpful, wouldn't it, in making sure all the possible locations are covered?'

'Exactly, Miss Cooper,' exclaimed Vera, excitedly. 'I mean Maisie. Yes, indeed, and I have just such a map that I offered to Constable Jasper to come in and peruse. But he was having none of it. Oh no, he knew what he was about and needed no advice from such as I.'

'Might I see it, Vera?' asked Maisie.

'Yes, yes. Please come in.'

'I'll just unburden myself of all this,' Maisie said, indicating the easel and canvas and the wicker basket of shopping. 'I'll be back in a jiffy.'

'Of course.'

Maisie walked quickly back to Sunny View, going round to the back door via the gravel drive under the copper beech, ducking her head so as not to get tangled once more in the lower twigs. She put everything down on the kitchen table, hearing voices close by but not wanting to get caught up.

She went back out, almost jogging up the lane to Vera Pond's cottage, between the Luscombes on the railway line and the Sturgess family on the corner of the L. The front door was open so she ducked her head and slipped inside, to a gloomy hallway with a threadbare carpet running up the middle of a hallway paved with worn red tiles. Vera Pond emerged from the back of the cottage with two cups of tea in fine white china with delicate saucers.

'In here,' she said, leading Maisie into her front room. Some enormous sheets of paper were laid out across the floor. 'You'll have to forgive the mess. I've been working on next year's timetable. Would you put on the lights? It's a dark room till the sun gets low in the west, then it's too bright.'

Maisie found the switch by the door and flicked it, bringing power to two ugly brass sconces, each with twin lamps, both trailing a braided electrical cable. The light was very yellow from the cloth shades that obscured the two pairs of bulbs.

'What a lovely room,' said Maisie.

'Thank you. The map is in the frame, just there,' said Vera. She put down the cups and saucers on a low side table and approached the far wall. Between the two sconces was the Ordnance Survey map that Maisie had been hoping for, but framed under glass. 'You'll need to come closer to avoid the glare.'

Maisie did so, taking a moment to orientate herself in relation to the compass points in the top right corner and the various symbols denoting public houses, churches, railway stations, dwellings and schools. Her practised eye took in the scale – one-to-two-thousand-five-hundred – and the contour lines indicating the height of the terrain. Trout Leap was to one side, meaning that the fields to the west – the ones Maisie was most interested in – were depicted in fine detail. It was even possible to see the path that led from a pedestrian crossing half a mile away on the railway line, through the fields. There was a mention of the direction to Gulthane and Colthorp, beyond the edge of the frame.

'If I follow the railway line to this point,' said Maisie, indicating where she meant, 'and go across country to the river valley, can I easily get back?'

'Very easily. There's a good bridge over the Wivel, then you'll find you're on a farm track that will take you back via the Tubbs' farm.'

Maisie studied the terrain, committing it to memory.

'I'll do just that.'

She felt obliged to stay and drink the cup of tea from the delicate china. Vera perched on a low leather pouffe and Maisie sank into a defeated fabric armchair that smelt of dust and damp. The tea was weak because Vera hadn't left it long enough to brew and, after her hike across the hills, Maisie would have preferred something cold.

She asked Vera about the racing prints on the walls. The school secretary became evasive, mumbling something about her father's 'regrettable penchant for gambling' and appreciation of 'a nip of Scotch'. Maisie switched to the issue of the school timetable, around whose papers they had skirted because it occupied most of the floor. Vera became voluble.

'I like to get ahead. Of course, the headmaster doesn't need me to provide complete detail until two weeks before the resumption. No one fully appreciates the complexity of the challenge. He, in any case, is on holiday in Frinton. Do you know where I mean?'

Maisie kept the conversation going until she had drained her cup and then politely left, confirming that the best way to get to the next pedestrian crossing across the railway lines was to walk beside the tracks.

'And I won't get into trouble for doing so?'

'Who is there to notice?'

'Good point.'

She went outside and slipped through the kissing gate, onto the gravel at the side of the rails. Looking east, she could see almost all the way to Kirton railway station and no trains were in view. Turning left, towards Barnstaple – about thirty miles distant – the two sets of tracks curved away out of sight after about a mile.

She set off. The stony verge was awkward to walk on because the large lumps of gravel slid and shifted beneath her sandals. Furthermore, the railway was lined with stinging nettles almost as tall as she was. At one point, she lost her balance and brushed the back of her hand across the poisonous hairs of a nearby plant, snatching it away in frustration, looking around for some dock leaves with which to alleviate the irritation. She found none.

With her hand throbbing, Maisie tried to pick her way more carefully. She cast her mind back to the map, framed and under glass on the wall of Vera Pond's front room, wondering if she had misjudged the distance.

I should have reached the pedestrian gate by now, shouldn't I?

The peace of the afternoon, made up of rustling nettles and occasional improvisations from invisible songbirds, was broken as the rails began to sing, very low at first, almost inaudible. As the sound grew in intensity, Maisie began to feel the vibrations, too. She looked left and right, unable to see from which direction the train was coming.

Because the nettles had been allowed to grow unchecked at the side of the tracks, there was nowhere for her to go. She felt a growing panic. If two trains happened to come at once, she would be completely trapped and have to burrow into the stinging weeds in order to avoid being crushed under the heavy steel wheels.

Am I in trouble?

Then, she realised, that was indeed the case. From both directions, visible about half a mile off in each direction, the passenger services were approaching, coming towards her with gathering speed and, it seemed, murderous intent.

Maisie tried once more to visualise the map.

Which way should I go? Whatever I choose, I'll be running towards the danger.

She made up her mind and began sprinting away from Trout Leap, towards the oncoming service from Barnstaple, hoping to reach the pedestrian gate before she met the train. The large stones slithered beneath her tread, making it difficult to maintain her speed, and every stride brought her closer and closer to disaster.

She began to be surrounded by noise, oppressive and intimidating. Glancing over her shoulder, she realised that it was the train from Kirton that was most dangerous, barrelling up behind her on the left-hand tracks, where she was awkwardly running and stumbling. And it was only moments away.

Trying to accelerate, she almost lost her balance. Still, she could see no gap in the forest of nettles. She thought wildly about running across the two sets of tracks to the far side where there seemed a little more room to cower in safety, but she worried about touching a live rail and receiving a deadly bolt of electricity through the soles of her sandals.

Her desperation mounted. The westbound service was almost on top of her when she saw it, the gap in the nettles where someone had attacked them with a scythe – probably Fred Luscombe – laying them low in a carpet of long stalks and shrivelling leaves in order to keep the gateway clear. With a surge of renewed energy, she covered the last twenty paces in just a few seconds and pressed herself against the warm timbers of the gate.

As the train thundered past, she caught a glimpse of the driver's eyes, wide and disapproving, and his incredulous shake of the head.

TWENTY

Maisie stayed where she was, her back to the gate, her arms slack, her palms pressed against the warm timbers, waiting for her heart rate to return to normal. Time passed and peace eventually returned to the valley of the Wivel.

The sun was warm, birds were singing and the tips of the stinging nettles were swayed by a gentle breeze. There was still a faint vibration in the air from the steel rails and a fading murmur of the receding trains.

That was danger of a kind I did not expect.

She turned and pushed through the gate, finding a fingerpost for a bridleway that led diagonally away through the fields, with a dry-stone wall to her left. She followed it, enjoying the firm path after the difficulty of running on the lumpy gravel.

The day was no longer quite so hot, but she was walking more or less directly into the sun, squinting her eyes so as not to be dazzled. With an idea of maintaining a sense of how far she had gone, she started counting her steps, then became distracted by a family of rabbits with five tiny kits, eating cowslips in some tussocky grass.

She strode on, wishing that she had asked Vera Pond for a glass of water as well as the cup of weak tea. Her left hand was throbbing from the aggressive poison delivered by the hairs on the leaves of the stinging nettle.

After ten minutes or so, the dry-stone wall made a sort of correction, shifting due south to avoid a lonely centennial oak in the middle of the pasture. She followed the wall, now able to see the Wivel in the distance. She could even make out the place where Norman Tubb had erected his barbed wire fence to stop people encroaching on his fishing grounds.

When she came to the riverbank and the aggressive barrier with its illegible sign, Maisie turned right, walking into the sun once more, away from Trout Leap. The field was deserted as she strolled on alone across the dry summer grass.

Because she was following the riverbank, the land was level and it was easy going. She found her mind wandering, imagining doing as Audrey and Russell had suggested, bringing Jack to Trout Leap for a holiday or, even, their honeymoon. She pictured herself walking with him along the lovely stream, the clear water burbling over flat stones and, now and then, deepening and darkening into sombre pools, beneath full-leaved branches.

We could borrow Audrey's wicker basket and bring a picnic and stay out all day, away from everyone and everything, alone and content.

The picture in Maisie's mind was so engrossing that she didn't see – until she was almost upon it – another well-constructed bridge, like the one near the barbed-wire barrier, with heavy timbers covered with chicken wire to prevent them becoming slippery in winter with mould and slime, supported by railway sleepers driven vertically into the bed of the river. The bridge linked two well-used farm tracks with ruts worn deep into the red soil. On the far bank, a herd of Jersey cows was spread out across the sward as if by an artist, concerned that they should each occupy their own patch of ground without any of them obscuring the view of another.

Maisie approached the bridge. One of the Jerseys – it was a lovely warm, rust-brown colour – wandered down to the riverbank. It bent its head to crop the grass, wrenching a thick tuft from a clump at the top of an overhang where two stunted oaks found their roots exposed by the erosion beneath.

167

In the shadows cast by these unhappy trees, Maisie could see a bundle of old clothes. At least, that was her first impression.

After a few confused seconds, however, she knew it must be something else.

I know it without knowing how I know.

★

Damp from the overnight drizzle, the blue-and-white stripes of Holly's fussy dress looked darker in the shade, her white legs protruding from the creased and crumpled hem, white, flaccid and lifeless, one foot still encased in a black buckle shoe, the other naked and limp.

This is awful. Holly was unhappy, difficult, flighty, hard to manage – but she didn't deserve this.

Maisie crossed the bridge, her sandals catching in a sticky-up bit of the chicken-wire mesh, causing her to briefly stumble. She approached the two stunted oak trees, growing out of deep clefts in an outcrop of hard limestone. She peered in beneath their moss-covered branches.

Poor woman.

Holly's face was awful, her mouth wide open, her eyes staring upon nothing. She had, of course, a dreadful blue-white pallor and her lips were bleached of warmth and life. The front fringe of her wet, blonde hair clung to her pale forehead, but it was also possible to see a patch of black blood coagulated on the side of her skull. It was not the first time Maisie had seen such an injury. From Jack's example and from sheer common sense, she knew it was always best not to jump to conclusions.

It's possible that Holly fell from the bridge, catching her toe in the chicken wire, perhaps, as I did, then losing her balance? Her position makes it almost likely.

Hearing the noise of an approaching tractor, Maisie straightened up. It was a miniature farm vehicle, dragging a trailer behind, piled high with hay. The driver was equally small, perched above the wide steering wheel, an expression of surprise on her face as she rattled and bounced down the rutted track towards where Maisie stood, creating an odd pause before Stella was close enough for Maisie to speak. When she did, her voice was obscured by the noise of the diesel engine. She waited for Stella to turn it off and call: 'Wasson?'

'It's Holly. I've found her.'

'What do you mean?'

'Just that. She's there, underneath the oak trees. Can you get help?'

'Is she hurt?'

Maisie felt frustrated that Stella didn't seem to understand what was, to her, completely plain.

'Holly is dead. She's been dead for some time, I think. And she has a wound on the back or the side of her head.'

'Oh, merciful heavens,' said Stella, putting her hands to her mouth.

'I know. It's awful, isn't it?'

'Something terrible, it is.'

'She may have tripped. The chicken wire is torn and treacherous. I can stay here to make sure that nothing is disturbed, but you need to drive back to the dairy and place a telephone call to the police station in Kirton, to summon the constable. I think his name is Jasper? He's out looking for her but someone will be able to get in touch by radio, I suppose.'

'That's right,' said Stella, looking appalled and frightened. Then, using a characteristic colloquial Devonshire enquiry, she asked: 'Where's she to?'

'Under those trees.'

'Oh, God,' said Stella, stealing a very brief glance. 'All right. But I'll be quicker if I leave the trailer behind. Are you able to help me detach it?' Maisie did so easily because the coupling was like one used on artillery pieces in the army. 'And will you spread the hay,' Stella asked, 'as evening feed for the ladies? The dry weather means there's nothing much growing.' She looked up at the sky. 'It'll soon be getting dimpsy.'

Maisie recognised 'dimpsy' as the Devonshire word for 'dusk'.

'Don't worry. We have plenty of light. I'll manage,' she said. 'You hurry away.'

Stella swung the little tractor round, off the track, then bounced it back into the ruts to drive uphill and was soon out of sight, over the first brow. Once she was gone, Maisie set to, lifting armfuls of hay out of the abandoned trailer and spreading them across the ground. There was evidence that the same thing had been done before on previous evenings close to a muddy beach beside the river with multiple imprints of cattle hooves, showing that this was somewhere the 'ladies' came down to drink. Seeing her at this work, the cattle lifted their heavy heads and focused their dark brown eyes on the delicious armfuls of dried grass, sluggishly congregating. By the time the trailer was empty, Maisie was almost surrounded.

She slipped away and returned to the stunted oak trees, growing out of the clefts in the limestone, peering in under the gnarled and twisted branches. From this new vantage point Maisie was able to see the wound to Holly's head more clearly. It was a gash about six inches long that gaped open, revealing the white bone beneath. She tried to see if there was evidence of where Holly's skull might have impacted the grey rock, if there was a sharp corner that might have 'done her a damage', as Russell would say.

It would require a magnifying glass or photographic enlarge-ments to make a proper examination. But, of course, it's been raining so the evidence might no longer be intact.

Maisie knew that she shouldn't get too close, that it was important not to disturb the scene. She had considerable experience of seeing Jack and his good friend Fred Nairn, accompanied by their forensics officers, Tindall and Wilson, taking great pains when approaching a body. By eye, however, she inspected the branches, hoping to discover a wisp of cloth or wool or perhaps some human hairs caught on the twigs. She found nothing.

At the base of the trees, she discovered some dock plants with juicy green leaves. She crushed some in her fist to release their sap and then pressed against the irritated rash on the back of her left hand, bringing immediate relief from the throbbing of the poison from the stinging nettles.

What if she didn't trip on the treacherous chicken wire?

Maisie contemplated the alternative theory of a murderous attack. She looked around for a possible weapon, her mind imagining a loose lump of limestone. She looked in the water within ten or twelve paces for a suitable fist-sized boulder, but found nothing of appropriate shape or mass. She pictured a heavy branch of fallen oak, telling herself that any assailant would have had the perfect means, close at hand, of disposing of a wooden weapon.

They could have simply thrown the branch into the river, watching it float harmlessly away downstream, far from the scene of the crime.

She glanced up the slope, listening for the return of Stella's tractor or the arrival of the Austin Princess police car. The valley seemed unnaturally quiet.

If Holly was murdered and it wasn't simply an accident, who's to say that this is where she was killed? It might have happened elsewhere, and her body brought to this place.

Maisie decided that, anywhere more than a hundred yards from this crossing point on the river, Holly's corpse might have lain undiscovered for a considerable length of time, especially in a shallow fold in the ground or where nettles or thistles or cow parsley provided cover. She, herself, hadn't intended to stray far from the track.

Most walkers wouldn't.

Thinking about Vincent Brent's fishing tackle, she changed her mind.

But if someone got a permit from Norman Tubb to fish the upper reaches of the Wivel – which Russell says are much richer in trout than the stretch down to Kirton – they'd walk the banks and, inevitably, come across Holly's corpse.

A new idea crystallised in her mind.

Or, if she was killed elsewhere – if it wasn't an accident – was her body left here on purpose, in order for it to be discovered?

There was still no sign of Stella on her way back. Maisie gave the Jersey cows a wide berth and walked three hundred yards upstream to a place where the river began to cut through between two steeper hills into a more densely wooded valley, the terrain more '*accidenté*'. She wanted to walk on but stopped, feeling the need to be close at hand when Stella returned, hopefully with the constable.

The valley ahead looked very lonely, as if no one ever went there. The land had not been cleared of trees to make it ready for agricultural use, perhaps meaning that the soil was thin over bedrock and, therefore, unproductive. She didn't know how far she would have to go before reaching Gulthane, the next hamlet. Assuming that her sense of direction and her memory of the map were both accurate, she had passed beyond the outer edge of the frame on Vera Pond's wall, between the two brass sconces.

Hearing the deep note of a diesel engine throbbing down the track, Maisie jogged back to the bridge. She arrived at the same time as Stella on her miniature tractor. They met by the oaks. Stella cut the engine and climbed down.

'I got through to the station,' she said, a little breathlessly. 'There was Mr Salmon, the special constable, on duty who promised to radio Seth Jasper in his patrol car. He won't be far away because he was out looking for her. Can you show me properly?'

'Are you sure you want to look?'

'I think I do. Happen it's worse not to know,' said Stella, her accent very pronounced. 'I've been imagining all sorts.'

Maisie was aware that the police were always interested to see how a witness or a suspect reacted to viewing a body or some other significant piece of evidence. She watched closely as Stella got down on her hands and knees in order to look beneath the lowest branches.

'Don't go too close,' said Maisie. 'You mustn't disturb anything.'

'Is this exactly how you found her?' asked Stella.

'Of course.'

'The sole of the foot without a shoe is completely clean, meaning she didn't walk around without it.'

'That's right. You're very observant. Or might the dirt have been washed off by the rain?'

'I doubt it. She didn't come down heavy.'

For a second, Maisie was confused by the use of the word 'she' to refer to the rain.

'No, I saw it out of my bedroom window, just drizzle.'

Stella reversed out from under the low branches. Maisie was surprised to discover a shifty expression on her face, as if Stella had been caught out in some misdeed. She made an immediate supposition.

'Did you perhaps see Holly out and about, late last night?'

'I have done before, coming up our lane, gadding about at all hours. How did you guess?'

'You looked like you were remembering something you regretted.'

'This night just gone,' explained Stella, sadly, 'I had a "lady" taken poorly with mastitis. The vet gave her the necessary, but the best you can do is bring it out through the udders with massage, or you'll end up with bad milk and perhaps even lose the beast.'

'What time was this?'

'I don't know for sure when the worry woke me. Dark, though.'

Maisie marvelled at Stella's dedication.

'So, you were in the barn? You didn't see Holly?'

'No, I didn't,' said Stella. 'After a bit of massage, my "lady" was doing much better so I walked her out to the top of the hill, up there.' She pointed. 'The brow, see? And I left her to wander down to join the others on her own. Then, I went home for a nap before breakfast.'

'Oh, I understand what you mean,' said Maisie. 'If you'd brought the cow all the way down to the water's edge—'

Stella interrupted: 'That's right. If I'd come all the way down, I'd have seen Holly and . . .'

Stella's voice trailed off. An unhappy silence folded itself around them. Maisie followed Stella's gaze to the small herd of what Russell would no doubt refer to as 'gurt hulking beasts'.

'You mustn't blame yourself for not finding her before me,' said Maisie. 'What's done is done.'

Stella indicated one of the Jerseys that was contentedly munching on an enormous bunch of hay, its big brown eyes focused on nothing.

'It were that one over there.'

They both watched the animal, Stella with a proprietorial, almost maternal air. Over in the west, the sun hid itself behind a cloud and, all at once, the river valley felt sombre and damp.

'Do you believe in the gold mine?' Maisie asked. 'You don't seem like the sort of person to be easily taken in by daydreams.'

'Everyone wants a better life, don't they? No one's completely satisfied with what they've got.'

Although Stella had spoken in a neutral tone, her words made Maisie suspicious, given what she knew of Norman Tubb's background and character.

How long could an optimistic and generous personality, such as Stella's, survive living alongside such a man?

'Do you have many friends round about?' Maisie asked.

'How do you mean?'

'People to talk to and share your troubles with – and your successes, your hopes and dreams.'

Maisie wasn't sure what it was that she was getting at and felt embarrassed that her conversational gambit was such a cliché. The response it elicited, however, was surprising.

'If there's one thing looking after animals teaches you, it's that every community needs a mix of new blood now and then. You can't just carry on with the same herd, never changing, till you pop your clogs. New people come in and they show you what you've been missing, perhaps.'

There was a look in Stella's eye that suggested she was on the verge of a kind of confession, something she had 'kept close' for too long and needed the comfort of saying out loud. Maisie thought about another police technique, encouraging a witness to make a confession by telling them: 'Get it off your chest. You know you want to.'

Will she regret telling me, though?

'Do you mean one person in particular?' asked Maisie.

Stella looked on the verge of speech, but the silence was broken and the moment passed. The white Austin Princess with police markings was coming carefully down the field, presumably driven by Constable Jasper. To protect its undercarriage, he had his offside tyres on the ridge in the middle, between the ruts, and his nearside wheels trundling along the grass beside.

'Before he gets here, is there anything you want to tell me?' asked Maisie.

'No,' said Stella, her eyes averted. 'I don't think there is.'

TWENTY-ONE

Maisie and Stella watched Constable Jasper, driving his 'jam sandwich' police car, carefully taking his time. Maisie thought back to the gala day ten years before, the commotion with the old man and his flashbacks to the war and being paraded round the town in her swimsuit on the back of a farm trailer, but remembered that was a different officer, the one who had since been promoted to sergeant.

'I'll be interested to hear what you think of Seth,' said Stella, with an air of needing to change the subject from Maisie's more personal enquiries. 'You'll not have met him previous?'

'What's your impression, Stella?'

'Jasper by name, jasper by nature.'

Maisie's heart sank. In the police force, she knew, were all kinds of people, some sympathetic, others less so. Constable Barry Goodbody of the Chichester police was a case in point, someone whose irrational antagonism towards Maisie had made two investigations more difficult than they had needed to be, until Jack's persistence and supportive management had made the young man turn a corner and understand better his responsibilities to his profession and to the public. Maisie knew, though, that many police officers joined the force because they liked the idea of being representatives of authority and power, rather than from a duty of service.

Constable Jasper parked on the dry grass alongside the miniature tractor and the empty trailer and got out, straightening his uniform and putting his regulation cap on his head, an expression of self-satisfied complacency on his face. Once he was content with his appearance, he spoke.

'What have we got here, then?'

Maisie introduced herself and told her story – how she had been concerned about Holly's whereabouts and had consulted Vera Pond's map and taken it into her head to walk up the river because of the potential clue of the shoe that she had picked up out of the water, which must have floated downstream with the current.

'And you say that was soon after ten o'clock this morning?' said Constable Jasper.

'I do,' said Maisie.

'Well, Miss Cooper, you dilly-dallied a good while before acting upon that information. I hope you don't come to regret your delay. It'll be a fine lookout if the doctor discovers she'd had an accident and could have been saved with a prompter response.'

'Once you've examined the body,' said Maisie in an even tone, 'you will see that she has been dead for quite a number of hours, making the delay irrelevant.'

'Are we a specialist, then?' asked Constable Jasper.

'No, but I do have some experience of police investigations, including several murders.'

Constable Jasper sort of twitched, clearly unused to being challenged. 'Who says it's murder?'

'No one,' said Maisie. 'I was merely sharing some of my own experiences. Holly may well have fallen from the bridge. The planks are uneven and the chicken wire torn and sticking up, so it's almost a death trap . . .' Maisie stopped, the expression sounding to her own ears in awfully bad taste. She went on: 'Anyway, Constable, I imagine not a lot of people die in unexplained circumstances in this lovely neck of the woods. How many unexplained deaths have you dealt with?'

Looking very uneasy, Constable Jasper said nothing in reply. His eyes down, he approached the stunted oaks, beneath which Holly's body remained clearly visible in the slant light of early evening. Finding his own shadow obscuring his view, he went round to the far side of the trees and crouched down as Maisie had done, keeping a careful distance. He took out his notebook, extracting the pencil from a loop on the side, and wrote something down. Maisie suspected it was simply for show, to give an impression of purpose.

'You may be right about the fall on this here lump of rock,' he grudgingly admitted. 'It looks awful sharp.'

'Neither Stella nor I have touched the body,' Maisie told him. 'I made a brief examination of the surroundings but could see no evidence of footprints or wisps of cloth or anything like that caught in the branches.'

He raised his eyes for a perfunctory glance: 'And me neither.'

'I've barely moved from this spot. It was quite by chance that Mrs Tubb came down in her tractor at just the right moment.'

Stella told them: 'It was time for my ladies' hay. Then, I would have brought them in.'

Hearing those words, Maisie realised that it was worth questioning if that were true.

Was it 'quite by chance' that Stella had turned up? If there's one thing I've learned, it's not to take coincidences at face value.

'I'll have to go and tell Fred Luscombe,' said Constable Jasper, sounding like he was talking to himself. 'It's my duty.' He stood up. 'And the poor lass will have to go into Exeter for the morgue and the post-mortem examination. Let's get her up into the trailer, there.'

'Will you not take photographs or conduct any other forensic investigations?' asked Maisie.

'Who do you think's going to do any of that?'

'We might have missed something.'

'You reckon I don't know?' complained Constable Jasper in a desperate tone. 'My sergeant's laid up in hospital with his strangulated hernia and I'm on my own in Kirton, except for my volunteer special constable on duty at the station to answer the telephone.' He gestured to the corpse. 'And she can't just be left here, can she?'

Maisie remembered the sophisticated camera hanging around Vincent's neck.

'I can wait here a little longer,' she told him. 'If you go via Sunny View, on your way to give the bad news to Fred Luscombe, you will find that Mr and Mrs Savage have a paying guest by the name of Brent who could perhaps take photographs before the body is moved. Don't you think that would be a good idea?'

'Who is this Brent?' he asked.

'Vincent Brent. He seems sensible.'

'And you'll bide along with the body?' asked Seth Jasper.

'Maisie, here,' said Stella, unexpectedly, 'is like a detective and Russell Savage can show you the stories in the newspapers sent down from that there Sussex to prove it.'

'But you'll need to hurry, Constable,' said Maisie, always uncomfortable with her adventures being talked about in her presence. 'The light's fading and I don't know if Mr Brent has any flash equipment.'

There was an expression of mingled resentment and doubt on Constable Jasper's face, but he seemed to have no alternative to Maisie's plan. She wondered why he would kick against her idea.

Is it possible he has something of his own to hide? Does he want the scene cleared as soon as possible for guilty reasons of his own?

She wondered if there was something she could say to him that would allow her to probe his circumstances and his relationships with the residents of Trout Leap more deeply, but he was already walking away, telling her, over his shoulder: 'All right, then. Have it your own way.'

He got back into the Austin Princess, swung round and drove back up the field, choosing the dry grass rather than risk the rutted track.

'I'll have to go, too,' said Stella. 'For evening milking. I've got to bring the ladies in, but I'll leave the trailer behind for . . . Well, you know why.'

'Yes, Constable Jasper was right about that. We might need it later if there's no ambulance available before it's dark.'

'Are you sure you'll be all right, being left and all?'

'Of course,' said Maisie. Stella gave her a smile of sympathy, which encouraged Maisie to repeat her question from earlier on, just before the police constable had arrived. 'You said: "A place needs new blood." Who did you mean?'

'It makes no difference,' said Stella, with a sad smile, 'if neither one's free.' Her expression closed up, as if she knew she had said too much. 'Never mind.' She turned and approached the cattle. 'Come on now, ladies, up,' she called in a high, sing-song voice.

One or two of the cows began moving towards their mistress. Stella jumped up onto the high metal seat of her tiny tractor – it was little more than a precarious perforated tray – turned the engine over and trundled up the slope, probably in second gear, at a pace that the Jerseys, with their heavy udders full of milk, could keep pace with, drawn on by routine and, perhaps, the promise of richer feed while the suction mechanisms of the dairy machines did their work.

Maisie watched them go, glad when the diesel tractor finally disappeared over the brow of the hill, leaving the river valley quiet, apart from the song of the water and the birds proclaiming their territories with evening tunes. Two blackbirds were particularly noisy, improvising their multiple variations on a simple melody that hopped from note to note, like the birds themselves, foraging through the grass for beetles and worms.

Maisie turned back to the corpse of poor Holly Luscombe, feeling sympathy, of course, but aware that her experience of other deaths – including one person very close to her – meant she was inured to the deeper emotions of fear or revulsion that others might feel, had they been left alone with a dead body in the deepening 'dimpsy' dusk.

Though untroubled, Maisie still felt inclined to keep her distance, if only out of respect. She left the corpse and went to sit on an overhanging portion of eroded riverbank, with her legs dangling above the water, and imagined, in her mind's eye, the black buckle shoe being dragged away by the stream, unnoticed by whoever had brought Holly's lifeless form to this place.

Maisie frowned, uncertain why it was that she felt so sure that Holly had been carried to this place after death.

Why do I keep thinking that she did not die here?

Under the trees, the low sun was creating alternating bands of light and shade, revealing with more precision something she had observed earlier on, but not paid any attention to.

Of course – the creased and crumpled hem above the sad white legs.

Unbidden, a macabre and dramatic image came into her mind, comprised of two strong fists grasping the damp, blue-and-white-striped fabric, dragging Holly Luscombe under cover of the oaks, leaving the cotton scrunched up, ready to tell its story.

And there can only be one reason why someone should do such a thing.

The murderer had moved the corpse and placed it some-where it would easily be found, perhaps by an angler or by one of the Tubbs, delivering hay to the cattle grazing the parched and unfruitful summer pasture.

Why?

The answer was obvious, surely, even to a mind as closed and self-satisfied as Constable Jasper's.

Because the place where she was killed was a clue in itself and had to be concealed.

Maisie remembered the conversation, under the hedge where the terrier Bertie had died, when Holly had told her: *'I see all sorts when I'm out late.'*

Maisie had asked: *'Do you want to tell me what?'*

Frustratingly, now, Holly had refused.

What did Holly see? Something that led to her death – perhaps her murder?

Maisie's hand was beginning to throb once more so she found another dock leaf.

There's no way now for me to find out.

Alone in the dusk, she thought about how the countryside needed balance, epitomised by the equilibrium between the nettles and the dock plants.

Is it foolish, though, to be embroidering a drama out of a crumpled hem when the theory of an accident might be much more likely?

She contemplated what she had noticed since being at Sunny View – above all, the tension amongst all the neighbours. The idea of the gold mine had caused a shift. It seemed to have the potential to magnify even the smallest of resentments, or resurrect old griefs that had long been forgotten.

Isn't the key to an untroubled life one without change? It's when things are shaken up that bad intentions are revealed.

Maisie sighed. Her own life had undergone enormous change: her brother's death; the dramas of several murder investigations; the stop-start resumption of her teenage relationship with Jack; his proposal of marriage and her delighted acceptance; the demands of his career suddenly taking him away from her, just when they were finally 'declared', as his Grandma Florence had it.

Maisie took a deep breath, the fragrance of the falling dew rich in the air. She recognised that she was still on edge from the almost-argument with Seth Jasper. By coincidence, a wasp – the other kind of jasper – buzzed past, looking for evening flowers. She thought about what she had said to Russell, riding in the asthmatic 'Victoria and Albert' from the railway station.

I sometimes wonder what's the point of wasps.

Stella had compared Constable Jasper to a wasp, a 'jasper' in Devon slang, meaning someone apt to sting. And Maisie had promptly put him in his place. With a vague shadow of guilt, she realised that she had deliberately got up on her high horse and used her poshest voice to assert herself.

He deserved it. He had no call to criticise the speed of my actions.

Of course, that wasn't entirely true. She felt self-critical, too. Constable Jasper's comment stung, like the nettles to the back of her hand, precisely because Maisie feared that he was right, that she ought to have acted sooner. Not to save Holly's life – she was sure that she would have been too late for that – but to begin investigating what had happened to her.

Maisie sighed again, becalmed in the lonely field beside the river, wishing she had someone with whom to discuss the accelerating events, Jack or perhaps 'Auntie' Phyl Pascal, whose no-nonsense countrywoman's wisdom was a valuable counterpoint to her own deep – and sometimes misplaced – empathy.

On the far bank of the trout stream, beside the heavy planking of the bridge, all her competing ideas came together, watching what was probably the same wasp buzzing from flower to flower on a stand of nettles.

Perhaps the point of them both is that they're symbiotic? The nettles blossom, providing pollen and nectar for countless insects, including wasps, helping them to flourish and propagate themselves.

Maisie was aware that some people considered nettles highly nutritious and processed them into soup for human consumption. Idly, she wondered if their fibrous stalks might be useful, woven into mats or ropes, then realised she didn't know how cooking removed the toxins in the fine hairs on their leaves. By a vague train of thought, her ideas drifting in the dusk, she thought about the role that poisons had played – or not played – in her previous murder investigations.

Poisons are insidious. In murder mysteries, they say that poison is a woman's weapon, because it doesn't require physical strength to administer. But, out here in the country, women aren't shrinking violets. Some do manual work, like Stella, managing large, heavy animals, or Geraldine, confidently operating the railway gates and signals.

Thinking of Mrs Sturgess brought Petunia back into her mind, Timothy Sturgess's secret mother, though the family behaved as though Petunia was his older sister.

If Timothy attends Queen Elizabeth Grammar School, he must be eleven, going on twelve, meaning . . .

It was an uncomfortable train of thought. The question of the age of consent was one that Maisie had read about in her favourite French newspaper, *Le Monde,* one Sunday morning at the Café des Phares in Paris. The long article had discussed the laws in different countries because consistent regulation across the European Economic Community was a live issue. She remembered that the rules in the UK weren't exceptional, beginning with an act of parliament in 1275 setting the age of consent at just twelve years old. Six hundred years later, in the Victorian era, it had twice been raised, first incrementally to thirteen then, ten years later, to sixteen, where it had stayed.

If the relationship that led to Petunia giving birth to Timothy was legal, she would have to be twenty-seven or even twenty-eight years old today.

Maisie frowned.

Can that be right? Doesn't she look younger?

There was also the question of who the father was. Maisie knew from the same newspaper article that, in underage pregnancies, the most likely person wouldn't have been a stranger, but someone known to Petunia, such as a boy at school or a neighbour – even a family member. She had a horrible thought that it might have been Petunia's own father, the man who had run out on the family soon after Timothy's birth.

Surely not.

Russell had spoken of the absent Mr Sturgess with frustrated sympathy, almost affection, as 'a pleasant mild man otherwise'.

Maisie's ruminations were disturbed by the noise of a vehicle. She turned to see the 'jam sandwich' Austin Princess police car coming over the brow of the hill.

This death isn't the end of the story. Upsets – like the nettles and the wasps and the thorns – are everywhere and I wouldn't be surprised if there wasn't something more for me to deal with before the end of my time at Sunny View.

TWENTY-TWO

When Vincent Brent got out of Constable Seth Jasper's police car, Maisie's first impression was of competence and purpose, which seemed at odds with the idea that he was just a passer-by, a guest at Sunny View. The task, after all, was unexpected: photographing a blue-and-white corpse with a visible wound clotted by dark coagulated blood clinging to wet hair.

How is it that he's taking all this in his stride?

'Will you be able to get anything worthwhile?' Maisie asked.

'I had a roll of fast film in my bag,' said Vincent. 'It should do, even though we're losing the currant bun.' Maisie frowned and he explained: 'I mean we're losing the sun. The images will come out quite grainy.'

Maisie was also impressed by Constable Jasper's focus and organisation. To her surprise, he directed Vincent in such a way that every possible angle was captured on the film inside the sophisticated camera. Two or three times, he took up a position where he would create shade in order that the glare of the low sun shouldn't flare on the lens and spoil the pic-torial evidence.

Before they had finished, an ambulance appeared over the brow of the hill – an old-fashioned converted Bedford van with bulbous fenders, chrome bumpers and headlamps. It was almost identical to the one Maisie had seen in the midst of the investigation into the murder at Church Lodge. It gave her a disagreeable flashback to those terrible moments when she had been too late to save another young woman from the worst of all crimes.

Constable Jasper went and spoke to the ambulance driver while a second uniformed orderly got down and went round behind to open the back doors and, so he said, in rhyming shorthand: 'Fetch the stretch.' Maisie heard the police officer and the driver discussing the traffic in Newton-St-Cyres on the road between Exeter and Kirton, then the performance of the local football team, Exeter City, that they referred to by a nickname, 'the Grecians'. They went on to the weather and the driver remarked: 'She's fallen heavy and sudden up on Exmoor but there's nothing for the likes of us where we wants it so very bad.'

Maisie wasn't shocked at their inconsequential chatter. She knew they didn't mean any disrespect by it.

Vincent got up off his knees and told them that he had finished.

'Are you sure, sir?' asked Jasper.

'I've no more film in any case, Constable.'

The police officer wanted to know if Vincent had any equipment with which he could develop and print the photographs, which seemed to Maisie unlikely. The answer, as she expected, was negative.

'There's a camera shop in town, though,' said Constable Jasper. 'Happen I might knock them up in the morning and ask for them to do it.'

'What do you expect to see?' asked Maisie.

'It was you wanted the job done,' Jasper retorted. 'Didn't you have no reason for asking, after all?'

Normally, Maisie would have snapped back, but she felt distracted by a strong impression that Vincent was hiding something – perhaps knowledge, perhaps some unknown intention. She had noticed an expression of displeasure on his face.

Was that simply gallantry, not liking to see bare-faced cheek to a lady? Or is there another reason?

Vincent took out his tobacco pouch and wandered away, filling the bowl of his pipe, preparing to smoke. Meanwhile, the ambulance driver and his companion moved the body of Holly Luscombe onto the stretcher and carried it to the open rear doors of the ambulance. Their behaviour was brusque but – again – not disrespectful. Once Holly's corpse was loaded, they wasted no time in climbing back into the cab, turning a wide circle across the grass and driving away.

'So, the ambulance came all the way from Exeter?' Maisie asked.

'What are you asking for?' demanded Constable Jasper.

Maisie noticed another fleeting expression cross Vincent's face. Had anyone asked, she would have described it as frustration.

'Because it was so quick.'

'They were delivering a patient home to Kirton,' Constable Jasper told her.

'What will you do next?' she asked, making an effort to remain patient.

'I'll do my duty.'

'I expect you will. What exactly?'

'I'll have to write a report.'

'Will you share it with your sergeant, even though he's in hospital with his strangulated hernia?'

'I will not. He can't be troubled. It's proper serious, with blood poisoning and I don't know what.'

'That is unfortunate.'

Maisie pursed her lips. If Holly's death turned out not to be an accident, she felt an intellect more acute than Seth Jasper's would be required to solve the mystery.

'Miss Cooper,' said Vincent, 'you've been out a long time. You should jump in the constable's car and let him run you back to Sunny View. I ate too much of Mrs Savage's supper and could do with some fresh air. Am I right that I can walk back on the far side of the river and come out on the lane in the centre of Trout Leap?'

'No, actually you have to walk along the railway line and that might be a mistake now. It's almost dark and a train can thunder along at any time. If you go the other way, through the fields, you'll have to climb a dry-stone wall and there are two bulls over there on the far bank of the river. They took a close and intimidating interest in me when I crossed their territory.'

'Ah,' replied Vincent, with a smile. 'You're not keen to repeat the experience and suggest I might not enjoy it either.'

For the first time, Maisie realised that Vincent was a hand-some man – or, if not exactly handsome, attractive, as Stella Tubb was attractive, because he had an engaging personality and a forthright gaze.

'That's right,' she told him with a smile.

'Will you let me take your camera, sir,' interrupted Constable Jasper, 'and see if I can't get the film developed? Maybe I'll go by the shop this evening, after all, and strike while the iron's hot.'

'Yes,' said Vincent, 'you take it and drive on. Miss Cooper and I will follow you on foot, the way we drove over, the long way round, via the dairy farm.'

'Right you are, sir.'

Maisie looked from one to the other in what seemed to her an odd little wordless pause. Meanwhile, Vincent removed the leather strap of the camera from around his neck, closed up the leather case around the device itself and put it in the police officer's hands. For a second, Maisie wondered if Constable Jasper had found some aspect of Vincent's behaviour suspicious or if, looked at another way, Vincent was worried for the safety of his belongings.

Or is there something peculiar about the way Constable Jasper seems to want to defer to Vincent? Is that it?

The odd hiatus came to an end. Seth Jasper nodded, mooched silently away and got back into his car. He drove uphill in a low gear and Maisie and Vincent set off after him, walking briskly, each of them stumbling once or twice because the uneven track was becoming harder to see as the evening progressed into night.

In order to make conversation, Maisie asked Vincent about trout fishing, elaborating on one or two details that she happened to know, such as the fact that the scales of each fish were as unique as fingerprints or that the handmade tying of flies as lures was considered an art-form by aficionados. Oddly, for an angler, Vincent didn't seem interested to share his own knowledge. Maisie tried a different topic.

'Are you aware of the gold mine? I can't remember if I've heard anyone mention it to you?'

'It sounds very unlikely,' said Vincent.

'Mr Savage has a number of documents pertaining to it that you might find interesting.'

'He did mention them,' said Vincent – warily, she thought. 'And some interesting books in his library.'

'How did you come to know about the guesthouse, Sunny View?'

'From the RAC listings.'

Maisie recognised the phrase as precisely the same as the one Ida had used and found it suspicious.

Are they in league, somehow, Ida and Vincent, like actors with the same pre-rehearsed lines?

At the brow of the hill, they stopped because Vincent wanted to turn and examine the landscape. Maisie did the same, contemplating the deep shade of the more sheltered valleys. The gorgeous sky to the west was still full of colour despite the sun having dipped below the horizon, painted lilac and orange and mauve, as if by a watercolour painter of great sensitivity and skill.

'Where do you think this gold mine might be?' Vincent asked, his eye scanning the folded landscape. 'You know the country round about pretty well, don't you, and you're an outdoors sort of lady. I imagine, ten years ago when you lived here, you were often out and about on hearty walks.'

Maisie didn't answer straight away because she had recognised in Vincent's tone something beyond simple conversation.

He's probing for something.

'It was a busy time. I didn't often go far. We should press on,' she told him.

They continued in silence and soon the lights of the farmhouse became visible. Maisie wondered what life inside was like.

How does Floyd Tubb spend his evenings? Watching television, perhaps? Would it be Dr Who? No, that's a teatime show. Some kind of variety entertainer, perhaps, or the American murder-mystery show that Grandma Florence likes, with the crumpled detective, Frank Columbo? And what about Norman Tubb? Would he even be home? Perhaps he's in the habit of going out to a pub somewhere nearby, once Stella has served him his tea?

Maisie imagined that Stella herself would spend the time between dusk and going to bed doing something useful, sewing or ironing or perhaps boiling up jams, preserving the glut of summer fruits for the winter to come.

'You're very quiet, Miss Cooper,' said Vincent. 'Of course, it must have been an awful shock to discover . . . Well, you know.'

They had passed the farmhouse and were walking down the drive to the cattle grid. Maisie successfully picked her way across it in the gloom, but Vincent half tripped. She put out a hand to help him regain his balance, grasping him just above the elbow. His arm was firm with thick, well-defined muscles, which seemed at odds with Maisie's first impression of his character.

'I'm not upset or distressed,' she told him. 'It's very kind of you to ask, but there's no need to worry. By the way, I don't think you said what you do for a living? Are you a photographer?'

'I'm a representative, a travelling salesman. I place fancy goods in department stores. I've recently been to Taunton and Exeter.'

For some reason, his answer sounded rehearsed.

'Do you have any samples with you?' asked Maisie as a kind of test. 'I would very much like to see them.'

'I'm afraid they're in the boot of my car, which is in for a service and MOT at a garage near Exeter Saint David's railway station. I thought I'd take advantage of my little holiday at Sunny View to get it fixed up. I can't get by without a reliable vehicle but, when I'm on holiday, the last thing I'd want would be to go motor touring.'

They were just crossing the humpbacked bridge and the slight elevation meant that the last light in the sky illuminated Vincent's unremarkable but appealing face. With an odd feeling that the answers he was giving were too pat, Maisie smiled and told him: 'That makes complete sense.'

'Is that you, Maisie?' came a voice.

It was Russell, standing outside Sunny View, in the lane, waiting for them, shuffling from foot to foot. He greeted them with three or four confused questions and insisted they answer all of them before they were allowed to go inside. Eventually he was satisfied and led them through to the kitchen where Audrey was waiting with some thinly sliced cold toast, a pat of butter, a wedge of hard cheese and a clay pot of home-made pickles.

Vincent accepted only a glass of cider because he had eaten before Constable Jasper came to fetch him, but Maisie was very hungry. She took care, however, not to overeat because she was tired and wanted her bed.

'I take it Ida has already gone up?' she asked.

'Not ten minutes ago', said Russell.

Audrey insisted that Maisie and Vincent repeat what they had seen and done, by which time Maisie had satisfied her appetite. Both Audrey and Russell assumed that Holly had met with a terrible accident.

'Those awkward shoes,' said Russell.

'And no socks,' Audrey confirmed. 'She was always clumsy, poor thing.'

Maisie helped her hosts to put the supper things away on the marble cold shelf in the pantry. Vincent went outside into the garden to 'live in peace with my pipe' – which was, apparently a line from a television advert – and Russell said he would keep him company. Audrey went with them, remarking that the smoke would 'keep the midges at bay'.

Maisie bid them all goodnight. She went upstairs to the bathroom and washed and brushed her teeth. She changed into a nightdress in her bedroom – 'Caesar' – and turned the key in the lock for privacy.

As she had done the previous evening, she opened the window, leaned her hands on the sill and looked out into the lane. The sky provided a featureless black background to a delightful array of twinkling white pinpricks – a dense scattering of stars. In the next-door room, 'Pompey', the light was on and the curtains open. An orange glow spilled out, illuminating the leaves of the copper beech tree. Maisie wondered what Ida might be doing – perhaps working on her surprisingly accurate sketch of the valley.

I haven't quite got the measure of her. Like Vincent, she seems to have an ulterior motive. Or am I making something out of nothing?

Maisie stayed very still, listening to the sounds of the night, hoping to see the beautiful, silent nocturnal assassin – the barn owl – once more. Then, instead, in a strange echo of the previous evening, when Holly had come twirling by, she heard a shuffling tread and Fred Luscombe staggered into view, the light from Ida's window just catching the bottle in his hand.

That looks like whisky. Maybe Bell's.

Fred seemed to be weeping or perhaps moaning to himself.

And why not? What a terrible thing to happen to a man, to outlive his own daughter, for her never to make old bones.

Fred stopped, raised the open bottle to his lips and drank deeply.

Where might he have got that from, though? I'm sure he said: 'We never have spirits in the house.'

Once the whisky bottle was empty, he threw it backhand into the hedge. What Maisie had thought to be moaning or weeping became more distinct. Fred was singing.

> *'Abide with me; fast falls the eventide;*
> *The darkness deepens. Lord, with me abide.*
> *When other helpers fail and comforts flee,*
> *Help of the helpless, O abide with me.'*

Maisie felt deeply sorry for him, drunk and lost, shaken by grief, unaware that he was observed, sort of shipwrecked, just two hundred yards from his own front door.

Then, her mind began to whir, wondering what precise combination of emotions had made him resort to unaccustomed spirits, sending him out in public, singing a hymn of despair, desperate for God's guidance in the gloom.

Might it be guilt, after all? And, if it is, guilt for what, precisely?

IV

BITING SPIDERS & POISONOUS PLANTS

TWENTY-THREE

Maisie woke on Sunday morning with a series of questions on her lips, but with no one to whom she could address them. She lay in bed, her eyes unfocused, vaguely gazing at the ceiling, reflecting on the interaction between Constable Jasper and Vincent that had puzzled her.

Why was Constable Seth Jasper so keen to show respect to Vincent Brent, calling him 'sir' and giving a distinct impression of deference?

The obvious explanation was because he had prevailed on the older man's goodwill, his sense of civic duty. It wasn't just that Constable Jasper had taken advantage of Vincent's expensive camera equipment and his photographic expertise. He had also asked a civilian to do a police officer's work, in close proximity to a corpse.

Those are good enough reasons, aren't they?

Maisie wasn't certain why the question still bothered her. She was troubled, too, by the traditional conundrum, the one usually summarised as: 'Did she fall or was she pushed?'

In this case, the question ought to be: 'Did Holly trip and tumble and hit her head, or did someone bash her with what the police would no doubt call a "blunt object"?'

There was also the issue of whether her corpse had been brought from somewhere else and dumped by the limestone outcrop, under the oak trees, to give the impression of an accident. Maisie regretted not examining the chicken wire that covered the timbers of the bridge more closely. The sticky-up bit she had tripped on herself could have been caused by someone deliberately cutting it to make a hazard, specifically to clothe a murder with the trappings of an accident.

It's possible that I only think that because of all that I've seen since Stephen was killed.

Maisie roused herself, climbing out of bed, going to the open window to pull apart the curtains. It was another lovely day, but the sun didn't seem quite so warm, veiled by thin cloud, and it was still quite low in the sky. She checked her watch on the bedside table.

Crikey, it's nearly nine. I'm becoming a sloven.

Maisie chose a different dress from the wardrobe, one with a similar shape to her polka-dotted one, with a narrow-ish waist, but in a slightly heavier mustard-coloured fabric. She put on her grey woollen cardigan over the top and chose some matching grey socks to wear with her sandals, thinking she ought to put her dirty white socks in soapy water to soak.

But I need tea.

Leaving 'Caesar', she heard voices from the kitchen and went down to find out who was up. Ida came to meet her in the doorway, obscuring the room, greeting her with an enquiry as to how she had slept, but not letting her answer.

'What a terrible thing to have happened, though,' she told her, her London accent very pronounced. 'And you having to stand guard for hour after lonely hour. Dear oh dear.'

'It was fine, really.'

Ida was wearing an apron with pictures of apples on it and a lacy edge. Her hands were covered in flour.

'I'm making my cobbler for after church,' Ida announced.

She stepped aside and indicated the stovetop, where a saucepan of apples was cooking.

'Miss Cooper's made of sterner stuff,' came Vincent's voice. 'And, as you see, we're both keeping busy and up to snuff.'

Maisie was surprised to see that he was cleaning and servicing a shotgun, laid out on the kitchen table on a few sheets of newspaper, looking very dramatic next to the teapot and sugar bowl.

'That's a vintage James Purdey side-by-side, isn't it?' she asked.

'You have a good eye,' said Vincent.

'I've seen some before, back when I used to be a beater on the pheasant shoots in Sussex, when I was a teenager.'

'Have you ever fired one?'

'Yes, I have, or something very like it. So, that was what was in your long bag. I thought it was fishing equipment, a rod in two parts or something.'

'No, my Purdey,' he told her. 'I don't carry it disassembled in a heavy box, just a slip case. How did you find firing one? They have quite the kick,' he said quietly, his eyes leaving hers and travelling along her body. 'People are often shocked.'

'That's true,' she agreed, turning away. 'Those apples smell marvellous, Miss Anderson.'

'Cinnamon and cloves. I was glad to find some spices in the pantry. And honey and sultanas, of course.'

'Delicious. Where have Mr and Mrs Savage got to?'

'They were up very early,' said Ida, 'doing a bit of gardening, round the foxgloves on the river edge and—'

'Don't tell Miss Cooper about foxgloves,' interrupted Vincent in a bantering tone. 'She'll start thinking about poisons.'

'I don't know about that,' said Ida, 'but there was a mishap of some kind and Mr Savage had to drive Mrs Savage into Kirton to see the doctor.'

'Oh, dear,' said Maisie. 'Nothing serious, I hope?'

'They were on the way out when I came down and Mr Brent – Vincent, I mean – wasn't yet in the land of the living.'

She laughed and Vincent replied merrily, as if there was a friendly implied criticism in her words: 'I am on holiday, after all.'

'Gentlemen like their beauty sleep,' said Ida, tittering.

'Actually, I was in the front room,' he told them, 'looking at the books.'

Maisie poured herself a cup of tea from the pot, finding it a little stewed, but she liked it strong, in any case. She excused herself and took it out into the garden. The foxglove border – tall green stems festooned with multiple bell-shaped purple flowers growing close together – was between the cider shed and the trees that fringed the river at the edge of the lawn. They seemed to be flourishing in the dappled sunlight. The dirt around their stems had been turned over and weeded, except at the far end where the flowers gave way to a pile of fallen branches, presumably left there as a habitat for over-wintering insects and hedgehogs and so on.

Maisie sat down at the garden table. To her dismay, Ida came to join her, wanting to know more about 'last night's adventure'. Maisie told her the bare minimum. Vincent brought his own cup outside to sit with them, listening in very attentively without saying anything much himself.

'Your apples smell very hot, Ida,' said Maisie, after a while. 'You don't want them to dry out and catch.'

'Heavens, I don't,' said Ida, bustling away.

Vincent drained his cup and said: 'I'll go and put my gun back together.'

'Where will you keep it?' asked Maisie.

'Mr Savage has given me permission to use the cupboard in the front room where he keeps his own.'

'Yes,' said Maisie, remembering seeing the padlock hanging loose. 'That's a good idea.'

Vincent followed Ida indoors. Left alone in the lovely garden with only birdsong and a warm breeze for company, Maisie allowed her thoughts to wander. The path they found was similar to earlier on.

Did Holly trip and bang her head or was she murdered?
Did someone move her body?

If so, why?

Who gave Fred whisky?

Was Fred's distress simply grief, or was there more to it?

Why am I unable to take Vincent and Ida – individually and severally – at face value?

Before she had finished her tea, Russell and Audrey returned and the mystery of their hurried departure to the general practitioner in Kirton was solved. Audrey had been on her knees in the dewy grass, grubbing out weeds from the area by the woodpile, and had been bitten by a spider on her little finger. The doctor had disinfected the wound, dressed it and given her a rust-red rubber stall – like a finger cut from a washing-up glove – to put over the top and keep it dry.

'How horrid,' said Maisie.

Audrey told them that she still felt 'odd' and wanted to lie down. Russell said he would make her a flask of tea to take up but the thermos was nowhere to be found. Ida protested that she had definitely brought it back from her sketching expedition.

'I took the liberty of borrowing it,' said Vincent. 'I'm planning to be out for a few hours this afternoon. I'm sorry. I'll fetch it.'

'No, don't you worry,' said Audrey. 'A cup will do me just as well.'

Maisie poured Audrey's tea while Russell accompanied her upstairs.

'Where will you be trekking off to like an intrepid explorer?' asked Ida in an oddly flirtatious voice.

'Up hill and down dale,' said Vincent, playing up to her. 'I'm quite the Captain Scott when the mood takes me.'

'I bet you are.'

Maisie took the tea upstairs and met Russell halfway. He took it from her, saying: 'Perhaps you'll help me finish in the garden?'

'Of course.'

Back in the kitchen, Ida was telling Vincent about a dance hall in New Cross, south London, that she liked to attend. Vincent replied with wide eyes and a delighted expression: 'I know the place. We might have been there on the same day.'

'To think,' said Ida. 'How about that, Miss Cooper?'

'Call me Maisie, please.'

'Life is a sequence of missed opportunities,' said Ida, coquettishly. 'And that's a fact.'

To Maisie's relief, Russell came back downstairs, looking for his gardening gloves. Maisie went and found some leather fire gauntlets in the front room, by the open fireplace. Together, they went out across the lawn to the foxglove border and moved the pile of old branches to the far end of the garden, all the time keeping a sharp eye out for potential eight-legged attackers. Several times, Russell seemed on the verge of sharing a confidence or a concern but, on each occasion, he hesitated and changed the subject.

Happy to be busy with physical tasks, Maisie spent the next hour attending to a short list of smaller chores: cutting the long grass on the edge of the lawn with shears, letting the stalks float away on the crystal clear water of the Wivel; running the push-mower up and down the lawn, leaving tidy stripes; snipping off one or two suckers growing from the boles of the trees; turning the compost heap of garden prunings and leaves and so on, to encourage it to rot down to use as mulch later in the year.

Once all that was complete it was time to 'smarten up for church', as Russell put it. Maisie, Russell, Ida and Vincent each got ready in their respective rooms, then foregathered in the kitchen, by which time Audrey was downstairs, looking pale, but she told them: 'I'm more or less myself.'

'Have you had a bad reaction to a spider bite before?' Maisie asked.

'I have,' said Audrey, with a vague laugh. 'I fainted right away up in the loft. Russell was looking for me for hours, not knowing I'd gone up for the summer dresses I'd put away for winter.'

Getting all five of them into the weary Vauxhall Viva would have been a squeeze – and Maisie had intended to make room by telling them that she would cycle – but, because Audrey didn't feel up to it, they would only be four. Russell drove with Maisie alongside, plus Ida and Vincent behind, taking the roundabout route out past the Tubbs' dairy farm, then left towards the railway station.

'I've come this way,' Russell said in a quiet voice, 'because there's no need to go bothering poor old Fred Luscombe.'

'I saw him in the lane last night,' Maisie remarked. 'Did you?'

'No,' Russell told her. 'We're at the back, remember.'

'I heard him singing a hymn,' said Ida. 'I hope it brought him comfort.'

'He'd been drinking,' said Maisie.

'Can you blame him?' asked Russell.

'That isn't usual though,' Maisie insisted.

'No, that's true.'

He parked the Viva and they all got out on the High Street, to the accompaniment of a descending three-note bell chime, repeated over and over to summon the faithful to worship. They walked together up the pathway to the impressive door. A large panel alongside gave its full, verbose name – the 'Collegiate Church of the Holy Cross and the Mother of Him Who Hung Thereon' – along with its date of foundation and a reminder of its original purpose as Kirton's cathedral, before the diocese was moved to Exeter in the eleventh century.

'But this version must have been built much later,' said Maisie.

'Tudor,' said Russell.

On the way in, he introduced them all to the presiding priest, Canon Greig, who shook Maisie's hand with dispiritingly limp fingers.

'If you don't mind, Reverend,' said Russell, 'Norman and me have rearranged for him to read the lesson instead.'

'No, not at all,' replied the minister, before hurrying away.

Cherry Atwill was there and briefly spoke to them. Her husband, Clive, was apparently out fishing. Over Cherry's shoulder, Maisie saw Vera Pond in the front pew, near Norman, Stella and Floyd Tubb, among at least a hundred worshippers.

Maisie, Russell, Ida and Vincent found an empty pew three-quarters of the way back, just before the Linton family arrived, all dressed in their Sunday best, giving Maisie a first sight of the Maltese mother, who gave an impression of feeling lost, like a child in a new school. Though she didn't look at him directly, Maisie felt Patrick Linton's eye upon her, not exactly leering, but not far from it.

Mr and Mrs Linton sat down in a nearby pew, but their teenage children disappeared into a robing room at the west end of the nave. Russell told Maisie a confused story about them having changed their names.

'They're Paul and Maria, now, though those names are just English versions of the foreign ones they had before – you know, similar but different.'

'And the mother?'

'I don't know if I've ever found out. I just call her "Mrs Linton" when we meet – which isn't often.'

The descending three-note chime gave way to a single tolling bell, then that, too, ceased and Paul and Maria emerged, changed into red cassocks and white starched surplices, looking very handsome, processing up the aisle with the priest behind. Maria was acting as crucifer, carrying a cross on a staff, while Paul took the role of thurifer, swinging an incense ball on three silver chains, sending perfumed smoke through the impressive nave. Once they reached what the poet Philip Larkin called – dismissively – 'the holy end', Paul and Maria stood beneath the pulpit as Canon Greig began the service with a prayer of welcome and announced a well-known hymn.

The Kirton congregation clearly enjoyed singing in community and Maisie was delighted to join her mellow contralto with theirs. Then, with a voice considerably stronger than his handshake, Canon Greig read the 'Collect for the Eighth Sunday after Trinity':

> *O God, whose never-failing providence ordereth all things both in heaven and earth: we humbly beseech thee to put away from us all hurtful things, and to give us those things which be profitable for us; through Jesus Christ our Lord.*

Maisie joined in with the congregation's 'Amen', thinking about the incongruity of the word 'profitable', given the well-known biblical warning about the 'love of money' being 'the root of all evil'.

But perhaps it's a different meaning of the word 'profitable'.

The service continued with Psalm 105, sung beautifully by a decent choir – two-thirds women and one-third men – to a stately 'modal tone', provided by an unseen organist. The choir included all three members of the Sturgess family and all three Topes. Each one had their eyes on their psalters, because the text was quite long and obviously hadn't been learned by heart. It concerned the Israelites' flight from Egypt – comically referred to as 'the land of Ham' – and God's punishments thereon, making Maisie silently smile at the surreal sequence:

> *He turned their waters into blood and slew their fish.*
> *Their land brought forth frogs, yea, even in their kings'*
> *chambers. There came all manner of flies and lice in their*
> *quarters.*

Of course, as the story continued, it became more serious:

> *Grasshoppers came, and caterpillars innumerable and*
> *did eat up all the grass and devoured the fruit of their*
> *ground. He smote all the first-born. Egypt was glad at*
> *their departing for they were afraid of them.*

Maisie wondered how the Lintons felt, hearing a story not of expulsion – as they had been expelled – but of voluntary exodus from bondage, into the harsh freedoms of the 'Promised Land'.

After the psalm, Norman Tubb got up heavily from his pew and strode forward to ascend a small dais where an enormous Bible was lying open on an ornately carved lectern.

'The Book of Mark, chapter ten, verse one,' he announced. 'And the Pharisees came to him, and asked: "Is it lawful for a man to put away his wife?" And Jesus answered: "From the beginning of creation, God made them male and female. For this cause shall a man leave his father and mother, and cleave to his wife; and they twain shall be one flesh. What, therefore, God hath joined together, let no man put asunder." And his disciples asked him again and He saith: "Whosoever shall put away his wife, and marry another, committeth adultery against her. And if a woman shall put away her husband, and be married to another, she committeth adultery." Here endeth the lesson.'

Norman Tubb came lumbering down from the little dais, making his way to his pew alongside his wife, Stella, whose hands were clasped and whose eyes were closed in prayer or contemplation.

Or sleep, if she's been up all night again, with her sick 'lady'.

Next came the formal Confession, recited in chorus by the entire congregation, followed by the Absolution, delivered in a self-righteous tone by Canon Greig, as if it were his own indulgence, rather than God's. Then Maisie recognised Herbert Peckham, the editor of the *Kirton Courier*, as he ascended the dais for a second reading, a famous one, beginning: 'Beware of false prophets, which come to you in sheep's clothing, but inwardly they are ravening wolves.'

Maisie became distracted, thinking about the supposed gold mine and the fact that her friends and many of their neighbours had invested in the – surely illusory – promise of unearned wealth. Then, she was tugged back to the present as Herbert Peckham concluded: 'This is the Gospel of the Lord.' The congregation replied: 'Praise be to Thee, O Christ.'

The Gospel was followed by the avowal of faith – the Creed – then an offertory hymn that Maisie didn't know so she had to read the depressing – almost-suicidal – words from a little hymn book:

> *If death my portion be,*
> *It brings great gain to me;*
> *It speeds my life's endeavour*
> *To live with Christ forever.*
> *He gives me joy in sorrow,*
> *Come death now or tomorrow.*

The plate came past, escorted from pew to pew by Norman Tubb, who she assumed must be a church warden. Maisie found a fifty-pence piece in her purse and added her coin to the healthy collection of silver and a few green pound notes.

In a pause between verses, Maisie heard the heavy south door of the church open and slam shut.

All heads turned towards the sound. As luck would have it, Maisie's view was unobscured.

It was Fred Luscombe, dressed in his British Rail uniform but exceedingly dishevelled, his tie half undone and the tails of his shirt untucked. While the congregation persisted with the doleful hymn, he staggered up the aisle in the centre of the nave, stumbled and threw himself on the steps before the altar rail, calling: 'Have I missed it? Am I too late? Can I be absolved?'

Surprisingly quickly, Russell was out of their pew and attending to his neighbour, helping him to his feet and escorting him away through a side door into the vestry, as the congregation glanced at one another, but completed the final verse.

The last notes of the organ faded, their vibrations hanging on the air. It was time for the sermon, a mercifully brief one, perhaps shortened because Canon Greig was as shocked as his congregants by Fred's obvious distress, prostrating himself on the cold stones, desperate for forgiveness.

Maisie was unsettled herself – not only by the heart-rending display, but also by what it might mean.

Forgiveness for what, exactly?

TWENTY-FOUR

The concluding elements of the church service all had a perfunctory air, as if everyone was now impatient for the routine of worship to be over. After the Blessing and Dismissal – as everyone got to their feet in a hum of unrestrained gossip – Maisie suggested that Ida and Vincent should wait outside: 'I'll go and see what Russell thinks is best.' The paying guests agreed, slipping unobtrusively away with the rest of the congregation.

Maisie went 'dreckly' to the vestry, a small room furnished with a desk, some built-in cupboards in dark oak and a large metal safe. An unshaded electric light bulb hung from a braided wire and was turned on because the light was poor from the north-facing window of small leaded panes.

As well as Russell, both Canon Greig and Norman Tubb were present, making it seem crowded despite the fact that an outer door was ajar. Through it, Maisie could see the green churchyard, with old stones marking places of Christian burial that had endured for nine hundred years. Fred, however, was nowhere to be seen.

'I couldn't get him to stay,' said Russell.

'Did you speak to him?' she asked. 'How was he?'

'Sober as a judge, but broken in spirit.'

'Amen,' said the priest, which Maisie thought pious and pointless.

'What did you expect?' said Norman Tubb, gruffly, in Maisie's direction. 'And don't go thinking people haven't heard that it's your fault, putting ideas in Holly's head, sending her off on a spree.' Maisie wanted to reply, but he didn't let her, gabbling on, flecks of white in the corners of his mouth. 'Yes, he told me, poor old Fred, how you made her think she should take her own decisions and decide what was best for herself. Then what? Off you'll skip without a backward glance for the damage you've done.'

'Now, Norman—' Russell began.

'I don't know what Fred told you, Mr Tubb,' interrupted Maisie, 'but I didn't encourage anything of the sort. I'm afraid the poor man is simply lashing out and I, as a recent arrival, am the undeserved focus for his grief.'

'Don't you talk nice,' said Norman, contemptuously.

Maisie realised that, under pressure, she had once again used her 'posh' voice, as she had with Constable Jasper.

'How I speak is not material.' She turned to Russell. 'Should someone go after him?'

'He's all right. He's out there, by his wife's grave.'

Maisie took two steps to the door and looked outside. Fred was kneeling on the dry grass in the far corner of the churchyard, his hands clasped in front of his breastbone, facing a dark-grey tombstone.

'Poor man,' she said, quietly.

'A lost sheep,' said Canon Greig. 'I will attempt to bring him back unto our flock. Will you excuse me?'

Maisie stood aside to let him go out, watching the skirts of his cassock just skimming the tightly mown lawn.

'I expect you wish you'd never come back,' said Norman.

She turned to face him and said: 'On the contrary. I think I'm precisely where I'm supposed to be.'

'Standing in judgement over others, is it?'

'Doing what is right,' she told him, levelly, 'to the best of my ability and knowledge.'

He made a scoffing noise and ran a heavy hand over his whiskers.

'I've read all about you in the papers Russ showed me. You're what I'd call a busybody, peering into others' business with no right. Who's to say those you got convicted were guilty after all?'

'Happily, in each case, it was the responsibility of the court to make that judgement, not mine.'

'But rumour and hearsay can be judge and jury, can't they. You came upon me in a moment of weakness and turned even my wife against me.'

'I don't know what you mean by that, Mr Tubb. To all appearances, Stella is devoted to you and, in any case, I've never discussed what I saw – not even with Russell or Audrey, as he will attest.'

'Maisie's telling the truth,' said Russell, with a desperate edge to his voice, clearly distressed at the anger in the room. 'Shall we step outside. This isn't right for Sunday or for the house of God.'

'I don't have nothing else to say.' Norman indicated the offertory plate. 'Anyway, I've still my duties to do.'

Maisie assumed he meant he had to add up all the notes and coins and consign the total in a book of accounts, squirrelling everything away in the safe. Paul and Maria Linton came in, looking very handsome back in their Sunday best, having changed out of their cassocks and surplices, returning the valuable paraphernalia of their offices as thurifer and crucifer. Maisie took advantage of the interruption to go outside, watching from a distance as Canon Greig bent over, speaking close to Fred Luscombe's ear.

Russell came out to join her and, together, they agreed that there was nothing useful that either of them could do. They went round to the south side of the church, looking for Ida and Vincent, who had found a bench to sit on, facing the sun. Vincent leapt up at their approach.

'All's well, I hope? Mr and Mrs Tope stopped and talked to us – and others have been by. What a sad story.'

'Isn't it awful,' said Ida, fanning her face with her hand.

'Poor bugger,' said Russell.

Maisie couldn't suppress a moment of doubt.

Everyone keeps saying 'poor' Fred Luscombe. But is he?

*

Lunch at Sunny View was a delicious lamb hotpot from the fridge that Audrey had prepared two days before and put in the Aga to reheat while they were out. Having shared the extraordinary events at the church and, less dramatically, the weather forecast, a good chunk of the conversation turned around countryside sports, there having been a recent protest in London about fox-hunting and related pastimes. Maisie was pleased to be able to probe why Vincent had his shotgun with him.

'I couldn't leave it in the boot of my car,' he explained.

'But why did you have it with you while out on the road, visiting department stores with fancy goods?' asked Maisie, trying not to look like she was prying. 'The season for pheasant and partridge and so on are a long way off, aren't they?'

'October first and September first, respectively,' said Vincent. 'Ducks are September, too. Grouse are earlier, of course, on the "glorious twelfth" of August, as are snipe. There's a lot you have to know. Sometimes, there are additional local rules.'

Maisie found his precise knowledge unconvincing.

It's as if he's learned it by heart.

'But you're travelling with your shotgun in late July?' Maisie insisted.

'Deer,' he told her. 'Without hunters to reduce the populations, they eat all the underbrush and the saplings, even the bark from young trees. Stags and bucks – males, you see – can be shot from the first of August. For the hinds you have to wait until November. But roebucks can be shot any time from spring onwards because they're considered vermin. I thought I might have a pop.' He turned to Audrey, a broad smile on his face. 'No good for the pot, though, Mrs Savage. It would need to be hung at least a fortnight.'

Maisie appreciated the argument about culling animals that could, in large enough numbers, become pests and would have been pleased to take what he was saying at face value, but couldn't.

None of this quite fits with his character.

'I dare say any one of the Kirton butchers would be pleased to take the carcass off your hands,' said Audrey.

'Those poor creatures, Vincent,' Ida protested. 'I don't know how you can.'

'Because it's always been a part of my way of life, I suppose,' he told her. 'I was brought up to it.'

'Where was that?' asked Maisie.

'Edge of London, Epping.'

There followed a discussion, instigated by Russell, in which they were apparently all more or less agreed – that different people had different lifestyles and ought, within reason, to be tolerant of one another's choices.

Maisie helped Audrey clear away the main course so they could move on to Ida's superb apple cobbler. The cake-like topping was golden and crisp on top, but gooey below where it met the spiced-apple compote.

And there was no more talk of shooting innocent – though troublesome – fauna.

★

Once they had all finished and the washing-up was done and the dishes dried and put away, Maisie helped Audrey clean the week's tea towels and napkins by immersing them in boiling water with half a teacup of Omo washing powder, stirring the mixture with wooden laundry tongs.

In the overwarm kitchen, Ida sat with them, at first watching them work, then reading Russell's scrapbook that she had asked for especially. Maisie took advantage of the boil-wash to add her white socks, hoping the bars of dirt they had acquired through the leather straps of her sandals would come out.

'How is it that you've been involved in three murder investigations?' Ida asked, guilelessly, once she had read all three write-ups.

'Pure coincidence,' said Maisie, drying her hands and straightening the kitchen towel on the chrome bar of the Aga.

'And there's a fourth to come from Bunting Fair,' said Audrey.

'Bitling Fair, not Bunting,' said Maisie, then regretted it, not wanting to be drawn into more autobiography. 'What's Russell up to?'

'He'll be having a snooze in his garden chair,' said Audrey. 'We both wake early, then he needs a nap in the afternoon. It's age, you know.'

'Did Vincent go out?' Maisie asked.

'Some time ago,' said Audrey.

'Where on earth has he got to?' snapped Ida, then tittered and asked, rhetorically: 'What am I saying? Why shouldn't he be out? You know, it's time for me to make tracks and do the same as Mr Savage. I'm going to retire to my virtuous couch.'

She stood up, heavily, and plodded out into the hallway. Maisie heard her tramping upstairs.

'What about you?' Audrey asked. 'Would you like me to find you a book to read. I have some nice *Reader's Digest* abridged editions – lovely hard covers and gold tooling.'

'Actually, I would. Thank you.'

'And it'll be cooler at the front of the house.'

They went into the darker, damper living room – the one with the television – to inspect the bookshelves. On the lower one, there was what looked like a complete set of the *Encyclopaedia Britannica*. Above was a shelf given over to Russell's books of local and classical history, plus ten or twelve spines belonging to nicely bound *Reader's Digest* books, each one containing three abridged novels.

Maisie found a volume that included an abbreviated version of *Scales of Justice* by Ngaio Marsh. It happened to be the story from which she had learned the detailed knowledge of angling that she had shared with Vincent – with unexpectedly little response.

But he's not an angler, he's a hunter.

'I've read *Scales of Justice* before,' Maisie said. 'But I don't mind reading it again.'

'Take it with you,' said Audrey. She switched on the television, tuned in to BBC Two, and settled herself down in a comfortably sagging chocolate-brown corduroy armchair to watch a cricket match, the wide expanse of grass burnt beige and dry by the July sun. 'It's a forty-over John Player league game,' she explained. 'They dash about like mad things. It's not like test matches.' She picked up her knitting from the coffee table, removing the rubber stall from her finger. 'You go on and have a bit of peace and quiet. I'm quite happy here.'

'How's your spider bite?'

'I can barely notice it.'

'By the way, what happened to your dining table in the other room with the French doors? I remember a nice beechwood thing . . .'

'Oh, yes, we gave that to the Lintons, poor things. They arrived with nothing, not a stick of furniture, and we seldom used it. Russell and me always eat where it's warm in the kitchen.'

Maisie found that she was unwilling immediately to leave.

Somehow, events are passing me by – or I'm not catching their meaning.

'Are you looking forward to this evening?' she asked.

'The meeting? I must say I'm not, but people need to say what they're thinking, otherwise it all festers. And Russell needs to get it off his chest, too. He blames himself.'

'In what way?'

'You'll see, I don't doubt, when we get there. Now, go on with you. Have an hour to yourself.'

Feeling that Audrey, too, needed time on her own, Maisie left her and went upstairs to sit on her bed in 'Caesar', happily turning the pages of *Scales of Justice*. Interestingly, the plot was introduced with one of the secondary characters looking down on a river valley – rather like Ida on Break Heart Hill with her easel and canvas – picturing the imaginary inhabitants of all the houses: the working classes in their cottages, the middle classes in their detached homes-and-gardens, the nobility in a mansion with a private golf course. It was beautifully written, but Maisie found it hard to concentrate because certain details of the fictional circumstances kept reminding her of her own brutal reality.

She put the book aside, memorising the number of the page she had reached, then looked round the room.

I need to get my thoughts in order – just in case.

One of the many innovations Maisie had brought to the management of Sunny View was to provide headed notepaper and pre-printed envelopes in the rooms. She found both in a drawer in the beside cabinet, but there was nowhere she could comfortably sit and write because 'Caesar' had no desk. There was, however, a tray on top of the marble-topped chest of drawers, on which an empty flower vase stood. She put the vase on the floor, found her favourite fountain pen in her handbag, and propped herself against her pillows, the writing paper on the tray on her knees.

For a few seconds, she simply sat, imagining how a novelist might begin. Then she told herself that was silly. What she needed was a clear checklist of the people involved in Holly's life and – it was impossible to avoid it – the strange and incomplete story of the gold mine. She began by reflecting on her good friends:

> Russell is the one who wrote to me, despite Audrey's reluctance (why?); and he's refrained from telling me what it is exactly that he fears. Is that because he thinks it best that I should come to my own conclusions when I finally see how people behave at the meeting at six o'clock this evening, or is it because he's changed his mind and regrets bothering me? He certainly seems to regret investing in the gold mine. It would be good to know how much he's committed and if Audrey knows the precise sum.

Maisie paused for a moment, then began a new paragraph.

> Audrey is quite unchanged and – though she sometimes seems impatient with Russell – she doesn't appear troubled, either by today's upsets or what the future might bring. Is that a function of age? Can she sort of 'see the finish line', perhaps a quiet room in the St Lawrence Residential Home, a place to knit and watch the cricket and ...

Maisie stopped writing, a faint frown on her face, screwing the lid back on her pen so the ink didn't dry out in the nib. She was thinking back to a decade before, remembering

Russell's dynamism but rather unfocused drive. Alongside her husband's directionless energy, Maisie could picture Audrey's indulgence, going along with Russell's plans, but not much bothered either way.

Coming back to the present, Maisie unscrewed her pen, made a note of what Audrey had said about elderly people disappearing 'like a river meeting the sea' then moved on.

> *Fred Luscombe is a desperate character, guilty – like so many people who have caring responsibilities – not necessarily because they've done something so very wrong, but because they're always exhausted, can never do enough and, therefore, they become impatient with their burden. But, of course, that burden has been lifted, whether by accident or design, and Holly . . .*

Maisie paused, her pen suspended above the paper. She put a full stop instead of a comma after 'design', crossed out the following few words and began a new paragraph for the deceased daughter.

> *If Holly got into some kind of trouble, it must surely have been because she was in the habit of gadding about very late, perhaps seeing things she oughtn't. For example, there's a rift between Norman Tubb and Shane Tope around Shane's role as an agricultural inspector – something to do with rats. Could Holly have discovered something about that? Might Norman resort to violence to prevent it becoming more widely known?*

She crossed the last sentence out as irrelevant because she knew from Stella that the contamination or whatever it was had already been 'reported to the ministry'.

Maisie shivered, remembering once again, out of the blue, the horrible scene from ten years before when she had seen Norman on the verge – so it seemed – of trying to physically shake some sense into his senile father. She thought about Stella asking her to forgive and forget and felt a pang of guilt, recalling Norman's criticism of her in the vestry of the church, accusing her of 'standing in judgement over others'.

In her imagination, Maisie ran through her interactions with Holly, wondering if she could possibly have said or done anything to encourage the poor woman to run away or go 'a-gallivanting' further than was her habit. She honestly didn't think she had.

> *Or might Holly have found the mine? Is that possible? Does it even exist? If so, is it so very important that the location remains secret – important enough to kill?*

Again, Maisie crossed out the last clause, thinking it foolish and melodramatic. She turned her mind to writing down what she knew of the Tubbs' home life, leading her to Stella's odd, yearning tone when speaking of the need for 'new blood' in an established herd.

> *I'm sure she was speaking for herself and the only newcomer, surely, that she could have been referring to is Patrick Linton who I saw trundling up the drive to the dairy in his Moore's van and who has, I think, a 'roving eye'.*

Almost against her better judgement, she added:

> *Unless Paul Linton is who she means. I've heard him out on his motorbike in the middle of the night, haven't I? Would Stella be foolish enough to entertain the idea of taking up with a boy only just out of school?*

The other residents of the five Trout Leap cottages didn't detain Maisie long. She had already mentioned Shane Tope, of course, so she took the time to ask herself a few written questions about the set-up in the Sturgess household, with the grandmother, Geraldine, passing herself off as Timothy's mother and Petunia longing for escape from rural isolation.

> *Might the mother and/or the daughter have the wit to fabricate the whole gold mine story out of thin air? Geraldine, yes; Petunia, no. Together, yes, obviously. And their respective occupations – seamstress and shop girl – will never make them financially secure.*

Maisie described the Sturgesses' neighbour in number two.

> *Poor Vera Pond is a lonely fusspot, by turns intimidated by and resentful of men, whose entire focus and zest for life – if she can honestly be said to have any – seems sublimated into her work as school secretary.*

Maisie added a note about what Vera had mumbled about her father's 'regrettable penchant for gambling'.

> *Did Vera inherit his debts?*

Even if she had, Maisie could see no way for that fact to involve anyone else on her list.

She realised she hadn't made any mention of Floyd Tubb. She made a note that he thought it 'clever to be rude' and that his blue eyes, long lashes and blond hair made him look more innocent than he probably was. She wondered if he'd been at school with Petunia who seemed the same age. She listed a few others about whom she had nothing of substance to add:

Herbert Peckham, editor of the Kirton Courier
Clive and Cherry Atwill, shopkeepers
Constable Jasper of the Kirton police
Canon Greig

Finally, she had only Vincent and Ida to add to her list, noting her vague disquiet:

> *Neither of them truly convinces me. Ida seems to have some unspoken purpose, but I can't say exactly what. Vincent often seems to be hiding what he's really thinking in pipe smoke and silence.*

She read over all she had written. It covered six sides of the letter-format writing paper in her tidy cursive hand. But, she judged, it all seemed to lead nowhere.

She folded the thick vellum-style pages over and slipped them all inside an envelope embossed by a printer, using a script-like typeface, with the address of the guest house: *Sunny View, Trout Leap, Near Kirton, Devon*. Distractedly, she inscribed the envelope to 'Jack Wingard, 147 Parklands Road, Chichester, West Sussex', realising as she did so that it was pointless. Jack wasn't in Chichester – would not be in Chichester for eight or nine weeks.

She took another sheet of paper and made a sketch of the hamlet of Trout Leap, including the railway line, Break Heart Hill, Sunny View and the dairy farm, plus the lanes and bridleways fanning out into the countryside beyond. Then, becalmed, she gazed out of the window, through the twigs of the copper beech, seeing the sky darkened by cloud and the passing of time.

She felt herself swamped by a wave of bittersweet nostalgia. She was missing her fiancé very deeply. She had an address for him in Newcastle, but that was no use without a telephone number. He had promised to call her from the hostel, once he was established, but that hadn't happened yet. She felt, inexplicably, terribly alone and sad, caught up in events that – as Norman Tubb had so forcefully argued – were categorically not her business.

They are, though. Russell wrote to me for help and I'm blowed if anyone's going to be able to accuse me of letting him down.

TWENTY-FIVE

Maisie told herself to buck up. Whether or not the events she had been drawn into at Sunny View were her business, Audrey and – especially – Russell had asked her for her help and she was obliged to provide it.

I'm not interfering. I'm responding to an appeal from old friends.

She went downstairs, wanting a cup of tea before they set out for the Masonic Hall and the meeting about the gold mine. Audrey was dozing in the front room with the cricket match still wending its way towards its low-key conclusion.

In the kitchen, Maisie put on the kettle, then found the tea towels and napkins and her white socks had been rinsed and were all lumped together in a metal colander in the sink. She took them outside and pegged them up on the line, noticing that the afternoon had become very close. She remembered what the ambulance driver had told Constable Jasper.

'She's fallen heavy and sudden up on Exmoor but there's nothing for the likes of us where we wants it so very bad.'

Looking up at the sky, she supposed he was right. There was a veil of cloud, but nowhere near enough to bring rain.

Russell emerged from the cider shed, looking ruffled and sleepy but pleased to see her, wanting to show her something.

'It's that nest I told you about, under the planks.'

He led her over the stile into the orchard and pulled aside the rough timbers that covered the manhole into the culvert. Sure enough, down in the dry gloom, Maisie could make out a handful of five or six slender slithering snakes, writhing in and around one another.

'Are they newborns?' she asked.

'Baby adders,' said Russell. 'I ought to get down there and kill them but I haven't got the heart.'

The whistle kettle summoned them back indoors. Audrey came through. Maisie made the tea and each took theirs with them to their rooms to get ready to go out, Maisie wanting her grey cardigan but otherwise just feeling the need to wash her face and hands and brush her curly hair. Doing so, her thoughts focused on whether there might have been enough rain on Exmoor to raise the level of the water in the Wivel.

That might change everything.

When she came back downstairs, Audrey was showing Ida how to operate the old-fashioned television, tuning it in with a dial to select the channels, a little like on a radio. There was copy of the *Radio Times* on the coffee table that she could consult to find out what was on offer.

'I'll be all right,' said Ida. 'You get along now.'

'I'm sorry this meeting can't be avoided,' Audrey apologised. 'Shall we bring you back some Chinese? They're the only one open on a Sunday evening but they do lovely pork balls with sweet-and-sour.'

'If it's all the same to you, I'll finish off my cobbler with some of that cream from Tubb's dairy farm. I won't need anything else.' She tittered. 'I can't speak for Mr Brent, however.'

'Is he back?' Maisie asked.

'Not that I'm aware of,' said Ida.

'Once I'd rinsed the tea towels, I fell fast asleep. I wouldn't have heard,' said Audrey apologetically.

There was a pause while Maisie – inevitably – began to feel a knot of anxiety, hoping Vincent hadn't come to any harm. The two older women looked vague.

Russell came clumping down the stairs, having added some kind of pomade or perhaps Brylcreem to his unruly hair. He told them he'd knocked at Vincent's door – 'Hannibal' – without reply.

'I tried the handle and found it locked.'

'Could he have shut himself in?' Maisie asked.

'We provide a key for each one. He might be in or out. If he's in, he's either asleep or concentrating so hard on something he's not noticed. It might be his maps.'

'What maps?' asked Maisie.

'He showed me. He's got three of those large-scale Ordnance Surveys for finding places round about where he's allowed to look for deer.'

'I see,' said Maisie, thoughtfully.

'What worries me, though,' said Audrey, 'is what will he have for his tea?'

'Don't trouble about that,' said Ida. 'If he doesn't know how to forage for himself, I'll help him and I expect we'll watch *The Good Old Days* together on the telly. I love the Black-and-White Minstrels. Don't they make you smile?'

Maisie began to feel impatient. Though she had picked up some interesting new fragments of information, there was somewhere – elsewhere – that she wanted to be.

'I have time to walk round by the river, don't I?'

'If you set off right away and don't dawdle,' Russell told her. 'Not that you're a dawdler. We laid that garden smooth this morning, didn't we?'

'We did, but I still feel I've not been out much and could do with the fresh air, especially now the evening's promising to be close.'

'Audrey and me will drive, though,' said Russell, 'and be on hand to bring you back after. You don't want to be walking down the lanes or across the fields in the dark.'

'I could take a torch and come back by the river?'

'Even so, maid.'

Maisie allowed herself to be persuaded because Russell seemed very concerned for her safety, going on at some length, discouraging her from walking home through the 'dimpsy' countryside alone. She tied her cardigan round her waist and set off, towards the Trout Leap cottages, but branching right just before them, over the stile and into the river field. Instead of clinging to the hedgerow, though, she crossed the tussocky pasture down to the river bend, the place where Timothy had embarked on his raft and where she had plucked Holly's lost shoe from the water.

This is a very far-fetched idea.

Coming in sight of the river, although the sky was veiled with high cloud, it was still broad daylight. The water looked as innocent and clear as ever. The cows on the far bank were placidly chewing their cud, taking no more than a passing interest in her presence.

Maisie picked her way down the slope to the river's edge, wondering if she was imagining that the river was running a little deeper and that the shallows were configured differently. She remembered the oil drums of Timothy's raft grating against the pebbles and thought that, were he there right now, he might have managed to manoeuvre without scraping the bottom.

Staying close to the red, undercut bank of Devon soil, she followed the current for five paces, managing to keep her sandals and her clean grey socks dry.

Am I merely convincing myself that there are more twigs and leaves floating past when, in reality, nothing has changed?

Then she saw it, trapped by the current on a sort of gravel mound in the midst of the flowing water – a length of worn

228

construction timber with a hole for a mortice-and-tenon joint at one end and two flat old-fashioned nails sticking out of the other.

Not so far-fetched after all.

The length of timber was about two feet long and too far away to reach out and grab, on the far side of a channel that ran at least a foot deep. But she was sure that she could see evidence of what it had been used for: dark blood congealed on the sharp corner by the mortice hole, with a few human hairs still adhering.

How can that be if it's been in the water all this time?

Maisie reconstructed, in her imagination, the likely sequence of events.

Whoever wielded this ancient length of hand-cut timber must have tossed it into the river, as I surmised, to get rid of it. It must have floated away out of sight and come to rest on a bank or a gravel mound, like this one, giving the blood time to dry. Later on, as the river rose with the rainwater coming down from Exmoor, the current tugged it back out into the stream, bringing it down to this river bend where the repeated shallows were always likely to beach it for a second time.

Maisie pictured the run of the river, as she had walked it upstream, under the humpbacked bridge, along the lawn of Sunny View and across the straight reach until she got to Norman Tubb's barbed-wire barrier. The timber might well have floated unimpeded all that distance.

Or maybe it's been here all along, even back when I met Timothy and helped him with his knots and found the buckle shoe? I didn't go searching. Why would I have? Or would Timothy have seen it? No, he was too busy getting under way.

Maisie sat down on a grassy part of the bank to take off her sandals and socks. Stepping into the water, running almost up to her knees, she was surprised by how cold it felt, compared to the heavy, warm evening. She paused, examining the timber, wondering how best to get it onto a dry part of the bank, perhaps sheltered from potential rain showers that might otherwise destroy the important evidence.

I can't very well carry it into town, but I mustn't miss the meeting.

She wanted very badly to hear everyone's point of view. Somehow, her stay at Sunny View had been building to this moment, six o'clock on Sunday evening.

Will Constable Jasper be there, I wonder? I hope so. That would be the easiest way for me to 'make my report'.

Maisie returned to dry land in her bare feet and searched the riverbank for a thin but sturdy stick. She found a length of hazel that she thought would do and stepped out into the fast-running channel once more, pushing the stick through the mortice hole, changing the angle in order to get some traction and hook the timber out of the stream without touching it. Gingerly, she turned, stepped onto the pebbly shore and lowered the timber carefully beneath an undercut bank of red dirt where it would be sheltered from any rain.

Satisfied that what she thought must be the murder weapon was sufficiently concealed, she climbed up onto the wiry grass of the field, using it to dry her feet, checking her watch, realising she was now at risk of being late.

With quick, efficient gestures, she pulled on her grey socks and tightened her sandals. She was so absorbed in her thoughts that the sound, when it occurred, took a moment or two to register. She raised her eyes, wondering if it had come from the cattle on the far bank, a heavy hoof treading on a twig and snapping it, for example. The direction, though, seemed to have been farther upriver, near one of the deeper pools where the trees grew more thickly, drinking deep from the generous water supply, creating thick cover.

Maybe it wasn't a broken stick? Maybe it was the sharp flap of a bird's wings?

She set off at a steady jog across the tussocky pasture to the hedge line and away past the place where Bertie the terrier had died in the collapsed rabbit burrow. She maintained her pace, ducking her head as the dragonfly swooped across the path.

A few minutes later, she reached the railway station, just in time to be frustratingly held by the gates as a train trundled out of Kirton station, on its way to Exeter. As soon as it was gone, the traffic gates opened and a pale-blue car pulled up alongside and wound down its window. It was Audrey in the passenger seat, encouraging her to get in, wondering why she had taken so long.

'I'll tell you later,' said Maisie, with a smile, then offered a white lie. 'Nothing sinister.'

She got in the back for the short uphill journey. Russell parked on a side street close to the St Lawrence Residential Home, opposite the police station. Before Maisie got out, she saw Constable Jasper, carrying a leatherette holdall, crossing the road on his way to the Masonic Hall where a small crowd of local people had assembled on the pavement. The keyholder appeared to be the newspaper editor, Herbert Peckham, in white shirtsleeves and braces as if he had just come from his office.

I don't want to wait till after the meeting to speak to Seth.

Trying to lock the car, Russell dropped his keys in the gutter. Once he'd retrieved them, Maisie saw that his hands were not quite steady. She wanted to ask him what the trouble was, but she thought she knew. In any case, there was no more time. He was walking away, his head bowed, with Audrey at his side.

My poor old friends.

Before she followed them across the road, Maisie thought back to the sound she had heard, back at the river bend, the sharp noise that had broken into her thoughts as she dried her feet and put on her socks and sandals. Reliving the moment in memory, she realised that there was a fragment of knowledge that – at the time – she hadn't allowed fully to crystallise.

There was someone there, watching me.

TWENTY-SIX

Maisie was interested to see the interior of the Masonic Hall for a second time. She knew there were many people who were wary or distrustful of freemasonry as a pointlessly secretive organisation that attracted men with a predilection for special handshakes and odd customs of dressing up. She had the advantage, from living in Paris, that the 'order' in France was much more open than the obscure English version. Senior French masons were acknowledged for their organisation's charitable work and their opinions were canvassed on important social and political issues. In England, her impression was that the secrecy constituted, for many members, a fundamental part of the charm – which seemed to her rather childish, like little boys devising arbitrary passwords for controlling access to their treehouses.

The Masonic Hall in Kirton didn't resemble a treehouse. It resembled a large, stolid double-fronted house, with nothing to suggest it was a grand place of worship or conspiracy. Set back only a few feet from the pavement, it was built in red brick and the front door and windows were all surrounded by pale stonework, smudged grey with dust and traffic fumes. Maisie had been in once before, to the robing room on the ground floor, the building having been opened for the town fête ten years back, providing her with somewhere to change into her swimsuit before being paraded round the streets – against her better judgement.

The spacious meeting room occupied the entire first floor, accessed by a landing at the top of the stairs from which it was separated by two solid oak doors. The ceremonial chamber was not especially impressive, apart from the lovely chequer-board floor. The ceiling was insulated with ugly polystyrene tiles and the seating reclaimed from an abandoned cinema – plush tip-up chairs in dusty and faded red velvet, arranged in traverse, north and south, with three wooden 'thrones' at the west end.

Maisie found most people on their feet, milling about, with drinks in their hands. Russell had one of his large clay cider jugs grasped firmly in both fists and was making a determined circuit, serving and topping up, with Audrey beside him carrying an emptying tray of glasses. Maisie looked for Constable Jasper, hoping to draw him aside to tell him what she had discovered, but couldn't see him.

Maisie checked her watch. It was gone six but no one seemed in any hurry to commence proceedings. She wondered if they were waiting for someone in particular to arrive and frowned as she went through her mental checklist of friends and neighbours of Sunny View. Doing so, she regretted that she hadn't thought to try and contrive a way for Ida and Vincent to be present, in order to gauge their reactions to all that was said. She knew that, in a large gathering, people often found it difficult to consistently mask their emotions, some of which could then be read on their faces.

She fell into conversation with Geraldine and Petunia Sturgess, asking them straight out if they had invested in the mine.

'I put in my savings,' said Petunia, guilelessly. 'I had twenty-eight pounds.'

'I topped it up to the round thirty and matched the sum myself,' said her mother.

'We both did it on Timothy's behalf,' said Petunia. 'We thought it might serve him well if . . .' She stopped, looking uncertain. 'Well, you know.'

Maisie smiled and told her: 'I hope it works out.'

Geraldine was frowning. Maisie thought it was because Petunia had almost absent-mindedly spoken of Timothy as her son, rather than her brother.

Thirty pounds is a lot of money for many people. But surely not enough to commit murder?

Canon Greig came in, looking sheepish, as if he feared that he was advertising his own sinful behaviour to his flock. He spoke with a half-smile to Herbert Peckham, his eyes darting round the room. The newspaper editor replied with a very serious expression and Maisie wished she could hear what they were saying to one another, but Geraldine was making that impossible by telling a complicated story about how little people were prepared to pay for pattern-cutting and sewing up.

Russell came by with his cider jug, offering to top up their glasses. Knowing how strong his home-made scrumpy was, Maisie demurred while the others accepted. She saw Cherry and Clive Atwill arrive and wondered if they were the late-comers whose attendance seemed to be delaying the start of the meeting. It seemed not, however, as they both took a drink and sat down in two of the recycled cinema seats, looking like they regretted being there as much as Canon Greig. Maisie excused herself to Geraldine and Petunia and went to sit next to them, greeting them warmly – especially Clive who she hadn't seen since she'd been back – then chose a different gambit.

'When did you first find out about the mine?'

'Poor Holly, though,' said Cherry, ignoring her question. 'What a thing to happen. It just shows, you have to look out and no one knows what's waiting for them just around

235

the corner.' Cherry shook her head in appalled disbelief. 'And you were simply out walking and found her where she fell and banged her head?'

Maisie wasn't sure how much the Atwills knew, so she commiserated and reassured them that the experience of finding Holly's corpse hadn't been 'too bad', that she had seen worse in the army. She repeated her enquiry.

'We got to know about it like everyone else,' Clive told her, speaking across his wife. 'There was the article in the *Kirton Courier* and, then, the next week, the advertisement.'

Maisie thought there was something shifty in Clive's eye.

'So, Herbert Peckham is the person at the heart of it?'

'Yes, well, no. I mean, I think Herbie just received the information and published it, like we might place an advert when we get in a new line of stock.'

'But when you place an advertisement, you are known to Mr Peckham. I get the impression that the share issue was anonymous?'

'I've asked him about that. There wasn't a named person, if that's what you mean.'

'How did you all submit your investments?'

'By postal order sent to an address in London.'

Maisie didn't say so, but she thought that sounded very unwise. A postal order wasn't like a cheque with a named person as creditor. It was almost like sending cash, redeemable at a post office, and couldn't be traced, therefore, either for its sender or its recipient.

'Do you remember where precisely you sent the money in London?' asked Maisie, thinking about both Ida's and Vincent's distinctive accents.

'It was a post office box – I remember that,' said Cherry.

Maisie couldn't help a note of exasperation entering her voice. 'Did that not seem odd to you, that you didn't have either a name or a proper address?'

'We did have the name of the company,' said Cherry, sounding aggrieved.

'Oh, good. That could be important,' said Maisie. 'What's it called?'

'Auraria Ltd.'

Maisie got Cherry to spell the name, then she repeated it: 'Auraria Ltd – Latin for gold mine, in fact.'

'Yes, Russ said,' Cherry agreed. 'And everyone invested. We all agreed that it was a wonderful opportunity.'

'You encouraged one another and shared your optimism. But what do you think now?'

Clive looked sheepish. 'We don't know what to think except that it's all gone a bit quiet.'

'You've had no news from this company, Auraria Ltd?'

'There was a date for opening up the mine for inspection.'

'And that date has passed?'

'Couple of weeks, now,' said Clive.

'I see.'

That probably coincides with when Russell wrote to me.

Clive pursed his lips. 'You were always a bright spark. What would you have done, Maisie?'

'I'm not sure,' she answered, though she hoped she would have taken more steps to investigate where she was sending her hard-earned savings. 'I wasn't here.'

'It was like the tulips,' said Cherry, surprisingly. 'You know, in the seventeenth century, when everyone went piling in. I read about it in the *Reader's Digest* magazine.'

Maisie knew the story. It was usually referred to as the 'tulip mania'. For a brief period, the bulbs of the colourful spring flowers became more valuable than gold or another contemporary Dutch craze, coffee. Then, their prices suddenly collapsed as people saw through the madness.

'A speculative bubble,' said Maisie. 'You all wanted to get on board because you all seemed to want to get on board.'

'I wish,' said Clive, 'that you'd been here to say that out loud when it started.'

'But what was the foundation for everyone's enthusiasm?' Maisie asked.

'I'm sorry to say it was your good friend and mine.' He glanced towards Russell, who was on the far side of the room, serving Geraldine and Petunia who had sat in the front row of dusty red-velvet seats opposite. 'It was a thing Russ used to talk about. You know, he's always on about history and generals and the Romans and all the rest of it? The tale of the legions finding gold in the valleys round Kirton two thousand years ago was one he liked to tell and, because he banged on about it, it became like a fairy story that no one quite believed in. But then, when it appeared in the newspaper, it sort of . . .' Clive stopped, his eyes becoming vague, as if he was trying to remember exactly what came next. 'It sort of crystallised.'

'People just started talking more and more about it,' said Cherry. 'When the advert came out, everyone saw it and could speak of little else, meaning it seemed silly not to . . .'

She, too, stopped, uncertain or perhaps embarrassed to express what she meant.

'It snowballed,' said Maisie. 'Every mention made it seem more real until it became fact, not speculation.' Neither of them answered. The hubbub in the room was still quite loud. Maisie asked: 'When I dropped in to the shop yesterday, you were out fishing, Clive. Where do you go, usually?'

'I have a permit from Norman Tubb for the upper reaches of the Wivel.'

'And were you out on Friday as well?' Maisie asked, thinking about Holly.

'Why do you want to know that?' he asked her with an edge to his voice.

'I was just making conversation,' said Maisie, intrigued by his defensive tone.

'Not because you're checking up on me?'

'Now, Clive,' said Cherry. 'Why would you be saying that?'

'Maisie's a private investigator, isn't she?' he asked.

'Who on earth told you that?' Maisie asked, exasperated.

'Well, it was Russ, wasn't it, showing us the pages from the newspapers that he had Herbie send down from that Sussex.'

'I'm not anything of the kind,' said Maisie. 'It's like the tulips and – dare I say it – like this frankly unbelievable story of a gold mine. The truth is, I've been present where a number of mysterious events have taken place and, quite by chance, I've had information that's been useful to the real investigators, the police. Nothing more. Out of that, the fanciful idea that I'm a professional investigator . . .'

She stopped, leaving her thought incomplete as Cherry and Clive had both done, fully aware of how it must look from the outside. She had been present at the scenes of several crimes. She had a close association with the Chichester police. She had provided crucial testimony in several criminal prosecutions. And now, here she was, turning up at Sunny View just when—

'These glasses are all empty then,' said Russell, jovially, looming over them with his heavy cider jug. 'How about I refresh them?'

Cherry and Clive accepted but Maisie put a hand over the top of hers.

'Did Constable Jasper come in?' she asked.

'Yes, he's here somewhere,' said Russell. 'Perhaps in the robing room downstairs, getting out of his uniform for being off-duty.'

'I see. What are we waiting for, by the way? Wasn't the meeting due to start at six?'

'Six for six-thirty,' said Russell. 'We've still got a few minutes to get comfortable.'

He moved on. Maisie excused herself and crossed the room to reintroduce herself to the Topes.

'How is Deborah? No more scares with the cows, I hope? I almost got into a scrape with the two bulls in the west pasture, you know, down the railway line?'

Maisie hadn't meant her words to provoke the Topes' curiosity about Holly, but they did. In her replies, she encouraged them in their supposition – already shared with the Atwills on the far side of the chequerboard floor – that Fred Luscombe's daughter's death had been an accident.

'I take it you've invested in the mine as well?' she asked, making her voice light.

'We have,' said Shane Tope. 'But no more than we can afford. We're not gamblers so we've not wagered any more than we can safely lose.'

'We'd rather not lose, though,' said Jane.

'No, we wouldn't,' agreed Shane whose right fist, Maisie noticed, was clenched tight around his glass.

'This cider is delicious,' said Maisie. 'Apples are the real treasure of the West Country, don't you think? And the rich green grass bringing forth good milk and butter and cream. You must know the countryside well in your work as an agricultural inspector?'

'I go to the farms,' said Shane, an intelligent gleam in his eye. 'But I think I see what you're getting at.'

'You do?' asked Maisie.

'You're wondering if I might have a clue to the location of the mine if I'm out and about in all weathers to all parts.'

Maisie smiled and agreed: 'I suppose I was.'

He shook his head and told her: 'I drive to the farmhouses and the barns and collect samples and send them for analysis. I get the forms filled out properly – and that's no easy task with all the red tape we're tied up in and it'll be worse next year once we go into Europe, you mark my words – then I'm back at my desk in Exeter. I've no time to be exploring the nooks and crannies of forgotten vales.'

'That makes sense. Why would you? But you must have an inkling?'

'How many of us,' said Shane, measuring his words, 'still believe that it exists?'

'What do you mean?'

'Just this. If, as seems every day more and more likely, it's all a hoax and it's not really out there,' he told her, holding her gaze, 'how would you find it?'

He almost sounds as if he's made up his mind. When his suspicions are confirmed, what will he do?

'Miss Cooper?' Jane began, breaking in to her thoughts.

'Yes?'

'If we've all been duped, can you use your connections with the police to get someone more senior to take an interest?' She gestured to the doorway where Seth Jasper had just shuffled in, wearing jeans, a denim shirt and a sleeveless crew-necked jumper. 'Is he up to it, do you think?'

'I'd say no,' said Shane. His gaze shifted to Russell. 'Russ looks in a state. I hope he doesn't have a funny turn.'

'Audrey's sticking close to him with the worry,' said Jane.

'And look at Stella Tubb,' said Shane. 'Talk about a rose between two thorns.'

Maisie followed his gaze. Stella was sitting between her husband and son, but that wasn't what had caught her attention. Rather it was the unabashed nosiness in Shane and Jane's conversation. It sounded almost malicious.

Is that true? Or am I just on edge myself?

'Will you excuse me?' asked Maisie.

She got up and crossed the room to the far end. The hubbub was considerably quieter as the majority of friends and neighbours had taken their seats as six-thirty approached.

'Constable Jasper,' she said quietly, 'could I speak to you for a moment?'

'What is it?' he asked, without much curiosity.

'Please come with me,' she insisted, without raising her voice, giving him the bright smile she used when she needed to be persuasive. 'It's extremely important, regarding last night's business. It will only take a moment.'

'Can't it wait?'

'No,' she told him, surprising him by taking his arm in order to lead him outside to the landing. 'The sooner the better.'

TWENTY-SEVEN

'Here you are then,' said Russell, loudly. 'That's everyone.'

With a small sigh of frustration, Maisie let go of Constable Jasper's arm and turned to see who he meant. Patrick Linton had pushed the double oak doors open, looking tall and lean and handsome in a narrow, out-of-date 1960s suit in charcoal grey, accompanied by Fred Luscombe who was shabbily attired in his faded British Rail uniform. Patrick apologised for their lateness, announcing: 'Marthese had to get some tea ready and set up Paul and Maria for babysitting Timothy Sturgess and Deborah Tope, watching telly next door. We fetched Fred and came the long way round before being held at the gates for two trains.'

'Never mind,' Russell reassured him. 'You're here now. We can get started.' He addressed the room more generally, making Maisie uncomfortable by using a Cold-War phrase that referenced the imminence of an atom bomb attack. 'Shall we say that's our four-minute warning?'

Audrey approached with three or four remaining glasses. Patrick and Fred both accepted and drank. A small, diffident woman with mousy hair and a nervous expression followed them into the room, wearing a summer dress with a long loose-knit cardigan over the top. Maisie recognised her from the church as the person Patrick had referred to as Marthese, his wife, from whom neither Paul nor Maria had inherited anything apart from their darker skin tone. Maisie remembered their athletic, upright physiques, just like their father. Weak and weary-looking, Marthese refused the cider.

Seth Jasper had slipped away. Russell was talking in a forced avuncular tone, rattling on, hiding his nervousness in chatter. Neither Fred nor Patrick seemed to be listening until he mentioned Vincent Brent.

'Who's that?' asked Fred.

'One of our paying guests.'

Fred's eyes returned to the tiles of the floor and he held out his glass for an immediate refill. Patrick's gaze flicked round the room, coming to rest on Stella Tubb, seated in the back row of velvet seats between Norman and Floyd. Maisie was struck once more by Stella's inescapable charm and a kind of radiant energy that seemed to envelop her, even including her unprepossessing son and her heavy and hot-tempered husband with his riot of dark-blond hair and whiskers.

'Come on then,' said Seth Jasper, reappearing at her elbow. 'If it's that important.'

Maisie led him out onto the landing, carefully closing the two oak doors, sealing them off from the mediocre ceremonial chamber. With no one within earshot, she told him about her rationale – how she had imagined the rise in water levels on the Wivel and the possibility that the heavy rain on Exmoor might have delivered another piece of evidence to the river bend, the place where Holly's shoe had beached.

'The reach of the river to the west of Sunny View runs very free and straight. The only stretches where a buoyant object should end up stuck are between Sunny View and the pasture by the Trout Leap cottages. West of the humpbacked bridge, it's hard to get down to the edge because there are so many trees, so I suppose it was caught up there in some undergrowth or on a ledge. I was lucky,' she explained.

'How were you lucky?' he asked. 'You're not making sense.'

Mentally, Maisie acknowledged that she was talking in circles and told him what she had found.

'It's a length of ancient construction timber with what looks to me like dried blood and several human hairs, the right colour to have come from Holly's head. Now, if that's right, we know it must have gone into the water . . .' She stopped in order to calculate. 'Well, more than thirty-six hours ago. Isn't that right? In which case it must have found a dry spot where the blood and hairs adhering to the grain of the wood weren't washed off.' She described how she had removed the timber from the gravelly mound without touching it with her hands and how she'd hidden it below the undercut bank, concluding: 'I imagine you will want to secure it as evidence and put it somewhere safe.'

'I will,' he told her, his expression a combination of gravity and nervousness. 'Does anyone else know about this?'

'No,' said Maisie. 'I went down to look on my own and haven't told a soul. It changes everything, though, doesn't it?'

'It does.' He bit his lip. Maisie wondered if he was contemplating drawing her into his investigation. Eventually, he sighed and said: 'I don't know what to say to you, Miss Cooper.'

What does that mean?

'I'm extremely discreet, Constable. You can have confidence in me. Do you want me to take you there now?'

'We could, I suppose.'

'Although it might cause unnecessary and unwelcome comment.' He didn't answer. She asked: 'Do you want to tell me what's in your mind?'

'What if I've not got the right?' he complained in a worried tone, almost as if talking to himself. 'What if I've got orders?'

'Orders concerning me?' asked Maisie, surprised.

'Why should it be about you?' he retorted, impatiently, then changed the subject. 'Is Mr Brent coming?'

'Why would Vincent be here?'

'I don't know. Taking an interest?'

245

'Not as far as I'm aware, unless Russell has invited him for reasons of his own, without telling me. He didn't accompany us. I suppose he might have made his own way.'

'Has he spoken to you?' asked Seth Jasper.

'Vincent? About what?'

'He was there, wasn't he? He saw what happened to Holly. What was his opinion?'

'Actually, I haven't seen him since lunch. He's been out ever since. Did you get his photographs printed?'

'The shop was shut with a note on the door to say that they're away for their week's summer holiday.'

'Oh, that's a shame,' said Maisie.

Or is it? The photos were just a formal record, weren't they? Neither Constable Jasper nor I actually saw any clues that needed to be recorded.

Maisie thought about Russell trying Vincent's bedroom door and wondered if he had done so for a more concrete reason than wanting to know: *What will he have for his tea?*

'Hang on,' said Seth. 'He's been out all this time and no one's seen hide nor hair of him?'

'That's right,' said Maisie, lost in her own foggy thoughts. 'I mean, just since lunch.'

I'm missing something.

'Did he leave a note?'

'Not that I'm aware of.'

Why would Vincent be out all afternoon? Could he have gone fishing? No, he's a hunter, not an angler.

She heard Russell's loud voice calling his meeting to order.

'We should go back in,' she said.

'All right,' said Constable Jasper. 'I'll give you a lift back after and you can show me the place.'

'That might arouse just as much unwanted attention as disappearing right now,' said Maisie. 'I'll go back with the Savages as planned and meet you at Sunny View.'

'Fine. Have it your own way.'

'Before we go back in, are you an investor in Auraria Ltd, too?'

'I'm here, aren't I? What do you think?'

Despite his repeated truculence, Maisie was beginning to feel some sympathy for Seth Jasper. He was overworked because of his sergeant's absence in hospital and had the same anxiety as everyone else about having been duped by what she could only think of as 'the gold-mine scam'.

She told him: 'Don't worry. The evidence I told you about is quite out of sight. It will still be there later on.'

She remembered the noise in the undergrowth and the uncertain impression that she had been seen.

At least, I hope it will.

Looking reassured and even a little grateful, Constable Jasper nodded and pushed open one of the two oak doors, standing aside to allow Maisie to go through first. She chose a seat close at hand, at the end of the front row, from which she thought she would be able to turn and see every face. Constable Jasper was on the verge of sitting next to her but she gave him a tiny shake of the head. He understood and took up a position two rows behind her, at the back.

He's under pressure but he's no fool. All the same, if Holly's murderer is in this room, it's for the best if he and I don't look like we're a team.

Russell was making a final circuit, refilling glasses. Maisie noticed that there were now three clay jugs on the floor beside the big wooden thrones, meaning some of those present would be tipsy, at the least. Russell put the fourth jug beside the others and sat down in the largest carved seat.

Herbert Peckham was already alongside him in a slightly smaller – but equally ornate – chair. The editor stood up, adjusting his braces and the cuffs of his white shirt, preparing to address the meeting. In the time it took for everyone to stop talking and focus their eyes upon him, Maisie felt oddly like she had in the train, when it had started moving without her expecting it, carried forward into an uncertain future, not of her own volition, with no choice but to accept.

'Thank you all for being here,' Herbert began. 'Given this is, after all, the Masonic Hall, it is fitting that we should begin with a few words from one of our most distinguished members, who accepted the laureateship of the Nobel organisation, but declined that of the British monarch. I refer, of course, to Rudyard Kipling.'

He paused and Russell stood up to declaim:

> *'We Masons prize that noble truth, the Scottish peasant told,*
> *That rank is but a guinea stamp: the man himself the gold.*
> *We meet the rich and poor alike, the equal rights maintain,*
> *Happy to meet, sorry to part, happy to meet again.'*

Maisie half-expected everyone to say 'amen'. She wondered if either Herbert or Russell had chosen the verse for its suggestion that the people around you represent 'the gold', just as she had suggested to the Topes that it was the apples and the green grass. Then the editor was speaking once more.

'It is also right that Canon Greig should provide an opening prayer.'

The priest was in the seats on the opposite side of the room from Maisie, among six or seven residents of Kirton that she didn't know, presumably also investors in the mine. He stood up to deliver a paragraph of words he knew by heart. Maisie was interested to hear that they were strongly flavoured with Masonic ritual.

'Dear Father, Great Architect of the Universe, fount of all gifts and graces, we rejoice in Thy promise: "Where two or three are gathered together in Thy name, Thou wilt be in their midst, and bless them." We beseech Thy blessing on all our doings.'

This time, there was an 'amen' while Maisie pondered if it was really appropriate for the priest to be invoking God's assistance in such base and earthly 'doings'.

'Thank you, Canon Greig,' said Herbert. 'Now, Russell has asked us all here this evening to discuss—'

'We know that,' interrupted Norman Tubb from the rear of the room. 'Enough shilly-shallying. We wants to know what you've found out, Herbie.'

'What I've found out . . .' said Herbert, looking taken aback.

'Haven't you been looking into things?' Norman insisted, lounging in his recycled cinema seat, his heavy frame pinned between the arms.

'I have, I believe,' said Herbert, 'shared with you, most of you, the sequence of events, as I understand them.'

'Not with me,' said Norman. 'And speak up. We can't all be craning in to catch what you're saying, always assuming it's worth listening to in the first place.'

Herbert cleared his throat. Russell gave him a nod and said: 'Happen we could hear it from the start and make sure we're all on the same page.'

Herbert spoke more loudly. 'The sequence of events is as follows. I received information in the form of a press release, which is quite normal, quite common, addressed to me at the *Kirton Courier*, providing the content of the article that you all have read. I had no reason to doubt its authenticity and took the trouble to verify its gist with Mr Savage who is a student of these things.'

'You mean you took Russ's word for it that it was genuine?' asked Shane Tope, politely but firmly. 'You took no other steps to confirm the information, as a journalist should?'

'The news was valid,' said the editor, looking uncertain. 'As I said, a press release from a limited company is a normal—'

'I've got your article with me,' said Norman, taking a scrap of folded newsprint out of his waistcoat pocket, screwing up his eyes to read. 'Here 'tis. The mine will "put Kirton back on the map" with "results that must be taken seriously" and we "must all be very excited". You call it an "unforeseen manna". That's why we're here today, because you've gulled every one of us.'

'Done up like kippers,' said Floyd, unexpectedly, reminding Maisie of Vincent's London colloquialisms.

'As I said,' the editor insisted, 'it is quite normal to print a story based on such a press release. A small concern such as the *Kirton Courier* cannot run teams of juniors, fact-checking every item that crosses my desk. And no one, not one of you, came to me to question the veracity of the article.' He left a brief silence for this to sink in and Maisie saw that his assertion must be true, because no one disputed it. Herbert resumed: 'And then, when the advertisements were placed in the following two editions, it was for you all to make your own judgements with respect to the probity of investing, of buying shares.' He mumbled something and Norman told him to speak up once more. '*Caveat emptor,*' said Herbert more distinctly, then translated the Latin phrase. 'Buyer beware.'

Norman stood up, readying himself to make a speech. Russell didn't let him, however, cutting him off by announcing from his carved throne: 'I know what you're going to say, Norman Tubb. The same things you said to me when I came up to have a chat in your kitchen when you summoned me like a naughty schoolboy and I didn't kick up a fuss, though I might have, the way you laid it all at my door.'

'And with good reason—'

'Sit down, sit down,' said Russell in a surprisingly strong and authoritative voice. Norman did so with a shake of the head. Russell resumed: 'I came up good-neighbourly to take on the chin whatever you had to say but it's not my fault that you, many of you, asked me about the gold the Romans found. And that's a matter of fact and public record, academic record, pieced together by men with their noses deep in books a sight too difficult for you and I. But, yes, I'll admit, and happily, that I regret ever opening my mouth on the subject, now all's gone quiet and it looks like we've been – what was the word you used? – gulled. Me and Audrey not the least among you. Let me broadcast it out loud. I did it behind my wife's back and how do you suppose I feel? Sick to my stomach with the guilt and the shame.' Audrey, who was sitting on his opposite side from Herbert, put a hand on his shoulder, but he stood up and shook it off. 'That's not what we're here for. We've come together to think about what next, not what's gone afore. And I've a plan.'

'What is it, then?' growled Norman.

'We should make a list of all the investments everyone's made and, if you all can, which you should be able if you've been prudent, show the receipts for the postal orders so it can all be verified and tidy. Then, we should get a lawyer and an investigator and the police to take a proper interest – no offence, Seth, it's not for you to deal with such things. I know that, we all know that – so that's why I wrote to Maisie, there, and she'll have ideas perhaps of who we can approach.'

Russell sat down and, very uncomfortably, Maisie saw that all eyes were now upon her. There was a long moment when she contemplated refusing to get any more involved. The expression of urgent appeal on both Russell's and Audrey's faces changed her mind.

She stood, because she thought that would be the best way to speak without being interrupted, and immediately had a flash-back to the patrician Lady Catherine Peahorn of Bitling Village in Sussex, reminding her in haughty tones not to 'gabble'.

'I think it would be a good idea, Russell, to review in more detail how you all got to this point. I'm not sure that I can help, but I do have some contacts in the Sussex police force and a very good lawyer, Maurice Ryan. If he cannot help himself, he will at least be able to advise on the next steps. I will happily call Maurice on the telephone tomorrow morning, if you really think it will be useful. In the first instance, though, could we just establish how many of you sent postal orders to the PO box in London?' After a pause, every hand went up, except for Audrey and Stella and several other wives who, Maisie supposed, considered themselves represented in their husbands' gestures. Maisie went on. 'Thank you. Now, this will seem indelicate, but have any of you borrowed in order to invest?'

'What's that got to do with anything?' demanded Floyd Tubb.

Maisie smiled at him, not wanting to cause any more upset.

'In the Great Crash – in fact, in any financial crisis – one of the biggest accelerators is always from people borrowing to buy shares, with the misplaced confidence that future dividends will allow them to meet the repayments. When the market turns and shares begin to decline, the dividends dwindle and the whole speculative bubble collapses. People lose their jobs, their homes, even their lives.'

'But why should we tell you?' insisted Floyd.

'There is no "should". I'm simply offering the suggestion that you all pool knowledge to share with people much better equipped than I to help you. That is what you want, isn't it: for me to find you professional and legal assistance? That's why I came so quickly when I received Russell's letter, requesting my visit.'

'When was that?' asked Patrick Linton.

'It was when things went quiet,' said Russell. 'I told you, Paddy. When there were no more adverts and no receipts for payments were forthcoming and, one after another, you all came asking me what I was going to do about it as if it was my idea in the first place, instead of me being a bystander like the rest of you, and hadn't I chipped in more money than we can afford myself?'

Russell sat down heavily and allowed Audrey to put a consoling hand on his shoulder without shaking it off. It struck Maisie that none of the women – except her – had spoken since the beginning of the formal part of the meeting and wondered if there was a kind of invisible barrier in the air, because the Masonic Hall was used to receiving all-male congregations.

'Perhaps it might be a good idea,' she proposed, 'for someone trustworthy to collect all the information and put it together in a single document. You might all submit your details – including the size of your investments and any borrowings – to that one person, who would have the knowledge alone, collate it and seal it in an envelope for me to hand over.'

'Why don't you do it?' Russell asked.

'It would be better, I think, if it's one of those most closely affected.'

Russell nodded.

'Fair enough. Vera should do that. She's got the brains for it.'

All eyes turned to the school secretary, sitting at the far end of the room in the front row, entirely alone, separated by two empty seats from Geraldine and Petunia Sturgess, a large tan handbag lying on its side on her knees. Several people made noises of approval.

'Would you do that, Miss Pond?' asked Maisie.

Vera's eyes darted round the room, her hands clasped over the ends of her armrests. Geraldine reached over with her long arm and touched Vera's white knuckles, giving her a smile but not speaking, which Maisie found rather touching.

'Miss Pond,' said Herbert Peckham, in his habitual fussy tone, 'you are equipped by your profession and by your Christian name, from the Latin, meaning "trust" or "truth".'

Maisie didn't think that was true. As far as she knew, 'Vera' was a Russian name popularised by nineteenth-century novels with characters like the compelling Vera Rostov in *War and Peace*. She didn't argue, however.

'If you're willing, Vera,' said Russell, 'we could do it this evening, write things down, all of us. There's paper and pens in the office downstairs, next to the robing room. We can fetch it up in a jiffy.'

He waited.

'Well, I'm not sure,' said Vera in a small voice, clutching up her large tan handbag like a shield.

'It would be no more than an extension of the organising you do at the grammar school,' said Herbert.

'It's for the good of all,' said Russell. 'What do you say then?'

'If you are sincerely asking and if you are all agreed?' Vera asked.

'We are,' said Russell to a slightly more emphatic chorus of agreement.

'Then, yes,' said Vera, looking slightly smug.

'Now, then, just a minute,' called Norman. 'What about the maid's idea for telling it all out here and now?' he asked, referring to Maisie. 'Are you trying to skip over that?'

'I think,' said Maisie, 'on reflection, that we should leave that to the official investigator, in the fullness of time. I apologise for suggesting it. I was putting the cart before the horse.'

'Good,' said Russell, with an air of relief. 'Let's do what we've said and we can all be on our way.'

'I'll fetch the necessary,' said Seth Jasper, who clearly knew the Masonic Hall well, crossing the chequerboard floor and pushing out through the double doors. Because the room was stuffy on the warm overcast summer evening, Maisie followed and pinned the doors back on shiny brass hooks at ankle height. Behind her, conversations became general, divided into seven or eight clumps, mostly made up of family members but some across friendship groups. She wished she could listen to all of them, one at a time, instead of merely overhearing snatches from each.

'I knew there was something funny about it.'

'This is a right kerfuffle.'

'How was anyone supposed to know?'

'Is it true that Miss Cooper can sort it out?'

Maisie noticed that Shane and Jane Tope were not talking, that they were gripped by the same thought as she, paying close attention to what was being said, eavesdropping in several directions at once.

They really are wickedly nosy.

Shane felt her gaze and turned towards her. She recognised the gleam of intelligence in his eye as he said: 'We will simply have to hope that everyone tells the truth.'

Maisie moved closer to him and asked: 'I don't think Jim Moore is here, you know, the man who runs the garage?'

'No,' said Shane. 'Jim's one of the few not to have been tempted.'

Seth Jasper came back upstairs with two lined A4 notepads, like those used by students. He gave Maisie a handful of cheap Biros and began tearing off sheets to pass round. Maisie distributed the ballpoint pens and all the friends and neighbours dispersed to private corners to note down their names, their addresses and the moneys they mostly – Maisie thought – couldn't afford to lose.

She thought about how Jack would be keeping a beady eye on every one of them, looking out for hints of self-doubt or suspicious glances.

This is my chance. They're under a kind of pressure. Someone, I hope, is going to give themselves away.

TWENTY-EIGHT

Maisie watched the residents of Kirton and Trout Leap annotating their unwise investments in the – surely imaginary – gold mine, some resting their sheets of paper on their handbags, others using their cheque books balanced on the narrow arms of their recycled cinema seats. Russell called out: 'Write very clear, friends, perhaps in capital letters.'

Maise waited, thinking that the atmosphere in the drab ceremonial chamber at the Masonic Hall was somewhere between a beetle drive, a public examination and a polling station. Everyone was trying to work in private but everyone also kept glancing round the room to see what the others were up to. And, like in an election – where a single cross has to be consigned to a slip of official paper – it actually took very little time for people to write out their details, fold their sheet of A4 paper twice over to conceal the information, and hand it to Vera Pond.

To give the nervous – but also self-important – school secretary some moral support, Maisie stood close by while the sheaf of folded papers grew in Vera's hands. At the same time, she noticed that people were leaving, again like voters who had discharged their civic responsibilities in the election booth and were glad to be on their way home for their tellies and their tea.

While all this was going on, Maisie was thinking about her checklist. Everyone on it, after all, was or had been present. At the same time, she felt a hard knot of anxiety tightening beneath her diaphragm.

Only Constable Jasper and I know – or believe we know – that Holly was murdered. And I alone have seen the murder weapon.

She remembered a conversation with Jack's colleague, Inspector Fred Nairn, halfway through the investigation into the murder at Chichester Festival Theatre, warning her to be careful.

'And, as we say in the force, crime causes crime. One bad deed leads to another, if you see what I mean.'

Maisie had seen what he meant and, of course, his prediction had come true. A second murder had taken place, live in front of a theatre audience of twelve hundred souls, a mystery in plain sight that she had helped to solve.

Patrick Linton approached, gave Vera his piece of folded paper and said: 'Thank you for taking on this responsibility, Miss Pond.'

Vera embarked on a verbose reply and Maisie took advantage to speak to Patrick's wife who was standing self-effacingly behind his right shoulder, as if hiding.

'Mrs Linton, we've not been introduced. I'm Maisie Cooper, a friend of the Savages. Perhaps Paul or Maria mentioned that I met them yesterday at the ice-cream van in town? They're very handsome young people. You must be very proud.'

Mrs Linton's nervous face softened and her eyes creased into a gratified smile.

'Thank you, Miss Cooper,' she replied, her foreign intonation noticeable even in that short phrase.

'Mr Linton, please accept my sympathy,' said Maisie, turning to Patrick. 'What an upheaval to have to go through. Did you have any idea it was coming?'

'You mean the expulsion from Malta?' he asked, his expression grave.

'Yes. I have friends in Sussex who experienced something similar, just a couple of years ago, losing everything, homes and livelihoods. They're of Indian descent, expelled from Kenya.'

'Everyone's just trying to get by,' he told her. 'Mr and Mrs Savage have their paying guests, for example.'

'True.'

'Where are they from, out of interest?'

That was a question Maisie had asked herself.

'Both from London.' Maisie noticed that there was a band of pale flesh around Patrick's third finger. She wondered, with sympathy, if he had had to sell his wedding ring to make ends meet. She almost asked him out loud, before telling herself that would be inappropriate on such brief acquittance. 'Perhaps I might come in and speak to you both tomorrow?'

'Will you excuse us? My wife is not strong and she's tired.'

He extended his arm so that Marthese should take it, turning away. Maisie wondered if she had been snubbed, but didn't think it was deliberate rudeness, just a consequence of the upset and tension of the strange meeting.

He'll need to explain everything that was said to his wife. I don't think she'll have been able to follow. Although she might understand more fluently than she speaks.

Maisie watched the Lintons leaving. Russell was at the double door and spoke to them with forced heartiness.

'It'll all come right. You see if it doesn't.'

He held out a hand for Patrick to shake and the other man took it. Maisie was struck by the disparity in ages and physiques, Patrick tall and lean, Russell appearing slightly stooped and rather overweight in comparison.

The ceremonial chamber was now almost empty. Audrey had collected up all the cider glasses and taken them away on her tray to wash up. Seth Jasper joined Russell at the doors to the landing as Cherry Atwill handed in her folded note, asking Maisie: 'Do you really think you can help?'

'I can only try,' she replied. 'Can I come in and speak to you tomorrow? Will you be in the shop?'

'We don't open on Mondays but there's a bell that rings in our flat upstairs.'

'Good. I will. Perhaps mid-morning?'

'What's the matter, Maisie?' asked Cherry. 'You look very troubled.'

Maisie gave a weak smile. 'I'm sorry, I'm running everything through in my mind, trying to make sure I've got it straight. It's important to understand the precise sequence of events.'

'This is a burden on you, isn't it,' said Cherry. 'My poor love.'

Maisie felt a moment of doubt.

I don't know you very well, Cherry Atwill. We've not met for a decade and you're behaving as if we're bosom friends. Why is that?

Maisie remembered the scraps of newsprint and Sellotape on the inside of the display window at the Atwills' shop.

'Did you have any part in promoting the idea of the mine?' she asked.

Cherry looked taken aback. 'How did you . . . ?'

'You stuck up the article from the paper and then the adverts calling for investment, didn't you?'

Cherry sighed and admitted as much.

'We thought it was a good idea. Clive said: "If we get in early and everyone piles on, the value of our shares will rise and we'll be laughing." We're not laughing now.'

'Is that for me, Mrs Atwill?' asked Vera, holding out her hand for the final folded sheet of A4 paper.

'Yes,' said Cherry. 'Here you are.'

She smiled ruefully, turned away, crossed the chamber and exchanged a few words with Russell at the door. Maisie thought there passed between them a glance of shared guilt.

They both have a responsibility in drawing in their neighbours and friends, creating the buzz of excitement that everyone now regrets.

Vera opened her capacious tan handbag and put all the information inside.

'Perhaps I will go into school tomorrow, Monday, and type all this up. I might then put the handwritten originals in the office safe. No one will mind.'

'Who has access to the safe?' Maisie asked. 'It might be better to burn them?'

'But they might be important later,' insisted Vera. 'Imagine that one or another of our neighbours has lied. It would be useful to have the evidence in their own handwriting, wouldn't it?'

'You make a good point,' said Maisie, though she found the idea depressing.

'Before placing them in the safe,' said Vera, 'I will, of course, seal them in a good-quality envelope, signed across the gummed flap so any form of tampering would be apparent.'

'You've thought it all through, Vera.'

'It is a responsibility I never asked for but which I will discharge with due care.'

She turned away without another word but with the same characteristic aura of self-importance, her oversized tan handbag hanging from the crook of her elbow. It struck Maisie that Vera was now in a position of considerable power.

I hope she doesn't abuse everyone's trust.

Maisie went to join Seth and Russell by the doors. To her dismay, she heard the police officer telling her friend the story of her finding what he unequivocally referred to as 'the murder weapon', making Maisie nervous.

'Did we not decide to keep this information between us?' she asked, unable to conceal her disapproval. 'It may not be relevant. Tests will have to be carried out.'

'I was asking Russ to go down and watch over the place.'

'Why?' said Maisie. 'Are we not going straight there?'

'You need to give a statement, official-like.'

'What?'

'Back at the station, so it's all writ down in proper order.'

Maisie stifled a sigh and acquiesced.

'Fine. Let's get it done.'

They went downstairs, finding Herbert Peckham at the front door, waiting to lock up. They bid one another good-night and crossed the road. Audrey was waiting by the pale-blue Vauxhall Viva, her weather-beaten countrywoman's complexion picking up the orangey rays of the evening sun.

Russell and Audrey got in and pulled away. Maisie guessed that Russell would inevitably tell his wife about the job he had been given. What was supposed to be a secret between her and Seth would be known still more widely.

The police station was close at hand, with a blue lamp outside the door and two steps up into a functional hallway with a counter separating the inner sanctum from the world outside. A volunteer special constable in a very smart uniform greeted Seth with a friendly smile and a remark that there was 'very small news'.

'Go on then, Mr Salmon,' said Seth.

'There was a complaint from someone away beyond Trout Leap, you know, near Gulthane, the hamlet that was flooded out a few years back and lost its electric and is abandoned.'

'Who was the complaint from, then?'

'Cyclist campers, would you believe, in their tents.'

'In Gulthane itself?'

'No, they're on the hill on the other side of the road.'

'What sort of noise?'

'Motor engines in the night, more than once. They called me from the pub over Colthorp. I wrote it all down but I asked them: "Why shouldn't someone be going by? It's a public road." They said it wasn't the noise, it was the "likeli-hood of something nefarious".'

Special Constable Salmon laughed. He had a jolly round face and, Maisie thought, had probably served in the army in World War II and was now enlivening his retirement with further public service in uniform.

'What else?' asked Seth.

'There's more potential nefariousness, though happen I don't know what to make of it.'

Seth sighed and told him: 'Miss Cooper and I must get her statement down and make our way back out. Can it wait?'

Special Constable Salmon shrugged and told them: 'Do as you must, young Jasper. I'll still be here. There's a bobby coming over from Barnstaple for the night shift at ten.'

'This will only take fifteen minutes,' said Seth.

He lifted the hatch in the counter and led Maisie into a corridor with several identical doors off it, giving access to offices and interview rooms. She was struck by how similar it felt to Chichester police station where she had learned of her brother's murder. Also, it reminded her of backstage at Chichester Festival Theatre, a private space only accessible to those who took their rightful places behind the magical divide of the safety curtain. Although, in the case of a police station, witnesses and wrongdoers were also welcomed 'behind the scenes'.

Seth opened the second door on the right and invited Maisie to sit on a dark grey polypropylene chair on the far side of a scratched and stained Formica table. He slumped down opposite, drawing to him an official notepad, pre-printed with small boxes for dates and times and names and addresses, but with a large lined area below for the actual statement. Maisie gave him her personal details, watching him taking pains to fit his rather flamboyant handwriting within the lines.

'Now, the statement,' he said, his ballpoint pen poised. 'Could you give it to me in the order it came to you?'

'I could write it myself. I'm used to organising my thoughts for an investigation. It might be quicker?'

Seth hesitated then passed her the Biro, using the same abrupt phrase he'd employed earlier on: 'Have it your own way.'

Determined to ignore his rudeness, Maisie set down in her own neat hand, in succinct phrases, her thought process, her actions and her discovery. To her surprise, as she finished, Seth – who had been reading what she wrote upside down – told her: 'That's a proper job, that is.'

'Thank you.'

'Very clear.'

They left the interview room and returned to the front desk. Seth put the statement in an in-tray and asked Special Constable Salmon what else he had to report.

'Like I told you, very small news. But there was a telephone call from down Trout Leap.'

Maisie felt a lurch of dread. 'What is it?'

In answer to the special constable's glance of enquiry, Seth told him: 'You can tell Miss Cooper. She's in it up to her neck.'

'Well,' said Mr Salmon, consulting his notes, 'it was a Miss Anderson, a paying guest with the Savages, you know, over at Sunny View, to say that a fellow guest has been out all day and, now that the dark is coming in, she's worried he might be the victim of some mishap.'

'What name?' asked Seth Jasper, a frown on his face.

'It's Vincent Brent,' Maisie told him. 'Who else?'

V

SNAKES

TWENTY-NINE

Travelling back to Trout Leap in the Austin Princess 'jam sandwich' police car, now and then dazzled by the low sun as it dipped between the trees beside Long Lane, Maisie felt conflicted. On the one hand, her brain was whirring, trying to fit everything that she had learned into an unseen pattern that would explain the death of Holly Luscombe, tying it in with the drama of what everyone now seemed to think of as 'the gold-mine scam'. At the same time, she felt guilty.

Is it really my fault that Holly is dead, as Fred and Norman both think? And, if something has happened to Vincent, should I have been able to prevent it?

An image came back into her mind. It was Russell, heaving aside the heavy planks, revealing the abrupt drop into the culvert below the orchard. She saw, in her imagination – the mental picture incredibly vivid, as if she was actually there – the subterranean concrete channel and the slender baby adders, writhing in and through and around one another, disturbed by the sudden light from above.

All these local people, friends and neighbours, have been stirred up and, perhaps, turned against one another by avarice, excited by the potential gleam of gold.

Driving responsibly slowly, Seth seemed to have nothing to say, leaving Maisie to think. She was glad, because there was a set of ideas she could not reconcile. If, as she believed, Holly had been killed because she'd been out gallivanting across the countryside in the dead of night, discovering something that her murderer needed to keep secret, could that mean that the mine was real? But Maisie wasn't convinced. Speaking to Shane Tope earlier that evening in the Masonic Hall, she had felt in complete agreement with him when he had said: *'How many of us still believe that it exists? If, as seems every day more and more likely, it's all a hoax and it's not really out there, how would you find it?'*

Because Seth was taking the windy Long Lane carefully, Maisie had time to find an answer to the two – apparently contradictory – ideas.

Could it be that the thing that's out there, waiting to be found – that perhaps Holly found – is like a stage set, giving the impression of a working mine and a viable gold deposit, in order to keep the scam going and encourage more people to invest?

Maisie thought about the hour or two she had spent alongside Holly's corpse in the 'dimpsy' dusk. She had felt drawn to the valley to the west, beyond the frame of Vera's map, in the direction of the abandoned hamlet of Gulthane that Mr Salmon, the special constable, had mentioned.

Seth pulled up at the end of Long Lane, the bonnet of the Austin very close to the railway gates, closed to traffic since it was after six on a Sunday. Maisie wished she could slip away somewhere, with nothing to disturb her train of thought. In particular, she wanted to consult one of the multiple volumes of the *Encyclopaedia Britannica* that she had seen on the shelf in the damp living room, beneath the row of abridged *Reader's Digest* novels, or perhaps—

Seth opened his door, asking: 'Are you coming, then?'

'Yes, I'm coming.'

Maisie got out and shut the door. Then she simply stood for a moment as the silence of the countryside flowed around her on the sticky air.

'What is it?' asked Seth.

'I'm just thinking.'

'What about?'

'All of it.' Maisie heard him sigh. She knew she was being frustratingly obscure, but it wasn't deliberate. She decided to challenge him. 'You know something about Vincent Brent that you haven't shared with me. Isn't that right?'

'Why do you say that?'

'I'm good at reading people, understanding the things they don't say as well as the things they do. You spoke to him with an unusual deference, unlike how you were with me. I assumed that was just because you thought I was a busybody – but it was also unlike how you were with Stella and with the ambulance driver.'

The sun was setting, but there was still plenty of light in the sky for her to see the expression on the police constable's face. He was frowning, reminding her of Timothy Sturgess when he was concentrating hard, trying to follow her nimble fingers as she demonstrated how to tie the special knots.

'Like most folk,' he told her, 'I've read the reports in the newspapers sent down from Sussex that Russ Savage would insist on showing to everyone. Happen it's true, then? You really did all that?'

'Yes.'

'And were allowed, by the police, I mean?'

'If you're asking if you can take a leap of faith and trust me, you can,' Maisie told him. 'I quite understand how, for a professional, my interest and my involvement might make you wary. I imagine that you are man enough to admit that you've been, shall we say, a little dismissive of my ideas? I hope you appreciate the fact that I haven't retaliated, that I have continued to try and help. If you do have information about Vincent that might contribute to understanding everything that's happened, you should tell me.'

Seth made another childish face, expressing frustration and regret. 'But it's like I told you: I've got my orders.'

Maisie sighed and used the expression that Seth had employed twice before: 'Have it your own way. I suggest we go to Sunny View first to see if there's any news of Mr Brent, then down to the river.'

She opened the pedestrian gate and crossed the railway lines, checking left and right for oncoming trains, knowing that she wouldn't see one without hearing it first, because the night remained extremely quiet with only now and then a rustle of undergrowth or a flap of nocturnal wings.

The lights were on in all three of the cottages to the left-hand side of the lane. She supposed that Fred was in his kitchen, perhaps also listening to the impressive silence, aware that his daughter would never again be around to break it. Next door, in number two, the curtains were closed.

Is Vera already focused on collating all the information that we collected from the disappointed and – some of them – desperate investors in the fictitious mine? I wouldn't put it past her.

Through the window of number three, Maisie caught a glimpse of Geraldine, Petunia and Timothy, sitting on the floor on a thick-pile Axminster carpet, clustered around a board game. Maisie smiled to herself. It was such an innocent image. But experience had taught her that such impressions were not to be trusted.

That family has already seen drama – and practised deception.

She walked on with Seth two steps behind, finding the front door of Sunny View hanging open, presumably because the evening was so close. She went inside, along the corridor and into the kitchen. Audrey and Ida were seated at the kitchen table.

'He left a note,' said Ida, showing her a scrap of paper torn from the edge of the *Kirton Courier*. 'Vincent left a note.'

'What does it say?' asked Maisie. 'Can I see?'

Ida proffered it.

'I don't think it's anything we've done,' Audrey chipped in, smiling.

The message was succinct, written in block capitals.

Called away. Will see you all soon. Mr Brent

Somehow, Maisie thought it didn't chime with the pattern of Vincent's conversation. It was too terse, too 'telegrammatic', and—

'Can I see?' asked Seth.

Maisie handed over the scrap of newspaper. In what she hoped was an undramatic tone, she asked the ladies: 'Did Russell go out?'

'He's gone to watch over the place,' said Audrey.

'Is it true that it's the weapon?' asked Ida.

Maisie's heart sank, understanding that Russell had shared the crucial information about the new evidence even more widely than just with his wife. She was about to warn them both that they shouldn't tell anyone else, when she realised something.

The expression on Ida's face is completely guileless. She's utterly confused by everything that's going on.

'Did you know Mr Brent before you met one another on the train?' Maisie asked. 'You did meet on the train, didn't you?'

'Yes, we did. Wasn't that lucky? Of course, there were only a couple of carriages. It would have been hard to miss one another. I understand there have to be either two or four, because only every other one has brakes. Is that right?'

'I've no idea—'

'Where was this note left?' interrupted Seth. 'You rang my special constable at the station, Miss Anderson, but you didn't mention no note. Now, I find you have more information than you let on over the telephone.'

'It was here on the table all along,' said Ida, plaintively. 'Beside the newspapers. I just didn't notice.'

'Why were you so concerned for Vincent,' Maisie asked, pursuing her own train of thought, 'if he was unknown to you until you bumped into one another on the train?'

'Oh, you know,' said Ida, her face flushing red in the orange light of the kitchen pendant fitting. 'One is concerned for one's fellow man, is one not?' She laughed her twittery laugh. 'He and I were in harmony, on the same page, *simpatico.*'

'I could see,' said Audrey, 'that you thought you'd found a new friend, Ida.'

Maisie nodded to herself, putting two and two together. But time was pressing, the darkness closing in. She turned to Seth.

'We should go and find Russell, don't you think? And we'll need something to transport it in.'

'Mrs Savage,' he said, 'might you have a large clean bag, for fertiliser or what-have-you?'

'I can let you have a paper potato sack. I've got two or three in the cider shed. They've been used, but you could perhaps turn one inside out.'

'That's a good idea,' said Maisie. 'I'll go and look.'

She stepped outside onto the lawn, casting a faint shadow from the dusky sky on the damp grass, fresh with the dew that had fallen with the humid evening weather. She opened the door to the shed and, despite the gloom, found the thick paper sacks tidily folded on the top shelf of the apple racking. She tried to turn one inside out but it was too inflexible and doing so risked tearing the heavy paper. In the end, she took two, thinking the weapon could be wrapped inside one then the whole package slipped inside the other.

Back in the kitchen, she found Seth Jasper looking impatient with the older ladies' conversation.

'You know,' Ida was saying, 'it isn't every day one meets someone with whom one shares so many ideas, one's way of seeing the world. Vincent seemed to take an interest in my small doings, too, which isn't common at my time of life.'

Maisie smiled to herself. What Ida was describing was a technique that she knew Jack was very good at employing – giving a witness the sense that he and they were 'in harmony, on the same page, *simpatico*'. It was, of course, merely good interview technique. Thanks to his mastery of it, Jack was adept at encouraging confidences.

And Vincent Brent has the same ability. Talking to Ida Anderson on the train, he took her in and she, poor thing, fell for him in rather a sad and touching way.

Maisie glanced at Seth, reaching another conclusion as Ida rattled on.

The reason Police Constable Jasper showed Vincent such deference is because Vincent is a policeman, too, and Seth knows it. Is that possible? If so, the question becomes: 'Why has Vincent come to Sunny View anonymously and what's he been up to all day?'

'We'll be getting on,' said Seth, interrupting Ida in full flow, just as she was telling Audrey about all the places in London that she and Vincent both knew. 'I've come without my uniform or my truncheon or my torch because I got changed at the Masonic. Might you have a flash lamp, Mrs Savage?'

'I know where to find them,' said Maisie.

She opened the drawer called 'chaos', excavating both torches from the riot of useful things. She flicked both switches to make sure they worked, finding that the one held together with Sellotape had a stronger beam. She gave that one to Seth and led him to the front door, telling the ladies they wouldn't be long, putting Vincent's note in the pocket of her dress.

The night outside was fragrant with all kinds of country smells, including pittosporum, which she knew was a boon for nocturnal insects. She led Seth to the stile into the tussocky field and they crossed it without needing the torches because the sky was still light enough for them to pick their way. As they reached the river, however, the land dipped a little and they found themselves in greater shadow, with Russell no more than a dark blob, low to the ground – lying on the ground, in fact.

Maisie had a sudden fear that her friend might have come to some harm. She turned on her torch and picked him out.

'Who's that, then?' he mumbled, leaning up on one elbow.

'It's us,' said Maisie, flicking her torch away from his eyes and illuminating herself and Seth. 'Is everything all right?'

'Oh, it's been a long day, what with one thing and another, the gardening and the church and the guests – and the doctor early doors, you remember? I had to lie down.' He sat up and Seth kindly stepped in to haul him up onto his feet. 'Mind, I never could see it, though I was here afore the light began leaving the sky.'

'What's that?' snapped Seth. 'You didn't find the weapon?'

'Hold these,' said Maisie, putting the paper potato sacks in Russell's hands.

Using her torch to find solid footholds, she crept down off the grass onto the gravel and mud of the bank, edging along the running water to the undercut part.

Where is it?

She played the torch beam over the whole stretch of sheer red dirt, five paces from where she stood in either direction, upstream and down.

'It's gone,' she said. 'Someone's taken it.'

'Who could have taken it?' said Seth. 'You told me no one knew.'

Maisie thought back to her suspicion that she might have been seen and decided a white lie would be best.

'If someone was watching, I wouldn't necessarily know, would I?'

'Or is it your fault, Russ?' said Seth. 'I asked you to stand guard but you had to lie down for forty winks. Someone could have followed you across the pasture and fetched it away while you were dreaming in the land of Nod.'

Russell shrugged and told him: 'I'm not as young as I was.'

'It isn't important who's to blame or not to blame,' said Maisie. 'The fact remains, it's gone.'

'And all we're left with is hearsay,' said Seth.

She and Seth both turned off their torches so the conversation continued in near darkness, the moon not yet up and the stars veiled by hazy cloud.

'Couldn't it be gone for an innocent reason?' asked Russell. 'Looking at the Wivel, there, I'd say there's been a rise in water levels and—'

'Yes,' interrupted Maisie. 'You're right, but I put it well away from the edge. There's no way the river could have taken it.'

'And there's no way of saying when it happened,' insisted Seth. 'From when you found it, Miss Cooper – you said that was a bit before six – and "now" o'clock, there's only been a few moments when it was properly watched over. Russ, did you at least look for it before you lay down?'

'Now then, Seth,' said Russell, 'no need to go on. I didn't go nosing in close because, you'll recall, you were at pains to tell me not to disturb anything but to stand by at the bend and wait for the two of you to come and join me.'

'Yes, all right,' said Seth.

'How did everyone get to the meeting?' asked Maisie. 'Did anyone else walk, like I did?'

'I don't think so,' said Russell. 'Do you want chapter and verse?'

'Please.'

'All right, then. Seth, you came from the station on foot, of course, and the other Kirton people would have done

275

the same, but the Trout Leap folk came by car, the Lintons bringing Fred. Next, I suppose, Vera and Geraldine and Petunia squeezed in the back of Shane Tope's Ford Escort. The Tubbs would have trundled over all together on the front bench seat of their farm truck, you know, the milk lorry, with the empty churns rattling behind.'

'Why do you ask, Miss Cooper?' said Seth.

'I'm just getting the timeline straight in my mind,' said Maisie.

She asked Russell to continue.

'Herbie probably came from his office on the High Street. He's always busy, that one. Canon Greig had vespers and might have wandered over from the church without going home first.'

'Home where?'

'A flat in town,' said Russell. 'Am I helping?'

'If someone saw me retrieve the . . .' Maisie hesitated, searching for the right word. 'If someone saw me retrieve the object from the gravel mound and hide it under that bank, they could have crept over once I'd gone and taken it or chucked it into the river further down where it's deeper and would have floated away out of sight. Because I was on foot, if they drove, they could still have made it to the meeting before or just after I got there.'

'I expect I'm terrible slow to understand, but tell me why that's important,' said Russell.

'Because murders aren't done by strangers,' said Seth. 'That's what Miss Cooper's getting at, isn't it?'

'That's right,' said Maisie.

'Why's that though?' asked Russell.

'Because there's got to be a reason,' said Maisie. 'Find the reason – the connection between the murderer and their victim – and everything becomes clear.'

THIRTY

Maisie didn't enjoy saying the words 'murderer' and 'victim' out loud. She hated articulating all the suspicions that were writhing in and out of one another in the back of her mind, like the baby adders in the culvert. Among her potential suspects, she knew that she should first examine the circumstances of those closest to the potential victim – family members.

It's hard, however.

Her natural humanity meant that she didn't want to express the unhappy possibility that Fred Luscombe might have dealt the murderous blow in order to be rid of his difficult and troubled daughter.

Had he done so, though, would he have been able to put on such a convincing pretence of grief and regret, including prostrating himself at the altar rail in the church?

'What next, then?' asked Russell, his voice almost disembodied in the gloom.

'What happens to the Wivel after passing the railway station at the bottom of the town?' asked Maisie.

'There's a weir,' said Russell, 'to perk it up.'

'To oxygenate the water,' elaborated Seth.

'Then it flows on, becoming a tributary of the Ex?' Maisie asked.

'And down to the sea,' confirmed Russell.

'Blow me if I didn't think of that,' said Seth. 'I'll follow the Wivel, looking along the banks. If I don't see it, maybe it'll be caught up on the lip of the weir.' He shook his head, a pale oval in the darkness. 'But there might not be any evidence left to recover, even if I find it.'

Maisie had already thought of that, too. Whoever had moved it would surely have tried to wash off the accusatory blood and human hairs.

If they had time . . .

'How can we get in touch with you?' Maisie asked. 'Later on, if there's news?'

'I'll sleep at the station. You can call, using the local number, not the nine-nine-nine, and the overnight bobby will roust me out.'

'Good. Thank you. Now, Russell, I have one or two more things to say to Constable Jasper. Take my torch and get back indoors and let the ladies know . . . Well, don't tell them anything else. Just say that all is well but there's no news.'

'They'll question me closer than that,' said Russell.

Maisie heard the rueful tone and imagined the matching expression that she could not see.

'I know. How about you say I'll put them in the picture when I get back? Will that satisfy them?'

'Fair enough.'

She gave him her torch and he picked his way out of the hollow by the riverbank, then made his way more nimbly across the pasture.

'I'll be off, then,' said Seth.

'Before you go, can you tell me what your relationship is with Vincent Brent?'

'That's not your business.'

'You don't want to tell me about how you know him?'

'No, I don't.'

'So, you admit you know him?'

'I never . . .' He gave a short laugh. 'All right. Very clever. You tricked me.'

278

'I'm not trying to trick you, Seth. I just want things clear. Was it perhaps you who got in touch with him when you began to be worried about the money you invested in the mine?'

'Who told you that?'

'No one told me,' said Maisie, with exasperation, wishing she could see his face – also, that he could see hers and be reassured by her frank expression. 'I'm just working it all out as I go. I'm guessing that Vincent is someone you know from the police?' He made another noise as if about to demand once more who her informant was, but she continued. 'You see, you spoke to him as a junior officer might address someone senior. You did well to hide it, but it isn't easy. The habit of respect is ingrained and does you credit.'

'I gave myself away though,' he mumbled. 'Was that all?'

'There's also his manner, by turns affable and then sharp. Do you know what I mean? He wants to get people to talk, then he wants to be given time to think through what he's learned. Is he from the fraud office?'

'This is like witchcraft,' said Seth. 'Do you promise no one's told you nothing?'

'Honestly, it makes sense from the outside, once you start to think it through. I simply put myself in your shoes, wondering what I would do if I thought I'd been tricked by a clever scam, assuming I had direct access to someone with the authority and experience to do something about it. That is what happened, isn't it?'

There was a brief silence, during which Maisie looked across the field to the cottages, seeing lights in the windows of numbers three, four and five. She would be glad to question the inhabitants more closely.

'Yes, all right,' Seth suddenly told her. 'It was back when everything went quiet. Others were worried before I was. I didn't want to believe it. Russ got onto me, wanting me to do something, but with my sergeant out of action . . .' He sighed.

'Then Russ told me he was going to write you a letter, telling everyone how you were "bright as a button" and all you'd done in that Sussex and "she'll know what to look for". I suppose that got my goat, the idea that an outsider, a civilian, would be able to sort it out – and me caught up in it like a rabbit in a wire.'

'That's why you were so fed up with me for being on the spot and trying to tell you your business.'

Maisie heard him sigh.

'No, you never. You were polite and I was . . . Well, you were there. Excuse me, Miss Cooper, for my behaviour.'

'Thank you, but it couldn't matter less. So, Vincent is a fraud squad officer. You called him in London and he thought there was something to investigate.'

'I'd only written and spoken on the telephone, never met him, so I just knew he was Inspector Brent. I never made the connection with your Vincent Brent till I went and picked him up with his camera.'

'What information did you give him?'

'All I knew. What was said at the meeting.'

'Nothing more?'

'I gave him the characters of all the people involved, so far as I could. It's not easy, though, to say what people are like when they're your neighbours and you've known them all your life.'

'I understand. They're just people that you happen to know. It's hard to be objective.'

'He was very patient with me. I gave him all the gen I could think of and he didn't seem to come to any particular conclusion. It was me who suggested he come down and stay, given it's the holidays. That was my idea.'

'A very good one, too,' said Maisie.

'I got him the name and address of Sunny View and . . . Well, there 'tis.'

'Do you know where he might have gone when he left this afternoon?'

'When we were taking the photographs, he mentioned to me, quiet like, because he didn't want you to know who he was, that he was going to keep obbo, I mean observation, because he had an idea of a place to look, but he couldn't tell me where exactly because you and Mrs Tubb were right there close by.'

'On foot or more distant?'

'He didn't say.'

'Oh, another thing. Why did Jim Moore, Patrick Linton's employer, not invest?'

'Perhaps because he's the only one with a bit of sense? Now, I'd better get off and see what I can find.'

'Yes, you're right. Thank you for telling me all that.'

'It doesn't sit well, going against orders.'

'I would feel the same, Seth. I was in the army. As I told you, it would give me a queasy feeling. In fact, I wanted to correct a false impression I gave earlier.'

'What's that then?'

'I didn't pay attention at the time, but I did hear a sound, when I was hiding the weapon under the bank, like a twig snapping underfoot.'

'You might have heard whoever saw you? Is that what you're saying?'

'It's possible.'

'But it didn't come into your mind that was what it could have been till later?'

'Exactly.'

'Well, there's just one thing I've got to say about that.'

Oh dear, he's going to tell me off and no doubt it'll be very embarrassing for both of us.

'Go ahead, Constable.'

He took a step closer to her and she found that she could make out the expression on his face, despite the darkness. He looked very serious indeed.

'Then we're lucky – I mean you're lucky, but me too, for the help you're giving – that you slipped away before he bashed you on the noggin as well.'

★

Three thoughts were in Maisie's mind as Constable Seth Jasper crept away along the river, flashing his borrowed torch across the water and along the banks. The first concerned her own safety.

If he's so very worried that I might get bashed 'on the noggin', he should have escorted me back to SunnyView, instead of leaving me here on my own in the dark.

The second was, of course, to do with the identity of the murderer.

Seth said 'he' but a woman might easily have used the weight of the heavy timber to cause a fatal injury, especially one used to physical activity like little Stella Tubb or tall Geraldine Sturgess.

The third arose out of a sense that she was trapped in a way she hadn't been before.

This doesn't feel like my other investigations. To start with, I'm much more on my own. Seth has come round, but he's not the brightest button in the box. Plus, the big showdown where everyone unburdens themselves of their grievances and I explain what I've deduced – that seems to have already happened in the Masonic Hall.

She set off across the field, moving slowly because her mind was so busy.

I've definitely discounted Ida, though, as no more than a genuine holidaymaker who just happens to have found herself drawn to Vincent due to their chance meeting on the train and the fact that he exerted all his charm upon her.

Reaching the stile, she paused but with no feeling of being observed or followed.

And I suppose I knew from the start that Vincent wasn't what he pretended to be – a salesman for 'fancy goods'. Like I told Seth, he was, by turns, too sharp and then too affable. Plus, he's physically strong in a way no one would associate with a commercial traveller, as I discovered by grasping his arm when he tripped on the Tubbs' cattle grid.

She climbed over the stile and paused once more in the lane, thinking about handwriting and the clue it might represent.

Might that be something concrete, at last?

Determined to follow up on her new idea, she went to knock on Vera Pond's door. The secretary came to answer, calling out without opening.

'Who is it?'

'It's me, Maisie Cooper. Can I come in for a moment?'

She heard two bolts slide back, the door eased open and Vera's face appeared, backlit by the hall light, looking creased and tired. Frightened, even. She didn't let Maisie in.

'I don't like it,' she said.

'I beg your pardon?'

'I've made the list already, but I don't like having it in my house. It seems like an invitation to more trouble and upset.'

'You mean you've already collated everything?'

'I have a typewriter here at home, of course, and paper and carbons. I've made a top copy and a duplicate.'

Maisie gave her a bright smile. 'Would you like me to take it all away?'

The worry left Vera's face, like creases falling out of laundered bed sheets on the line.

'Oh, I would. Yes, please.'

Without another word, she turned away. Maisie followed her indoors, contemplating the stale smell from the gloomy, low cottage, wondering how much worse it would be for the Lintons in number five whose home had been left empty for a number of years before they moved in. That made her think about Gulthane, the hamlet to the west of Trout Leap that Mr Salmon, the 'special', had described as 'flooded out a few years back and lost its electric and is abandoned'.

It's sad to see the countryside depopulated but it's true, what Petunia said – and I felt it myself in my own adolescence – that it can be stultifying and narrow.

In the corner of the low-ceilinged front room was the low glazed cabinet that Maisie had noticed before. She bent to look through the dusty glass, seeing half a dozen bottles, including Harveys Bristol Cream, Cinzano and Dubonnet. Vera returned with three large envelopes.

'I was typing in the kitchen where the light is better. They're sealed,' she said, sounding pleased with herself, 'and I have signed across the edge of each gummed flap. I didn't know to whom they should be addressed, but I did inscribe them "Top Copy", "Carbon Copy" and "Originals".'

'That all seems very wise and efficient. I hope you soon feel better for me taking them off your hands.'

'I will – and I intend to keep my doors and windows locked.'

'Good.' Glancing again at the drinks cabinet, Maisie remembered Vera mentioning her father's appreciation of 'a nip of Scotch'. 'Vera, did you give Fred a bottle of whisky?'

'Yes. I don't drink myself but Fred was so very unhappy and I know that my father used to find solace in a nip every now and then.' She sighed. 'Since he died, I've not been able to bring myself to throw his old half-finished bottles away, though a man shouldn't overindulge.'

'No,' said Maisie, thoughtfully, wondering if that was a direct quote from Vera's father. 'So, you went round and offered it to him, on your own initiative?'

'Fred's been kind to me,' said Vera, 'always happy to chat. I thought I was doing the right thing. Was it an error?'

'Fred's not used to strong liquor,' said Maisie. 'But perhaps it helped in the immediate aftermath of his terrible news. How many of your father's half-finished bottles did you give him?'

'Just the small one of Bell's. Is it important?'

'Perhaps not, but I like to get things tidy in my mind.'

Maisie returned to SunnyView, entering the quiet house by the front door, finding Russell's keys on one of the hooks on the oak panel, inscribed with the terse prayer: *Bless this house.* She went into the living room on the north side of the house, the one with the television, the bookshelves and the lockable cupboard. She turned on the pendant light in the centre of the ceiling and saw the padlock was hanging open, as before. She unhooked it from the hasp and put the envelopes inside the cupboard. Before locking it, however, she thought about the fact that there was no point if the keys were always to be found within easy reach by the front door. Then her eye was drawn by the multiple volumes of the *Encyclopaedia Britannica*, alongside Russell's books of Roman and local history.

Maisie crossed the room and crouched in front of the shelves. All the volumes of the encyclopaedia had a thick layer of dust on the top edges of their pages, as if they hadn't been read for several years. The local history books had been consulted more recently, in particular one concerned with early Roman settlements in the first century after the birth of Christ.

Maisie drew the book from the shelf and let it flop open in her hands, finding that it was an alphabetical list of towns, villages and hamlets, with only a few lines of sparse information on each, but it was hard to read because her own head and shoulders were casting a shadow on the text.

This page is important.

She went to sit on the arm of the chocolate-corduroy armchair in which Audrey had dozed while watching the cricket, beneath the pendant lamp. In the better light, she read:

Gulthane – a hamlet in the parish of Kirton, founded by the Saxons in the sixth century during their period of agricultural expansion, but with archaeological evidence of previous habitation in the Romano-British era. The name – apparently unique – may be derived from Proto-Germanic 'gulthan', meaning 'gold', suggesting a link to the Roman exploitation of precious metals in the region, resources sadly depleted and, in the jargon of the mining industry, 'worked out'.

Because she was sitting so quiet and still, Maisie heard sounds of distant voices, Audrey, Russell and Ida. She returned the book to the shelf, sliding it in between its fellows, thinking about what Seth had told her about Vincent's plans.

'. . . *he mentioned to me, quiet like, because he didn't want you to know who he was, that he was going to keep obbo, I mean observation, because he had an idea of a place to look . . .*'

She went to lock the gun cupboard, going so far as to insert the key into the padlock, before persuading herself that she ought to look more closely at the information collected at the meeting in the Masonic Hall.

I'm alone in this business. I'm the investigator to whom this evidence should be addressed. I have the right.

She left the keys hanging in the lock and found the envelope marked 'Originals'. The flap was stuck down and Vera's name signed across it, but the glue was old and brittle. Maisie was able to get her finger beneath it and prise it away. She thought she might even be able to reseal it without anyone knowing.

She shuffled through the papers, not looking for the details of loans or investments, but seeking something else, a different sort of clue – of a kind a murderer might regret.

It's lucky Russell asked people to use block capitals.

She felt suspicious of the delay in Ida finding the supposed message from Vincent and took it out of the pocket of her dress to compare handwriting. Frustratingly, there were several 'investment notes' of equal validity where the shaping of the letters seemed to match. She began to doubt herself.

Am I making too much of this? I'm not a graphologist, after all.

She returned the papers to the envelope, dampened the gummed strip and smoothed it down, finding it did re-adhere. She placed it underneath its fellows in the bottom of the gun cupboard so that the pressure of the other two would help while the glue dried. Only then did she notice the absence of Vincent's Purdey shotgun.

Good heavens. He's taken it with him.

Her mind flipped back to what had seemed an unimportant moment, climbing Break Heart Hill with Ida, when her mind had wandered to the intriguing idea that her amateur murder investigations had called on only four of the five important skills, honed in her army days, competing in the modern pentathlon: horse riding, fencing, running and swimming. Reaching the brow of the hill and turning to look back down on Trout Leap, she had seen Ida, toiling along thirty paces behind, and had wondered if the neglected fifth skill – shooting – would ever be called upon.

Like a fool, I tempted fate.

In the same moment, her hand on the open padlock, she remembered the business with the missing thermos flask that it turned out Vincent had borrowed.

He was planning to go out before we went to church. He knew he might be on his own in the hills – over at Gulthane, surely? – for some time.

Maisie was struck by the thought that she and several others had spent so much time tramping through the fields and valleys, over the hills and along the water courses. She remembered a fragment of conversation she had overheard between Russell and Vincent as her friend showed his paying guest to his room on the top floor. In addition to the story of the nest of jaspers, Russell had told him: *'Perhaps you'd like to look at the book I mentioned . . . ?'*

Somehow, while Maisie had been removing the disgusting tick from her calf, Russell must have embarked on one of his conversational hobby horses: the presence of the Romans in the landscape round Kirton and their exploitation of its precious metals. Subsequently, in a quiet moment, Vincent would have crept into the front room to look at the book of place names, before consulting his own Ordnance Survey maps and recognising that Gulthane was worth investigating.

Maisie shook her head, trying to dispel a compelling vision of gold dust in the red Devonian dirt – perhaps in the dark shaft of an ancient mine – somewhere near the abandoned hamlet.

There is no gold. The whole thing's make-believe.

She locked the gun cupboard, removed the key from the ring, putting it in the deep pocket in her dress, under her handkerchief and Vincent's note, then returned Russell's other keys to the panel inscribed *Bless this house*, then stopped, her mind awhirl.

Or is it not make-believe? If the gold were real, wouldn't that be an even stronger reason for murder?

THIRTY-ONE

Before she went to find Russell, Audrey and Ida, Maisie's mind went back to her rough notes on the characters in the mystery, in particular Floyd Tubb.

Blue eyes, long lashes and blond hair . . .

She remembered telling herself he must have been at school with Petunia, meaning he was by far the most likely candidate for Timothy' father.

She placed a telephone call to the Tubbs' dairy farm, hoping Russell wouldn't hear and come and interrupt. It was Stella who answered.

'It's Maisie. Do you mind if I ask you a personal question?'

'Is it about Norman's dad again?'

'No, not at all. And it's not necessarily anything to be ashamed of.'

'All right, Go on then.'

'It's about Floyd and Petunia.'

'Oh, is that all,' said Stella, the relief audible in her tone. 'Yes, to all appearances Timothy is his child and, one day soon, everyone might need to know it, the more the lad gets to look like him.'

'But Floyd doesn't—'

'Oh, my son can't see any further than the end of his own nose. And, of course, everyone's been told the boy is Geraldine's not Petunia's. Does that satisfy you, Maisie?'

Maisie could hear Stella's resentment at her prying.

'I'm sorry to, well, to put you on the spot. I just needed to know.'

'Is that right?'

Maisie tried to engage in some polite chit-chat to soften the intrusion, but Stella was curt in her replies and soon hung up.

Keen to test another idea, Maisie climbed two flights of stairs to the top floor, hesitating between the doors of the two bedrooms. On the wall above the dado panelling were their names, each carved into a small panel of oak, like the one with the key hooks by the front door. The one to the right was 'Scipio' and the one to the left was 'Hannibal'. Maisie tried the door handle of the latter, finding it locked. She bent down to look through the keyhole, seeing that it was empty.

I wonder ...

The door to 'Scipio' was unlocked and the key was inside. She took it and tried it in the door to Hannibal. The mechanism clicked and she was able to push inside.

Even before she put on the light, she could see that the room was in complete disorder, as if a hurricane had blown through. The drawers were open and Vincent Brent's clothes were strewn about the floor. His shaving kit and hairbrushes were tossed across the bed whose mattress was misaligned, as if someone had lifted it up to see if anything were secreted underneath. His luggage was upturned and his Ordnance Survey maps – the ones Russell had mentioned, before Maisie had set off for the Masonic Hall via the river – were unfolded, spread across the top of the chest of drawers.

Maisie remembered asking Vincent whether he knew anything about the gold mine, just after he had photographed Holly's corpse down by the river. His answer, on reflection, should have given her pause. Without hesitation, as if it was something he had been thinking about himself, he had replied: *'It sounds very unlikely.'*

Maisie turned on the light and laid the maps on the untidy bed, side by side, trying to make them into a whole. As it happened, Kirton was on the boundary between two of them, making it hard to orient herself in the patterns of contour lines, abbreviations, river courses, roads and railways. Once she'd got it straight, she saw that Vincent had taken a particular interest in the area to the west, including the abandoned hamlet of Gulthane that he had ringed in soft pencil.

Someone broke in here and searched the place, wanting to find out more about who Vincent is. And, from the map, they must have discovered the place where Vincent is 'keeping observation'. But who, out of all the people caught up in this business, has met him? Almost none of them, surely?

Then she mentally corrected herself.

No, on the bench after church, almost everyone spoke to him ...

She took the note out of her pocket.

If it wasn't Vincent who wrote it, if it's a forgery, when might that have happened? It must have been after I left on foot, followed by Russell and Audrey in the car, and Ida was asleep upstairs or perhaps busy sketching.

She searched the untidy room for an example of Vincent's handwriting, but found none.

As a police officer, he would keep his notebook on his person, not leave it lying around for anyone to discover.

Maisie backed out of the room, mentally rebuking herself for having disturbed another crime scene – or, at the very least, an invasion of Vincent's privacy. She realised that she had left her feeble torch in the front room. She locked up 'Hannibal' with the key she had taken from 'Scipio' and put it in the deep pocket of her dress, alongside the one for the padlock of the gun cupboard.

Whoever searched Vincent's room must have locked it from the outside and taken the key away with them, unaware that the one next door would also open it.

She quickly descended the two flights of stairs, fetched the torch and made her way along the corridor to the kitchen. To her surprise, she found it empty. Then she heard voices from the garden.

That's why they didn't hear me making my phone call to Stella.

Russell, Audrey and Ida were sitting round the table on the lawn, their faces illuminated by two fat citronella candles, lit to discourage biting insects, exaggerating the contours of their faces and reminding Maisie of the dramatic chiaroscuro in paintings by Rubens or Caravaggio.

'Can I get anybody anything?' she asked.

Audrey was quickly on her feet.

'We've been so worried. Where did you get to?'

'I'm sorry I've been longer than I meant,' said Maisie. 'I had to talk to Seth Jasper and then something else came up.' They all looked at her, expectantly. 'I'm afraid I can't tell you what it is. This must be very annoying, to be kept on the outside.'

'The important thing is that you're safe,' said Russell. 'Take the weight off, why don't you, my handsome. I didn't like leaving you back there in the dark.'

'All's well that ends well,' said Maisie, sitting.

'But nothing has ended,' bleated Ida, 'let alone "well".' She was leaning in over the table in a pose that suggested anxiety. 'There's that girl who must be lying cold and alone in a morgue somewhere, and no one knows if she fell or who did her a mischief, and poor Vincent's gone off, who knows where or why.'

'What did he mean by "soon" do you all think?' asked Russell.

Maisie realised that the three of them had decided Vincent was coming back to Sunny View, that his absence was temporary.

'Before bedtime, you'd have thought,' said Audrey, trying to raise a smile.

'But it is bedtime,' said Ida.

Maisie contemplated sharing what she had deduced. She frowned, visualising the scrap of paper.

Called away. Will see you all soon. Mr Brent

'I don't believe he'd have gone off for good like that,' insisted Ida. 'Without a word.'

'It does seem odd,' agreed Audrey.

They chattered on and Maisie became absorbed by her own thoughts.

It's reasonable to think that Vincent might write such a note and leave it on the kitchen table, not wanting Audrey and Russell to worry. But there's something wrong with it, isn't there?

Finding no answer to that niggling question, Maisie saw another possibility that turned her ideas upside down.

I know that Vincent must be a fraud squad officer because of Seth Jasper's official connection, but what if he has a regional responsibility and knows Kirton because it's his 'patch' and the whole gold-mine scam is actually something that he—

Russell's voice broke in, talking with more emphasis.

'Why do you call him "poor Vincent", Miss Anderson? He's a fine figure of a man, isn't he?'

'I suppose he is,' Ida replied, blushing.

Maisie wanted to tell them that she was certain that she knew where he would be found, that he was carrying his shotgun for protection or, perhaps, as a kind of bluff, a suggestion that he was out hunting roe dear rather than hunting a fraudster or even a murderer.

But could he be a murderer himself?

She remembered the special constable relating the complaint about 'motor engines in the night' and realised that her mind had gone straight to the angry-bee buzzing of Paul Linton's motorbike.

But it could have been a car. Vincent might have come down to 'salt' the mine with gold dust, making it look more prosperous than it really was. The maps in his room would have been preparation for doing just that. Then Holly wandered in so he killed her, then drove back to Exeter to leave his vehicle at the garage in order to cover his tracks. Then he got on the Kirton train with Ida.

'I want to ask you all about what you've said to whom,' she told them, decisively. 'I don't mean to criticise. It just might be important.'

'How do you mean?' asked Russell.

'For example, you went up to the dairy and talked to Floyd and Norman and Stella. Was there anything odd about their conversation?'

'In what way?'

'Did they seem on edge?'

'I'm not good at this,' said Russell. 'I'm a simple man. I can't see what people are thinking behind their eyes.'

'Was the conversation solely focused on the mine, though, nothing else? When I arrived, I thought there was an odd atmosphere. I'd been speaking to Stella outside in the garden. She, too, seemed in a strange mood – not that I know her well.'

Russell pursed his lips, narrowing his eyes. 'Now you ask, well, maybe there was something between the three of them.'

'Can you remember any details?'

'It was something Floyd had mentioned that put Norman's nose out of joint, and it had to do with Stella, too.' He leaned back, making his garden chair creak. 'You know Norm summoned me up there to talk about the mine but also because they're all three very worried about what Shane Tope is going to do because of the rats and the taint that Shane's tests have shown up in the milk.'

'Shane doesn't have a choice,' said Audrey. 'He submits his report and then there'll be a command comes down from on high.'

'It'll be a full inspection,' said Russell, with a weary shake of his head. 'No one likes that, outsiders poking their noses in.'

'Although,' said Maisie, gently, 'that is what you've asked me to do.'

'You're different, maid,' said Russell.

'Of course you are,' said Audrey.

'But look at the time,' interrupted Ida, her eyes wide, flicking between the three of them. 'Where can he be? That's what I want to know.'

'Perhaps his little note actually meant he was off for good,' said Russell. 'And he's taken his key with him by mistake. People do that.'

'Actually,' said Maisie, 'the key to next door opens his room. I checked. His things are still all there. He means to come back and, I think, Vincent can look after himself.' She thought again about when she had sent Ida and Vincent to sit alone outside the church – while she and Russell talked to Canon Greig and Norman Tubb in the vestry. 'After the morning service, you told us that the Tope family came and talked to you. Isn't that right? Did anyone else?'

'Oh, yes,' said Ida. 'You know how it is after a service. People sort of mill about and, of course, the gatekeeper had made such a performance that everyone wanted to give their two-penn'orth.'

'Who, exactly, did you both talk to?'

'Who didn't we?' Ida replied, following it up with half-hearted titter, a sort of ghostly shadow of her habitual affability. 'The Tubbs, the Lintons, the ladies from the cottages, you know, the one with the bottle-black hair and the other tall one with the daughter and the little boy.'

Maisie was aware that it was important not to 'lead a witness' so she kept her voice neutral as she asked: 'Did any of them make any kind of special impression on you?'

Ida replied in an unexpectedly critical tone: 'I thought they were all very inquisitive, almost rude, wanting to know who we were and why we had decided to come and stay at Sunny View. Somebody assumed that we were brother and sister. People shouldn't make assumptions.'

Maisie nodded, gravely. 'No, they shouldn't. Do you remember who it was?'

'The little Maltese lady.'

'And what did her husband say?'

'What I was thinking – that it wasn't right to pry.'

'What about the Tubb family from the dairy?'

'They weren't very happy with one another but didn't Mr Savage already explain that was to do with the contamination of the milk?' She put a hand to her mouth with a little gasp. 'Is it the milk that we've been drinking?'

'It was only one batch,' said Audrey. 'They've been tested again since. You've nothing to worry about.'

'What are you getting at, though, Maisie?' asked Russell, looking confused, with too many competing questions in his head.

Maisie didn't answer directly. 'Ida, was there anyone who struck you as uneasy, unable to look you in the eye or to look Vincent in the eye, or who was especially inquisitive?'

'The shopkeepers – what are they called?'

'The Atwills.'

'They didn't have a word for anyone. They were the only ones who couldn't get away quick enough.'

'Do you have any idea why?'

'No, but Vincent went after them. Very friendly, he was, wanting to know all about their business. Apparently, he has a brother in the retail trade.'

'Is that what he told them?' asked Maisie, not believing it for a moment.

'Yes, it's extraordinary how Vincent always seems to have some connection to one's own experience. He's lived a very broad and varied life. Whatever one says, he can find a link.'

Ida spoke with a sort of naive innocence, but Maisie thought she knew that Vincent's mercurial conversation was, in fact, a cleverly disguised technique for collecting information.

'Where are we, then, Maisie?' asked Russell.

She wondered about telling them that Vera Pond had given her all the documentation from the meeting in the Masonic Hall – and, with it, a potential clue – but decided against it.

'One other thing. Why did Jim Moore not invest in the mine? I don't think I've ever met him.'

'Jim's got some very firm ideas,' said Russell.

'He doesn't believe in lending or borrowing,' said Audrey.

'He calls it usury,' said Russell.

'So, I don't need to look him up tomorrow? I intend to have some more chats with . . . Well, everyone who's available and willing.'

'No,' said Russell. 'There's nothing suspicious about Jim not being involved. I wish I had his sense.'

'All right, then. Now, I think it must be bedtime,' said Maisie. 'We've all had a long day.'

'But what about Vincent?' demanded Ida. 'Could there be another reason why he's gone, something he didn't want to put in his note?'

'There's no point worrying about it, my lovely,' said Audrey. 'The best thing we can all do is—'

'I don't believe it, though,' interrupted Ida.

'What don't you believe?' asked Maisie.

'That he would just disappear. I don't even know where he's from. How will I get in touch with him?'

Ida's face was crumpled and sad. Maisie felt hurt on her behalf. She remembered her own idea from much earlier, when she had imagined that Ida might have an 'ulterior motive'. Now, she knew what it was.

Poor Ida had believed herself liked, appreciated, by a handsome man of her own age and had, it seemed, embroidered a kind of fantasy of late-blooming romance out of their brief acquaintance.

Maisie thought that Audrey saw it, too, but Russell looked even more confused at the unexpected emotion.

'Was he a friend of yours, Miss Anderson?' he asked. 'I thought you had only met on the—'

'It isn't easy making friends later in life,' interrupted Ida.

Her tone was so desolate that nobody seemed to have anything to say in reply. In any case, Maisie's mind was clearing, thinking about the idea of 'late-blooming romance' and how that might impact a tiny community, such as the one clustered around Sunny View and the hamlet of Trout Leap. Maisie thought again about the idea of such a place having a fragile equilibrium. Unexpected dramas could provoke unaccustomed peaks of emotion, destabilising the web of everyday relationships – sometimes even leading to murder.

THIRTY-TWO

Above all else, after Fred Luscombe's performance on the steps of the altar, Maisie wished she hadn't been trapped in the vestry, arguing with Norman Tubb. She would have learned so much more had she been able to see the sequence of events outside the church as Vincent insinuated himself cleverly into conversation with all the friends and neighbours who she, too, was interested in. Her ideas, though, teetered between two competing possibilities.

I thought at first that Ida and Vincent were in league somehow. But that's clearly not the case. It's still possible, though, that Vincent is behind the scam. He came down to SunnyView 'under cover' but that might be a double bluff. He might have been collecting the monies at the London post office box – and he is a Londoner, after all – he would want to probe and find out if anyone has seen through his plan.

Maisie frowned to herself, wondering if she was making too much of her suspicions.

If, on the other hand, Vincent is honestly investigating on 'information received' from Seth Jasper, he would still have good reason to be extra chummy and look us all in the eye and judge us.

She, Russell, Audrey and Ida remained in the garden, with the citronella candles burning down, for another half an hour. Then they all decided to go upstairs to bed – or, at least, to their bedrooms.

Alone in 'Caesar', Maisie didn't get undressed, but sat on her folded counterpane, looking through the six pages of the letter she had written to Jack.

This will be out of date by the time I send it.

She wondered about adding a long *post scriptum*, detailing all the new knowledge that had yet to resolve into a decisive pattern.

Perhaps that isn't how this mystery is going to play out.

Turning the letter-sized pages, thinking about the secrets she had already uncovered, remembering her discomfort when 'gossiping' about Petunia Sturgess. She had asked Russell: *And people think that Timothy is the son of Mrs Sturgess and that Petunia is his big sister, just far apart in ages?*

Russell had thought the idea absurd and scoffed. What had he said?

'No one with eyes to see.'

From her brazen telephone call to Stella, she now knew and wondered why Russell hadn't categorically pointed her in the correct direction. Was it consideration for his neighbours' privacy or hadn't he noticed himself? But the obvious candidate for Petunia's teenage lover – Timothy's father – had always been the one person with whom the young woman would have attended school and who shared Timothy's distinctive floppy blond hair, pale skin and long eyelashes.

Floyd Tubb, obviously. But Floyd doesn't know, even though his intelligent mother, Stella, has worked it out? And what, if anything, does that have to do with Holly or the gold mine?

Maisie decided that she knew the answer to that question.

Nothing – it's just one of those random mysteries that it's important to clear away in order to understand what's truly important.

She looked at the last page, her sketch map of Sunny View and the surrounding area and spent a couple of minutes adding new details. Then her mind wandered and she felt herself drifting into sleep, unsure of how much time was passing as late evening became stark night.

★

Maisie's fully clothed doze was interrupted by the sound of a motorbike, buzzing past beneath her window. She jumped off the bed and ran downstairs, opening the front door in time to locate the direction from which the sound now came, hearing the engine decelerate then swing away to the west, far up the lane, beyond the entrance to the Tubbs' dairy farm. For a second, she stood transfixed by a new thought, remembering Patrick's hungry eye looking at Stella during the town meeting.

If either Patrick or Paul is carrying on with Stella, might her halting story about being up all night with her sick 'lady' have been a kind of pre-emptive alibi? Or am I becoming distracted by questions that have nothing to do with Holly's death?

The sound was fading. Before she lost it completely, Maisie decided to act.

She pulled the bicycle that Russell had serviced for her out of the porch and swung her leg through the frame, grateful that it was designed for someone wearing a dress or a skirt. Pushing off on the gravel path, she tottered unsteadily because Russell had left it in a difficult gear. On the smooth tarmac of the lane, however, she quickly picked up speed, standing on the pedals, driving athletically over the hump-backed bridge and out into the countryside.

The night was quiet and still. Maisie arrived at the junction and headed west, towards Gulthane and Colthorp, covering perhaps a mile before recognising that she was cycling down dangerous, unlit country roads, between deep hedges of bramble and nettles, without any lights, not even a torch.

For the time being, that's not a problem.

The moon had come up above the horizon, illuminating everything with a faint silver-grey light. All the same, the world seemed devoid of colour like an old-fashioned film.

She pedalled on, her mind focused on the future – her arrival in . . .

Well, it has to be Gulthane but I can no longer hear the motor-bike up ahead. Whoever it is, they've been too quick for me . . .

Thinking about her destination made the distance she had yet to pedal seem longer, like watching a kettle, impatient for it to boil. Meanwhile, apart from the hissing of her rubber bicycle tyres on the tarmac and the creak of her chain, the countryside was very quiet.

Is it possible that Geraldine Sturgess, for example – as a strong and enterprising woman, the sort who might know how to ride a motorbike – has access to the Lintons' shed?

The road began descending and she thought about the fact that Gulthane must be in a hollow because it had been flooded out. She knew Jack would be making similar deductions and wished that he was there with her.

Jack would definitely want to be here protecting me. He would be properly appalled at me plunging onward into the unknown. But I just feel I have to. What if more bad things happen because I failed to act?

She pressed on. The road dipped further, into an even darker valley whose sombre forms she could only just perceive: outcrops and hollows, inky-black silhouettes of trees against the greyer sky, no white lines on the unmarked rural lane. The air began to smell different, heavier, damper, telling her that she was approaching the course of the river.

There was a dark bulk of hills to her left and, a third of the way up, she could see a faint light, maybe two hundred yards away. She remembered Special Constable Salmon talking about the cycle campers who had complained about the noise and the possibility of 'something nefarious' taking place in the abandoned hamlet and supposed it must be the remnants of their fire from their evening meal.

Maisie forked right and was surprised, suddenly, to be cycling between two low buildings, each roofed with slate, visible because the dark stone was damp and not so much reflecting as enhancing the faint light. Then that was the end, for the time being, of the bright moon. A bank of clouds rolled in from the north, from Exmoor, shutting out the stars and darkening the skies.

No one will see me coming – if there is anyone – but, also, I will not be able to see them.

Maisie allowed her bicycle to glide to a halt and got off, very alert, listening more than looking, but also attuned to that sixth sense that might tell her if she was alone or if someone else had come, under cover of night, to the abandoned hamlet. She leaned her bicycle against a wall, stumbling slightly in the verge where loose stones met rampant weeds beneath a broken windowsill. She stepped into a doorway where the shadows were deepest, her shoulders against the timbers, roughened by age and neglect.

She heard nothing, saw nothing but the looming dark shapes of half a dozen cottages, several with shutters, two whose dirty windowpanes gleamed slightly, despite the gloom. Beyond the hamlet, the land rose in dark smudges but it fell away to the right. She stood still long enough to perceive faint sounds of running water from the Wivel.

The valley beyond the hamlet is where I need to go, surely?

Maisie set off, walking carefully on the broken ground, vigorous weeds brushing against her calves, a little worried about disturbing nocturnal snakes. Depending on the victim's physiology, the venom of an adder could be dangerous.

Her vision was improving as her pupils dilated, hungry for light. She came to a gap between the hulks of two dark cottages with invasive plants growing indistinctly from gaps in the stonework. The ground beneath her feet became more uneven and stony, awkward to walk on but lighter and slightly easier to make out.

She passed between the two cottages, her eyes finding a rectangular printed sign that, though filthy with age, was slightly fluorescent, with a bolt of lightning in a black triangle on what looked like a yellow background.

That must be the electrical substation that failed in the flood.

The substation was protected by a fence of galvanised metal, rough to the touch. She picked her way past, along the path. It led her closer to the trout stream. The sound of the running water became louder and more insistent, almost intimidating in the darkness.

The path petered out, overtaken by brambles that she recognised not because she could see them but because they snatched at the hem of her dress. She doubled back and found there was a fork she had missed, leading slightly uphill between more substantial undergrowth and midsized trees, probably hazel and hawthorn.

From the road, faint with distance, she heard a stuttering petrol engine and wondered if it might be the motorbike again. Standing very still, Maisie became aware of an animal moving through the leaf litter, perhaps a weasel or a pine marten or a hedgehog. It was eerie, to be aware of the rustling noises but not to be able to pick up the precise direction. Then, due to a peculiarity of the topography with the road higher than the pathway she stood on, wary and uncertain, she was shocked by the beams of two headlamps playing across the tops of the trees, making her look away from the sudden brightness. Before she did so, however, she caught a clearer glimpse of the terrain, with the path dipping beyond the hazels and hawthorns into what seemed a substantial bowl of land.

Much more quickly than she expected, silence and darkness returned.

Did whoever it was drive on, or did they park close by, killing their lights?

Both ideas felt suspicious – even threatening.

Stillness returned. She realised that there was another sound, very faint, a regular scraping, carrying on the stillness of the night, evoking a memory her mind couldn't quite retrieve.

Oh, I know. It sounds like someone filing their nails.

She frowned.

But that's ridiculous . . .

Maisie felt that her breathing had become shallower, her pulse accelerating. She filled her lungs, held the breath for a count of five, then allowed the air to flow gently out again. She repeated the trick twice more until she felt properly in control of herself.

Where is Vincent?

The clouds seemed to be thinning slightly and the terrain was becoming more visible as the moonlight re-emerged.

Surely, he's here somewhere? Should I call out?

The odd-but-faint rhythmic sound stopped and – perhaps forty or fifty yards away, between the hazels and hawthorns – she saw a movement of darkness on darkness, making her muscles tense with anticipation. Ahead, there was a person-sized gap in the trees. She slipped through, finding a brief pathway to the edge of the river where the water ran vigorously over stones.

If I clumsily make a sound, perhaps the Wivel will mask my approach.

Maisie wondered if she was, potentially, in danger. She had been through all the possible suspects – friends, neighbours and incomers – and felt convinced that Vincent Brent must, indeed, be corrupt, that it was he who had created the mirage of the make-believe gold mine, collecting the local people's subscriptions at his London post office box, making Constable Seth Jasper doubly his dupe.

He's the only one who seems to me to have the right sort of sharp intelligence.

The bank of the Wivel where she found herself was an inside curve, so the ground was fairly level, like a gravelly beach. She followed, with the land rising to her left, beyond the fringe of midsized trees. After thirty or so paces, running parallel to the dark hollow, the river course altered and she had to climb up above a scooped-out deeper bank, wrapping her fists around the smooth trunks of a hand of hazel to haul herself up, finding herself still forty paces from where she had seen the shadowy figure. Moving away from the stream, she stopped and heard it again, the sound that reminded her of someone filing their nails.

What on earth does that mean?

The sky lightened a little as the clouds began to separate, no longer a solid bank, becoming ragged in east-west strips. Still, the moon remained hidden but, at any moment, it might peep out and betray her.

I need to know what's happening. I can't just creep away and tell Seth that there was someone here in the dead of night, but I have no idea who or why.

Just beyond the hazels and spiny hawthorns was a small, low building, with a broken silhouette as if the single-storey structure was tumbling into ruin. She thought it might be a bothy, a kind of shelter often found on the edge of a village or hamlet, for use in bad weather for both shepherd and flock. She made for it, picking her way very carefully, hesitating when the ground beneath her feet was uncertain, not wanting to dislodge any stones and give herself away.

She reached the bothy, placing her left hand flat on the stonework, feeling the softness where it was clothed in moss. It struck her that this would have been a perfect place to 'keep observation', like a birdwatcher's hide.

No, that could just be a ruse that Vincent used to put Seth off his scent.

Maisie heard shuffling footsteps, someone moving with impunity, believing themselves unobserved, still thirty yards away. She crept along the mossy wall to the corner of the low building, finding an opening with an angled, collapsing lintel, beneath which she had to stoop to pass. Cloaked in shadow, she found herself in a space about eight feet square with no roof, a clutter of fallen timbers and slate around her feet, making it unsafe to move.

She had a brief flashback to finding the length of ancient construction timber that she believed was the weapon with which poor Holly was struck.

That might well have come from this ruin. But there's something else . . .

The moon emerged from between the ragged strips of cloud.

Oh, no. How awful. I was wrong.

THIRTY-THREE

Maisie crouched down, feeling irrational guilt that she had been too slow, too dim, worried about not upsetting people with her prying questions.

And, all the time . . .

She subsided onto her knees, contemplating the pale face of Vincent Brent, turned up to the sky, illuminated by the cold moonlight. Vincent was lying awkwardly, his limbs untidy across the uneven heap of fallen roof timbers and slates. She felt for a pulse in his wrist.

It's there, but faint.

Maisie paused, allowing herself a few moments to reassess what she knew, noticing that Audrey's thermos flask was lying beside him, a homely touch alongside his stunned form.

So, I was wrong. Vincent isn't the author of the fraud. I wonder how he gave himself away.

Maisie imagined Vincent hiding in the bothy all afternoon and late into the evening, waiting for someone to come. Feeling a sense of guilt, she tried to reorganise his awkward-looking limbs. She was reassured by a faint moan in reply, but he remained unconscious. She touched her fingertips to the back of his head and they came away darkened and damp.

Blood.

She cleaned her fingertips on the mossy wall then glanced at her wrist, but the light wasn't good enough to see what time it was.

It feels like well after midnight. I need to get Vincent away from here or summon medical help.

The reiteration of his name made her realise what it was about the supposed note that had bothered her. It was the way it was signed, using his surname, 'Mr Brent', instead of 'Vincent' or 'Vincent Brent', as were his habit.

She focused once more on the timeline.

In the end, the meeting at the Masonic Hall only lasted an hour or so, with people arriving from six, properly beginning at six-thirty and finishing with the collection of the slips of paper for Vera to type up. And there were three that I looked at whose handwriting seemed similar to the note that Vincent purportedly left – which must have been a fake because here he is, stunned, with no opportunity to come back to Sunny View and leave it on the kitchen table for Ida to find.

For a few moments, Maisie wondered why she had convinced herself of Vincent's guilt. She came to the conclusion that it was due to her deep empathy, being faced with Ida's disappointment and distress. She had been turned against Vincent by the idea that he had played up to the lonely Ida Anderson, deceiving her as to his motives.

That doesn't matter any more. The key is that the handwriting of the fake note resembles either that in the investment details noted down by Floyd or Norman on behalf of the Tubb family – I wish I'd noticed who actually did the writing – or those submitted by Patrick Linton or Geraldine Sturgess.

She told herself not to rely completely on her impression of those similarities, reminding herself once more that she had no experience as a graphologist and might be leading herself astray. At the same time, she now knew conclusively that Vincent wasn't the author of the scam and had to reassess the sequence.

Holly was killed on Friday night into Saturday morning. Vincent arrived undercover on Saturday, running into Ida on the train quite innocently, but using his natural charm and police officer's technique to draw her out in case she had anything to do with his investigation. He must, quite quickly, have come to the same conclusion that I reached much later – that Ida had nothing do with any of this. She's just a lonely spinster on holiday in the West Country who thinks she's made a friend.

Maisie looked round – in vain – in the silvery moonlight for Vincent's Purdey shotgun. But she did find another dark object, lying like a shadow on the rubble beside Vincent. It was a torch of a kind Maisie recognised from her association with the murder at Bitling Fair: a regulation police-issue flashlamp, coated in a sheath of black rubber, with a cylindrical handle containing the batteries and a wider bulb-and-reflector section to produce the beam. She had seen one just like it in the hands of Sergeant William Dodd when he had caught up with her in the dark chestnut wood, contemplating the body of a battery-farmed turkey, nailed up as if crucified against one of the enormous trunks.

She picked up the torch, not daring to turn it on – though she dearly wished she could, shining it across the hollow to reveal the truth of who else was there. Then she returned to her imaginary reconstruction.

Vincent left Sunny View quite soon after lunch, taking his shotgun with him either as a pretext – because it was plausible that he might be out hunting roe deer, considered vermin hereabouts – or in order to be able to defend himself, knowing from his experienced eye as he photographed Holly's corpse that she must have been the victim of a murderous assault.

She remembered the maps and the conversation with Russell.

Vincent was a clever man. From a few sparse clues – the book of place names, the conversations he had with neighbours, including those he buttonholed after church – he homed in on this place as the most likely location for a fake mine.

Maisie frowned, putting together the noise of 'nail filing' and another clue that she hadn't known was important and, therefore, hadn't focused on until this moment.

It's the sound of someone salting the mine. It must be. Does that mean . . . ?

Her train of thought was interrupted by the hoot of an owl, very close and shocking. Vincent moved slightly, his lips parting as if he, too, wanted to join in Maisie's imaginative reconstruction.

Okay, whoever is behind all this must have snuck into Sunny View, perhaps while everyone was asleep in the afternoon. The front and back doors have been left open for the fresh air since I arrived. Or maybe it happened after I left on foot and Russell and Audrey set off in the asthmatic Vauxhall Viva. The murderer crept upstairs and looked in Vincent's room, 'Hannibal', perhaps doing the same as I, using the key from 'Scipio', and . . .

Maisie heard another more abrupt sound, like someone standing and sighing and shuffling their feet, as if taking a break from some arduous task. Handily, to her right, the low moss-covered stonework of the bothy was pierced by a small window. Very carefully, she moved towards it, peering round the edge, for the first time able to make out the lie of the land because of the unobscured moon.

Once again, she saw a smudged black shape moving against the deeper darkness, making her picture the mouth of a cave or some other kind of opening.

A disused mine shaft? Or perhaps a natural hollow in the hillside, carved by a small tributary out the hills, running down into the Wivel?

Behind this obscure tableau, the hillside rose quite steeply, darker areas of grass or vegetation broken by lighter outcrops of limestone, like silvery knuckles.

If only I could get closer . . . But there's no cover.

Maisie had an irrational urge to point Vincent's torch through the small opening and turn it on, dazzling whoever it was, clarifying her thoughts.

But, if the Purdey shotgun isn't here with Vincent's stunned form in the bothy, it must be in the hands of a murderer.

Hoping that the delay wouldn't be important – either for Vincent or for the solution to the mystery – she went back to trying to put her ideas in order.

Sometime in the afternoon, before the meeting, Holly's murderer saw Vincent's Ordnance Survey maps with their pencil annotations and knew that he had identified Gulthane as a likely place. At the church, the murderer might have learned that Vincent wouldn't be at Sunny View, that he intended to go out after lunch and – clearly – he hadn't returned.

Maisie tried to remember who knew that and who didn't, but had no clear memory to rely on.

Anyway, after the meeting, the murderer would have been able to approach this abandoned hamlet, having an advantage on Vincent from knowing the lie of the land and . . .

Maisie nodded to herself.

Yes, whoever it was would have done what I did, following the course of the Wivel with the sound of the water covering their approach. And it would have been in the 'dimpsy' dusk. Perhaps Vincent gave himself away with a clink of his thermos flask. Or perhaps that wouldn't have been necessary. There's nowhere else but in this bothy to hide and, everywhere you look, there are bits of old timber and stone to serve as a weapon.

Maisie contemplated the pale face of the fraud officer in the moonlight. His pale features seemed calm.

He, like Holly, must have been struck from behind. But he's survived, for the moment, at least.

Abruptly, the quiet of the night was broken by something moving more quickly, a pattering of feet, a fall of smaller stones and a rustle of leaves. It came closer and Maisie felt herself shrinking back, away from the low doorway, then suddenly there were two bright-orange eyes in the opening, looking at her, then darting away with a flash of white at the tip of the tail.

Maisie's heart was pounding. She told herself not to be silly, that it was just a fox on its nocturnal hunt. Silently, she breathed a long sigh, then looked uphill once more through the small square window opening. It took her a few moments to locate the dark figure against the black hillside because whoever it was had also frozen, utterly immobile. Maisie considered which of her suspects it could be, judging from what she could see of their physique.

Definitely not Norman, but it might be either Floyd or Patrick or Geraldine.

Maisie realised that there was someone she had discarded, because of the handwriting clue.

But that was a mistake.

Very still, she put her ideas in order.

It was Cherry Atwill who wrote down their investment details, not Clive, and he's the right build. Plus, people are used to seeing him out and about in the countryside when he's fishing, including upstream of Norman Tubb's boundary. And Cherry admitted that she and Clive popularised the idea of the mine by advertising it in their shop window.

Maisie gently shook her head, telling herself to make no more assumptions.

The truth is right there, in front of me, if only I could properly see.

Then she realised that there was another reason why whoever it was had become immobile. It was because there was another presence in the landscape, profiled on top of the rise above the location of the mysterious figure that she had assumed to be the murderer, engaged in salting the mine. And this second figure was much more distinctive, although just a silhouette against the sky – a big man, heavily built with a thick head of hair and whiskers.

It's Norman. So, the one nearer to me must be Floyd. They've planned all this together.

She thought back to the awkward atmosphere that she and others had noticed between the dairy farmer and his son and his wife – and the bald resentment in Stella's tone when she had rung up to discuss Timothy Sturgess.

Is Stella in on it as well?

THIRTY-FOUR

For Maisie, finally caught up in the moment of crisis, decision and revelation, time seemed to slow down. There were thirty paces of empty ground between the bothy and the entrance to the mine, darkened with another change in the configuration of the drifting night-time clouds, veiling the silver moon more fully. But not before she had seen the nearer anonymous figure – was it Floyd, though? – snatch up something long and slim that glinted momentarily as they raised it to their shoulder. She heard a man's voice, directed away from her, calling up towards the second person on the crest of the rise.

'Who's there?'

That doesn't sound like Floyd.

'Now, then, let's not do anything hasty,' came the reply, in a reassuring West-Country burr that Maisie knew well and which made her heart sink with fear.

'Who is it?' demanded the other.

'Can't you recognise your good friend and neighbour?' called the man on the top of the rise.

What are you doing, Russell?

Maisie was craning through the tiny window opening, trying and failing to see precisely where he was. Very carefully, she crept out of the bothy and saw the dark outline of the motorbike leaning against the slope beside the opening. A trickle of water was indeed running down the slope towards the river.

So, it's not an old mine shaft, it's just a natural cave in the limestone, carved by a tributary stream – the ideal setting to salt with gold to lend credence to the scam. The connections to the old Roman workings have long gone, but they were a sort of hint that such a thing was possible. And, of course, gold is often revealed by water running through what that pamphlet called 'auriferous' lands.

The man in the shadows of the cave entrance replied: 'Come down and see what I've found.'

I don't think that's either of the Tubbs.

'Now, I don't think that's a very good idea,' said Russell, calmly. 'You don't seem like the sort of article I should trust, after all, Paddy.'

Patrick Linton.

'We could share it, Russ,' said the murderer. 'I wouldn't mind that. No one need know. We could both benefit. Isn't that the sensible thing to do?'

Maisie advanced a few steps, treading gingerly on what she hoped was solid ground, avoiding the noisy litter of twigs and leaves. Her eyes strained in the darkness. She thought she could tell where Russell was, crouched on the crest of the slope, not quite concealed by one of the lighter knuckles of limestone, but unable to move for fear of becoming a target for the shotgun. As they spoke again, she crept forward.

'That's just silly talk,' came Russell's disembodied reply. 'You'll have to go to prison for what you done to poor Holly, Paddy. And what you've perhaps done to my guest, to Mr Brent. Have you mischiefed him, too? I shouldn't wonder.'

'I don't want to hurt you, Russ. I never wanted to hurt anyone; I just needed a leg up, to get a new start . . .'

Patrick's voice faded and Maisie froze.

'You "needed"? It's not "need" to steal from us all,' said Russell, his voice drifting down the slope. 'And after everyone made you welcome. Didn't Audrey and me give you our old beechwood dining table because we always eat in the kitchen these days?'

Torch in hand, Maisie crept closer as he spoke, covering a little more ground. She wondered if she could run and jump him. But Patrick was a strong figure of a man, athletically built and – of course – armed with a shotgun.

'We lost everything when we were thrown out,' said Patrick. 'You have no idea – house, car, savings, pension, turning up here with fifty quid in our pockets and just the clothes we stood up in.'

'No, I don't know what that's like. But I don't know neither what it is to hurt a poor innocent like Holly Luscombe who never did a hair's harm to no one. I can't see it, Paddy. And you and your wife and youngsters, all sleeping in the sheets and blankets your neighbours donated, including poor old Fred.'

'Listen, Russell,' said Patrick. 'You're not a wealthy man. Have it all. I'll give you every penny.'

'Did you think it would make you happy, Paddy?' Russell asked, shifting position slightly, a smudge of blackness behind the paler stone. 'Did you not think about how it would eat at you, ever after, what you'd done?'

'There was no need for Holly Luscombe to come poking her nose into other people's business in the middle of the night.'

'That's just her way,' said Russell, sadly. 'Or it was her way. When she came mooching up here – is that how it happened? – you ought to have seen that the good Lord was giving you your chance to give up on it. You could have let her go on her way.'

'Rubbish. She would have told Fred and anyone who asked.'

'But, if you'd left her alone, you might have told us all that you were out looking for the mine. No one would have doubted it. Others have been searching, I dare say, like Clive Atwill, maybe, who knows the lanes and the hills from his angling, or Shane who visits all the farms.'

'What would that have achieved?'

'I'm telling you that was your invitation to turn back. That was fate letting you off the hook, giving you room to retreat.'

Why is Russell talking to him? Maisie wondered. *Does he know that I'm here – or suspect that I might be, having checked my room back at Sunny View? Is he trying to distract Patrick so I can slip away?*

'Did you know you'd find me?' asked the murderer.

I'm not leaving.

'I blame myself,' said Russell in a conversational tone. 'I should have guessed you might not be the "honest John" everyone hoped when I saw you making your advances to Stella Tubb, pretty thing that she is, but a married woman, after all. Didn't you hear the lesson in church? I was supposed to read today, for it being my turn, but Norman wanted me to let him so you might take it to heart.'

'Take what to heart?' asked Patrick.

Maisie could see Patrick moving leftwards, trying to get into a position from which he might be able to get off a shot at poor Russell, who remained pinned down, behind his meagre cover.

'The lesson of the *Bible*, Paddy,' Russell replied. 'You heard as we all did. "What, therefore, God hath joined together, let no man put asunder." Didn't you think it might be for you to ponder?'

'I never touched her,' said Patrick, moving back the other way.

'But you never missed an opportunity to nip up to the dairy and try and make yourself welcome.'

'They've a lot of machinery needs attention from a trained mechanic . . .' he began.

Maisie saw Russell move. Patrick jumped to the left and, suddenly, the quiet of the night and the back-and-forth of the odd conversation was broken by a violent explosion with a flash from the muzzle of the shotgun that Maisie saw fly up with its violent recoil.

That's good. That means Patrick's not used to firing such a weapon.

As the reverberations echoed in the damp valley, Maisie crept four or five paces closer, then lay flat on the ground, hoping the dip she had found would disguise her presence. Then she realised that, since the shot, Russell hadn't spoken.

Oh, no. Has he been hit?

'Ah,' came her friend's voice, finally. 'That's the way it is, then? You're doubling down.'

'It's not too late,' said Patrick. 'I didn't aim to hit you. I just wanted you to know I'm serious. Let's come to an arrangement, Russ.'

'Don't you "Russ" me. I'll not have a murderer talk to me like I'm his bosom friend.'

'Then I'm coming up and that'll be an end of you.'

Maisie saw Patrick's silhouette lurch up the slope, grappling with a few bits and pieces of tough undergrowth with his free hand, struggling to get purchase. She could see that it would only take him a few seconds to reach the top where Russell cowered defenceless.

She jumped up out of her shallow hollow, holding the torch out in front of her, flipping the switch and calling out his name.

'Mr Linton, I heard every word,' she shouted.

Patrick spun round and looked directly into the beam of her torch, screwing up his dazzled eyes. He fired the second barrel from Vincent Brent's Purdey shotgun as Maisie threw herself left and full length onto the ground. The pellets of lead whistled past.

I'm okay. I'm unharmed.

At the same time, the beam of her torch caught Russell staggering to the edge of the slope, his big hands high above his head, holding aloft a boulder. He let it drop and it landed on Patrick's head and shoulder, striking a glancing blow. The shotgun fell out of his hands.

Maisie sprang to her feet and ran forward to pick it up. Although both barrels were now empty, it would be a useful weapon in a pinch, used as a club. But Patrick was no longer a threat, too groggy to confront her, the blow from the heavy limestone boulder leaving him concussed and vague.

Russell climbed backwards down the slope while Maisie stood warily observing the murderer of Holly Luscombe. She part-obscured the torch beam, so there was light, but not so bright as to dazzle.

'Did you know I was here?' she asked her friend.

'Not for certain-sure, maid,' said Russell. He reached the flat. 'But I'm not surprised. What a life you do live.'

Yes, thought Maisie. *You can say that again.*

EPILOGUE

By the light of Vincent's police-issue torch, shining through her fingers, Maisie watched Russell take off his tweed jacket and unbutton his braces from the waistband of his trousers. He crouched and tied Patrick Linton's hands together behind his back, rolling him onto his side: 'So that he doesn't choke or nothing.'

'We need to get in touch with Seth,' Maisie told him.

'I've already done that,' said Russell. 'I told Audrey where I was going, didn't I, and that she should ring the station and roust him out, like he told us to.'

'So, he's on his way?'

'I wasn't sure I could keep Mr Patrick Linton talking long enough for our constable to arrive, but I was doing my best. Anyhow, are you safe and unharmed? I want to hear everything about how you ended up here afore me.'

'I'm fine and I'll happily tell you, but I was about to ask how you came to be here, too.'

Russell made slightly comical figure, holding his trousers up with his right hand, gesticulating with his left.

'I got to thinking about my book of place names and – I don't know why I never thought about it before – that this here Gulthane is where I or anyone should look. I did what you told us you'd done and went into Mr Brent's room with one of the spare keys and, luckily, it let me into "Scipio" and I saw his maps spread out across the bed with Gulthane ringed and standing out like a sign.'

'When was this?'

'A fair bit after going up. I couldn't sleep. As you know, I've been feeling guilty and ashamed to be a part of this mess. Then something disturbed me, maybe a buzzing insect.'

'That was Paul Linton's motorbike going by, but with Patrick on board,' said Maisie. 'I heard it before in the night but, perhaps, you didn't because your bedroom is at the back of Sunny View.'

'Are you saying you heard it on Friday night, when you arrived, and poor Holly was killed some time before Saturday morning?'

'Exactly. I think he used it to confuse things with people assuming it was Paul going out to meet his girlfriend. Perhaps it was Patrick who put it about that his son was a bit of a tearaway, in order to seed that idea. And, of course, the Moore's van would have been too easy to recognise.'

'Was it Patrick Linton that you expected to find here?'

'Not at all,' said Maisie. 'I was completely in the dark, going round in circles. It crossed my mind, of course, that there might be other reasons for young Paul to be out and about. I considered Clive and Floyd and even Geraldine. I never felt I had enough information. I was intending to go round all the houses tomorrow and – in a sociable, friendly sort of way – interrogate them all.' She briefly laughed. 'That seems ridiculous, now.'

Patrick was coming back to himself. He swore at them, struggling with his bonds. They moved away so as not to be interrupted and Maisie showed Russell the bothy and Vincent's unconscious form, telling him what she thought must have happened. In the torchlight, she could clearly see that Vincent had more colour and seemed to be breathing more deeply, as if asleep, rather than unconscious. Russell crouched down with a creak of his knees and Vincent opened his eyes.

'Hello,' came a befuddled voice. 'It's me, Vincent Brent.'

Maisie smiled.

'Don't you worry,' said Russell. 'You just rest a while. Help is on its way.'

'Good . . . er . . . yes . . .'

Vincent's eyes closed and they stepped outside the bothy.

'Was there a brilliant clue, though?' asked Russell. 'I bet you saw something like Sherlock Holmes would have done, an article no one else noticed.'

'Well, sort of,' said Maisie. 'But it was after the event. Shall we go and see what Patrick was doing?'

Using the bright torch to guide them on the uneven ground, beside the little stream that had carved the opening in the limestone, she led Russell towards the mouth of the cave. On a flat area alongside, with the powerful beam, she picked out a metal file with coarse teeth and a gold wedding band of which only a third remained. The rest had been ground to powder. There was also an old bit of copper tubing that Maisie supposed Patrick had used, too.

'I'd been thinking about someone wanting to salt the mine,' said Maisie, 'to give an impression of it being productive and potentially profitable. At the meeting in the Masonic Hall, I noticed that Patrick wasn't wearing a wedding ring and I assumed that he must have sold it because they were so short of money – you see, at that point, I was still feeling sympathetic towards him. When I crept up here, into the abandoned hamlet, I heard a noise that I thought was somebody filing their nails, although that was ridiculous because . . . Well, obviously, it couldn't have been that. I don't suppose I would have heard the file on the ring, but that bit of pipe, being hollow, would have made a louder noise. I honestly didn't make the connection, though, until you brought him out into the open by challenging him from the top of the slope. How did you get up there?'

'If you've been here for some time, which is what it sounds like, you must have noticed me drive past? I parked up, quiet like, beyond a little way, and I walked back from the road at the top of the slope, not knowing what I would find.'

'I'm very glad you did.'

They both looked round as the sound of a police car with its siren wailing broke the quiet of the night. Several birds flew up out of the trees, frightened of the unnatural noise. Looking away towards the road, Maisie saw pulsing blue lights above the deep hedgerows.

'That'll be Seth,' said Russell.

'Good,' said Maisie. 'We need to get Vincent away from here.'

'There's a thing I'd like to know, though,' said Russell.

'What's that?'

'Will we get our money back?'

'Oh, I think you will. I shouldn't be telling you this so please don't pass it on. Vincent Brent was summoned by Seth Jasper to investigate on behalf of the fraud squad. I'm sure they will have the resources to find out from the post office where your money has been hidden and return it.'

Russell pressed her, wanting to know more, but Maisie wasn't keen to discuss details that she had been told in confidence.

'Turns out Patrick Linton's a proper snake, isn't he?' she told him.

'He is, maid,' said Russell with a frown. 'But there was a reason why Patrick was late to the meeting with Fred and his missus, wasn't there? It was because he crept in to Sunny View and forged a note so we wouldn't fret about poor Vincent. Or did he bash him one earlier?'

'No, I don't believe so,' said Maisie, 'because I think he was watching me when I found the weapon that killed Holly, over which we asked you to stand guard.'

'I made a mess of that,' said Russell, ruefully.

'No. By the time you got there, I think he'd already flung it into a deeper part of the river once more, around six o'clock.'

They heard a crunch of tyres on gravel and Maisie called out to reassure the constable the moment he opened his car door.

'We're down here,' she shouted. 'All's well. It's quite safe.'

'Why didn't he come after you, seeing that you'd fished the weapon out of the Wivel?'

'It was just lucky that, almost in the same moment I heard the cracking of the twig or whatever it was, with him in the undergrowth of the river, not knowing it was him at the time, I literally ran off, thinking I was going to be late for the meeting.'

'Wanting to be punctual might have saved your life, then?' said Russell, with a laugh.

'Perhaps,' agreed Maisie, though she didn't feel it was funny.

Police Constable Seth Jasper came galumphing in through the trees. He was back in uniform and, while he stood getting his breath back, Maisie told him about Vincent. He immediately radioed for medical assistance. Maisie resumed the story. Seth listened in silence, now and then nodding his head, then he put Patick Linton in handcuffs, gave him the official warning and got him onto his feet to take him away to the waiting 'jam sandwich' Austin Princess police car. Maisie touched his arm.

'Did you find the first weapon at the weir?' she asked.

'No,' said Seth. 'I reckon that's gone for good. Now listen, I've made it a priority-one emergency for the ambulance to come out for Mr Brent and there'll be a patrol car from Exeter for the forensics, too. Can one of you wait? Perhaps I can drop you back, Miss Cooper?'

'No, thank you,' said Maisie. 'I'd rather wait with Russell. I've got my bike and he's parked up above the hill, there.'

'In that case, I'll take Mr Linton into custody. Perhaps tomorrow morning you can both come in to the station? It's past midnight so shall we say ten o'clock tomorrow morning for you to give your statements?'

'Of course,' she told him.

'Whatever needs to be done,' said Russell.

Seth moved away, guiding Patrick – who looked unsteady – with a hand under his elbow. As they disappeared between the hazel and hawthorn trees, Russell said: 'I did wonder about Ida and Vincent.'

'In what way?'

'They were very chummy, weren't they? Perhaps he felt something of what she felt?'

Maisie considered the idea that Vincent hadn't merely been 'playing' Ida.

'You think they might remain friends?'

'I wouldn't be surprised. Audrey agrees,' said Russell, as if that settled the matter. Then he sighed and told her: 'You never know what's going to turn up.'

Generally, thought Maisie, *for most people, the future is a closed book that only the passing of time can open. I, on the other hand, can almost always predict that mystery will find me and—*

'What are you thinking?' Russell demanded, interrupting her train of thought, sounding hurt. 'Is it that you'll never want come back to Sunny View ever again? Is it all spoilt for you, for a second time?'

Maisie touched his hand. 'No, Russell. Certainly not.'

'I don't believe you, Maisie. We've lost you for good, this time, haven't we?'

'No, Russell. I'll be back – and sooner than you think. Jack and I will come together and banish all the unhappy ghosts.'

'Will you, really?'

'That's what new happiness is for, isn't it right? To drive away the shadow of past sorrows.'

'I hope that's true,' he told her.

'Jack and I,' she said with a twinkle, 'will be back "dreckly".'

'How so?' he asked her, smiling broadly.

'I'm not going to wait for months and months of engagement and dress fittings and banns and preparations. I've decided that I'm going to marry Jack Wingard before this summer is out and we'll take you up on your offer to have a lovely honeymoon, here, instead of a murder at Sunny View.'

The End

ACKNOWLEDGEMENTS

Thanks to Luigi Bonomi whose idea it was that I should write cosy crime, and to the team at LBA; to my magnificent editors Cara Chimirri and Audrey Linton, plus all their colleagues at Hodder & Stoughton; to the booksellers, festival co-ordinators, podcasters and all the others whose dedication and enthusiasm are so essential to a flourishing book industry; to all the generous writers who have supported this playwright's unexpected transition to novel writing.

And, of course, to the person from whom I learnt to write books – the best and only Kate Mosse.

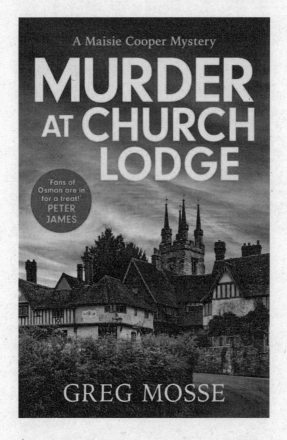

Something is afoot in the little village of Bunting . . .
Luckily, amateur sleuth Maisie Cooper is on the case.

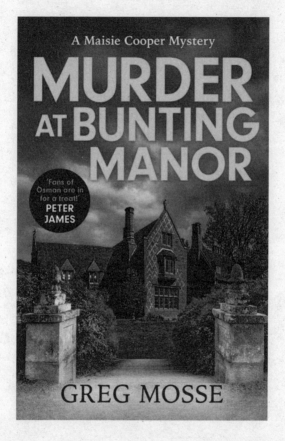

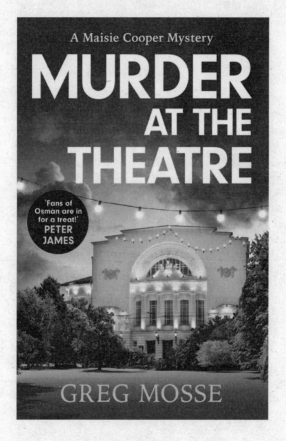

**It is a lovely day at the fair,
but someone thinks it is a lovely day for murder . . .**

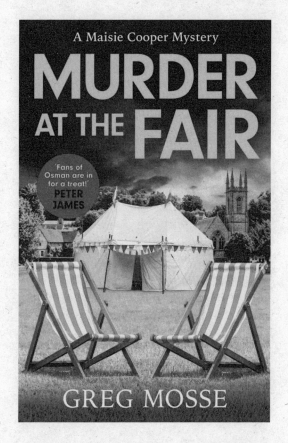

**Don't miss the fourth book in the
Maisie Cooper mystery series, available now!**